I

NEVER

KNEW

YOU

A NOVEL BY
PATRICK HIGGINS

I NEVER KNEW YOU
COPYRIGHT © 2020 PATRICK HIGGINS

All scripture quotations are taken from the Holy Bible, New King James Version (NKJV) © 1979, 1980, 1982 by Thomas Nelson.
English Standard Version (ESV) and
New International Version (NIV) © 1973, 1978, 1984.

Library of Congress
Cataloging in Publication Data
ISBN 978-0-9992355-6-0

Published by
www.ForHisGloryProductionCompany.com

Manufactured in the United States of America.

For Your Consideration

In light of the widespread chaos and rapidly diminishing race relations in our world, I felt it appropriate to add this *For Your Consideration* piece regarding the book cover, as the issue of race has mushroomed to such an extent that even the color of Christ's skin has become an increasing topic of debate in some circles.

Before I share my thoughts on it, which will come solely from a Christian perspective, allow me to first tell you about an experience I had back in 2015, while watching the Floyd Mayweather—Manny Pacquiao fight with friends.

As a long-time Pacquiao fan, the fight didn't go as well as I had wanted it to. After Floyd was declared the winner, the knot in my stomach tightened even more when I logged onto Facebook and read a bevy of harsh criticisms made by a handful of Filipino netizens—about Mayweather—to include racist comments.

Most were online acquaintances whom I did not know. Some I knew fairly well. Or should I say, thought I knew? To say I was dismayed would be putting it mildly, especially since some of them professed faith in Christ.

Anyone who knows me knows I have a deep affection for the Filipino people and their culture. Many of my closest and dearest friends are Filipinos. They are among the nicest, kindest, most endearing people I know. Which was why the mean-spirited words I read from a few of them online shocked me so much.

I messaged them in private telling them I understood their frustration over the fight, but I found their words extremely offensive.

Like them, I was equally frustrated with the outcome, but never once did Mayweather's skin color enter into my frustration.

After sharing my disappointment with everyone in the "real world" about what I'd just encountered in the "virtual one", my shock took on even greater heights when a dear friend of mine, for more than 30 years, suddenly blurted out that he believed we're all a little racist.

I winced, then raised an eyebrow in protest. My first thought was to denounce his comment as utter nonsense. What made it so strange was that my friend is black.

Naturally, I needed no convincing that some people were racist. Perhaps even many. But all people? As a lover of all cultures, I had great difficulty accepting his words as truth.

Now, this doesn't mean I never have disagreements with people whose skin color is different than mine. Of course, I do, especially when it comes to politics and religion—mostly stemming from differing views of the Word of God.

If you spend enough time with people from any culture—including your own—disagreements are bound to happen. But skin color should never be the reason for it...

Well, it's been five years since my friend uttered those words, and I must say I still wrestle with them to this day. This present climate in which we find ourselves has only served to fan the flames of my thinking on this topic even more.

The reason I'm sharing this past experience with you is that racism isn't only a black-white American thing. It's everywhere! No country or ethnicity is exempt from this grievous sin.

So, the question begs, is it true that all of us carry, at the very least, small traces of the plague of racism in our hearts? I don't know about you, but the very thought makes me want to get on my knees and repent before a just and holy God.

If true, Heaven help us, especially those of us who identify as Christians! If no one is racist at birth—which I wholeheartedly believe to be true—how has society sunk so deeply into the "race" cesspool into which we now find ourselves?

Do you think small children care if someone is black, white, brown, yellow, red, or any color in between? The answer is a resounding no. All they want is a playmate. Like you and I, they are born of sin, but not born racist.

We can only conclude that racism *is* a learned behavior. I must reiterate, this "learned hatred" toward others exists on all sides, meaning all cultures are guilty of it, not only some. Anyone who tells you otherwise is being dishonest.

The reason? It's a sin issue, a heart issue, which means there will always be racial injustices in the world, coming from all sides. Jeremiah 17:9 states: *The heart is deceitful above all things and beyond cure. Who can understand it?*

What makes racism such a strong indictment on the entire human race is that the Bible makes it crystal clear that we're *all* made in God's image. Not only that, we are the way we are because God chose to make us this way.

Which leads me back to the book cover and the One who walked the earth 2,000 years ago, healing multitudes, giving sight to the blind, and saving the souls of all who would trust in Him from the very real and horrific place called hell.

Jesus was a Jew. This is an undeniable fact! Now, whether He was a dark-skinned or light-skinned Jew, I don't know; nor do I need to know.

All I know is that Christ died for me, a sinner. His red "sinless" blood was shed for the forgiveness of my many sins. Not only did He suffer a brutal death on a bloody cross for every bad thing I did in life—past, present, and future—He died willingly for me as if He Himself had committed them, not me.

When He was raised from the dead three days later, the resurrected King then went on to resurrect sinful old me from the grave. God's "substitute" for my sin became my blessed Savior, Redeemer, and Mediator in Heaven.

He even prays for me, just like He does for all who trust in Him for their salvation. Wow! Just wow!

So, let me ask, if Someone did all that for you, would you care what color His skin was? In the end, if it turns out Messiah's skin color was a shade or two lighter or darker than how the world perceives Him, it still won't matter to me one iota. All that matters is that He died for me, a once lost and hopeless sinner!

With that in mind, if you have an issue with what color you think Messiah's skin was, or should be, perhaps you need to repent of whatever is causing you to think that way, because it's not coming from a good place.

Let me just say, friend, if you are a Christian struggling with racism, it's as destructive to your walk as all other sins—lust, hatred, gossip, pornography, drugs, alcohol, sorcery, fornication, gambling, "self", to name a few.

But, in my opinion, what makes the sin of racism so bad is, just like gossiping and bearing false witness, racism is a judgmental sin that is projected onto others who were made in God's image, just like we were.

Imagine that—hating someone who was knit together in their mothers' wombs by the very same God who knit you together in your mother's womb...

Borrowing from something I wrote a few years ago, let me just say that if you have an issue with the color of someone else's skin, the sobering truth is that your issue isn't with them as much as it is with God.

Again, we are the way we are because the Most High chose to make us this way. Humanity had nothing to do with it. Sure, God uses humans in the procreation process, but I assure you if He didn't want you to be the color you are, you wouldn't be that color! It's as simple as that...

With that truth hopefully settled in your mind, imagine standing before the great I AM on that inescapable day, and trying to explain to Him the mistake *you* thought *He* made with someone else's skin color.

Talk about shallow! One thing I can say is I wouldn't want to be standing anywhere near you on that day...

If you want a glimpse of what the true church will look like in Heaven, all you have to do is read Revelation 7:9a: "*After these things I looked, and behold, a great multitude which no one could number, of all nations, tribes, peoples, and tongues, standing before the throne and before the Lamb...*"

Did you catch that? A great multitude that no one could count, from *every* nation, tribe, people, and language! The thought of having multitudes of eternal brothers and sisters from different mothers, yet all having the same Father, excites me to no end! How about you?

So, if you are a Christian struggling with racism, I challenge you to go in search of others outside of your culture—either in person or online—then tossing all pre-conceived notions you may have out the window, and treating them with the same level of respect you would want from them.

Naturally, I'm not talking about embracing or tolerating their sin, or agreeing on things for which you disagree—neither should they with you—but accepting their skin color as God's personal choice for them.

If you'll only do that, you may be shocked to learn just how much you really have in common. The fact that we're all part of the human race shouldn't make this too difficult to believe.

On the other hand, if you keep following worldly causes, which are all headed by Satan and only serve to pit us against one another, chances are good you will keep nurturing the plague of racism in your heart.

Don't get me wrong, in many cases, I understand where the pain and anger come from. But certain radical groups on both sides of the political spectrum are very good at putting hate in peoples' hearts.

The most ironic part about these groups who loathe each other with a venomous hatred, is that they are actually fighting on the same team—team Satan!

How foolish!

Let me close this out by saying, as Christians, we must lead the way in this worthy campaign, by embracing people for how God created them. If we don't, how can we expect others to? I believe we owe it to our Maker to do just that.

In the final analysis, on that great and glorious Day, we'll all see that it was God's "grace" that saved us from hell—through Christ Jesus—not "race".

Think about it, if the exact color of Christ's skin was so important, wouldn't God have inspired one of the writers to include it in His Word? But He didn't.

Neither should we...

So, if you are focused on the pigmentation of Christ's skin tone, let me stress again that you're looking at Him for all the wrong reasons. Bottom line: His skin color cannot save you—only His shed blood can! Are you getting this?

As an eternal optimist, I'm of the mindset that, with God, whatever can be "learned" can also be "unlearned". This even applies to the horrible sin called racism. Know what I mean?

God's grace and peace be multiplied unto you all...

One More Thing...

While the *Blessed and Highly Favored Full Gospel Church* represented in this story is fictitious, it shows what can happen when self-centered individuals who "proclaim" to be Christians twist the scriptures to get what they want from God, as if He were a genie in a bottle.

Let me just say there are many solid charismatic preachers in the world, who truly love the Lord. When it comes to God's salvation, these kind, generous and tenderhearted pastors preach belief in Christ and repentance from sin as the only way to be saved from hell, without ever sugarcoating it.

They challenge their flocks to seek the Lord with all their hearts, minds, and souls. They speak of God's saving grace and His limitless mercy. They reach out to their communities in love. In short, the Gospel they preach is spot on...

But there is a growing number of charismatic preachers in our world today who preach the Word with one foot in the Word and the other in the world. The most extreme among them have both feet in the world, and have zero understanding of the Gospel of Jesus Christ.

Instead of teaching the things that best represent God's salvation—obedience, sacrifice, denying self, and Godliness with contentment—they focus on things that have nothing to do with the Gospel and everything to do with accumulating as many temporal "worldly" possessions as they can, which, for many, puts great distance between themselves and God.

Such individuals preach a savior from hell but not a savior from sin...

The story you are about to read represents the "prosperity gospel" on steroids, pushed to the farthest limits. Sadly, tragically, there are churches on the planet practicing the very things you will read about in this book...

The false teachers of these churches preach a gospel that is self-centered, not Christ centered. The difference between the two is eternal, because the god they serve and preach on isn't the God of the Bible.

My prayer is that no one reading this book is involved in a church like that...

> *For what will it profit a man*
> *If he gains the whole world*
> *and loses his own soul?*
> *(Mark 8:36).*

7

Is the

God you serve

the true God

of the Bible?

1

AT 6:15 A.M, THE Bose surround system roared to life, streaming Gospel music all throughout the 3,500 square foot house located in Bellevue, Washington—situated across Lake Washington from Seattle—rousing Charmaine DeShields from a deep slumber, short as it was.

Mouth stretched in a yawn, even though she felt tired and wished she could sleep a little longer, the successful real estate agent swung her legs off the bed and lowered her feet onto the plush carpeted floor.

Charmaine rubbed sleep from her eyes, then stretched her arms high above her head, eager for this day to begin. "Good morning, Jesus!" she shouted skyward. "Thanks for another day to shine for You. Bless me richly today, so I can be a blessing to others, Amen!"

This had long since been her daily morning prayer...

Saturday mornings used to be the one day of the week that Charmaine could sleep in. But ever since her city bus advertising campaign began three years ago, her schedule had swollen to the extent that the free time in her life had shrunk considerably.

These days, she was lucky to get five hours of sleep each night. But how could she possibly sleep soundly when there was always so much going on? If she wasn't out showing a property to perspective buyers, meeting someone for a closing, attending a church event, preparing for the Wednesday night Bible study—she was in charge of at church with her boyfriend Rodney—something else always kept her busy.

As part of what she liked to call her personal 'monthly ministry', Charmaine fed the homeless once a month and visited incarcerated women at a state prison just outside Seattle, to encourage them and share the Good News with them. She also visited the senior assisted living home at which her late parents had spent their final days on earth, to have lunch with the few remaining patients she met when her parents resided there.

She told anyone who asked her that she did these things to help keep herself grounded, humble...

At 31, Charmaine DeShields was well put together. Her face was thin, her eyes were brown and almond-shaped. She had a medium size mouth and full lips. Her hair was shiny black and naturally curly.

Thanks to bi-weekly spa treatments, where she received facial and body scrubs, her ebony skin was silky smooth.

But her most distinguishing feature was her smile. Due to constant brushing, her teeth were so white they practically glowed; they never needed bleaching. She attributed her near-flawless skin and encompassing smile to the Spirit of God living inside her.

Because she was so ambitious, sociable, and outgoing, whenever she walked into a room, one glance at her black, springy coils—as they danced on her shoulders with each confident stride she took—caused heads to turn and others to gravitate toward her.

As a blessed and highly favored woman, Charmaine was expecting a long, healthy, and prosperous life. To keep her 5'9" athletic body fit, she loved rigorous exercise, and seldom had to push herself to stay motivated.

Ever since her track and field days in high school, exercise was the one constant in her life. It provided a powerful release, physically, mentally, and spiritually.

The proof was that she still maintained the same athletic build she had in high school and college, with very minimal body fat.

The past three years, especially, were nothing short of life-altering for Charmaine DeShields. Her real estate business took off like a rocket and her social status in the community had risen to semi-lofty heights. Her future was so bright, it was difficult sleeping most nights.

And it all started with the city bus campaign...

She attributed her sudden rise to her membership at the *Blessed and Highly Favored Full Gospel Church*. By far, it was the most opulent and successful megachurch in all of Seattle, and beyond!

Charmaine became a member a little more than 7 years ago, a month before they moved into the building they presently occupied. Without a doubt, joining the church was the best decision she'd ever made in life.

After exercising and showering, it was off to church for the monthly intercessory prayer meeting at 10 a.m., giving her three hours to get ready.

After that, she had a house to show that was listed in the half-million-dollar-range, followed by a closing at 4 p.m., on a house that sold for $1.7M—which would net her a cool $50K commission—her largest to date. To celebrate, she had a reservation for two at SkyCity Restaurant at the Space Needle, in downtown Seattle.

Charmaine beamed at the thought. Days like this were what real estate agents lived for. It was when all their hard work was finally rewarded.

It was the main reason she found herself staring at the bedroom ceiling fan in the middle of the night, arms flailing wildly, feet stomping the mattress, giddy with laughter, as she shouted praises to her God.

Once Charmaine left the house, she didn't expect to be home until after midnight. Even so, she would be at church in the morning, at 8 a.m., bright-eyed and bushy-tailed, to praise God for His many blessings with thousands of her brothers and sisters in Christ.

Then on Monday morning, it would start all over again. Yet, amid the constant flurry of activity in her life, the one thing Charmaine DeShields seldom was, was still...

But she didn't mind. She liked keeping herself busy helping others and diligently striving for the blessed and highly favored life God was skillfully and lovingly carving out just for her. Not only did she desire this sort of lifestyle, according to her pastors, she deserved it.

And she was only in the beginning stages...

Charmaine changed into exercise gear, mounted her home cycle, and logged onto the site of her favorite online trainers, along with best friend and fellow real estate agent, Meredith Geiger, and a handful of other women from across the country.

Watching each other on the screens before them as they pushed their bodies to the limit—five days a week—by some of the best online coaches and instructors on the planet, provided them with that added motivation to survive the 45-minute session.

Instead of positioning her cycle in front of a ceiling-to-floor mirror, like most did, Charmaine's bike was pressed up against one of her corner bedroom windows, so she could drink in the stunning view of downtown Seattle out in the distance, which she called her business playground.

Meredith said, "You're glowing today, even more than most days. But I don't have to ask why..."

A bright smile broke across Charmaine's face. Through heavy grunts, she said, "It's going to be a great day, Bestie!" Sweat covered her skin, illuminating it to the extent that she practically glowed.

Meredith Geiger was 33. Three years divorced, the best thing she walked away from her failed marriage with was a 7 year old freckleface daughter, named Bethany, whose hair was as golden as the sun.

Meredith was quite attractive. The half Irish, half Native American woman was well toned. She stood 5'7", with light brown hair and soft brown eyes. She had a thin face and a long but thin nose.

Her natural wavy brown hair flowed past her thin shoulders down to the middle of her back. Blonde streaks could be seen all throughout.

Meredith was a caring, sensitive woman. She was also known to be moody at times. She was more laid back and reserved than Charmaine was.

After the 45-minute session concluded, Charmaine wiped perspiration from her face with a clean towel she kept on a small table next to the stationary bike, then reached for the bottled water she also kept there.

Taking a few gulps, with the sun slowly making its early morning ascent, she glanced out at snow-capped Mount Rainier in the far distance.

Even 60 miles south of the bustling city of Seattle, it was clearly visible. Now magnified by the radiant sun, it was so majestic, so stoic, so awe-inspiring, she wondered why she never took more time to appreciate it. Charmaine knew the answer: her busy schedule.

She checked her phone for messages, to make sure there were no cancellations or delays, then sent a voice text message to the Stoddards, congratulating them in advance on the closing, followed by a text message to a prospective client, confirming their 3 p.m. appointment.

Before showering, Charmaine opened her website and saw her image plastered on a city bus, something she did every morning to help keep her motivated.

Perhaps it was from seeing her face on so many transportation buses, as one of Seattle's up and coming real estate agents, but she couldn't help but feel like a vital part of her city.

Without a doubt, two of the biggest blessings in her life were Julian and Imogen Martín. Not only were they the lead pastors at her church, they also served as her spiritual mentors and life coaches.

The Martíns were essential to getting Charmaine to take the big plunge three years ago, by investing tens of thousands of dollars she didn't have at that time, into the city bus advertising campaign.

Even when she confessed that an investment of that size would drain her bank account and max out all her credit cards, her pastors insisted that God would honor her commitment by going out before her and fighting all her battles, ultimately clearing a pathway of success just for her.

As usual, their advice had paid off...

What would I ever do without them?

After a quick shower, Charmaine started her car from inside the house, so the engine would be warm by the time she gathered the things she would take with her.

Halfway to the church, she called her boyfriend—and praise and worship team leader at church—Rodney Williams. "Good morning, sweetness! Ready to praise the Lord and be blessed by Him?"

"Of course, my love! I'm pulling into the church parking lot now."

"I may be a minute or two late, so save a seat for me in the cafeteria."

"Would you like me to order breakfast for you?"

"Aww, what would I ever do without you, Rodney? Mwah!" Charmaine kissed her boyfriend through her cellphone. "See you soon, sweetness! Love you."

"Love you back. Be careful driving."

"I will." The high-spirited woman cranked up the Christian music and backed her black four door Mercedes GLE Coupe out of the driveway, singing with a voice that was glad.

Charmaine had a full list of prayers to be offered up to her Maker, including the six-bedroom house she first saw three years ago, at a Labor Day picnic, at the Wilshire residence on Northlake Way.

One glance at the huge backyard and perfectly manicured lawn was all it took for Charmaine to start speaking the house into existence, as she had been taught by her pastors, whenever seeing something she desired.

The sprawling mini-mansion was situated four doors down from Norm and Nancy Wilshire, owners of a large construction company, and the wealthiest members at the *Blessed and Highly Favored Full Gospel Church.*

Even though the lakefront house wasn't on the market and, according to the owners, wouldn't be anytime soon, Charmaine nevertheless wanted it and kept claiming it as her own.

As it was, many of her friends and neighbors thought the house she lived in was already too big for someone living alone. Now she wanted a six-bedroom mansion?

But according to her pastors, that's how the truly blessed were supposed to live.

Charmaine eagerly anticipated the two huge announcements Pastor Julian would make to open the monthly prayer session. She was fairly-sure she knew what one of them would be, but not so sure about the other one.

Charmaine would be making a big announcement herself at church; only she didn't know it yet. *This is going to be a great day!*

2

THE SANCTUARY WHICH HELD 7,000 people per service was full of worshippers this day. While this was nothing new at the *Blessed and Highly Favored Full Gospel Church*—it happened at each of the four services held every weekend at the megachurch—what made it so newsworthy was that they weren't gathered for a church service, but for their monthly prayer meeting.

Increasingly, when it came to gathering for the sole purpose of praying corporately, most churchgoers in the world—including many who faithfully volunteered their time for all sorts of church functions and activities, and seldom if ever missed a Sunday service—were usually too busy doing other things to attend, or they opted to pray at home instead.

Worse, attendance at these gatherings was on the steady decline at most churches worldwide. Even many of the megachurches dotting the planet experienced shrinking numbers.

It was an alarming statistic...If prayer was the most powerful tool in the Christian toolbox, these constantly declining numbers further confirmed it was the least used tool in the box for most who called themselves followers of Jesus Christ.

But this couldn't be said about the "Personal Blessings" monthly prayer service at the *Blessed and Highly Favored Full Gospel Church*. It had become so popular that a second service was recently added.

Many likened it to a life-altering event, even placing it above the Sunday services, powerful as they were. So much so that tickets had to be issued in advance, to ensure that only 7,000 members showed up for each session.

The Seattle-based church was so mixed, so alive, so hip, that a quarter of those in attendance represented the Gen-X demographic.

Even the praise and worship music was mixed. It wasn't uncommon hearing an old Gospel hymn being sung on any given Sunday, followed by a grunge, pop, rock, hip hop or rap song of praise, performed by musicians who were fairly well known throughout the Seattle-Tacoma area.

Bottom line, it was all about appealing to the masses...

After singing a few songs, Julian Martín approached the lectern. The lead pastor was 38 and stood a lean 6'4". His wavy light brown hair was shampoo-commercial worthy and was always combed to perfection.

His soft brown eyes rested beneath bushy eyebrows. Even though they were soft, they were intense at the same time. So much so that if he glanced in your direction, they commanded your undivided attention.

His nose was slightly turned up, but otherwise well-designed. He had deep-set dimples and a squared off jawline.

Because an equal mix of Asian, Black, Caucasian, and Hispanic blood pumped through his heart, Julian easily identified with each member of this thriving mixed ethnicity church.

Miraculously, all it took was one good look at him, and all those heritages were put on full display. As usual, he was highly energized, dressed in a blue three-piece pinstriped suit, soft blue shirt, and gold necktie that was covered in deep blue polka dots, which looked purple from a distance.

Pastor Martín opened the session with a lengthy prayer for those who were sick in the church and needed healing, as well as for their family members and friends. He then prayed for continued provisions for the church God had blessed him and Imogen with, followed by the city, state, and country in which they lived, their President, and all leaders and government officials, regardless of political affiliation.

Once he was finished, Julian let his soft brown eyes settle on the large body gathered before him. With face aglow, he said, "Now for the two big announcements you've all been waiting for!"

He shot a quick glance at his wife and co-pastor, seated up on the stage. Imogen, too, was all smiles.

"First, after so many years of trying, God has finally answered our prayer. I'm happy to announce that Imogen is with child!"

The sanctuary erupted in thunderous applause.

"Praise God!" Jeremiah and Sophia Ogletree both exclaimed. Jeremiah was one of the associate pastors, and next in line if it ever came to that.

Charmaine DeShields was seated next to them. She shouted, "I knew it! Even told Rodney at breakfast in the cafeteria!" She pointed to her boyfriend up on stage seated at the organ.

Rodney smiled and mouthed the words, "You nailed it!"

15

Once they settled down, Pastor Julian continued, "It's too soon to know the child's gender. We're not sure we wanna know. But what should surprise none of you is if we have a boy, his name will be, 'Prince'. If it's a girl…"

Bonnie Devlin yelled, "Princess?"

Julian squinted in her direction. "Exactly, Bonnie! Isn't God good?!"

"Yes, He is, Pastor!" Tears of joy flooded the eyes of the longtime member, who owned a bakery a few miles down the road from the church.

"So good!" someone else yelled from the balcony level.

Pastor Julian paused a moment so those standing could be seated again. "Now for the second big announcement. It's time to expand again! Simply put, we've once again outgrown our building."

There was more thunderous applause.

"Can you imagine how much more of an impact we'll have in our community, with three thousand more seats for each of our four services? That would mean an extra twelve thousand souls being exposed to God's goodness, and His richest blessings, every week! Talk about good fruit? I'm excited just thinking about it!"

"Yes, Lord, we receive it!" someone shouted.

"Now, I know what some of you are undoubtedly thinking. One of the biggest complaints we receive from so many is with parking. It's gotten so bad that if you don't arrive thirty minutes before service begins, it's next to impossible to find a parking space anywhere on campus."

"True that, Pastor!" someone yelled.

"Fear not, help is on the way! Part of the seed money we raise will be used to purchase the parcel of land we've been renting across the street all these years, for parking. The owners finally agreed to sell it to us.

"Once it's ours, the first thing we'll do is level the three dilapidated buildings and build a multi-level parking garage equipped with LED lighting, security cameras and guards, for all of our evening services, concerts, and all other events."

"It's about time!" someone yelled in a joking tone.

"Hey, I feel your pain." Julian chuckled, then went on, "The three thousand additional seats in the sanctuary, plus the added parking spaces, will allow us to expand our reach and better compete with other large arenas in the area. Imagine having concerts for top Christian performers at our place of worship every month?"

Thunderous applause filled the sanctuary again.

16

"We also plan on adding a third prayer service each month, for ten thousand folks at each service instead of just seven! How cool is that? As it is, we could have easily issued fifteen thousand tickets for this event alone..." Julian's voice was smooth, calm, persuasive.

"The rest of the funds will be used to build larger classrooms for our students, add another childcare facility on the campus, expand the cafeteria and bookstore, and refurbish our offices and conference rooms."

Heads nodded all throughout the church.

"But it's not gonna be cheap! Eight-point-six million dollars will be needed to achieve our goal. As you've heard me say many times, a second-class effort will never produce a first-class result! Nor will a first-class effort produce a second-class result. Amen?"

"Amen!" came the vociferous reply of everyone, in unison.

Julian said, "It's a rather large sum of money, to be sure, but God has never failed us in the past when funds were needed. He won't fail us this time either..."

This was said with a boldness and confidence few other pastors possessed. "Let us pray. Lord, as we begin our new fundraising campaign, I ask that you fill each heart with the spirit of generosity, just as You have been so generous to each of us. We know it's coming, Lord, and we thank You in advance for the funds we seek, in the mighty name of Jesus, Amen!"

"Amen!" came the reply.

"By sowing into this costly renovation project, the harvest your generosity will yield will be quite vast. Just like our last expansion project, if we build it, they will surely come! Remember this when filling out the commitment cards you were given on the way in.

"Since we still have ongoing fundraisers for other endeavors, we're only taking pledges for now. But come January, we'll start collecting for this project. So make sure you honor God by following through on whatever pledges you make today. For everyone livestreaming with us, simply text your intent to the number on your screen. Amen?"

"Amen, Pastor!" many shouted.

Julian smiled brightly for all to see. "How about a rousing hand clap for our awesome God!"

Loud applause and cheering once again reverberated throughout the sanctuary.

Not surprisingly, Charmaine DeShields' voice rose a little higher than the others. By being one of the church's top givers, she got to sit in the front rows each Sunday, among the rich and famous in the community.

Some were known the world over, including professional athletes from the Seattle Seahawks and Mariners. Norm and Nancy Wilshire also occupied front row seats. Just being seen online and on TV with some of Seattle's most influential citizens not only elevated Charmaine's social status, it was good for business. Very good!

Once everyone settled down, Pastor Julian proceeded, "Okay, on your feet everyone." Everyone rose from their seats in one accord. "Now, repeat after me, brothers and sisters, 'I am worthy!'"

"I am worthy!" they shouted.

"I am significant!"

"I am significant!" they shouted a little louder.

"I am set apart!"

"I am set apart!" they boomed even louder.

"I have all the talent I need to prosper in life!"

They repeated it in unison.

"As a blessed and highly favored child of God, I'm already prosperous in my mind!" Their voices were at fever pitch now.

Julian prayed again, "Lord, Father, God, as Your blessed and highly favored children, we ask that You supernaturally open our minds and imaginations to the fullest, so we can receive Your greatest and richest blessings—spiritually, physically, mentally, and most importantly, financially…"

A barrage of "Amens", "Hallelujahs" and "We claim and receive it, Lord!" could be heard all throughout the sanctuary.

"In faith, we speak into existence the things we desire, the very things that will bring more enjoyment to our lives! Daddy in Heaven, we hereby declare that You shower us with the blessings we so richly deserve. After all, we are your children and You own it all! We're ready and waiting to be blessed by You, in Jesus' mighty name, Amen!"

"Amen, Pastor!"

"Please be seated." Pastor Julian took a small sip from his water bottle, kissed his pregnant wife on the lips, and faced the crowd again. "The Lord gave me a message to share with you all today…"

Many shifted in their seats, eagerly anticipating his next words. "And that message is this: '*It's…Your…Time!*'"

There was more thunderous applause.

Rodney Williams struck a chord on the organ. The thick sound shook the air, filling every inch of the sanctuary, causing many to bolt out of their seats. Some jumped up and down. Others marched in place rather unevenly. Some younger members did what could be best described as an awkward calisthenics of sorts; their heads bobbed up and down, their arms flailed wildly in all directions.

Julian paced the large stage; his sparkling light brown eyes drank in the full crowd seated before him. "God loves each of you unconditionally, church, and wants to bless you all beyond your wildest dreams! With that truth firmly settled in your minds, are you believing God for a new car?"

"Yes, Lord!"

"A new house?"

Someone else shouted, "Yes, Lord! In Jesus' name, I pray!"

"Greater wealth?"

Someone else replied, "I receive it, Lord!"

On and on they went, one after the other.

Pastor Martín let it continue until the last voice was heard, before saying, "What were the last three words Jesus spoke on the cross, before breathing His last breath in human form, and becoming our unconditional Mediator in Heaven?"

Many shouted in unison, "It is finished!"

Julian asked, "What?"

"It is finished!" they bellowed even louder.

Signaling with his hands, he said, "I still can't hear you, church!"

"IT IS FINISHED!" came their full-throated reply.

Pastor Martín grinned for all to see. "That's more like it! Wanna know what this means for you?" Squaring his broad shoulders back, the lead pastor said, "You know that new house you want? Well, I'm here to tell you Jesus finished it for you two-thousand years ago on the cross! All you have to do is claim it, in Jesus' mighty, miracle-providing name! It's already finished, just for you. How awesome is that?"

"I receive it, Lord!" a female voice declared victoriously.

"Bring it, Lord, your servant is ready and waiting!" someone in the balcony yelled, not even realizing how ridiculous it was for him to be pleading with the King of Majesty to bless one of His lowly servants with great riches.

"Bless us, Lord!" someone else shouted.

Everyone perked up in their seats even more, their minds now working at Mach speed. Some rubbed their hands together with greedy glints in their eyes, as if at a craps table in a casino, or at a get-rich-quick seminar.

Pastor Martín stopped pacing and gazed out at everyone, greatly comforted seeing the many newcomers clinging to every word he spoke. Just seeing the mesmerized expressions on their faces satisfied him immensely. He fed off their energy as much as they fed off his.

He went on, "Brothers and sisters, what are the true desires of your heart? Whatever they are—you must draw them out from deep within, by expressing your faith, using only words that agree with what the Lord has already done for you!

"You must never lose sight of the fact that it's all there for the taking—all you have to do is name it and claim it, in Jesus' mighty name! Jesus Himself said in John fourteen, fourteen, 'You may ask me for anything in my name, and I will do it!'"

This declaration generated even more rousing applause from so many.

Someone yelled, "I believe, Lord, and I receive it!"

"Uhm, gimmie that new Mercedes, in Jesus' name!" someone working part time at a fast food restaurant shouted from the rear of the sanctuary, on the lower level. Had she made this declaration on the job, or at any other place than here, most would laugh at her or think she was slightly off kilter. But not at this gathering place...

"Fill my storehouse, Lord, your servant is ready!" another ignorant churchgoer with only self-centered desires, foolishly declared.

Julian shook his head in agreement, then continued, "I can't overstate this enough—in order for the things you desire to eventually become a reality, you must have total faith that you will receive it all without ever doubting! As in *never*! Do you hear me, church?"

"Yes, Pastor, we hear you!"

"Loud and clear, Pastor Julian!"

"Good, because only then will it ever become manifest in your life, and part of your physical experience! Never forget, if you lack in life, it's because you lack in faith!"

Another chorus of "Amens" and "Hallelujahs" ensued...

Pastor Julian gazed out at the congregation. "One more thing: don't insult God by thinking too small! Remember, He owns everything. This is your time to start dreaming big, people! Otherwise, how can you possibly expect to receive God's most bountiful blessings?

"But remember, the more seeds you sow into this church, which represents the purest and most fertile soil in the greater Northwest, the more you'll receive! Do I make myself clear?"

"Yes, Pastor!"

"Crystal clear!"

"Okay, good. Time to get busy making your petitions known to the One who saw your unformed bodies, before He breathed a single star out of His mouth. This same Creator who holds the entire universe in the palm of His hands is ready and waiting to bless you beyond your wildest dreams! It's time to ask Him to empty His storehouses just for you! Ready?"

"Yes, Pastor!" they shouted in unison.

"Let's get busy then..."

Julian Martín took his seat next to his wife on the massive stage. With her right thumb, Imogen tickled the back of the ring her husband recently gave to her as a tenth anniversary church memento, causing the 5-carat diamond to sparkle ever so brilliantly.

Everyone in the sanctuary marveled, seeing the full spectrum of effervescent colors exploding out of the stone, splashing on the walls and ceiling, easily rivaling the sparkling glow from the colorful blue sequin dress she wore, that would no longer fit her once she started showing a few months from now.

After many weeks of practice, Imogen knew how to best display it on her finger for maximum exposure. While she pretended not to notice all the attention her ring had garnered from so many, she did it just as much for herself as she did for them.

The optics spoke volumes. It was all part of the gig...

Rodney Williams played soft Gospel hymns on the organ to further stimulate the minds of his brothers and sisters in attendance.

The congregation wasted no time coming into agreement with everything their pastor had just loosed for them in Heaven. Some shouted their petitions to God. Others spoke in silence or in near whispers; confidently claiming the many material blessings that were theirs for the taking, as God's children, in Jesus' name.

Some were so overcome with emotion, they sobbed tears of joy. Many spoke in unknown tongues—declaring this and that—filling the air with what sounded like unintelligible gibberish, as they made their most grandiose desires known, by speaking them all into existence, without anyone there to translate it for them.

You name it—great riches, perfect health, new homes, fancy jewelry, exquisite cars and boats, first-class trips around the world—they claimed it all in Jesus' mighty name!

Charmaine fell into both categories. Sometimes she whispered. At other times, she boldly shouted her declarations, reciting key scriptures the Martíns had drilled into her head the past seven years, to solidify what she thought was hers for the asking.

After a while, she kneeled on the third step leading to the stage, and raised her hands toward Heaven for all to see. "For my new six-bedroom house on Northlake Way, I declare Psalm thirty-seven, four, which states, 'Delight yourself in the Lord, and he will give you the desires of your heart.'

"For the seven figure annual income I seek, I claim Jeremiah twenty-nine, eleven, which states, 'For I know the plans I have for you, declares the Lord, plans for welfare and not for evil, to give you a future and a hope.'

"As for the talent, discipline, and determination I'll need to obtain all these things, I once again declare, Philippians four-thirteen, 'I can do all things through Christ who strengthens me.'

On and on she went, with the confidence of a Lebron James on the basketball court, with five seconds left in the game and the ball in her hands, knowing for certain she would score, but never once considering whether the things she asked for—in prayer—would be good for her spiritual journey or not.

Her constant hope as one of the church's top recruiters was that God would keep prospering her, so she could use her material possessions to increase church membership once the new expansion was completed, and turn newcomers into believers as well.

Charmaine returned to her seat in the front row. A smile broke across her face. What other reason could there be for being blessed with so much?

It all made perfect sense to her.

Thy will be done, Lord...

3

THIRTY MINUTES INTO THE "name-it-and-claim-it" prayer session, Charmaine DeShields felt convicted by the power of the Holy Spirit and burst out of her seat in the front row.

Turning to face her brothers and sisters, she yelled, "Hold on, y'all!" It was loud enough that everyone heard her. She paused a moment for those whose heads were bowed in prayer, not wanting anyone to miss out on what she was about to say.

It was too important.

When all eyes were steadied on her, she declared, "When I leave here, I'm closing on a house that sold for one-point-six-million dollars. Which explains why I'm not so casually dressed!"

The sanctuary erupted into thunderous applause.

"Praise God, I sold it to a wealthy techie in one of the finer neighborhoods in the area. It's been a long time coming. Believe me when I say, I worked very hard on this deal." A smile lifted those full lips of hers. "The good news is my commission will be a cool fifty-thousand dollars."

There was more handclapping amid a foray of ooh's and aah's, mostly from those who didn't earn that kind of money in a year.

Charmaine craned her neck back to her boyfriend up on stage. Rodney removed his right hand from the ebony and ivory keys he was playing, and blew his girlfriend a flying kiss.

She beamed in reply, then faced the huge gathering again. "But here's the best part." She paused for effect before continuing, "I want you all to know I plan on giving my entire commission to help fund the new expansion project! God just put it on my heart now."

A loud collective gasp filled the room, followed by loud cheering and rejoicing.

Someone yelled out, "Whoa! Are you serious?"

"Totally!" Charmaine looked back again, to gauge her boyfriend's reaction. Rodney blinked hard and stopped playing the organ. He gazed at his girlfriend, totally stunned by her outrageous declaration.

Charmaine became teary-eyed. "Ever since I joined this church seven years ago, God has blessed me immeasurably!" Pointing to Julian and Imogen Martín, she went on, "Those two people are very special to me! I can't even imagine what the future holds under their unwavering leadership. I'm sure the next seven years will make the last seven, amazing as they were, look like nothing.

"Truth be told, had it not been for them, I don't think I would have had the guts to take the huge leap of faith I needed to invest so much money advertising my real estate business, which means all those images of me on all those city buses wouldn't be there now.

"This church, those two pastors, apostles, I mean, helped me step out of my comfort zone by giving me the courage to proceed with the plan. Not only that, they reminded me every step of the way that I was one of God's princesses, I was already successful, and God would surely honor my faith and commitment to Him by blessing my socks off!"

Proud smile on her face, she said, "I haven't broken the million dollar annual plateau yet, but that day's fast approaching, in Jesus' name!"

Many shouted, "Amen!"

"Believe me when I say, church, had Julian and Imogen not started speaking my success into existence, even before I did, my real estate business would be a small fraction of what it is now.

"Even my closing later today is with clients who contacted me after seeing my ad on a city bus. How awesome is that?"

Applause flooded the sanctuary again.

"But here's the point I wish to stress, much like the investment I made in my business, the fifty grand I'm pledging now to the church expansion project can very easily turn into ten times that much, when God blesses my faithfulness and obedience again.

"That said, I'd be foolish not to do it, right?" Heads nodded all throughout the sanctuary. "Well, the same can happen to you, too, if you faithfully sow into this amazing church! Like Pastor Julian said, remember this when you fill out your commitment cards."

More shouts of, "Amen!", "Hallelujah!" and "Praise God!" drifted up to the ceiling from the mouths of her fellow believers.

Many gazed at Charmaine like they did the celebrities seated with her in the front rows. What she saw on their faces filled her with a deep sense of pride. Some shed tears of joy for her, all the while hoping God would bless them so they, too, could give as generously as she was about to.

"In fact, let's make it official!" Charmaine retrieved her cellphone from her handbag, and called her investment banker.

As it rang, she glanced at the Martíns seated on plush chairs up on the stage. They weren't the slightest bit surprised that she was the first to commit to the project. But the entire commission?

Julian and Imogen shot thumbs-up gestures at Charmaine. Their surgically-repaired smiles were so wide, even the backs of their teeth were visible.

Judging by the looks on the many faces in the sanctuary, it was evident to the Martíns that Charmaine really drove the message home. She made everyone believe that sowing into this thriving ministry was a mere pittance, when compared to the countless riches they would soon receive from the very Throne of Heaven for their generous giving.

The fact that she had interrupted the session to publicly commit would surely spur others to do the same, including those in the front rows with the greatest means. Her timing had been perfect.

Her faith kept maturing more and more as the years passed...

The congregation grew silent when, after four rings, Kaito Fujimoto answered. "How's my favorite client today?" This was his usual greeting whenever Charmaine called. He knew how much she enjoyed hearing it.

"Blessed and highly favored, Kaito, as always," she declared, rushing up on stage and positioning herself in front of a microphone, so everyone could hear her banker's voice. "But you already know I'm God's favorite princess!"

Many burst out in laughter, not even caring that her declaration to her banker had just placed herself above them, as if she were more special in God's eyes than they were.

Fujimoto chuckled. He was having lunch in downtown Seattle with his good friend, Mark Lau, a Chinese American who'd moved to China after his wife died, to preach the Gospel over there.

They just finished thanking God for the meal when his cellphone rang. "So, what can I do for you, Charmaine?" Kaito cupped the phone and whispered to Mark, "She's the one who will be selling your house..."

Mark nodded, but remained silent.

Charmaine declared, "Just wanted you to know I'll be closing on a big sale later this afternoon. My commission will be somewhere in the neighborhood of fifty-thousand dollars."

"Wow, congratulations! Will it be your largest commission to date?"

"Yes, but as God's favorite princess, it's just the tip of the iceberg! I expect even greater commissions in the future!" The smile on her face was so bright, it lit up the sanctuary even more than Imogen's flashy sequin dress and diamond ring.

"I'm so happy for you, Charmaine, but not the least bit surprised to hear this. Was this sale generated from your city bus campaign?"

"Yes, sir!"

"Those ads are really starting to pay huge dividends. The future keeps getting brighter and brighter for you!"

Charmaine waved her right hand victoriously above her head. "I receive that, Kaito, every word of it! Keep speaking it into existence on my behalf."

Fujimoto grimaced at her words. Worse, hearing so many shouting positive declarations meant she had him on speaker phone again, even though she knew he was uncomfortable with it.

Mark Lau saw him shaking his head. Whatever Kaito had just heard, he didn't like it.

"Anyway, the reason I'm telling you this is, once the money's been deposited, I want it transferred into a separate account, to be set aside for the new renovation project at my church."

The investment banker's eyes widened. "The entire fifty grand?"

"Yes, sir! Since the funds won't be needed until early next year, I want whatever interest is earned during that time to also be given to the church."

More shouts of, "Amen!" and "Hallelujah!" drifted up to the ceiling from Kaito's former church family, only it was louder this time.

Fujimoto remarked, "That's very generous of you, Charmaine."

"Glory to God!" Another proud smile pressed onto her lips, seeing the wealthiest members in the front rows all aglow, showering her with silent praise. Her heart swelled in her chest. It felt good to be one of them...

Rodney Williams also noticed and resumed playing the organ. He, too, would be giving to the expansion project, but nowhere near what his girlfriend had just pledged. As a single father of three kids, even a check in the amount of $1000 would be a stretch for him.

A small part of him was upset because his girlfriend had made the announcement without telling him first. Or was it jealousy because Charmaine out-earned him by a long shot?

Rodney couldn't discern between the two. Then again, like she'd said, the Lord had just put it on her heart to do it...

Meanwhile, Kaito Fujimoto scratched his head thinking, *If it really was for the glory of God, why is she telling me, not to mention the many others listening? What about not letting her left hand know what her right hand was doing?* He brushed the thought aside and played along. "When do you expect to receive it?"

"If all goes well, it should be in my account within a week."

Kaito cupped the phone when the waiter brought their salads. "Don't wait for me, Mark," he said softly to his friend. Then to Charmaine, "Okay, noted. Anything else I can do for you?"

"Yeah. Come back to church!"

"You know I attend church every week, Charmaine."

"You know what I mean, Kaito. My church! You and Lucy are terribly missed here. We'd love to have you back. I can't tell you the many blessings the two of you are missing out on! We're not the largest church in the greater Northwest by accident, you know..."

Kaito shook his head again. He knew exactly what Charmaine was doing. This was yet another recruiting ploy on her part, to hopefully persuade him to reconsider coming back.

As a former member himself, Fujimoto knew success stories like this were what had built the foundation of the *Blessed and Highly Favored Full Gospel Church*, ultimately transforming it from a small shopping center meeting place into a vibrant megachurch, in just a few short years.

Fujimoto had used the same recruiting tactics himself when inviting new people, often claiming that his membership there was at the heart of God's generosity toward him.

His words were only partly true. While his investment business did greatly expand during his time there, the unspoken rule was the more he tithed to the church and gave to other church projects, the more clients the Martíns sent his way.

This was something Kaito understood with even greater clarity upon leaving the church. He cleared his throat. "We miss you too, but we're perfectly happy at our place of worship. Even though we live on half of what we once did, Lucy and I couldn't be happier."

Charmaine grimaced, then turned the throttle to full speed. "You wouldn't believe the growth we've experienced since you left; I'm telling you, Kaito, miracle upon miracle! You, of all people, know how greatly I struggled with my real estate business when you left three years ago. Now look at me!"

"I admit your recent success is commendable…"

"I can't stress enough that God's hand is really on the Martíns. Their messages are even more powerful now!" Charmaine glanced over at her two spiritual and financial mentors. "Did I tell you they were recently appointed as apostles?"

"Doesn't surprise me in the least." Fujimoto was tempted to ask if their new titles were self-appointed, or did they attend some prosperity "apostle school", or merely donate a sizable amount to some particular cause. Even though his suspicion wasn't without foundation, he left it alone…

Julian Martín listened, hoping no one saw him gritting his teeth. He knew more than anyone that Kaito's remark wasn't meant to be taken in a positive light. The prosperity gospel he preached, the very one that had blessed the Fujimotos so richly over the years—when they were still members—was now seen by them as a false gospel message.

Charmaine said, "That's what I can't understand. If you really believe that, it makes me wonder again why you left us in the first place? All I can do is keep praying that God will change your mind, and you and Lucy will come back soon."

Another chorus of "Amens" filled the rafters.

Fujimoto wanted to counter, by telling her he and Lucy prayed just as diligently that God would open her eyes to the true Gospel message, like He did for them, and pluck her out from underneath the Martíns' false teachings. But now wasn't the time…

Instead, he said, "Congratulations, again."

Charmaine wanted to keep pressing the issue, but with so many of her fellow congregants listening—including many newcomers—she didn't want them to witness a possible crash and burn.

"Once the money's in my account, we can discuss a short-term investment strategy until I transfer it to my church."

"As you wish," Fujimoto said to his only remaining client at the *Blessed and Highly Favored Full Gospel Church*. "Changing topics, I had actually planned on calling you today…"

"Oh, yeah, why's that?"

"A good friend of mine is visiting from China. Mark is from the States, but he moved to the Far East to preach the Gospel over there ten years ago. He'd like you to put a house he owns on the market after his father-in-law passes, which should be any day now…"

"Aww, sorry to hear that…"

"At least we can rest assured knowing he has eternal assurance…"

Charmaine smiled warmly. "Amen to that!"

"Why don't you stop by the house later, so the two of you can meet."

"Hmm, my schedule's tight for today. The only possible window would be on the way to dinner. I'm taking Rodney to SkyCity Restaurant at the Space Needle, to celebrate the big sale."

"Good choice."

Charmaine winked at her boyfriend. "He's never been there. Our reservation's at nine, so we won't be able to stay long. Will seven work for you?"

"That would be great. We'll be home all night."

"Okay then, tell Mark I greatly appreciate the opportunity. I'll be happy to help him any way I can."

"I will. Make sure to bring a seller's agreement with you."

"Already have one in my car. Thanks again for thinking of me."

Kaito grinned. "It's the least I can do for my favorite client…"

Charmaine loved the added attention his comment had generated from the many who were listening. "Aww, so sweet of you, Kaito. See you a little later. Enjoy your lunch."

The call ended.

"See what I mean? God's timing is always perfect!" Charmaine declared. "My pledge is already paying dividends! Isn't God good?"

The congregation roared to life once more.

The Martíns were thankful for the powerful object lesson Charmaine had just provided on how God rewarded those who sowed into this church.

Once again, her timing had been perfect…

Rodney shook his head in awe. *Simply amazing!*

MEANWHILE, JUST AS THE call ended, as if on cue, a city bus passed by with Charmaine DeShield's image plastered on it. Pointing at it, Kaito said to his friend, "That's her right there!"

Mark Lau said, "Talk about timing! I saw her image on another bus on the way here. The woman's everywhere."

After bringing his good friend up to speed, Kaito sighed. "The good she could do for God's Kingdom with that kind of money!"

Pastor Lau said, "Has she forgotten what Jesus said in Matthew six, about Christians practicing our righteousness in front of others? Is she even aware that the praise she just received from so many nullified any further rewards she would have rightly stored up in Heaven for her generosity, had she only kept it between herself and God?"

"I'm afraid not, Mark. Sharing good works with each other is the standard at her church. It's what drives the machine, so to speak. Preachers like Julian and Imogen Martín do all they can to shield their mostly uninformed flocks from anything they feel might hurt them.

"You know the type, avoid negativity at all costs, by preaching God's love and blessings only, and never the other side of the coin, namely God's justice for sin."

Mark Lau was familiar with the Martíns' brand of preaching. "Yeah, well, not to sound disrespectful, but I struggle to address them as two of God's anointed preachers."

Kaito swallowed the forkful of pan-seared tuna in his mouth. "Can't argue with you there, brother. That's why Lucy and I pray for them every night before going to sleep. We pray for everyone at that church, in fact."

Lau felt a pang of guilt stabbing at his insides for what he'd just said. *The weakest Christians are just as saved as the strongest ones*, he reminded himself. "Why don't we pray for them now…"

The two men dropped their heads at the restaurant table and prayed that God would convict the Martíns of their false teachings, and rescue Charmaine from the church Kaito had been completely dedicated to, until God changed his heart three years ago and placed him elsewhere…

AS THE PRAYER SESSION wrapped up at the *Blessed and Highly Favored Full Gospel Church*, more than seven billion dollars' worth of worldly, material possessions had been claimed by their many members. And thanks to Charmaine's kind generosity, another $1.3M was pledged to the new renovation project, on top of her $50,000 commitment.

Everyone left the church feeling fortunate to be blessed with fearless pastors like Julian and Imogen Martín. There was no one like them anywhere in Seattle! Were there prayer warriors like them anywhere in America? They seriously doubted it…

Thanks to them, their heads were full of even bigger dreams for the future. Why would anyone want to miss out on this must-attend life-altering event?

For those who were fairly new to the church, and totally ignorant to the Bible, whatever this man was offering, they wanted in. He had a gift of explaining things in such a way, they couldn't help but feel motivated by him. If anyone had God's ear, it was him!

Knowing this, why would any believer in Seattle attend any church other than this one? The blessings they were missing out on...No wonder a third monthly prayer service would be added once the new construction was completed.

Yet, for all the praying they did, never once did Julian, or anyone else among the large gathering, openly repent of their unconfessed sins, or ask God to help them to become more holy and obedient. Nor did they pray for a deeper understanding of His ways, so they could become better soul winners, and know their Maker more intimately.

In short, there wasn't a shred of genuine repentance offered up to a just and holy God by anyone in that frenzied environment!

It was all about prospering themselves first, then helping others do the same...

Yes, it was all about "self", the very thing Jesus told His true followers to deny...

4

AFTER BATTLING THROUGH LATE rush hour traffic, Charmaine and Rodney arrived at the Fujimoto residence a few minutes after 7 p.m.

Lucy opened the front door. It was impossible to ignore the glow on their faces. She greeted them both with hugs. "Nice to see you both again. Please come in."

Kaito and Mark Lau were in the living room waiting for them to arrive.

"Greetings! Welcome back to our humble abode. It's been a while."

"Yes, it has, Kaito," Rodney said. "It's good to see you again!"

"Judging by your blooming faces, I assume everything went smoothly with the closing…"

Charmaine flashed a captivating smile. "Signed, sealed and delivered!"

Kaito shot a thumbs up gesture at her. "Can't say I'm surprised. I can only imagine how you must feel."

"What can I say? It's been an amazing day, Kaito, from start to finish! And to think the day's not even over yet. God is good!"

Lucy asked Rodney, "You must be so proud of your girlfriend?"

Rodney grinned. "Couldn't be prouder, Lucy!"

His comment caused Charmaine to blush. "Aww, thanks, baby…"

"I'd like to introduce you both to our good friend, Mark Lau."

Rodney extended his right hand. "Pleasure meeting you, Mark."

Charmaine did the same.

"Pleasure meeting you both as well." At 5'8" Mark Lau was of average height. Then again, from the Fujimoto's vantagepoint—since Kaito was 5'3" and Lucy was 4'11"—both begged to differ with that assumption.

In Lucy's opinion, Mark Lau was a giant which, on many levels other than his height, was certainly true.

The Fujimotos were both in their early 60s. They recently celebrated their 40th wedding anniversary. After throwing a memorable party for their parents, their three children—all in their 30s—sent them to Hawaii for a week. The best characteristics their children used to describe their parents were loving, caring, polite, respectful, prompt, and strict.

Now that all three were married with children of their own, they appreciated their strict upbringing infinitely more now than when they were living under their parents' roof.

Kaito and Lucy really enjoyed themselves in Hawaii. It was the perfect gift. The only gifts they enjoyed receiving more from their children were the seven grandchildren they had blessed them with.

Kaito's face was so thin it was as if his cheekbones were trying to press through his skin. This wasn't due to sickness or disease, it's just the way he looked. His black eyes were deep and penetrating, enough to easily intimidate others. Yet, he never used them for that purpose.

He was too friendly for that. His wiry salt-and-pepper hair was gradually thinning at the crown of his head.

Lucy's face was much fuller than her husband's. Also of Japanese descent, the shape of her head resembled an upside down pear. Her hairstyle was a silver-white bob with bangs. She had big soft eyes which were a shade or two lighter than her husband's, a well-proportioned nose, and small ears. Her skin was soft and on the pale side.

She didn't smile nearly as much as Kaito did, but that didn't mean she wasn't happy in life. She *was* happy, and extremely grateful for the life God had blessed her with. Whereas Kaito looked every bit his age of 64, Lucy looked ten years younger than her age, which was 61.

Mark Lau was 55 and on the lean side. His eyes were kind, friendly and expressive. He had a full head of black hair. But up close, it was easy to detect the few wisps of gray in some places. He had a flat nose and an engaging smile that often served to put many minds at ease.

Without a doubt, his most distinguishing feature was that he was a generous and deeply thoughtful individual.

Lucy said to Rodney and Charmaine, "I know you can't stay long, but I've prepared a little something to hold you over until dinner. Please help yourselves."

Rodney saw the fruit and cheese tray on the coffee table and wasted no time digging in.

"Don't eat too much, sweetness. You'll ruin your appetite."

"I won't, baby…"

Charmaine put a piece of sharp cheddar cheese on a wheat cracker, and took a bite. Swallowing, she asked, "So, how'd the two of you meet?"

Lucy sat next to her husband on the couch opposite their guests, which was separated by a coffee table.

Lucy was so tiny that if she wanted her feet to touch the floor, she had to lean all the way up in her seat. And even then, it was just barely. If she leaned back on the couch even one inch, her feet would dangle.

Charmaine silently chuckled at the thought. *So cute!*

Kaito said, "I met Mark at a men's Bible conference in Southern California. Yes, the one that caused me to leave your church..."

Rodney and Charmaine exchanged brief glances. The smiles vanished from their faces.

Mark Lau shook his head. "Life was anything but easy for me at that time. The conference took place a few weeks after I lost my wife to an aggressive form of breast cancer."

Charmaine frowned. "Oh my, sorry to hear that..."

Mark sighed. "Six months after Alli was diagnosed, she was gone, leaving me and my two children little time to absorb it all, let alone prepare for a future without her. She was in her early-forties.

"Part of the reason I'm back in the States was to recognize her tenth year death anniversary with my two children, Rachel and Samuel.

"As you can imagine, I was so overcome by grief that I took an extended leave from work. During that time, I started drinking alcohol again and questioning my faith in God.

"A month after I buried Alli, I confessed to my longtime friend from Portland, Oregon, about my constantly wavering faith. Tristan wasn't surprised to hear me say this. Much like Alli, he sensed my faith wasn't as genuine as I proclaimed it to be. Since he and Alli shared the same Biblical viewpoint, both were concerned about my spiritual well-being.

"When Alli was told she had six months to live, knowing she was Heaven-bound, she accepted it more quickly than I did. Tristan promised my wife on her deathbed that he would look after us when she was gone. This was meant from a spiritual standpoint.

"Inviting me to the men's conference was the first step in the process. He even paid my admission. In truth, I didn't want to go. I was still wallowing in self-pity, and didn't want to be surrounded by a large group of people.

"It turned out being one of the best decisions I ever made. By being exposed to sound doctrinal teaching from keynote speakers who were true theologians in every sense of the calling, and staunch defenders of the Gospel, I realized that weekend the salvation I always thought I had, I never had at all.

"Alli was right all along—I really was going through the motions of what I thought best represented true Christianity. I had profession without possession, as the saying goes. The conference changed everything...

"A month after my beloved was in Heaven, God answered her prayer, by using those speakers to open my eyes to the true Gospel message.

"Crossing over from spiritual death to life was the most remarkable transformation of my life. As God would have it, Tristan and I ended up being seated next to Kaito."

Mark glanced at Kaito. "We've been the best of friends ever since."

Kaito smiled in reply.

Charmaine was touched by his gesture. "Aww, how sweet!"

Mark continued, "Not too long after that I felt called to the ministry. When God opened my eyes to the persecution Christians in China were suffering for their faith, I felt called to join my brothers and sisters in preaching the Gospel over there."

"Very noble of you..." Rodney plopped a few grapes in his mouth. When it came to chips, nuts, or grapes, he wasn't a one-at-a-timer.

Kaito interjected, "Prior to taking that trip, while Mark's faith was floundering, as you both know, life was seemingly perfect for me. I was a full-fledged member at your church, my investment banking business was booming, and my family was in good health..."

Charmaine and Rodney both nodded yes.

He sighed. "My way of thinking quickly changed that weekend. After listening to just one speaker, I realized how little I understood about the Word of God, and how much of my own prideful, self-centered will I had placed on the parts I *was* familiar with.

"The simple truth is, the three of us went to that conference all professing faith in Christ. But only one of us was truly saved. And it wasn't either of us. Only Tristan was..."

Charmaine stopped chewing the food in her mouth and shot her investment banker a sideways look. *What?!*

Kaito shook his head. "Oh, I thought I was saved alright. But, in truth, I really wasn't. I assure you this wasn't an uplifting self-discovery on my part. Like Mark said, the conference changed everything. The knowledge and command those men had of the Word of God was entirely different than what Pastor Julian preached on each Sunday.

"So different, in fact, that it was hard to believe they read from the same Book. God used each speaker to open my eyes a little more and light a fire in my soul that has only intensified since. Like everyone else fortunate enough to attend the retreat, we left Southern California with a new, more balanced, understanding of the true Gospel message."

Rodney reached for Charmaine's hand as they sat on the couch and listened, hoping neither of them would overreact.

"Things really got interesting when I returned home and told Lucy about my life-altering experience, and how transformed I felt."

Lucy giggled. "That would be putting it mildly. When he told me the gospel Pastor Julian preached was a false one, based entirely on self-centered wants and desires, I stared at him as if he hadn't been enlightened, but brainwashed.

"If that wasn't enough, he blurted out that his days at the Blessed and Highly Favored Full Gospel Church were over. I was caught completely off guard. My mood soured even more when he told me one of the keynote speakers had recommended a church an hour north of our home, up in Everett, and that he would be attending that following Sunday.

"I admit I was angry. How could he make a decision that would alter our lives without asking me first? When I called to tell the children, they were equally concerned and agreed their father had been brainwashed down in the San Fernando Valley, even though he kept insisting nothing could be further from the truth."

Kaito frowned. "Talk about feeling ganged up on! Things didn't improve much when I arrived home after my first visit to Grace Bible Church. When I tried explaining the many vast differences between the two churches, Lucy shot me a look as if to say, 'You must be joking!'"

Kaito took a sip of tea. "After a few uneasy moments, she told me Pastor Julian wanted to see me before the evening service that night..."

Charmaine leaned back on the couch. "I still remember like it was yesterday."

Kaito nodded. "I remember seeing you there. Both of you. I wasn't surprised to see the conference room full of church elders and deacons. Even my three children showed up to pray for me."

Rodney said, "I still remember how upset Pastor Julian was. He refused to believe God wanted you to leave the church you were a member of for so many years, after just one conference and a visit to a church that could never compare to ours."

Charmaine interjected, "Imogen was even more upset. For the life in her, she couldn't accept how you were willing to walk away from the church that had blessed you so much. She agreed with Lucy and your children that you had been brainwashed..."

Kaito chuckled softly. "Of course, I understood why some of you thought that way. But I was very much in control of my senses at that time, and made it clear that no matter how hard they tried, my decision was final and nothing would change my mind."

Charmaine exhaled deeply. "That's when the room grew icy cold."

Lucy said, "You can say that again! I remember lowering my head in shame. The way he openly rebuked the two pastors I greatly admired and respected so much was mortifying. I was consumed by sadness and despair.

"I honestly thought he had a mental breakdown, especially when he kept praising God the whole ride home, for giving him the strength to overcome all attempts to get him to change his mind..."

Kaito smiled at Lucy. "It was a difficult time for us to say the least. But even three years later, my convictions haven't changed. They've only been strengthened. I still don't believe in the prosperity gospel the Martíns teach. With respect to the two of you, I still reject it as a false gospel."

Kaito leaned up in his chair, his eyes settled on Charmaine and Rodney. "Even before I attended the men's conference, I found myself questioning the Martíns' approach to the Word of God. Would you like to know what started the beginning of the end for me at your church?"

Charmaine glanced at Rodney. He shrugged his shoulders. "Sure. Tell us..."

"A few months before that time, your pastors invited me to accompany them to New York City, for one of the many wealth-building conferences they attend; on a private jet, no less.

"To say I was honored, and excited, would be an understatement, especially since they'd hinted about introducing me to new clients."

Kaito sighed. "Everything was going great until I offhandedly expressed to one of the featured speakers, a female pastor, of my desire to one day become a pastor myself.

"Without hesitation, and with a prideful expression on her face, she said she had the power to ordain me right then and there.

"When she first said it, I nodded my gratitude as if being a pastor could be obtained so easily. At that time, I considered myself fairly-well versed in the scriptures. But in truth, I'd never seriously studied the Bible let alone read it all the way through, so how could I possibly preach on it?

"The more I thought about it, the more her words rubbed me the wrong way. I mean, could being a pastor really be obtained so effortlessly, without having a broad knowledge of the inspired Word of God?

"It took many years of schooling and training before I could be licensed as an investment banker. Yet this woman made what I now believe is the highest calling anyone could ever have seem so cheap and flimsy.

"It forced me to question so many things, including the church I attended, and my faith in God in general.

"Not too long after that, I heard a message online that basically confirmed what I had thought in New York about the copious amounts of time pastors needed to spend in the Word, if they are to be worth their salt.

"The man on the radio stirred something deep inside me. He caused me to look outside my church for guidance and leadership. That's when I first learned about the conference in Southern California. It was the icing on the cake, so to speak."

Rodney was confused. "Wait! Are you saying you got saved by switching churches?"

"No, Rodney. With all due respect to your church and pastors, I switched churches *because* I got saved. I wasn't brainwashed in Southern California. I, we…" he said, glancing at Mark, "…were redeemed."

Kaito removed his glasses and massaged the bridge of his nose, before his eyes settled on Charmaine and Rodney again.

"Jeremiah twenty-nine, thirteen says, 'You will seek me and find me when you seek me with all your heart.' Not *may* find Him, *will*! So, the question is, are you seeking God that way?"

The house grew silent for what seemed like an eternity.

Charmaine was the first to break the silence. She glanced at Mark. "So, where's the location of the house you want me to sell?"

Mark was sitting on the couch with the Fujimotos. He crossed one leg over the other. "Kenmore."

Charmaine's bright eyes lit up. "I sold a house in Kenmore last year to someone working at Amazon. It's a good location."

Mark added, "It's a four bedroom, two-and-a-half bath rancher with full basement, and a two car garage."

"Square footage?"

"Just under three-thousand square feet of air-conditioned space. It's already been appraised at five-hundred and eighty five thousand dollars."

Charmaine raised an eyebrow. She was impressed. "Kenmore's becoming a real hot spot. I may be able to start a bidding war and get even more than the asking price."

"I'll leave that up to you. As my agent, I'm sure you'll do the right thing." Mark glanced at Kaito and Lucy. "According to my dear friends, I should have every confidence in your ability…"

Charmaine nodded her professional appreciation to the Fujimotos. "I'm grateful for the opportunity, Mr. Lau, and appreciate the confidence you're placing in me. I promise to sell it as quickly as I can."

Mark leaned back in his chair. "I'm sure you will. I'm really going to miss that house. Compared to my tiny studio apartment in China, it's a mansion. But since I live alone, the transition from four-bedroom house to tiny studio apartment wasn't difficult for me."

"Kaito said earlier that your father-in-law lives in that house?"

Mark nodded yes. "It's been vacant since he was placed in hospice care two months ago with stage four liver cancer. I'm told he won't survive the week."

Charmaine's eyes doubled in size. "You know better than to say that! Let's speak total healing over him right now, in the name of Jesus."

"Yes, Lord!" Rodney shouted.

Mark glanced at Kaito. His eyes quickly shifted back to Charmaine.

"Don't get me wrong, Mark, I'm not trying to push away your business. Nothing would please me more than selling your house for you. But God is able and willing to heal your father-in-law this very moment!"

Pastor Lau studied Charmaine's face very carefully. "Yes, He is able. I have total faith in God's healing power. But when it's our time to go, nothing can prevent it from happening.

"Besides, my father-in-law's eighty-eight. He's a lonely old man who longs to reunite with his wife in Heaven. Mostly, he longs to be with Jesus. So why would I pray against his wishes?

"Wouldn't it be selfish on my part to want to keep him here, especially knowing we'll one day be reunited at God's appointed time? It's not like he's going to hell, he's going to Paradise!"

Mark was tempted to ask Charmaine if she really believed she could speak life into existence, why, then, did her parents die in their early 70s? He left it alone.

"Hmm…" It was as if the air had left the room again. Charmaine shot an uncomfortable glance at Rodney. Neither knew how to respond to that.

Finally, Kaito said, "Did you bring the seller's agreement?"

"Sure did. Right here." Then to Mark, "It's an exclusive listing agreement, which gives me six months to sell the house without any outside interference from other agents."

Knowing how driven and goal oriented she was, Mark cut to the chase. "Tell you what, if you sell it before the first of December, instead of the normal three-percent commission, I'll give you five percent."

Charmaine glanced at Rodney. His face was aglow. She did a little mental calculating. At 5%, her commission would be just under $30,000. *Sixty percent of my pledge earlier already recovered. Amazing!* Her face lit up. "Will you need my help finding a new home?"

"That won't be necessary. Kaito and Lucy will know what to do with the proceeds."

Charmaine smiled. "Okay. As you wish…"

"When would you like to stop by to photograph the house?"

She sat more erectly on the couch. "The sooner the better, right?"

Mark nodded yes.

Rodney jumped in, "Say, why don't you join us at church tomorrow? After service, the two of you can drive to your house and take pictures."

The *Blessed and Highly Favored Full Gospel Church* was the last place Mark Lau wanted to go. He couldn't hide his overall reluctance. But knowing how God worked in mysterious ways, perhaps He was opening this door for him to walk through.

He glanced at the Fujimotos. Their eyes pleaded with him to accept Rodney's offer. Apparently, they were thinking the same thing.

"What time's the earliest service?"

Charmaine answered, "Nine a.m. But if you meet us at eight-fifteen, we can have breakfast in the church cafeteria. My treat."

"I was really looking forward to going to Grace Bible Church in the morning, with Kaito and Lucy, but let's do it."

"Great!"

"But after I show you the house, I plan on spending the rest of the day with my father-in-law."

"Understood." Charmaine smiled excitedly at Rodney. "You won't regret coming to our church!"

We shall see… "I look forward to it, Charmaine."

"We gotta go now. See you in the morning, Mark." Rodney extended his right hand.

Charmaine gave him a hug. "Here's my card. Call me anytime…"

At that, the couple left for the Space Needle in downtown Seattle…

CHARMAINE RAISED HER GLASS. "Here's to a very prosperous day!" She took a sip of wine, feeling like she was on top of the world. The elevated majestic view SkyCity Restaurant offered all its patrons, as it slowly rotated before finally coming full circle, further punctuated her metaphoric thought all the more.

Rodney took a sip from his glass and gazed at the effervescent glow on his girlfriend's cheeks. "I'm so proud of you, baby!"

At 43, the sanitation engineer, and die-hard Seahawks fan, was 12 years older than his girlfriend. He had a buzz cut that gradually faded on both sides, and a beard that extended a few inches beneath his chin.

Rodney Williams was in good shape, but he still had a slight potbelly from eating so much fast food for so many years. Since becoming Charmaine's boyfriend, the middle-aged man had already lost 37 pounds.

Another big change that took place was, to honor his girlfriend's wishes, most of the tattoos on his body had been removed.

Charmaine made it known at the outset that, in her opinion, tattoos didn't match the image she had burned into her mind of what a blessed and highly favored couple should look like.

She wasn't judging him, per se, nor did she ever demand that her boyfriend remove them, she was only stating her opinion.

As much as Rodney liked his tattoos, since he planned on proposing to Charmaine this upcoming New Year's Eve, he would keep removing them from his body, one by one. It all came down to compromising with his girlfriend, whom he soon hoped to call his wife.

As of yet, only his teenage daughter, Wanda, knew of his intent to ask for her hand in marriage. He didn't feel he could trust his two younger children enough to keep it a secret. If asked, he knew they would blurt it out without hesitation.

Rodney glanced out the window and saw *Lumen Field* down below, the home of the Seattle Seahawks.

The team was in San Francisco this weekend to play the 49ers. Next week they would return home to play against Philly. As a longtime season ticket holder, he would be there three hours before kickoff, to tailgate in the stadium parking lot with his two brothers and sister-in-law, who loved the Hawks as much as her three brothers-in-law did.

Since Rodney wasn't one of the wealthy members at his church—not yet anyway—the bait he used when trying to recruit fellow tailgaters to come to the *Blessed and Highly Favored Church*, was by bragging that six of the players on the 53-man roster were members there.

As the praise and worship leader, he promised to personally introduce them to anyone agreeing to come to a Saturday night service, the same service the players attended during the season when the team had a home game scheduled on Sunday.

More times than not, it worked. But in the end, only one person from the dozen or so who took the bait became a member at his church.

The rest just wanted selfies with their heroes.

But right now Rodney couldn't think about football. All he could think about was when he first met Charmaine five years ago, when he earned nearly twice as much as she did.

In a flash, she had catapulted herself miles ahead of him, financially speaking. So much so that there wasn't much to compare. He simply couldn't fathom how far she'd come in just three years.

The city bus campaign changed everything…

5

SUNDAY MORNING

AT 8:15 A.M., RODNEY Williams spotted Mark Lau seated in the lobby, reading the Bible he brought with him. "Good morning, Pastor."

"Good morning, Rodney!" Mark Lau closed his Bible and stood.

"So glad you came. You're going to love it here. We're not the most prosperous church in the Seattle area for nothing!" Rodney squared his shoulders back. "There's just something about this place..."

We shall see... "I look forward to it."

"Charmaine just pulled into the parking lot. She'll meet us in the cafeteria. Hungry?"

Mark Lau smiled. "I am."

Rodney said, "Great! Follow me, Pastor."

When they arrived at the cafeteria, Charmaine waved to them. She was thrilled to see her new client again. "So glad you made it!"

"Likewise. Thanks again for the invite."

"Of course! Rodney and I usually have scrambled eggs with bacon and hash browns. With so many people always coming and going in between services, the selections are limited..."

"I understand. That sounds good."

"Would you like coffee, orange juice, or both?"

"Orange juice would be fine, thanks..."

Charmaine said, "Coming right up, Pastor."

Once they were seated, Rodney blessed the food.

Charmaine put a fork full of hash browns in her mouth. Swallowing, she asked, "Did Kaito and Lucy tell you many of the city's rich and famous worship here, including professional athletes?"

Mark took a sip of orange juice. "I believe they did."

Flashing one of her killer smiles, she boasted, "Seeing them occupying the front rows each Sunday fills my soul with great joy. Especially since I get to sit with them!"

Hmm... "With all due respect, Charmaine, that sort of thing would never be the reason for me to attend any church."

Charmaine took a moment to let his comment sink in. "I understand what you're saying. But you must admit it takes a special kind of pastor to attract people like them. When the Holy Spirit visits our church, the most amazing things happen!"

Pastor Lau looked confused by her comment. "When you say He visits, wouldn't that imply that He leaves at some point? How can that be when the Word of God teaches that at the point of salvation, the Holy Spirit indwells that heart without ever leaving?"

Charmaine shot him a sideways look, as if she wanted to say something, but she had no answers to his confusing questions...

Mark went on, "So long as there are true believers in your church, the Holy Spirit will always be there in your midst. We must never overlook that we are the true church, Charmaine, not the buildings at which we congregate."

Rodney said, "You make a good point, Pastor..."

"In truth, Rodney, my opinion matters not. All that matters is what the Word of God teaches, nothing more..."

Rodney shot Charmaine a confused glance. Neither knew how to reply to his outlandish statement. Unlike at the Fujimoto residence where he was warm and friendly, he seemed more serious now.

After breakfast, Mark Lau followed the couple to the massive welcome center. Everyone was impeccably dressed for the occasion.

Pastor Lau wore a brown tweed jacket, maroon color tie and beige slacks. It had been many years since he last wore a suit jacket to church. Even wearing a suit, he felt way underdressed at this place.

Charmaine made sure to introduce her guest to everyone within earshot. Everyone Mark met was happy, upbeat, and highly energized. Despite all that, he felt anything but comforted by them.

His discomfort worsened with each step he took, as they made their way into the massive sanctuary, to the front row of seats.

Rodney said, "See you both after the praise and worship ends..."

"Okay, sweetness." Charmaine blew her boyfriend a flying kiss. "Enjoy."

Rodney went up on stage and took his seat at the organ.

Mark's eyes wandered the cavernous sanctuary. Compared to his subterranean place of worship, this place overwhelmed him. But what concerned him most was this certain darkness he sensed in his spirit, that was skillfully hidden behind the bright lights.

He kept these troubling thoughts and feelings to himself...

"Pastor Lau, I'd like you to meet Pastor Imogen Martín."

Imogen was as amped up as a rock and roll musician getting ready to perform on stage. Confidence oozed out of her. She extended her right hand. "Nice meeting you, Pastor."

"Nice meeting you too..." Mark was quite familiar with this woman's over-the-top style of preaching. His first thought was that she looked so much taller on TV and on the Internet than she did in person.

Imogen Martín was quite attractive. She had short-cropped dark brown hair, that almost looked auburn. The way it hugged her beautiful face almost made her look like a porcelain doll. Her green eyes sparkled like diamonds. With exception to her rock-star nervous energy, everything else about her appearance dripped of class and elegance put on full display.

Though she was on the petite side, at 5'4"—which was a foot shorter than her husband, when it came to attitude and energy, she matched Julian stride for stride.

Charmaine said to Mark, "We were surprised to learn yesterday that Imogen's three months pregnant with their first child."

Mark's face lit up. "Congratulations! Do you know if you're having a boy or girl?"

Imogen beamed. "Still too soon for that. Hope to know soon enough."

Charmaine said, "Mark's visiting from China."

"Really? Nice having you here. You're in for a treat. My husband has a powerful message to share with everyone today."

Pastor Lau thought, *we shall see...*

Imogen sensed his uneasiness. "Welcome to our church. Enjoy the service."

"Thanks, Imogen. Nice meeting you."

"You, as well."

Pastor Lau took his seat next to Charmaine, then lowered his head in prayer. "Lord, quiet my spirit. Make Your presence known in this place, in the name of Jesus."

As he prayed, Charmaine confided to Imogen, "This is the man whose house I'll be selling. He's a good friend of the Fujimotos. He used to be an engineer at Boeing before moving to China to preach the Gospel over there. He's very nice, but some of the things he said at breakfast earlier seemed a little morbid to me, somber even.

"I sense he lacks energy and enthusiasm when it comes to the Word of God. I also sense he no longer feels worthy of the good life, if you can believe that. If anyone can reinvigorate him, I know it's you."

Imogen winked at Charmaine, "Got it..." Once she was seated up on stage with her husband, the service promptly began.

Jeremiah Ogletree, the associate pastor in his late 20s with shaved head and dark complexion, declared, "Welcome to the Blessed and Highly Favored Full Gospel Church, where blessings and prosperity become a reality for all of God's children!" The smile on his face was so infectious, it nearly lit up the entire sanctuary.

Charmaine took her seat next to Pastor Lau. The praise and worship team started playing the hymn, *Every Praise*.

Pastor Lau marveled at how beautifully their voices blended together, as they belted out the heartfelt lyrics to the Lord.

But when it came time to receiving the offering, Mark squirmed in horror, as dozens threw money on the steps leading to the altar, then danced on top of it, all but commanding God to greatly multiply what they had just given to the church. He was sickened by it.

If he wasn't seated in the front row with the rich and famous, with cameras rolling, he would have already left by now.

Charmaine saw him squirming in his seat, and kept praying that God would calm his spirit and open his eyes to the good life he was missing out on.

After one last praise and worship song, Pastor Julian approached the lectern. "Good morning church! Nice to see you all again. Today's message is titled, 'Don't anger and insult God by selling yourself short and living in squalor.' Our text can be found in Ecclesiastes five, verses eighteen through twenty. I'll ask you all to stand as I read the inspired Word of God..."

Mark Lau shook his head in disgust. *Don't anger or insult God by living in squalor? Really?*

Julian cleared his throat and began, "'This is what I have observed to be good: that it is appropriate for a person to eat, to drink and to find satisfaction in their toilsome labor under the sun during the few days of life God has given them—for this is their lot. Moreover, when God gives someone wealth and possessions, and the ability to enjoy them, to accept their lot and be happy in their toil—this is a gift of God. They seldom reflect on the days of their life, because God keeps them occupied with gladness of heart.'"

Hair slicked back to perfection, determined expression on his face, Julian Martín asked the congregation, "Do you think it makes God happy when those who openly hate Him get to thrive in life, while so many of His children suffer?"

Many in the sanctuary shouted, "No!"

Mark Lau cringed in his seat. He never heard anything more ridiculous in his life! If anything angered God, it was the sermon this man was preaching! No, it wasn't a sermon, it was a message—a prosperity message, to be precise. It was all about self-fulfillment in Jesus' name...

Lau had no problem with the Scripture itself. The simple truth was, just as the verse proclaimed, God did bless some of His children with great riches. And those who were blessed in that capacity were commanded to enjoy what they were given. But He never intended for *all* His children to be rich. All that would do is create lazy servants.

It was clear to the Chinese-American Pastor that in the thirty minutes Julian spent preaching on those three verses, he was merely twisting that scripture, and other passages he cross referenced in his sermon, as tools to further justify his self-centered approach to the Word of God, like many "word of faith" teachers did.

The proof was his emphasis on the three key points he extracted from the three verses. The first was that it was appropriate for a person to find satisfaction in life. His second key point was that God was the giver of all wealth and possessions. And his third key point was since these gifts were from God, they were to be enjoyed.

While all three of his key points were certainly true, he failed to include the "toilsome-labor-under-the-sun-during-the-few-days-of-life-God-has-given," part that Solomon had included in those verses. Nor did he mention the "accepting-their-lot-in-life-and-being-happy" part.

In other words, he never encouraged his flock to be contented with whatever God had already blessed them with, whether it was little or much. He urged them all instead to always want more...

These were subtle issues, to be sure. But Mark knew that's how Satan worked, layer by layer—like peeling an onion.

In fairness to Julian, he did mention about getting right with God, but without a call to repentance that led to salvation. And where was the denying self and carrying our crosses daily and following Jesus?

47

It was never mentioned...He was too focused on telling everyone what they wanted to hear.

Each time he declared to the congregation that God had great things in store for them, to include great riches, the praise and worship musicians played loud harmonious music, sparking many in the congregation to dance in the aisles again, waving their hands above their heads, speaking in tongues, claiming this and that. It happened on three separate occasions.

At times, Mark felt like he was at a 21st Century Woodstock concert, or at a carnival or the circus, not a church. Perhaps outsiders might think some at this place were drunk or high on drugs or even demon possessed.

It was disturbing to say the least...At least to him, it was.

At any rate, the way their pastor explained things to them, with such remarkable clarity, it was evident that he really was on God's good side.

How could they not love Jesus, after what their pastor had just promised He would do for them? How could they not shout His name from the rafters, when He was about to shower down His richest blessings on them from the very Throne of Heaven?

Mark Lau begged to differ. Was this man not taught in seminary school that the true gospel message was meant to be offensive to fleshly ears, because it exposed humanity as wickedly sinful beings who were deserving of hell?

Or did he deliberately choose not to share this biblical truth with them, because it ran counter to the prosperity gospel he preached on?

Mark Lau shook his head. *Am I the only person in this place bothered by these crucial omissions?* Even if he used all ten fingers and toes, it still wouldn't be enough to count how many times he found Julian in error, in the hour or so in which he spoke. This ate away at his soul...

But to everyone else in the completely full sanctuary, apparently their lead pastor's words were received like manna falling from Heaven.

So much so that another $800K was pledged to the new expansion project, bringing the total raised to just over $2M.

Not bad for two days of preaching the Word of God...

6

AFTER THE SERVICE HAD ended, Pastor Julian said, "Wait, everyone, before you go, I understand we have a pastor visiting us from China."

Mark Lau winced, then glanced nervously at Charmaine, who giggled under her breath. He was already on edge after hearing Pastor Martín's man-centered sermon. He shifted uncomfortably in his seat.

"It's okay, Pastor, don't be nervous," Julian said. "We're your family! Come join us on stage so we can pray for you."

Lau gulped in air, got out of his seat, and slowly trudged up the steps leading to the massive stage, silently wishing he could make a beeline to one of the rear exit doors. But with TV cameras steadied on him, he complied and did as he was instructed.

Pastor Lau reminded himself again that God worked in mysterious ways. If He was opening a door for him to preach the true Gospel message, Mark wouldn't hesitate. *This is mysterious, all right!*

Rodney Williams was still seated at the organ. He shot Mark a thumb's up gesture, hoping to calm his nerves a bit.

The Martíns positioned themselves on either side of their visitor. Pastor Lau felt great heat coming from Pastor Julian. What some might mistake as Holy Spirit fire pouring out of him—as if shooting out of a furnace—Mark deduced was nothing more than excess body heat from being so worked up throughout his sermon.

Julian said, "What's your name?"

"Mark Lau."

"I understand you were an associate pastor here in the States before moving to China…" Since his guest was Kaito Fujimoto's best friend, he probably wasn't a big fan of his preaching style. The way he squirmed in his front row seat at times during the service further dictated that much.

Julian knew it was risky inviting him up on stage unvetted like this. On the flipside, once they laid hands on him and prayed for him, perhaps God would use this moment to open his eyes and change his heart, so he could finally start living the good life again…

Pastor Lau said, "That would be correct." As a first generation Chinese American, his English was perfect.

"How long have you been over there?"

"Going on eight years now…"

"Marvelous!" Julian said, "Let's give it up for our brother sharing God's goodness halfway around the world!"

Applause thundered all throughout the sanctuary, accompanied by many "Amens" and "Hallelujahs".

"It's always an honor sharing the stage with another mighty man of God."

Lau waved off his words. "I'm a servant of the Most High God. Nothing more."

"Amen to that, Pastor!" Julian said, half-heartedly.

Mark wondered why Imogen kept gazing at him. Whatever she was thinking, it literally caused the hair on his arms to stand at full attention.

When Charmaine introduced him to her before the shenanigans began, something felt strangely off about her. Now up on stage with her, that troubling sensation only intensified.

Imogen said, "Where exactly is your church in China?"

"Shanghai."

She said, "Ooh, I've always wanted to go there. I hear the shopping's unbelievable…"

"You heard correctly. But our church is located on the lesser side of town, far away from the massive skyscrapers and ritzy shopping locations. That area's too rich for our blood…"

Ahh, the words she wanted to hear. Imogen closed her eyes and started shaking her head softly at first, then wildly, violently, as if having an epileptic seizure.

Pastor Lau observed in silence, already knowing this wouldn't end well. It went on for several seconds before she finally broke out of it.

With a determined expression on her face, she said, "I have a word for *you*, from God Almighty Himself!"

Someone yelled from the second level, "Bless him, Pastor!"

There were more "Amens" uttered from many.

Mark Lau flinched, then tilted his head strangely at her, wondering upon whose authority she was about to prophesy.

After a prolonged moment of still silence, Imogen answered his question—at least her version of what she thought to be true—when she screamed into the microphone in her hand, "I declare by the authority of Jesus Christ of Nazareth, that when you return to China many new doors will be opened for you that no man can close, to include newfound financial blessings!"

"Amen!" someone in the balcony shouted.

"Hallelujah!" someone yelled on the lower level.

"Praise Jesus!" declared a wealthy business owner, seated in the front row.

With her face mere inches from Lau's, Imogen started speaking in unintelligible tongues. Mark couldn't understand a single word she spoke. He felt certain no one else could either—there was no one there to translate for her—but she almost sounded angry.

Mark glanced over at Julian. Arms lifted skyward he, too, was speaking in tongues, but a little more softly than his wife.

Pastor Lau remained silent. He felt himself shivering, sensing her spirit was entirely different than his.

Had Charmaine told him in advance this would happen, he would have never agreed to join her in the first place.

Out of the corner of his eye, Mark noticed two men walking up on stage, positioning themselves behind him with a covering rag. He knew why they were there—in case he suddenly became "slain in the spirit", as they taught at this place, and he lost all control and fell backwards.

If so, they would be there to catch him in the covering rag.

Another shiver snaked through him, seeing some of the elders and church deacons form a tight circle around the three of them, to lay hands on him. It wasn't the laying on of hands that spooked him, even his church did that, it was the different spirit he felt behind it all.

Pastor Lau knew this was all part of the prosperity gospel that had enslaved so many churchgoers for so many years.

After a while, Imogen opened her eyes and shouted at the top of her lungs, "Stop selling yourself short over there in China! Why praise God in such squalor when you could have a place like this of your own to worship in someday?"

Looking her visitor square in the eye, she said, "You must cease from cheating your flock, my brother, by withholding the limitless blessings God's been trying to shower upon you all this time!

"Can you imagine the overwhelming disappointment you'll feel in Heaven, when God shows you the storehouses full of wasted blessings that were intended for you and your flock back on earth, but they were never received because of your lack of faith? How do you think the members of your church might feel about that?"

Mark Lau glanced out at the massive congregation. They were sad for him; pity was splashed all over their faces. He wanted to ask Pastor Julian why he had handed total control of the situation over to his wife, but his eyes were still closed as he spoke in tongues.

His eyes volleyed back to Imogen. She was sweating profusely. "Our Heavenly Father loves His children in China just as much as His royal princes and princesses here in America.

"As part of God's royal priesthood, it's time to start acting like it by increasing your faith! Once you do that, my brother, get out of the way so God can finally unleash His mighty power in your life, and the lives of everyone at your church!"

Imogen shot a quick look at Charmaine, and went on, "Another thing the Lord told me to tell you has to do with your overall approach, when sharing the Word of God with others.

"Simply put, the words you speak are weak at times, morbid even. And your lack of energy and enthusiasm is costing you dearly. Your church needs to be reinvigorated, not bored out of their minds!"

Imogen gazed deeply into Mark's eyes and shook her head sadly. "Trust me when I say, once you repent of the great sin of squandering away the very things God's been wanting to lavish upon your church for the longest time, it won't take long before He fully restores what the locusts have eaten away for so many years, due to your weak faith."

"Amen!" someone yelled, in reply.

"Hallelujah!" someone else yelled.

"As their pastor, it all starts with *you*! Now's your chance to repent in front of God, and your many brothers and sisters in the faith. You said yourself that the finer things in this life are too rich for your blood.

"That changes today! Doubt needs to be replaced with rock-solid faith, my brother. But first you must repent of your many spiritual shortcomings before you can expect God to bless you in this capacity!"

Finally, the word Pastor Lau wanted to hear all day—repent—only it was directed at him, not them!

The congregation once again erupted in thunderous applause. They praised God for blessing them with such spirit-filled pastors.

The way Imogen spoke into this man's life further proved that she was chosen by God to be one of His mighty prophetesses.

The sanctuary fell silent when their guest lowered his head and closed his eyes. While they were right, he was communicating with God, he wasn't repenting but praying that God would deliver this so-called body of believers from the clutches of Satan himself.

When he was finished, he opened his eyes to find Imogen still gazing at him, huffing and puffing loudly into the microphone in her hand, her face mere inches from his.

She was so close he could feel her breath on his face.

"Well done, brother! Now you can rightly claim the things you want—they're there for the taking, in the mighty name of Jesus of Nazareth!"

Glancing skyward, Imogen said, "Lord, I command You to release your countless blessings on this man, this very instant!

"May Your first miracle come in the form of physical healing for his father-in-law. We rebuke every cancer cell invading his body! Heal him, Lord, and bring him back to perfect health!"

With high heels on, Imogen's 5'4" height was elevated just enough to where their eyes were level. "Fear not, my brother, he's going to be just fine."

"Amen!" Pastor Julian shouted.

Another chorus of "Amens" and "Hallelujahs" filled the sanctuary.

Mark stood stoically silent, motionless.

Imogen didn't know what he was thinking. Their eyes remained deadlocked, as if both were trying to gain spiritual ground.

After a few more uncomfortable moments, she could no longer hold his stare. She tilted her head one way then the other; her counterpart's kind eyes earlier now looked deeply troubled. It was impossible to overlook. "Anything you'd like to say, Pastor?"

"Yes."

When Imogen handed him the microphone, most in attendance started handclapping. Mark knew it wouldn't last...*Give me the grace, Lord, and your strength, to say what I must...*

Gazing out at the congregation, Pastor Lau lowered his head. "Let us pray. Father, protect everyone in this sanctuary from the many lies this so-called prophetess just told. Seal her lips shut, so she'll no longer fill the ears of so many with such blasphemous words."

Imogen opened her eyes and glared at him. Anger surfaced on her face.

Mark's eyes were closed, but he wouldn't be surprised to see her reaction. He went on, "Lord, give everyone upon whom Your mighty hand rests in this place spiritual discernment to realize her message didn't come from You, but from the great deceiver, the devil himself."

A loud collective gasp fell upon the sanctuary. Many blinked hard and shook their heads in disbelief; they glared at him angrily.

The last thing anyone expected was for their beloved pastor to come under attack like this. They ached for her.

Pastor Lau went on, "Shield the hearts and minds of Your chosen ones in this sanctuary, whoever they may be. Lead them into the Truth by sending biblically-sound preachers to share Your Gospel with them, as only You can. This I beg of you, Father, in Jesus' name, Amen."

You could hear a feather drop inside the sanctuary...

Mark Lau opened his eyes. As if on cue, droves of congregants emptied out of the sanctuary, with menacing growls on their faces.

They refused to listen to any more of this man's vitriolic hate speech. It spewed out of his mouth like vomit. *How dare he disrespect our Pastor like that—especially with the cameras rolling!*

Julian watched his wife furiously storm off the stage. The humiliation on her face ripped through him like a knife in warm butter. His fists were clenched in a ball—he burned with anger. If looks could kill!

Usually when Imogen prophesied over someone, the recipients joined her in speaking in tongues as she delivered encouraging messages from God's lips to their ears, or they became giddy with laughter, or jumped up and down with tears streaming down their cheeks, like they'd just won a new car on *The Price is Right* game show.

But not this man...Their hearts were pierced within them.

And with more than 17,000 viewers watching on Facebook live, 8,000 more on Twitter, and another 4,000 on Instagram, how much potential collateral damage had this man just done?

One of the cameramen recording for their TV audience shot a desperate glance over to his female counterpart, as if to say, "What should we do?"

She shrugged her shoulders and kept the camera steady, thankful that all TV sermons were aired two weeks after they were recorded. There wasn't a chance this man's evil rebuke would make the final edit.

It didn't take long for loud choruses of boos to replace the dead silence that had filled the sanctuary for so long, from those who still remained.

Amid the constant shouting to get off the stage, Pastor Lau went on, "God's salvation isn't about miracles or financial gain; it's all about the shed blood of Jesus Christ, who alone has the power to cleanse repentant sinners and rescue their souls from eternal damnation. That's the whole premise of the Gospel message, not worldly possessions!

"Think about it, if God's sanctification was meant to make us more like Jesus, why should any Christ follower expect to be honored in a world where our Redeemer was hated to the point of being crucified as an innocent Man? Does that make sense to any of you? It doesn't to me.

"Once the miracle of salvation happens in a life, we're called to serve God, not be served by Him! In the end, when you stand before your Maker on that inescapable day, you will be judged on the things you did or didn't do for Him, not the other way around."

A handful of ushers rushed the stage. They glared angrily at Mark, as they slowly closed in on him. Rodney Williams ran his right pointer finger across his neck, signaling for the sound man to cut his mic immediately.

The problem was the sound man was completely transfixed by the words this man spoke. They convicted him deep in his spirit, as if his soul was hearing truth for the very first time.

He wasn't the only one. Others felt that same deep conviction in their souls and wanted to hear more...

Pastor Lau was mildly amazed the microphone was still turned on. Seeing dozens on the edge of their seats, hanging onto his every word, he took it as a sign that God had left it on just for them.

He would keep speaking until they muted it or ripped it from his hands, which he anticipated happening at any moment. "Everything your pastors strive for is nothing more than chasing after the wind. I assure you the many material things they want you to have won't mean a thing to any of you a hundred years from now."

"So, if you haven't truly been born again, I plead with you to stop chasing after worldly material blessings and get right with God! Since tomorrow's promised to no one, the day of salvation is at hand."

He ended with, "But for those of you who receive this woman's message as truth, and reject the true Gospel message, you will come to see that what she preaches will be God's judgment upon you."

Only no one heard it. Pastor Ogletree stormed the sound booth and turned the microphone off himself...

7

JULIAN MARTÍN GLARED FURIOUSLY at Mark Lau, then raced off the massive stage to console his pregnant wife.

The air was charged with negativity, the very last thing Imogen needed now. That went double for the baby.

It was always risky prophesying on live TV. This time it backfired on the Martíns in a very big way, leaving Imogen totally mortified.

Pastor Lau was briskly escorted off the stage by three bulky men. The man gripping his left arm squeezed so hard, it would surely cause bruising.

They were kind enough to let him grab his Bible off the seat he'd occupied in the front row. Other than that, his feet never stopped moving until he was out of the building...

Charmaine sat in the front row with her face buried in her hands, shaking her head from side to side, totally stunned by what she'd just witnessed. The stupendous high she felt the past 24 hours, after having her best day ever as a real estate agent, had just come to a crashing halt.

When they met at the Fujimoto residence, Mark Lau seemed like a perfect gentleman. He was the *last* person she ever thought could do such a mean-spirited thing like this. She was now having second thoughts about selling his house, even despite the lucrative commission.

She glanced up at Rodney. "What should I do, sweetness? Should I follow him out to his car, as planned, or just go home?"

Rodney was still seated at the organ, unable to fathom what just happened. He took a deep breath to calm himself, then shrugged his shoulders. "It's your call, baby..."

Charmaine took a moment to think things through, then gathered her belongings and left the sanctuary. In the end, by signing the seller's agreement, she wouldn't be the one to break the appointment or the contract. It wouldn't be the professional thing to do.

Jeremiah Ogletree rushed outside and caught up with the man who'd just perpetrated this unspeakable evil at his place of worship, just as he was getting inside his vehicle. "Pastor Lau, wait!"

Mark slid behind the wheel but left the car door open; his left foot was still planted on the cement parking lot. "Yes?"

"Who do you think you are coming to our place of worship and speaking judgment over our lead pastors, and over me as well, by extension?" Anger was prevalent in Ogletree's voice and on his face. "How dare you humiliate us like that! Who do you think you are?!"

"Like I said earlier, I'm a servant of the Most High God, nothing more."

"Yeah, well, Mister Servant of the Most High God, nearly thirty thousand viewers heard your judgmental words online! Some aren't even members yet. You better hope your actions didn't push them away!"

Mark Lau brushed off the threat. "Sorry if I offended anyone, Pastor. I certainly didn't come here looking to rebuke anyone. But when Imogen started prophesying falsely over me, she forced my hand…"

"How can you say that? Do you even know how far her reach extends in our community and beyond? Not only is she a well-respected prophetess, she and Julian were recently appointed as apostles."

"So I heard…"

Jeremiah snickered at his bland reply. "Okay, for argument's sake, what exactly did you mean when you asked the Lord to seal her lips shut to the many lies you claim she told?"

"I assure you if the things she prophesied over me ever came true, it would mean prison for me or worse. If God wants me to go to prison for my faith, and for His glory, I am willing. But being prosperous won't be the reason for it, Pastor."

Jeremiah shot him a sideways look. *Prison? Seriously?*

Mark Lau saw his confusion, but felt no need to elaborate on it. "According to Deuteronomy eighteen-twenty-two, if the things she spoke over me don't come true, that would make her a false prophetess."

"There you go again. What's wrong with you, man?"

"As a Pastor, you should know the Word of God makes this crystal clear."

Pastor Jeremiah grunted under his breath. "If Jesus was here, do you think He would approve of what you just said?"

"Yes, I do…" Mark said, without hesitation.

If Pastor Ogletree had sackcloth on, he would have torn it by now. "Your words are blasphemous!"

"Again, I'm not trying to sound mean or judgmental in any way. I'm merely standing on the authority of what the Bible teaches…"

There you go judging us again! Jeremiah rubbed his chin with his fingers. "What did you mean when you asked God to protect those upon whom His mighty hand rested in this place, whoever they may be? Are you actually saying some of us aren't saved?"

"I can't proclaim to know who among you are saved and who aren't, any better than you can. Only God knows the heart of man. Are you familiar with Matthew seven, twenty-one through twenty-three?"

"Yes, of course! I'm a pastor, too, remember?"

"Well then, there you have it…"

Jeremiah was astounded by Mark's blunt reply. "Have what?"

"Jesus said that *many* who think they are saved really aren't…"

Before Jeremiah could reply, his wife Sophia approached them. She glared angrily at Mark Lau, then said to her husband, "Pastor Julian would like to speak to you."

"Right away, honey…"

Pastor Ogletree glared at Mark Lau again. Before he could say something, Pastor Lau's cellphone vibrated.

It was a text message from his daughter: *Sorry to inform you, Papa, but Grandpa just died. I wanted to call but I know you're at church. Please contact me as soon as you can. Xoxo.*

Mark quick-replied to his daughter: *The service just ended, honey. Are you okay? Be home soon. Love you.* He sighed, then lowered his head. Not so much because his father-in-law had just stepped into eternity—as a true Christian, this was a cause for rejoicing—but if he needed further proof that Imogen was indeed a false prophetess, this confirmed it.

Jeremiah saw sorrow creep onto his face. "Is everything okay?"

Mark grimaced. "My father-in-law just died. Yes, the one your prophetess assured me would be totally healed…"

Just as the words came out of his mouth, Charmaine met up with them. She gasped loudly. Her eyes widened; her mouth was agape. She was more rocked by this news than what had just transpired in the sanctuary.

As it turned out, neither of them had to cancel the appointment—God just cancelled it for them, temporarily, anyway.

Charmaine was too shocked to speak. Now this, after Imogen had just prophesied saying God told her he would be completely healed?

Why then, did he die mere moments after she spoke those words over him? It's almost as if God had sided with Pastor Lau on this matter.

Suddenly, her rebuke for his giving up so easily on his father-in-law, at the Fujimoto residence, flooded her mind.

Jeremiah looked down at his feet. "Sorry for your loss..." *Talk about bad timing!*

Sophia thought to herself, *See what you get? It's all your fault! This is God's way of punishing you for embarrassing my best friend like that!*

Mark looked at her and quickly looked away, seeing the anger in her eyes to the point of hatred. To Charmaine, he said, "I'm afraid I'll have to reschedule."

Charmaine slumped her shoulders sadly. "So sorry for your loss, Pastor. Anything I can do for you?"

"Thanks, but no. His wish was to be cremated. We will have a simple service for him before I leave for China. But I'd still like you to photograph the house before I go."

His soft-spoken words once again resembled his tone at the Fujimoto's house. "Sure. Whatever time's good for you will be fine with me."

Mark nodded at her. "I have your card. I'll be in touch."

He shifted his focus back to Jeremiah Ogletree. "If you'd like to further discuss this all important topic, Pastor, you're welcome to stop by my house. Or we can meet at the Fujimoto residence."

I don't think so! Jeremiah paused. "I have a better idea. Why don't you come to my life group Bible study tomorrow night? Perhaps you can enlighten us all on *your opinion* on what Jesus said in Matthew seven..."

Jeremiah made sure to say, "your opinion" as sarcastically as he could.

Sophia nudged her husband's lower back with her elbow, hoping he would retract his offer. He didn't.

Mark knew she was upset. "In the final analysis, my opinion matters not. All that matters is what the Word of God teaches. My job as a Pastor is to share the Word, without adding or taking anything away from it."

Sophia nudged her husband again. It was time to end the conversation.

Jeremiah said, "So you'll come?"

"What time will it begin?"

"Eight p.m. Seven-thirty if you want to eat first."

Pastor Lau said, "I should have my father-in-law's affairs settled by then. So, yes, I gladly accept your invitation."

"Very good then. It'll be nice having a spirited Bible debate with you. Normally, five hundred people show up. But after this fiasco, I can't guarantee how many, if any, will be interested in coming, once they know you'll be the speaker…" the associate pastor said.

"I understand…" What else was there to say? "Now, if you'll excuse me, I need to call my daughter…"

"By all means. Please extend my condolences to your family."

Charmaine took a deep breath and exhaled. "Me too, Pastor…"

Sophia remained silent.

"I will. Thank you." At that, Mark pressed the ignition button, put the car in drive, and left for home…

8

MONDAY NIGHT

JEREMIAH OGLETREE APPROACHED THE lectern and did a quick silent head count. He seriously doubted if 100 seats were occupied now. After what happened 36 hours ago in the main sanctuary, the associate pastor wasn't overly surprised seeing 40 of the 50 round tables, which sat 10 each, void of people.

Even though he privately told his study group that this would be a wonderful opportunity to have an open debate and gang up on the man who'd caused such an uproar the day before—if that's what it took to finally set him straight—many were still too upset to come.

After what he did to Imogen, they refused to listen to anything else he had to share with them. Once was enough!

This included Jeremiah's wife. Sophia chose to stay at home, not wanting to be anywhere near the so-called preacher from China. After trying to console Imogen all day, she couldn't yet bring herself to forgive him for embarrassing her pregnant best friend the way he had, with thousands watching in person, and tens of thousands watching online.

His words were vile and reprehensible!

This was the first time Sophia had ever missed her own Bible study. Her absence didn't go unnoticed by anyone...

As it was, many remained in the sanctuary with her long after Mark Lau was escorted out of the building, to chase away every evil spirit their visitor brought to the church with him.

When Sophia got home, she was drained physically, mentally, and spiritually. She didn't have the strength to potentially repeat the process on consecutive days.

She was even more convinced now that Mark's lack of faith, plus his outright rejection of Imogen's words as coming from the Lord, was the chief cause of his father-in-law's death. Had he not done that, she was convinced he would still be alive and completely healed of cancer.

Those who showed up were strangely curious to meet the man who'd caused such an uproar, to see what he would say next. Only half were part of this life group. As for the rest, some weren't even members of this church.

Before the last part of the service could be taken off all social media platforms, critics of the *Blessed and Highly Favored Full Gospel Church* were able to download and reshare it online.

Many watched and couldn't believe their eyes and ears. It instantly became the number one topic of discussion, trending among netizens in many circles. One critic of the megachurch shared it with the caption, *Oops, looks like the Martíns failed to properly vet someone. A prophetesses' mistake, I presume.*

The last time Jeremiah remembered seeing a small crowd at one of his Bible studies was when the Seahawks played on Monday Night Football, back in September. But even then, the room was still half-full of people wearing their team gear.

Of the six NFL players who were members, three attended this Bible study group. Only one of them was in attendance now.

Once everyone was seated, Pastor Ogletree began. "Thanks for coming, everyone! Glad you could all make it. Did everyone have enough food to eat?"

Many heads nodded.

Shooting a glance at Mrs. Devlin, the associate pastor said, "We know the Fall season's officially upon us, when Bonnie bakes her famous pumpkin-filled cream puffs. They're so delicious I could eat them all!"

Laughter filled the room.

"I'm not kidding! If there's one good thing to having a smaller group than usual, there are plenty of leftovers." Pastor Ogletree rubbed his belly over his sweater. "You can be sure I'll be taking some of those yummy treats home with me."

The bakery owner, whose hair was dyed pink to honor breast cancer awareness month, smiled and sat more erectly in her chair. "Take all you want, Pastor…" Even though Bonnie witnessed the debacle with her own two eyes, for whatever reason, she wasn't turned off to the man.

In her mind, the jury was still out on him…

"Trust me, Bonnie, I will! Of course, the biggest challenge for Sophia and I will be finding a secret hiding place at home, so the kids won't find them!"

Pastor Ogletree burst out in laughter. Even in his early 40s, he still had the ability to laugh like a child. Only it wasn't as hearty as usual. Everyone knew the reason—a growing anticipation for what might happen in the coming minutes...

He continued, "It's a great honor having Charmaine DeShields and Rodney Williams with us tonight."

The couple received a warm round of applause. They weren't part of this life group—they were in charge of the Wednesday night Bible study class. But since Charmaine had invited Pastor Lau to their church in the first place, not to mention that she would be selling his house for him, she sort of felt obligated to come.

Normally at this time, Pastor Jeremiah would spend a few moments recapping certain key points from the past day's sermon. But if he did that, it would remind everyone too much of what had transpired at the end of the first service.

Instead, he focused on what happened on Saturday. "Charmaine, your generosity last weekend inspired so many, including me! I'm still trying to wrap my mind around it. Many said afterward you stole the show!"

"Glory to God," came the reply.

"How many of you were there for the monthly prayer session?"

A dozen or so hands were raised. Everyone else wished they could have been there, but there was only so much space.

Unlike now...

"Man, oh man, was it awesome or what?" Pastor Ogletree smiled, causing his ebony cheeks and bald head to shine even more. "One-point-three million dollars pledged in just one day! Shattered the old record by four hundred thousand! And another two million yesterday!

"We're well on the way to achieving our goal. Since you were the one to set the stage, so to speak, God's gonna bless your faithfulness big time, my dear sister!"

Charmaine's full lips curled into an easy smile. "I receive that, Pastor!"

Rodney stiffened up in his seat and put his right arm around his girlfriend. Like many others at the church, he still couldn't understand why this man, who certainly looked harmless enough, had reacted so poorly last time they were all gathered.

What true man of God would reject someone else laying hands on him while speaking blessings over him, of all things? Everything Imogen did was for his own benefit. The way he reacted was inconceivable!

Rodney's heart still ached for his pastor. So much so that he was reluctant to join Charmaine until the very last minute. In the end, he didn't want his girlfriend to go alone.

Pastor Ogletree looked at the clock on the wall opposite him. "Okay, let's get started. Next week, we'll continue our study on the book of Acts. But for now, help me give a warm 'Blessed and Highly Favored' welcome to a special guest who travelled all the way from China, just to be with us tonight…"

Jeremiah hesitated, then said, "He may be a little heavy-hearted after receiving news yesterday that his father-in-law had died…"

Bonnie Devlin flinched; her eyes doubled in size. "The one Imogen prophesied about?"

Jeremiah lowered his head, not quite knowing how to respond to the question. "I'm afraid so…"

Bonnie covered her mouth with her hands, as a hush filled the room.

Pastor Ogletree remained silent, hoping there would be no follow-up questions. He waited a few agonizing seconds, then said, "His study will be on Matthew seven, verses twenty-one through twenty-three. Please put your hands together for Pastor Mark Lau!"

Pastor Lau got up out of his seat in the front row, to a lukewarm ovation. It was nowhere near what Charmaine and Rodney had received, not even close. No one had to ask why…

They silently prayed the same vile spirits he brought to their place of worship last time, hadn't followed him back again.

The Chinese-American pastor shook hands with Pastor Ogletree, wondering why he said something that wasn't even true. *I didn't come to America just for them!* He brushed it aside and spread his notes out on the lectern.

The sadness in his eyes was noticeable. It was evident to all that the past 24 hours had been difficult for him.

"Hello everyone. I consider it a great privilege to share the Word of God with you all tonight. Let me begin by apologizing to anyone who may be thinking my actions yesterday came across as mean-spirited. I never meant to disrespect or offend anyone."

Pastor Lau glanced at Charmaine. "When I was invited to your church, I was there to attend the service only. I never expected to be a participant in any way. And I certainly didn't want to go up onstage. It was suddenly thrust upon me."

Charmaine looked away momentarily, before their eyes reconnected. *Please don't embarrass me again!*

Many gestured at him politely. Some still had slight traces of anger on their faces for disrespecting one of their own. But, having just lost a family member, it was replaced with sympathy for now.

Pastor Lau's eyes momentarily drifted to Rodney Williams. The praise and worship leader nodded at him, as if silently forgiving what he did to Imogen last time. *That's more like it!*

Mark Lau breathed air in through his nostrils and shifted his gaze back to everyone else. "While my apology for offending anyone is sincere, friends, I cannot and will not apologize for defending the Word of God. That's all I did yesterday. Nothing more."

Seeing many shifting uncomfortably in their seats again, it was time to build rapport with his audience. "But let me digress. A little about myself. I was born and raised in Portland, Oregon. After receiving an academic scholarship at the University of Washington, I enrolled at the main campus here in Seattle, at the ripe young age of seventeen."

"Go Huskies!" someone shouted, causing many to laugh.

Pastor Lau smiled. "I met my wife in my junior year, at the Huskies-Cougars football game, of all places. Alli was a sophomore at Washington State University. I'll give you one guess who she was rooting for…"

"Go Cougars!" someone shouted, causing a few mock boos.

"Go back to Pullman!" Rodney said, jokingly, referring to Washington State University's location 280 miles clear across the state.

Mark motioned with his hands. "I know, it's a wonder we were married at all, right?"

His comment elicited more laughter from the group.

"At least we can all agree on our beloved Hawks!" another man yelled, regarding the Seattle Seahawks. "Am I right, Cedric?"

The backup strong safety who played mostly on special teams shook his head up and down. "You better support us!"

Everyone laughed.

"Oh, and for the record, 'Go 'Canes!'" Cedric said, regarding his alma mater, the Miami Hurricanes.

They laughed even harder.

Two of his teammates were also part of this life group, but after last night's game in San Francisco, against the 49ers, they were too exhausted and too banged-up to attend.

Cedric sensed there was more to it than that, namely the gentleman standing before him. But after watching what happened online, with his own two eyes, he wanted to come to see how it would all unfold.

Jeremiah Ogletree was seated in the front row. He said to Pastor Lau, "Yet another reminder that Fall is upon us!"

Mark Lau smiled politely again, then went on, "In truth, aside from receiving Christ as Lord and Savior, marrying Alli was the best decision I ever made. She was the godliest woman I ever knew.

"After graduating, we were both hired by Boeing as engineers. We married young and remained in the Seattle area. In our twenty-two years of marriage, God blessed us with good careers, two beautiful children, a son and a daughter, Samuel and Rachel."

Lau lowered his head. "Life was seemingly perfect for us until my wife was diagnosed with an aggressive form of breast cancer. Six months after her initial diagnosis, she succumbed to the disease."

He looked up to the ceiling and frowned. "It happened ten years ago last Saturday. I still miss Alli everyday…"

Bonnie Devlin lowered her head. "Sorry to hear that, Pastor. I lost my mother and only sister to breast cancer, so I know how you feel." She let out a loud sigh. "Then to lose your father-in-law?"

Mark looked down at his notes. "I rejoice knowing beyond certainty that both are now with the Lord. But as you might imagine, Alli's death was the most difficult trial of my life, and the lives of my children, up to that point.

"A few weeks after we buried her, I attended a conference in Southern California. The impact it had on my life was nothing short of life-changing. Soon after that, I enrolled at seminary school.

"After receiving my degree, I was hired as the associate pastor at Grace Bible Church, up in Everett."

Some in attendance, mindful that it was the church at which the Fujimotos were members, looked as if something had just soured in their mouths.

Mark noticed but went on, "Not too long after my kids were enrolled at the University of Washington—for the record, both are staunch Huskies fans, Seahawks, too for that matter…" he said, winking at Cedric, "I felt God calling me to preach the Gospel to my fellow countrymen and women over in China."

Cedric nodded his appreciation, unable to comprehend how this man, of all people, had caused such a ruckus at this house of worship 36 hours ago. He seemed nothing like the monster some had portrayed him to be. If anything, he was kind and respectful and harmless as a dove.

"Believe me when I say, moving to China was the last thing I wanted. I fought it every step of the way. But the more I fought it, the more I felt the Holy Spirit convicting me deep in my soul that that's where God wanted me to go.

"What came as no surprise was that my kids had no interest in joining me. They loved Seattle too much. And they didn't want to leave the many friends they'd made growing up.

"They thought I was crazy for walking away from a job I'd loved so much, especially after just receiving a lofty promotion the year before. My children couldn't understand how I could be so willing to throw it all away just to preach the Gospel halfway around the world.

"From a financial standpoint, I was doing quite well. Throw in the million-dollar life-insurance settlement I received after Alli died, which I used to pay off the mortgages on the two houses we owned, and I guess you could say I was in pretty-good shape, as the saying goes."

Pastor Lau sighed. "One of the steep prices I pay for serving God so faithfully is that my children maintain minimal contact with me, often calling me their 'over the top' religious father.

"Sadly, the four years they spent studying at university had changed them both from self-professed Christians to outspoken atheists."

This caused a few nods, and even some confused sideways looks, from some in the audience.

"The changes in them were subtle at first. But the more time they spent at college, the more their faith in God dwindled. They stopped reading the Bible, going to church, and they refused to listen whenever I tried sharing the Word of God with them..."

Pastor Lau sighed again. "When I told them I was coming back to the States to visit Alli's grave, they were eager to see me again. But they warned me up front to keep my religious beliefs to myself. In short, they didn't want to be proselytized by me in any way."

The way he said it pierced Bonnie Devlin deep inside. Widowed, four of her five now-grown kids had long since departed from the faith, totally disconnecting themselves from all things Christian.

She got up out of her seat to hug the man who'd angered so many at her church the day before. Her skin was so pale, it looked like it hadn't been exposed to the sun in many decades. *No way this man's a monster!*

As far as Bonnie was concerned, the jury was no longer out on him. She took a seat, even more eager now to hear what he would preach on than when she first arrived...

9

"NOW, BEFORE I DELVE into my message, I know there are many opinions on what the Word of God teaches. I'll even go so far to say many parts are highly debatable and are difficult to comprehend.

"Which would explain the thousands of denominations in the world, equating to millions of people all reading from the very same Book, yet disagreeing so vehemently on so many vital issues."

Mark Lau paused a moment, then said, "For proof of this, we need not look any further than what transpired yesterday. It was a prime example of how we tend to deviate from the scriptures.

"After thinking about it all day, I'm convinced there's only one demographic who are in absolute agreement with everything the Bible teaches." Mark sighed. "Sadly, it isn't the church..."

Charmaine tilted her head one way then the other. "Who is it then?"

"Those who have already passed on to the afterlife, believer and atheist alike. Those souls believe every word the Bible teaches, from start to finish—whether their final destination is Heaven or hell!"

"Ooh, that's good!" Cedric said it loudly enough that everyone heard him. "'Those who passed on to the afterlife...' I gotta write that one down!"

Mark Lau smiled at Cedric, then steadied his gaze back onto the partially-filled room, a first at this place. "Let me be clear, in my nine years as a pastor, I've read the Bible all the way through several times. Truth be told, I still don't understand it all. I'll even confess some parts still make me scratch my head in utter confusion.

"But here's the thing: Even though I don't understand it all, I nevertheless accept it all as God's Word, and believe every word and syllable was recorded for a specific purpose. Nothing needs to be added to it or taken away..."

"Amen!" someone to Mark Lau's right, that no one at the church recognized, said loud enough for everyone else to hear.

"Friends, God never intended for His Word to become an item of debate among His chosen people. Everyone He chose to record His message, which was intended for our benefit, was written under His divine inspiration at that time.

"Paul said to Timothy in the third chapter of his second epistle that all Scripture was God-breathed and was useful for teaching, rebuking, correcting, and training in righteousness, so God's servants might be thoroughly equipped for every good work...

"And Peter said in his second epistle that no prophecy of Scripture came about by the prophet's own interpretation of things. He went on to say prophecy never had its origin in the human will, but prophets, though human, spoke from God as they were carried along by the Holy Spirit..."

Heads nodded throughout the room...

"True that...," the same man to Mark Lau's right opined.

"Even so, mostly because no one fully comprehends the Word of God, we tend to impose our will on what it teaches, by offering various interpretations and opinions on what *we* think it means, instead of letting it speak for itself.

"This is why the Bible has become such a highly-debated topic among us humans..." He paused a moment. "But not with God Himself. Since the Gospel message is the only part of the Bible that brings salvation, every message I preach always comes back to it. After all, how can anyone be saved without hearing it, right?"

Heads nodded throughout the room again.

"With that in mind, please open your Bibles or e-Bibles to the Gospel of Matthew, chapter seven, verses twenty-one to twenty-three. I'm sure you're all familiar with this powerfully sobering passage.

"Let me begin by saying that of all the messages I heard at the men's Bible conference in Los Angeles a decade ago, this one was the most powerful. Naturally, as someone who proclaimed to be a Christ follower back then, I was mindful of this passage.

"But the way it was explained to me that weekend drove me to my knees in repentance, which ultimately led me to seminary school. So, with that, I'll ask you all to stand as I read from the Word of God."

Pastor Lau cleared his throat. "Not everyone who says to Me, 'Lord, Lord,' shall enter the kingdom of heaven, but he who does the will of My Father in heaven. Many will say to Me in that day, 'Lord, Lord, have we not prophesied in Your name, cast out demons in Your name, and done many wonders in Your name?' And then I will declare to them, 'I never knew you; depart from Me, you who practice lawlessness!' Lord, bless the reading of Your word."

Mark gripped the lectern with his two hands and began. "As we delve into the text, my emphasis will be on one word, which happens to be the first word in verse twenty-two: '*many*'.

"By simply reading the text, it's evident the many Jesus warned about are those who think they're saved but really aren't. I can assure you that our Lord wasn't referring to alcoholics in a bar or prostitutes roaming the streets, but to churchgoers and religious individuals on every level—including pastors, preachers, priests, elders, deacons, praise and worship leaders, those involved in children's ministry, and on and on.

"The fact that they uttered the word 'Lord' twice meant they were quite emphatic that a mistake had been made. This would explain their desperate pleas, as they tried convincing Jesus of the many good things they did in His name—driving out demons and performing many miracles—as if God had somehow overlooked something, or that their constant pleadings might get Him to change His mind.

"I find it interesting how they repeated the words, '*in your name*' three times in verse twenty-two. On several occasions in the four Gospels, Christ said, 'If you ask for anything in my name, it will be done.' At first glance, it sounds like a contradiction in terms. But for all who have a proper understanding of what the Bible teaches, it makes perfect sense.

"Can you imagine the shocked looks on so many faces when this happens for real?" Pastor Lau paused before saying, "First let me remind you, friends, that this isn't a fairytale. All of us have a divine appointment with God someday. Let me also remind you that our Lord *never* makes mistakes or overlooks anything.

"In short, the people spoken of in the text are those who think they're doing the will of the Father, and have a full expectation of going to Heaven when they die, only to learn too late, I might add, that they are headed straight to hell...

"Sobering, I know. Even more frightening is that Jesus didn't say 'few.' Nor did He say, 'some', Our Lord said, 'many'. If we are to take Him at His word, which I always do, the tragic truth is that *many* who attend church each week will ultimately end up being separated from Him for all eternity. What can be more tragic than that?"

Lau became teary-eyed. "Does it break your heart as much as mine that many who sing *Amazing Grace* and *How Great Thou Art* in church—with all their hearts—will end up in hell? Have you ever given this serious thought?"

Many were suddenly crestfallen; they squirmed in their seats thinking, *This man can't be serious?*

Rodney and Charmaine exchanged shocked glances. Both knew what the other was thinking: *Here we go again!*

Pastor Lau noticed. "Please hear me out, friends. Imagine singing *'Amazing Grace, how sweet the sound, that saved a wretch like me,'* and still ending up in hell? Sad to say, Christians may not tell lies in church but some sure do sing them!

"Sounds mean, I know, but anyone can sing hymns in church that were penned by men and women who knew Jesus intimately, and loved Him with all their hearts and souls. But merely singing the hymns they wrote to God won't save your soul. You must be born again!"

Many shifted uncomfortably in their seats again. They didn't want him to continue. His words were too harsh for their delicate ears to absorb; they contradicted the collective blessed-and-highly-favored mindsets that were cultivated at this church, by eliminating all negativity.

Pastor Lau took a deep breath and went on, "Personally, the reason I was so impacted by this passage was that the Lord used that man to help me realize I was one of the 'many'", he said, using his fingers as quotations, "that Jesus had referred to in that passage.

"What you must understand is I honestly thought I was saved all along, when I really wasn't. I learned that weekend that I was merely going through the motions of being a Christian when, in reality, all I was doing was building my house on sand, not rock.

"Alli knew I was a false convert. While she never judged me with her suspicions, I can only imagine how many sleepless nights it cost her. She's the main reason I went to the men's conference in the first place.

"My friend, Tristan, invited me to the conference. He later confessed it was at Alli's insistence that I go. Turned out to be a lifesaver for me, soul saver, rather."

Pastor Lau looked down at the lectern. "Even in death, she still had one last thing on her 'Honey Do' list for me..."

His comment made Bonnie Devlin laugh and cry at the same time.

Smiling at the thought, Mark became serious again. "I can't wait to see her again. No doubt her joy will be multiplied when we meet face to face on the day of God's choosing..." He sighed, then shook his head sadly. "Just hope my children end up there as well."

72

With a sad expression on his face, he said, "And so, friends, I ask, are you part of the 'many' Jesus warned about like I was, without even knowing it? More to the point, if your life came to an abrupt end today, would Christ welcome you Home as one of His good and faithful servants, or would He say, 'Depart from me! I never knew you...'"

You could hear a feather drop again...

Pastor Lau went on, "Imagine breathing your last breath in the flesh with a full expectation of being welcomed Home by Jesus, only to hear those frightful words spoken to you.

"The tragic truth is 'many,'" he used his fingers as quotations again, "do everything in church but get saved..."

The room fell completely silent. This was *not* what their itching ears wanted to hear! Many were suddenly disgusted and wanted to leave, including the two wealthiest members of the church—Norm and Nancy Wilshire.

Pastor Lau saw the anger building on their faces, but this was too important. "If you have truly been born again and are part of God's eternal family, Hallelujah! But what about the person seated next to you? Not to come across as judgmental in any way, but are they truly your co-laborers? Or are they still part of the mission field without even knowing it?

"If this has never concerned you before, it should because Jesus' words apply to all generations. None will be exempted or given a free pass, including our generation..."

Jeremiah Ogletree craned his neck back to gauge the looks on the faces of those behind him that he knew were members. It wasn't pretty. He could almost hear them screaming, "Really? Once was bad enough, but twice in two days? That just ain't right!"

The associate pastor shot up out of his seat, silently wishing many more would have stayed at home, rather than being exposed to this man again. Perspiration covered his forehead.

"Whoa! Whoa! We're a positive church, Pastor, an upbeat one. We like building people up, not tearing them down with heavy-yoked messages. We're all about giving hope, not scaring our members into submission."

Heads nodded all throughout the room.

Pastor Lau was quick to reply, "I get that you like keeping things lively and upbeat always, but is that what the Bible teaches?"

Pastor Ogletree winced. "You said earlier there are many varying opinions regarding the Word of God, right?"

"Yes, but there can only be one truth, not a consensus."

"Like I said, we're a seeker-friendly church built on unity. Last thing we need is someone coming here trying to divide the flock with minor doctrinal differences. How could that ever be seen as productive?"

Mark Lau sighed. "Unity is a mighty blessing indeed, Pastor, but if it's purchased at the cost of truth, how could that be considered a good thing?"

Jeremiah was losing patience. "One of our goals here is to keep our church full of people, not lose anyone due to minor differences of opinion."

Pastor Lau said, "With all due respect, there's nothing minor about it. When it comes to the human soul, you're right to say that doctrine does divide—it divides truth from error!"

Pastor Ogletree was deeply offended by his words. "I'm sorry, I cannot and will not allow you to bring these scare tactics into our church. I think it's best that you leave now."

"As you wish," Pastor Lau said softly, humbly, closing his Bible. He took a moment to fish around in his pants pocket for the keys to his daughter's car.

Finding them, he held up a sheet of paper. "I had planned on ending the session by reading this short poem written by Geoffrey O'Hara. I took the liberty of making copies. I'll leave them here in case any of you would like to read it."

Without apologizing this time—he felt no need to—and without a trace of anger or arrogance on his face, Mark Lau left the 50 printed copies on the lectern, then said, "May God bless these truths to your souls. And may His grace and peace be with you all."

At that, with a deep concern for the souls of everyone in the room, he left them...*Open their spiritual eyes, Lord, as only You can!*

10

THE ROOM GREW EERILY silent again, as many shook their heads in disgust and disbelief, trying to piece it all together. They were completely rattled by what they'd just heard.

Rodney Williams was the first to speak. "Really? After all that, he has the audacity to pray God's grace and peace over us? If anyone needs those things, it's him! He was nothing like this when we met him at the Fujimoto's house. What a hypocrite he turned out to be!"

Pastor Ogletree bristled in annoyance. "What do you expect, Rodney? He's Kaito's best friend, not to mention the former associate pastor at the church the Fujimotos attend, before he relocated to China. Why should we have expected anything less from him?"

Rodney clenched his fist in anger. "He calls us his friends then proceeds to tell us many of us are going to hell. The nerve of him!"

Up until now, Rodney had been using the huge commission Charmaine stood to receive from selling his house, as a mental bargaining chip to tolerate this man's actions. *No more!*

Jeremiah gritted his teeth; his cheeks burned with anger. No one had to tell him anger wasn't a fruit of the Spirit, but this wasn't merely anger, it was righteous indignation. It was spiritual warfare!

He called Sophia. When his wife answered, he said, "Good thing you stayed home with the kids. What was I thinking by inviting him back?!"

Sophia muted the television. "Oh, no…What happened?" She wanted to say, "I warned you not to go through with it," but now wasn't the time.

"Tell you when I get home. Just glad I took your advice and didn't use Facebook live this time. You were spot on, sweetie." Jeremiah sighed. "Let me get back to our people. Time for more damage control. Hope to see you soon…"

"Take your time, darling. I'm busy getting the kids ready for sleep. I'm praying for you all…"

"Thanks. We need it."

Rodney overheard the conversation and sent a text message to Imogen Martín: *He did it again. Only to all of us this time! You're right; he must be demon possessed or something!*

Charmaine plucked her cellphone from her handbag, and sent a voice text message to Kaito Fujimoto. It would be too many words to type: *Your boy really did a number on us the past two days! Yesterday, he rebuked our anointed prophetess in front of a full congregation, not to mention thousands of others online!*

Tonight he openly proclaimed at Pastor Ogletree's life group that many of us won't be going to Heaven when we die. What's up with him? I appreciate that he asked me to sell his house, and all, but it gives him no right to come here and do such things.

Kaito was mindful of what had happened between Mark and Imogen—Mark told him all about it. He also watched it on Facebook, and knew what topic his best friend would be preaching on this night.

Kaito wanted to go with him but Mark told him it might not be a good idea. He replied: *Sorry his words weren't well received at your church.*

Charmaine replied: *Well received? How could they be when his message was filled with venomous hate speech! Is he even a true Christ follower?*

Instead of replying, Kaito called her cellphone. When Charmaine answered, he said, "He most definitely is…"

"I hear what you're saying, Kaito, but it's hard to see the love of God in his message. He seems like a kind and gentle individual. But once he starts preaching, it's like something goes off inside and his friendly demeanor changes."

"He preached on Matthew seven, right?"

"Uh-huh."

"Did he yell or scream or point his finger at anyone in judgment, or talk down to anyone as if he was better than them?"

Charmaine took a moment to think about it. "No, not at all…"

"I didn't think so. This may surprise you to hear me say this, but Mark's a tender-hearted pastor. I'm sure the message he preached was shared in love, even if it didn't seem that way on the surface…"

Charmaine silently scoffed at his reply, then said, "I assure you, Kaito, it *wasn't* preached in love. Even after what he did yesterday, Pastor Ogletree was still willing to give him another chance to redeem himself.

"More than a hundred people showed up hoping to hear something positive from him. This is the thanks we get? I know he's mourning the death of a loved one, but he didn't come anywhere close to being loving toward us. If anything, we felt judged by him."

Charmaine took a deep breath and exhaled. "Just glad most were so turned off by what he did yesterday, they never bothered showing up tonight. No doubt he would've angered them too!"

Fujimoto sighed. "I understand how you feel. Again, Matthew seven can be difficult to digest, especially for those who think they're saved but really aren't."

"Are you saying we're not saved?" *Have you forgotten that I'm your only client left at this blessed church?*

"Of course, not! Only God knows the heart, Charmaine. All I'm saying is it takes courage to preach on that soul-splitting topic."

"No disrespect, Kaito, but you weren't here! He should know better than to come to someone's church, then judge and criticize everyone the way he did, from the pastor on down."

Charmaine looked at Rodney. "His meanspirited approach may work in China, but not here in America."

Kaito scratched his head. "As one of God's servants, he was only repeating Jesus' words, nothing more. Don't hate the messenger, take it up with the One who gave him the message."

Jeremiah Ogletree said, "Is that Kaito?"

Charmaine lowered her head. "Yes..."

"Tell him his friend's no longer welcome at our church!"

"Did you hear that?"

Kaito said, "I heard."

Charmaine closed her eyes. "You need to have a serious talk with him. Hopefully, you can teach him proper church etiquette."

Fujimoto said, "Why don't you come over for dinner before Mark goes back to China, and tell him yourself? After all, you're sort of in business together, at least until you sell his house."

"Not sure I still wanna sell it. Not after this..."

"Sorry to hear that. I'd hate to see him waste the next few days looking for another agent before he returns to China."

Charmaine sighed, then looked at her French manicure. "Hmm. When's he leaving?"

"Friday. The funeral will be on Wednesday. Perhaps Thursday would be a good day. Whatever day works best for you, will be fine for us. Lucy will prepare your favorite this time—shrimp tempura and miso soup."

"Been missing that." Her tone was more subdued than usual.

"Well then, you must come! Bring Rodney too."

Rodney heard him and put his hand up in refusal. "Let me talk to him and get back to you."

"Roger that. Just make sure to leave enough time so Lucy can prepare the meal."

"I will. Tell her I said hi."

"Sure, when she gets home. She's attending a women's group at our church. I'm expecting her back soon."

Charmaine rolled her eyes. Even after all these years, she felt sorry for the Fujimotos. What could she possibly learn at that dead church? If it was anything like this experience, no wonder their church was so small in numbers...

She blinked away the thought. "You'll have an answer by tomorrow."

"Great! Be careful driving home later."

"Thanks, Kaito. Hope you have a good night."

"You, too." Charmaine placed her phone back in her handbag and rejoined the conversation. She quickly learned not everyone was angered or the slightest bit offended by Pastor Lau's words.

This was especially true with the group of people no one knew, who weren't even members of her church. They seemed to be in total agreement with everything that he said.

One middle-aged married couple, who'd slipped in just before Mark was introduced—who weren't big fans of the Martín's teachings—sat alone at a table toward the rear of the room.

Usually, when they saw Julian or Imogen preaching on TV, they changed the channel, and often prayed that God would humble the couple and use them both for His glory and no longer for theirs.

They never thought the day would come that they would ever step foot inside this place. But after watching Mark Lau's online rebuke of Imogen Martín, they checked the church calendar for upcoming events and learned he would be teaching the Monday night Bible study.

They couldn't resist...

Having just witnessed God at work through the humble guest speaker, both had broad smiles on their faces.

The husband said, "If I may, let me point out that anyone who professes to be a true child of the Most High God will never be offended by anything the Bible teaches, especially the words that Christ Himself spoke..."

His comment generated a few awkward glances from others.

Cedric played with his cornrows. He glanced at Julian. "Think you were a little too hard on him, Pastor? Like our visitor pointed out, he was only quoting what Jesus said in the Bible, word for word..."

Jeremiah became visibly defensive. "No, I don't. One of my duties as a pastor is to protect the flock from ravenous wolves."

Bonnie Devlin weighed in, "Ravenous wolf? I can't speak for anyone else but I, for one, was touched by his transparency. He seems like a perfect gentleman. He's kind, humble and respectful..."

Someone else said, "I agree. He wasn't being arrogant or meanspirited in any way. Never once did he point fingers at us in judgment, saying we weren't saved. If anything, he confessed to us that *he* was one of the many that Christ spoke of in the passage."

A young woman, and new church member, seated at the table next to Rodney and Charmaine said, "What's there to be mad about? Like Cedric said, all he did was share the very words Christ Himself spoke, as evidenced by the red letters. His explanation seemed logical to me. Makes me want to dig deeper into the Bible."

Jeremiah stiffened up and gritted his teeth again. "You mean, *his* interpretation of it. Come on, y'all, Jesus wasn't referring to *us* in those passages—not a chance! His words were intended for the 'many' so-called Christians" he said, using his fingers as quotation marks, as if silently mocking Mark Lau, "who are merely jealous of us.

"You know who I mean, the ones Pastor Julian says only criticize us because of how blessed and highly favored we are! I'm sure this man is part of that group..."

Norm and Nancy Wilshire occupied the same table as Rodney, Charmaine, and Pastor Ogletree. Norm weighed in. "I'm with you, Pastor. I'm sure he doesn't have two nickels to rub together. I'm certain his words came more from a jealous perspective than anything else."

Jeremiah winked his appreciation. "Well said, brother Norm. With that in mind, it's time again to rid the evil spirits that followed him into our church! Like Sophia keeps saying, if God's judging him for what he did yesterday, we must get out of the way and have nothing to do with him, and let God straighten him out!"

Norm and Nancy both nodded. "Agreed!"

After a moment of reflection, a middle-aged Hispanic man—also not satisfied with Pastor Jeremiah's explanation—said, "Not sure I still believe that Pastor. I agree with the others who said he was only sharing Jesus' words with us, word for word. What's wrong with that?"

Jeremiah was incredulous. "Again, his words weren't meant for us, but for those who think they're Christians, but really aren't…"

Cedric sighed. "I don't know, Pastor. He may be soft-spoken, but his words carried much weight. I think he came here to warn us all in love. Do you really think we're immune to Christ's warning?"

Bonnie Devlin was in total agreement with Cedric. Something didn't feel right about Pastor Jeremiah's explanation. It was too shallow, too clumsy, too vague.

And why did Pastor Lau's father-in-law die after Imogen had just prayed for him? Especially since she'd assured him that he would be fine?

Bonnie didn't believe for a second that a lack of faith on his part was the reason it happened. No way!

Her head was more full of questions than answers…

Pastor Ogletree, who had been pacing the front of the room, back and forth, stopped at the lectern and glanced at the poem the man had left behind. Reading it, he flinched; a shiver shot through him. He snorted, hoping it would divert all attention away from his initial reaction.

It didn't work. Bonnie got up out of her seat and read the short poem in silence, then read it loudly for everyone else to hear.

> "'Why call me Lord, Lord and do not the things I say?
> Ye call me the "Way" and walk me not.
> Ye call me the "Life" and live me not.
> Ye call me "Master" and obey me not.
> If I condemn thee, blame me not.
> Ye call me "Bread" and eat me not.
> Ye call me "Truth" and believe me not.
> Ye call me "Lord" and serve me not.
> If I condemn thee, blame me not.'"

Pastor Jeremiah's eyes wandered the room, trying to mentally gauge everyone's reaction. What he saw on most faces was sheer and utter confusion.

He gulped hard, then sent a text message to Julian: *I hope this man doesn't create a rift at our church. Some seem to think he was sent by God, including Cedric, if you can believe that…*

After spending a few minutes casting out the spirit their guest speaker had once again brought into their place of worship, Jeremiah prayed blessings over everyone, then dismissed them.

The associate pastor locked up and left for home with a throbbing headache, and a bad feeling inside. He would discover in time that his worst fears had been realized...

11

AFTER PRAYING FOR THREE straight days, followed by a lengthy conversation on the phone with Mark Lau, and later with Lucy Fujimoto, Charmaine finally agreed to stop by the Fujimoto residence, even despite Rodney's strongest protests. He flat-out refused to join her this time.

What ultimately drove her decision was something Lucy had told her, "You already know we disagree on some key doctrinal issues. If you came to our church and wanted to tell us where you disagreed with us, we would listen without judging you. So please don't let our differences stop you from coming for dinner."

It worked. Before going there, Charmaine met Pastor Lau in Kenmore, to photograph the house he owned. The two hours they spent together were rather enjoyable. Mark was as kind and gentle as the person she met the night they signed the seller's agreement.

The man she had thought might be bi-polar, really was normal after all. When they arrived at the Fujimoto residence, Charmaine was relaxed enough to let her guard down.

Kaito blessed the food, and asked God to remind them in their disagreements that this was a safe place for all of them, and that the Holy Spirit was in their midst.

When he was finished, Charmaine took a bite of the lightly-fried shrimp tempura. "Pastor Lau, since we're in our safe zones, can you explain why you have such a huge problem with my pastors?" She wanted to ask this question earlier when they were photographing the house. She decided to wait so Kaito and Lucy could also hear it.

"Let me start by saying I agree with much of what your pastor preached on in Ecclesiastes five. I have no qualms with the Scripture itself. God's not against us having things. What He's against is things having us!"

Charmaine liked the way he put it.

Mark dipped a fried jumbo shrimp into tempura sauce and chomped on it, leaving only the tail between his fingers. He took a moment to chew on it and swallow, then said, "Let me say there are many solid charismatic preachers in the world. When it comes to God's salvation, the Gospel they preach is spot on. They don't try sugarcoating anything.

"They rightly preach belief in Christ and repentance of sin as the only way to be saved from hell. They love their flocks and encourage them to seek the Lord with all their hearts, minds, and souls. They speak of God's saving grace and His limitless mercy.

"The problem is some preach with one foot in the Word and the other in the world. Others have both feet firmly planted in the world, and have no true understanding of what the Gospel stands for.

"The end result is that many preach a savior from hell but not a savior from sin, by teaching things that have nothing to do with Christian obedience or sacrifice, let alone Godliness with contentment."

Pastor Lau shook his head sadly. "I'm afraid your pastors fall into that category. They represent the extreme spiritually off-track demographic."

Charmaine stiffened up, then shifted her focus to the Fujimotos. "You know Pastor Julian always says we need to be saved, or born again, and that we all need God's grace and forgiveness…"

Kaito interjected, "Yes, he does. But saved from what? Sorry to say, but his approach is greatly flawed. Lucy and I know first-hand the gospel he preaches is designed to recruit people into the good life, not into a life of obedience or from a position of brokenness or true repentance…"

Charmaine looked at Mark. "Didn't I hear you say 'Amen' a few times during the service?"

He nodded yes. "I always say, 'Amen' when I hear truth being preached. But I also heard too many partial and watered down truths spoken, not to mention a few outright falsehoods. Too many for comfort. Would you like to know what grieved my spirit most at your church?"

"Sure…"

"It was seeing people dancing on dollar bills on the steps leading up to what's supposed to be the altar of God. I couldn't believe it. Defiling something that's meant to be holy is beyond reprehensible to me."

Charmaine couldn't argue his point. Even she was at odds with it. She wanted to confront her pastors about it once or twice, but since things were going so well for her, she refrained.

She backpedaled, "You know how greatly admired my pastors are."

Mark shook his head thoughtfully. "One thing I learned in the eight years I've been preaching in China is that Christians are not so much in danger when they are being persecuted as when they are being admired."

*Hmm...*Charmaine gulped hard. "Okay, let's say for argument's sake you're right. Did that give you the right to humiliate Pastor Imogen the way you did? You shook her confidence. Even now, she has difficulty making eye contact with some people..."

"I understand her anger, and I do feel bad for hurting her feelings. But that doesn't change the fact that I cannot call her a prophetess unless I put the word 'false' before it.

"I can give you two reasons for this. First, like I told Pastor Ogletree last Sunday, if the things she prophesied about me having a bigger and better church in China ever came true, it wouldn't end well for me.

"The simple truth is Chinese Christians have the same Savior we have here in the States. But what they don't have is the same freedom to worship Jesus like we do."

Charmaine shot him a sideways look but remained silent.

Pastor Lau paused. "I think you already know the second reason..."

"Your father-in-law?"

Mark nodded. "Don't you find it telling that he passed-away mere moments after she made her bold declaration?"

Charmaine grimaced. "Some at my church believe it happened because of what you did to Imogen. Sorry to tell you this but some think you're demon possessed."

"Doesn't surprise me. I'm sure that's what Imogen thinks too, right?"

"No disrespect, but how could she not?"

Pastor Lau leaned up in his chair and rested his elbows on the table. "Think about it, the woman who addressed me as a mighty man of God to the congregation before I rebuked her, now thinks I'm demon possessed. If she were a true prophetess, wouldn't she have known that up front?"

"Hmm..." Charmaine grew fidgety and shifted in her chair.

They finished their meals in silence, before reconvening in the living room for tea.

Lucy took a small sip and placed her empty teacup on the living room table. "You've heard my husband tell you why he left your church. Would you like to know what ultimately drove me away?"

"Sure..." This came out of Charmaine's mouth softly.

"As you already know, Kaito's decision to leave the only church we'd ever known as a married couple caused constant friction between us, especially on Sundays and Wednesday nights when he attended the weekly Bible study.

"It took six months before I finally agreed to join him one Sunday." Lucy sighed. "The moment I stepped foot inside that church, I felt entirely out of place. I admit I was standoffish and even a little cold toward everyone he introduced me to."

Charmaine leaned up on the couch opposite the Fujimotos. Seeing Lucy's feet tiptoeing on the floor again, she chuckled silently to herself. "How was it different from our church?"

"In all ways! For starters, it was plain looking, boring even. There was no massive stage, no indoor smoke machines, or bright lights streaming down from the rafters like we had.

"There was nothing but a lone piano, organ, a violin, and an acoustic guitar on the moderately size stage. The entire time I was there, I wanted to leave. I missed the high-octane praise and worship at our church, and the upbeat messages Pastor Julian preached."

Lucy glanced at her husband. "Kaito didn't know but I streamed the service on my phone, but kept it in my handbag so he couldn't see it."

Kaito belly laughed, then wrapped his right arm around his wife. "Oh, really, now!"

Lucy kissed him on the left cheek, then focused her attention back to Charmaine. "If going there did any good, it further reinforced how much I loved the Blessed and Highly Favored Church.

"Much like the Martíns had warned in advance, I found Grace Bible Church to be a weak church. Nothing about it impressed me in the least. I told Kaito on the drive home it was *his* church family, not mine. I silently swore I'd never go back there again, let alone ever become a member."

Charmaine nodded, as if in total agreement with what she'd just heard.

Lucy took another sip of tea. "It took another six months before I reluctantly agreed to join him again, but only because the Martíns were in Miami that weekend, for a Christian wealth accumulating conference at which both were featured speakers."

Charmaine said, "I was there with Rodney…"

Lucy said, "I had planned on going myself, but I cancelled at the last minute." She paused a moment. "Actually, the wealth conference wasn't the main reason I went back to church with my husband that day…"

Charmaine took a sip of tea. "What was it then?"

"I confess it was partly due to my growing disdain toward some at church who used to be Kaito's clients. A month after he left, even though I was still a member, fifty percent of his business was wiped out."

85

Lucy smiled wearily at Charmaine. "After three months, you were the only one left at church still doing business with my husband. Everyone else took their investments elsewhere.

"The fact that he worked on commission wasn't good. The loss of income caused unbearable stress at times. I couldn't help but ask myself if his clients were blessings from God, as the Martíns had always boasted, why were they so suddenly taken away? It made no sense to me. Had that not happened, perhaps I'd still be a member at your church.

"But in truth, it went even beyond the lost income. While many did their best to comfort me, others were cold and distant. I even overheard some saying my husband had lost his salvation for leaving the church.

"This wasn't the type of behavior I thought I'd ever encounter at a church that was supposed to be the greatest in all of Seattle. How would you feel if the roles were reversed and it was Rodney instead?"

Charmaine momentarily lowered her head in embarrassment.

Lucy said, "Don't feel bad, Charmaine. You always made me feel welcome until the very last day. But I admit I harbored resentment toward some of the others...

"But not Kaito. He refused to speak ill of anyone. He prayed for them instead. He was much more calm and understanding than I was. When I asked how he did it, I'll never forget his answer.

"He said now that he'd finally hit the 'self-evaluation' truth, he felt more comfortable describing himself as a 'redeemed wretch' than 'blessed and highly favored.'"

Charmaine blinked hard, as she softly mouthed the words, "Redeemed wretch?"

Lucy read her lips and giggled to herself. "That was the first big change I noticed in him. Other things I noticed was that he no longer tried singing louder than everyone else in church, or raising his hands higher than the person next to him, like he formerly did.

"He also left his Rolex and all other expensive jewelry he owned, and used as recruiting tools, at home where he said they belonged.

"And where he occasionally sent and received text messages during Pastor Julian's sermons, informing absentees of just how 'on fire' he was, his phone was always turned off, so he could give his undivided attention to the message being preached by Pastor Donnelson.

"That's what mattered most to him. In truth, I wasn't sure if the sudden changes in my husband were good or bad. In time, I came to learn they were very good. He was kinder, gentler, and infinitely more humble than he used to be...

"One week at his church turned into two. Then three. Then four. Whereas I always felt good about myself when Julian or Imogen preached, Pastor Donnelson's messages produced the exact opposite emotions in me.

"Instead of feeling fully empowered and ready to take on the world, I felt less entitled, less worthy, less significant, and more dirty and sinful after each service. At least initially...

"After being exposed to sound doctrine week in and week out, a lightbulb finally went off in my mind. It took knowing just how holy and just God was, and how my sins had caused eternal separation between us before I could finally understand His love for me.

"Up until that point, the love I experienced from God was one sided, one way, and totally distorted, because all focus was squarely on me.

"Think about it, if we don't preach about sin and God's judgment on it, how can we possibly present Christ as a Savior from sin and from the wrath of God?"

Charmaine bit the inside of her mouth. "Hmm..."

"In time, I stopped thinking so highly of myself and realized the 'blessed and highly favored' mindset I'd always harbored, was nothing more than pride on my part.

"And much like my husband a few months back, I started displaying a kinder, gentler, and more humble side. The more I understood God's salvation message, the more I understood it had nothing to do with obtaining material blessings.

"I also came to understand why Kaito was so comfortable describing himself as a 'redeemed wretch'. It took understanding the bad news, that I was a wretched sinner to fully embrace the Good News, that God loved me so much that even despite the great sin in my life, He sent His only Son to die in my place."

Charmaine silently gasped. Lucy's words nearly brought her to tears.

She continued, "That was when I stopped praying for worldly material things. My personal quest was to know all I could about the One who created me. I started hungering and thirsting for the Word of God and couldn't get enough of it. It was a remarkable turning point in my life.

"One thing I've learned is that we can never truly judge the growth of a church by the size of its building. Just because a church is large doesn't necessarily mean it's healthy. It could just be swollen with false converts...

"Pastor Donnelson isn't flamboyant like Julian and Imogen, and our church isn't nearly as big as yours, but the passion he has for the Word and sound preaching more than make up for it.

"So, in the end, the biggest disparity between both churches isn't the buildings at which we gather, but the messages that are preached. In that regard, sorry to say, there isn't much to compare."

Charmaine blurted out, "We're a praying church. All we do is pray."

Pastor Lau responded, "That's good to know. But what exactly do you pray for? In other words, what's more important to your church, praying for someone's physical healing or for their spiritual regeneration? For them to be delivered from sin or into a life full of prosperity?

"Put another way, what gives the members of your church the most anxiety? Is it their sins or their misfortunes in life?"

Charmaine was trying not to be offended. She took another deep breath. *Remember this is a safe zone!* "Go on…"

"I believe these are vital questions all Christians should have solid answers to before joining any church. They will determine whether that church is self-centered or Christ-centered, whether they're in the Word or still in the world, even if partly."

Charmaine folded her hands on her lap. "Like you said, we agree to disagree, right?"

Mark Lau nodded.

The Fujimotos glanced at each other. Both were impressed with his timely answer, especially since it served to put an end to the argument.

But Charmaine silently begged to differ. She left for home that night feeling even more confused, and frustrated. Weren't they supposed to be on the same side? The way they staunchly defended certain parts of the scriptures, without ever compromising, it made her feel like they were playing on different teams.

It wasn't a comforting feeling…

12

FRIDAY MORNING

CHARMAINE STOPPED BY THE Fujimoto residence still a little rattled from her jarring dinner conversation the night before. But after waking this morning to a half dozen text messages, from people interested in seeing her new listing, she managed to put her ill feelings aside and focus on the reason she was introduced to Mark Lau in the first place—to sell his home.

Lucy opened the door. "Charmaine, what a pleasant surprise!"

"I wanted to see Mark before he leaves, and give him some good news about the house."

"Please come in. He'll be happy to see you." Lucy didn't mention that they'd just finished praying for her. After the way everything unfolded last time, she didn't want her to take it the wrong way.

Mark was lounging on one of the two living room couches, his feet propped up on a pillow. "Someone's here to see you before you go…"

He sprung up off the couch. "Charmaine! How nice of you to stop by."

Mark shot a curious look at Lucy. She was ever mindful that he tossed and turned in bed most of the night, unable to stop thinking about the woman now standing before him.

Before Kaito left for work, Mark told his friends over breakfast that he woke this morning with the strangest thought. "We know she has no interest in going to your church," he had told them, "But I have this feeling, a premonition if you will, that if we could only get her to visit my church in China, God will do the rest. Perhaps that's why He kept me awake most of the night thinking about her…"

Now, just like that, here she was again, not looking downcast like she did 12 hours ago, but bubbling over with excitement and enthusiasm. *Was this confirmation from above?*

Lucy was thinking similar thoughts…

Charmaine smiled brightly. "Just wanted you to know more than a dozen people have already contacted me about seeing the house?"

"Wow! That's fantastic news! You don't waste time!"

"I try not to, Pastor. Time is money, right? Let the bidding war begin!"

"I suppose."

Charmaine was relieved to see the kind and gentle side of him again, after two disasters and a near third one last night. "I'm actually on my way to an appointment to show the house. But I wanted to see you off first, and thank you again for the opportunity you gave me."

"You're welcome." It was nice seeing her looking so happy again.

Lucy asked, "Do you have time for a quick cup of coffee?"

Charmaine checked her watch. "I have fifteen minutes, so any conversation we have needs to be short."

Lucy looked at Mark and giggled. Both knew exactly what Charmaine meant. "One cup of coffee coming right up…"

Charmaine decided that she would be the one to determine the direction of the conversation this time. Little did she know, it was God who was directing her path. "Are you eager to get back to China?"

Mark nodded yes. "As much as I'll miss everyone here, mostly my kids, my church family really needs me there."

"I'm curious, Pastor, what does your church look like?"

Mark was mildly shocked that it took until the day he was leaving before she finally inquired. "I assure you it's nothing like your church, especially when it comes to overall opulence. And our services aren't quite like yours."

"How do they differ from ours?"

"In all ways, actually."

Charmaine shot him a quizzical look. "What did you mean last night when you said Chinese Christians have the same Jesus we have, but not the same freedoms to worship Him?"

"You said you only have fifteen minutes, right?"

"Yes…"

"Instead of trying to explain it to you in such a short period of time, if you truly want to see how we worship, come to China and experience it for yourself," Pastor Lau said, matter-of-factly.

"A nice thought, but my schedule won't allow for it."

Sensing even more now that a trip to his church could potentially change her life, it was time to challenge her. "So, what you're saying is you have the financial freedom to travel, but your schedule won't allow you the time to do it? How successful are you really then?"

"Don't get me wrong, Pastor, I travel. In fact, I'm taking a ten-day trip to Paris in December, with my best friend, Meredith. We're going to celebrate our birthdays and do some Christmas shopping.

"We went last year, followed by a brief stop in London. The shopping we did! The year before last, we went to Vancouver, Canada for the weekend. We try to do something every year for our birthdays."

"Did you book the trip yet?"

Charmaine shook her head. "Not yet, Pastor. Why do you ask?"

"What do you know about Shanghai?"

"Not much, sorry…"

"What if I told you it's known as the 'Paris of the East,' only far more luxurious." No one had to tell Mark how much Charmaine enjoyed the finer things in life. It was evident in her demeanor.

"Seriously?"

Pastor Lau nodded. "I know you're in a hurry, but if you search Shanghai online, you'll discover it's one of the most cosmopolitan cities in the world. It's a place the super successful flock to just to shop."

"Really now?"

Lucy returned with coffee. "I can attest to that, Charmaine."

Charmaine blew into the cup then took a small sip. "Tempting as it sounds, Meredith would never agree to it. Paris is our favorite city on earth. The only disappointment we had was that it was too cold to enjoy Disneyland. We left after only two hours at the park. Total waste of money. Other than that, what can I say, it's Paris?"

"Did you know we have a Disneyland in Shanghai?"

"Hmm, really?"

Mark took a swig from his water bottle. "It opened in twenty-fifteen."

"Interesting. Have you been there yet?"

"Not yet. Too busy at my church."

"If I ever come there, Disney's on me," Charmaine said, more in jest than anything else.

"That's very kind of you, Charmaine. It will be quite chilly in December, but not as cold as France." Mark paused, then said, "But if you do come, more than anything I'd want you to worship at my church."

"Tell you what, if I sell your house before December first, and earn the extra two percent you so generously offered, if Meredith agrees, we'll go to Shanghai instead." Charmaine was shocked at her own words.

Mark glanced at Lucy. She raised an eyebrow. His eyes volleyed back to Charmaine. "That will be my daily prayer."

The way he said it, coupled by what she saw in his eyes, removed any remaining negative thoughts she had about him. "Let me discuss it with

Meredith. Probably be a hard sell though. Her heart's set on going back to Paris. Then again, she's an open-minded gal who likes experiencing new things, so perhaps she'll agree. But no promises, okay?"

Mark smiled warmly. "Of course."

Charmaine glanced at her watch. "I gotta run. I have my first showing in less than an hour. Wish me luck."

"No need. The house will sell in God's perfect timing, not a moment sooner."

"Yes, Pastor, keep speaking it into existence!"

Pastor Lau glanced at Lucy, who chuckled under her breath.

Charmaine sensed his uneasiness to her comment. "Meeting you has been interesting on so many levels. Sort of like riding on a roller coaster."

Mark Lau burst out in laughter. "I know what you mean."

"Even though my heart is set on going to Paris again, I promise to do my best to sell your house before the deadline. I'll also search Shanghai online. What can I say? You've piqued my curiosity..."

Mark Lau smiled brightly. "If it's God's will for you to go there, nothing or no one can prevent it from happening..."

Charmaine's bright eyes lit up, easily rivaling the smile on her face. "Amen to that!"

"Thanks for stopping by to see me off. I appreciate it so much."

"It's the least I can do for a fellow brother in Christ."

"Amen! Hope to see you again. Next time in my country."

"Enjoy the flight back to China. I'll be praying for your safe return."

"Very kind of you, Charmaine. I hope you sell the house before the deadline. I'd really love to welcome you to Shanghai and introduce you to how so many of us worship God outside the States."

Charmaine looked at him curiously. "Like you said, if it's God's will, nothing can stop it from happening, right?"

"Absolutely!" *Open this door, Lord...*

The way he said it earned him another smile. Not the professional smile Charmaine gave to prospective clients. This was more endearing, more from her heart.

Pastor Lau cautioned, "But a few words of advice if you do come. Many social media sites here in the States, Facebook and Twitter, for example, are blocked in China."

Charmaine raised an eyebrow. "Oh?"

"I'm afraid the access we have to the outside world online is extremely limited. So, if you want to access those sites, you'll need to connect to a virtual private network before leaving the States…"

The look on Charmaine's face told Mark she had no idea what he was talking about.

He explained, "Essentially, VPN's bypass all firewalls in China by masking your IP location, thus creating a secure connection between your device and a remote server. VPNs encrypt all posts made before routing it through a server in a remote location of your choice."

"Thanks for the tip. I'll be sure to check into it…"

"Good. And while you're at it, why don't you research the prosperity gospel online? You may be surprised by what you discover."

Charmaine winced. *Not again!* Since she was leaving, she brushed it aside, hugged them both, and left for her appointment…

LATER THAT DAY, CHARMAINE remained true to her promise to Mark Lau to search Shanghai online.

What she discovered was nothing short of spectacular. After watching several *You Tube* videos, she was completely blown away by the vibrant cosmopolitan city.

From what she could see, there was nothing like this place in America. *Wait until Meredith sees this!*

She sent a text message to her best friend: *Good evening, Bestie. If you have no plans for tonight, stop by the house. There's something I wanna run by you. I'm cooking eggplant parmesan…*

Meredith was out showing a house. She replied: *Yummy! What time?*

Charmaine typed: *Sevenish? Hope you can make it!*

Meredith: *See you then!*

Meredith arrived on time. "Come in, Bestie!"

Charmaine had always been a high-spirited individual. She was on full throttle now. "Wow! Look at you! Something good must have happened! Did you already sell his house?"

Charmaine burst out in laughter. "Not yet, but I already have lots of interest in it. What I have to share with you is indirectly related to that."

Meredith noticed the *YouTube* videos playing on the huge flatscreen TV in the living room, but she was too engrossed in conversation with Charmaine, as she put the finishing touches on her mouth-watering eggplant parmesan, to give it much attention.

It wasn't until Charmaine suggested that they eat their meals in the living room, instead of at the dining room table, that Meredith realized the video shorts were all about China. Shanghai, China, to be precise.

One video they watched was taken from a drone offering a sprawling view of the city. A voiceover boasted, "Shanghai, Hu for short, is located on the central coast, halfway between Hong Kong and Beijing, and is one of the wealthiest cities on earth. Known as the 'Oriental Paris', with its numerous bustling commercial streets and shopping centers, Shanghai has truly become a shopper's paradise like no other city on the planet…"

Meredith raised a curious eyebrow at Charmaine, before her eyes were drawn back to the TV screen.

The voiceover continued, "Situated on the edge of the East China Sea, Shanghai serves as the most influential economic, financial, cultural, science and technology hub in eastern China. In addition to its pulsating development and modernization, the city's multicultural flair endows it with a unique glamour.

"Here, one finds the perfect blend of cultures, the modern and the traditional, the western and the oriental. Western customs and Chinese traditions intertwine to form the city's culture, making a visitor's stay truly memorable."

After watching in silence, Meredith finally said, "Okay, I give up. Why are we watching videos about Shanghai?"

The way she said it made Charmaine burst out in laughter again. "I'm trying to subliminally entice you to change your mind about going to Paris in December."

Meredith snorted laughter. Realizing her best friend was being serious, her eyes widened. "What?"

"Crazy, I know, but hear me out. I stopped by the Fujimotos earlier to say farewell to Mark Lau. After inquiring about his city, he made it sound so amazing. At his insistence, I searched Shanghai online when I came home and started watching. Haven't stopped since…

"It's even better than I thought, Bestie! Shanghai's our kind of city—beautiful and clean! I can't explain it, but I feel called to go there. Besides, I'd like to visit Pastor Lau's church and see how they worship so differently from my church.

"I may not agree with his negative brand of Christianity, but that doesn't change that he is a kind and decent man. I'd also like to take him to Disney Land once we're there. It's the least I can do for letting me sell his house."

Meredith was about to say something. Charmaine held up her right pointer finger. "Before you say anything, watch this video. I saw it earlier. If we go, it's where I'd like to stay…"

The voiceover said, "The Waldorf Astoria Shanghai on the Bund is a luxurious hotel with legendary architecture, combining China's deep history with the prosperity of the twenty-first century. Our two-hundred and sixty luxuriously-equipped rooms and suites overlook the beautiful Pudong skyline."

As the voice kept speaking, recent accolades awarded to the vibrant hotel flashed on the screen. *"Voted by Trip Advisor's Global Traveler's Choice for six consecutive years," "Ranked among the top three Chinese hotels by readers of Condé Nast Traveler," "KOL Trustworthy Gold List City Classic Hotel 2019", "Forbes Tourism 2018 Guide five-star hotel," "2018 Forbes travel guide five-star spa," "2018 'Travel' China's top 100 hotels,"* and *"Winner of the Ctrip TOP Global Hotel Selection Six Diamond Hotel in 2018."*

Charmaine gazed deep into Meredith's eyes: "Nice hotel, huh?"

"Exquisite!"

"So, what do you say?"

Meredith played with her hair, twirling it around on her finger, as if it was a curling iron. "I dunno. It's a nice hotel, to be sure, but you know my heart's set on going to Paris."

"Mine too, at least before watching the videos. If we go, at least we can say we travelled to the far East. And imagine the serious shopping we could do there!"

Meredith's attention was drawn to the TV when she heard, "The number one menace to communism is social networking on the internet. Most foreigners visiting China cannot access Facebook, You Tube, Google and Twitter, to name a few, without first obtaining a virtual private network."

"That's not good, Charmaine…"

"It's okay, bestie. Pastor Lau warned me about it earlier. All we have to do is download VPNs here in the States before we leave. They bypass all Chinese firewalls by masking our IP locations, giving us a secure connection. That's what most travelers do when going there."

"You know I can't travel anywhere without social media access. I need to maintain constant contact with Bethany…"

"Of course. I need it too, for business and for Rodney. Don't worry, Bestie. I won't let us forget to download it before we leave…"

Charmaine scratched the back of her head. "So what do you say?"

"Hmm…"

"Oh, c'mon, Meredith, we can always go back to Paris next year."

"Hmm…"

"What if I pay for the trip?"

"What?"

"You heard me. If I sell Mark's house before December first, I'll use the extra two percent commission, roughly twelve grand, to pay for the trip. If I don't sell it before then, we can still go to Paris."

"Won't it be more expensive if we wait too long to book the trip?"

"Don't worry, if Shanghai falls through, I'll pay all additional costs to Paris." It was the hook, the dangler, so to speak…

"Hmm, free trip to Shanghai." Meredith rubbed her chin, deep in thought, going back and forth in her mind trying to decide what to do. "I admit, your offer's enticing. And the city does look fabulous!"

Charmaine smiled. The online searches and *YouTube* videos were working. They were quite persuasive.

Finally, with a loud exhale, Meredith caved in. "You know I'm a serendipitous gal, so here's the deal. If you sell the house by mid-November, I'll take it as a sign that we're supposed to go to China…"

"Deal, Bestie!"

As if on cue, Charmaine received a text message from one of the potential buyers interested in Mark Lau's house. She read it aloud to Meredith, "'Thanks for showing us the house earlier. My wife and I are very interested and are ready to make an offer.'"

Charmaine replied: *Great! Call you in the morning to further discuss it. Just so you know, I showed it to another couple after you left. And I have two appointments tomorrow.*

The man quick-replied. Charmaine smiled, then read it aloud again. "'Like I said, we're extremely interested. I'd appreciate it if you'll allow us to match or surpass the best offer. Thanks!'"

Charmaine replied: *You got it! Have a blessed evening.*

Meredith said, "Looks like we may be going to Shanghai after all…But not without the VPN thingy…"

"I know, Bestie, I know."

AFTER MEREDITH LEFT, CHARMAINE called Kaito's cell phone. "Hey Charmaine. How are you?"

"Just fine, thanks. Did he leave yet?"

"No. We just arrived at Sea-Tac. He's having a tearful embrace with his children. After that, Lucy and I will get to say one last goodbye before he checks in and goes through customs..."

"I won't disturb him. Just tell him a married couple is very interested in buying the house." The excitement in her voice was unmistakable. "A handful of others are also interested. Something tells me it's going to sell soon!"

"That's great, Charmaine!"

"Tell Mark it looks like we may be going to Shanghai after all. I already got the green light from Meredith. But only after offering to pay her way."

Kaito laughed into the receiver. "Mark will be delighted to hear this."

"Yeah. Shanghai looks amazing! Been watching *YouTube* videos all evening. Can't wait to see it with my own two eyes."

"I think going there might be good for you, Charmaine."

"Let's hope so. Whether it's Paris or Shanghai, I could really use a break."

Kaito saw Mark waving them over. "I need to go now, Charmaine. But I'll be sure to tell him the potentially good news."

"Thanks, Kaito. Give him another hug for me. Lucy too!"

"I'll be sure to do that, Charmaine."

At that, the call ended and Charmaine resumed watching *YouTube* videos, until she dozed off on the living room couch.

13

MID DECEMBER

CHARMAINE DESHIELDS AND MEREDITH Geiger were at Sea-Tac International Airport, waiting to board their flight. Both were dressed to the nines.

While neither looked forward to the long flight to Hong Kong—their connecting city—at least they would enjoy the many trappings of business class. For half the cost of first class it was luxurious enough, offering passengers lie-flat seats, video on demand, in-seat Wi-Fi, and USB outlets for their personal use.

Much like they did before going to France last year, both women notified their credit card companies that they were headed to China and would be spending thousands of dollars in the coming days.

The representatives were happy to oblige their valued customers.

To make room for the clothing they planned on bringing back with them, the suitcases they brought were lightly packed, but would be filled to the brim with newly purchased outfits upon returning to the States.

As the Boeing 777 jumbo jet roared down the runway at Sea-Tac International Airport, gaining speed with each new tire rotation, Charmaine and Meredith watched on their privates screens, from cameras that were mounted to both the tail and the belly of the plane.

Excitement oozed out of them.

Once they were airborne, it didn't take long for the West Coast of the United States to slowly fade from view, quickly changing the scenery from concrete gray to deep blue. The shadows from the scattered grayish-white clouds hovering above the landscape danced on the shimmering blue water below.

Charmaine couldn't help but smile. How could she not feel blessed with God's favor shining so brightly on her? Life was near-perfect! She credited her success to her strong faith and the amazing pastors God had blessed her with.

Meredith also professed faith in her Maker, but she wasn't nearly as vocal about it as Charmaine was. On the few Sundays she went to church, she took Bethany to the Catholic parish down the street from their home.

It was the only religious activity that took place among them all week, and even that was inconsistent. The bulk of their time was dedicated mostly to her real estate career and to Bethany's schoolwork.

Meredith was an avid reader but preferred reading steamy romance novels instead of the Bible. Once they'd reached their full cruising altitude and the seatbelt sign was turned off, she plucked the novel she was halfway through reading from her handbag. She hoped to finish it on the long flight.

At the very least, it would help the time pass by more quickly...

After nine hours flying over the Pacific Ocean and Bering Sea, the pilot announced, "From the flight deck, this is your captain speaking. Those of you seated on the left side of the aircraft should have an impressive bird's eye view of Hong Kong. At this time, I'll ask the flight crew to prepare the cabin for landing..."

After a two-hour layover at Hong Kong International Airport, the two Americans boarded their next flight to Shanghai, for the short 90-minute flight northwest.

As they started their descent into the cosmopolitan metropolis, the numerous high-rise buildings seemingly went on forever, neatly-arranged in perfect rows, almost like landing strips guiding the plane they were on straight to the airport. Everything looked to be in proper order on the ground below.

Looking out the porthole, Charmaine said, "We could make a killing in this city!"

Meredith fist-bumped her best friend.

They landed at Shanghai Hongqiao International Airport at 1:11 p.m. The flight attendant enthusiastically welcomed everyone to her home city, first in Mandarin, followed by English.

Had they flown directly from Seattle to Shanghai, without connecting, they would have landed at Pudong International Airport, Shanghai's other airport.

But Pudong Airport mainly served international flights, while Hongqiao Airport mainly served domestic and regional flights in East Asia. The benefit to landing at Hongqiao Airport was that it was only nine miles away from the Waldorf Astoria Hotel.

Pastor Lau had offered to meet them at the airport, but knowing the last thing on Meredith's vacation list was going to church, Charmaine thought it would be best to take the hotel shuttle instead, so they could enjoy Shanghai for a couple of days together, before meeting Mark at his church on Sunday morning.

Thankfully, they only had to wait ten minutes for the hotel shuttle to receive them.

Riding in the backseat of the vehicle, both women were completely exhausted. Even so, they couldn't help but marvel at the bustling city.

Meredith's mouth was formed in a yawn. "What a magnificent place! It's so alive, so vibrant!"

Charmaine pursed her lips, then motioned with her hands until Meredith finally confessed, "Okay, Bestie, you win. I'm glad we came here instead of Paris! It's even more beautiful than all those *YouTube* videos we watched…"

A smile played on Charmaine's lips. She high-fived her best friend.

In excellent English, the shuttle driver both women guessed to be in his mid-30s said, "In the last decade, Shanghai has become a city on steroids. Rumor has it that twenty-percent of the world's construction cranes were used to help transform the city into what you see now."

Charmaine was looking out the window, drinking in the huge metropolis. "Wow! Really?"

The man smiled, then shrugged his right shoulder. "Not sure. Like I said, rumor has it…"

Charmaine and Meredith both cracked up.

"What I can say for sure is, what you see out there," he said, pointing toward Pudong skyline, "was nothing but swampland and factories twenty years ago. The city has grown six-fold since then. I was a young teenager at the time. But I still remember like it was yesterday."

The driver shook his head. "A quarter century ago, we were a relatively small city. Now Shanghai's the largest high-rise city on earth! And with twenty-five million people, it's the second most populated city on earth. And this is only the beginning…"

Meredith said, "That would explain the serious traffic problem you have…She glanced at her watch. It's not even rush hour yet."

The driver looked in the rearview mirror and chuckled. "It's always rush hour here. Even with the best elevated highway system in the world, traffic is a big problem in my city. But you get used to it after a while. It's one of the prices we pay to live in Paradise…"

"What about air pollution?"

The driver sighed. "Also a problem. But it's not nearly as bad here as it is in Beijing. Many living there are forced to clean the insides of their noses four times a day, due to the smog. Hope it never happens here…"

Meredith looked out at the Pudong skyline. "It's quite remarkable. I've never seen a city like this place. The human ingenuity is mind-boggling. It's so futuristic."

The driver nodded agreement. "Shanghai is quickly becoming a global center for finance, technology and innovation. The goal of my government is to be the richest and mightiest on the planet. Like I said, ladies, what you see is only the beginning…"

Charmaine said, "Looks like you're off to a good start."

The driver smiled proudly. "The hotel you will be staying at is a prime location. It's right in the middle of everything, right at the edge of the Bund historical waterfront promenade.

"The Bund represents the very heart of Shanghai. Visitors get to experience the charm of the old city, with its many colonial-era buildings, as they contrast with our, as you said earlier, 'futuristic skyline,'" he said, shooting a quick glance at Meredith. "Personally, it's my favorite part of the city. You won't be disappointed."

Charmaine leaned up in her seat in the back. "We've watched so many videos, it feels like we already know your city like the back of our hands."

The driver laughed. "I think the experience will be so much better than watching it on *YouTube*…"

Charmaine replied, "Amen to that!"

The driver shot her a curious look. Her reply had stunned him. *Amen? Does she not know?*

Forty-five minutes later, they arrived at the Waldorf Astoria Hotel on the Bund, where they had a reservation for the next seven nights.

Constructed more than a century ago, at first glance, it very much resembled some of the buildings they saw last December in Europe.

Meredith's jaw dropped. "Now I see why it's called the Orient Paris! It's like we're getting both cities for the price of one!"

Charmaine beamed. "Exactly, Bestie! It reminds me more of jolly ol' England than Paris, especially seeing it decorated for Christmas! I almost expect to see Charles Dickens walking the streets with his top hat on!"

Meredith smiled at the thought. Even completely exhausted from the long flight, it was invigorating. A pulse of energy soared through her. "Can't wait to see it lit up at night!"

They went inside to register. Their eyes were drawn to a 20-foot Christmas tree in the lobby, covered entirely in red decorations. A thick red ribbon was draped around the tree from top to bottom.

Next to the Christmas tree was a table full of gingerbread houses. An even larger house made completely out of chocolate stood next to it. The words HAPPY NEW YEAR were engraved on the roof.

The aroma wafted in the air, tantalizing their tired senses...

If there was one minor eye-sore amid the stark opulence, the tree decorations and holiday wreathes hanging inside and outside the hotel were all red in color, not green.

To Charmaine and Meredith, it was a bit too much. It looked rather odd to them.

Aside from that, the Waldorf Astoria on the Bund was the perfect place to spend the next seven days.

Their excitement soared to new heights upon checking into their suite. The room was just as luxurious as advertised, with its separate living room, huge walk-in closet, marble framed bathroom, and sprawling view of downtown Shanghai. Everything about this place dripped of elegance.

Looking out the window, their eyes feasted on the many mind-blowing edifices assaulting their senses. Marvelous as it all looked earlier from up in the air, it paled in comparison to being down on the ground.

Meredith couldn't stop yawning. "I must say, this is the most beautiful city I've ever seen!" *Can't wait to go shopping!*

Charmaine plucked a complimentary Belgian chocolate off the table and put it in her mouth. "I agree. And for the record, whatever weight I gain will be gone a week after I get back home!"

A smile formed on Meredith's face, followed by another hearty yawn. "Can't wait for my birthday cruise tonight!"

Since Meredith's birthday was on the eighth of December and Charmaine's was on the 22nd, they always travelled in-between both dates, and celebrated Meredith's special day on the first day of the trip, and Charmaine's on the last day.

"Me too. But right now, I need a nap." Charmaine put her left arm around her best friend, and yawned into her fisted right hand.

"I heard that..."

After changing into comfy pajamas, they settled into bed.

Much like when they travelled to Paris, the burst of energy they both felt upon checking into their hotel in the *City of Lights*, quickly dissipated when their heads touched the soft pillows on their beds.

Within minutes, both women were sound asleep. They slept straight through the night...

14

IT WASN'T UNTIL THEY received a 7 a.m. wakeup call the following morning, that they realized Meredith's birthday celebration cruise never happened.

"Don't worry, Bestie, we'll make up for it tonight after shopping."

Meredith smiled. "Sounds perfect."

"Ready for breakfast?"

"Let's do it…"

When they left their suite, the aroma wafting in the air from the Grand Brasserie Restaurant filled their senses with yumminess.

Charmaine ordered eggs benedict. Meredith had a Belgian vanilla waffle and a bowl of fresh mixed fruit. The floor-to-ceiling windows overlooking the interior courtyard garden weren't only beautiful to look at, they provided a sense of peace and tranquility.

After enjoying a scrumptious brunch-style breakfast, Charmaine and Meredith changed into exercise gear, then spent an hour side by side on elliptical bikes in the gym, burning a few calories, followed by a swim in the indoor heated pool. They also scheduled massages for Sunday.

After showering, they took the hotel shuttle to Nanjing Road—the main shopping street in Shanghai, and one of the largest on the planet.

Charmaine and Meredith had never seen a high volume shopping mecca so spotlessly clean in their lives. As far as the eye could see, there wasn't a single piece of litter anywhere. It was incredible.

Nanjing Road was mostly used as a pedestrian street. The only vehicles ever seen driving on it were mopeds, trams, and trolley cars.

The shops and stores seemingly went on forever.

Meredith wanted to facetime with Bethany, but it was 4 a.m. back in Seattle. She already planned on calling her on the river cruise later.

The Americans walked up and down Nanjing Road for an hour or so, drinking it all in, before finally hitting paydirt, upon finding the location they were looking for—Plaza 66.

With its many world-famous upscale fashion locations, Plaza 66 was recognized by most Shanghainese as the top shopping mall in their city. It was the tallest building in the Puxi district.

Three hours later when they left the mall, Meredith's credit card was charged more than $3K, most of it at her favorite store, *Prada*.

Charmaine spent slightly less than that, just over $2K.

But it was only day one...Her main purchase was a light-orange, pea-soup green checkered dress she planned on wearing to church in the morning. She made the purchase at *Chanel*.

Sure, it was mid-December, and the store racks and shelves were filled with their new winter collections, but Charmaine justified her "late Fall collection" purchase by reminding herself that while it very much looked and felt like wintertime, according to the calendar it was still a week away.

The 30 percent discount she received on the dress was also nice.

From there, they had lunch at the Shanghai Restaurant. It was the first time either of them had tried Shanghainese food. It was similar to the Chinese food they both enjoyed back in the States. But being on vacation made it taste even more delicious.

With full bellies, they strolled Nanjing Road again and did some Christmas shopping. One stop was at the Adidas apparel store. Charmaine purchased two matching warm-up suits, one for her and one for Rodney.

Looking into the floor-to-ceiling mirror, she said to Meredith, "Now I know what I'll be wearing on the long flight home! Talk about comfy!"

Meredith laughed.

An hour later, with many bags full of purchases—Meredith had three bags for Bethany alone—they called for the hotel shuttle to fetch them.

After quick showers and a change of clothing, Charmaine and Meredith grabbed their coats and walked the short distance to the port.

Charmaine purchased two tickets and they boarded the boat.

The weather turned cold and foggy. But it wasn't enough to dampen Meredith's "belated" 34th birthday celebration. For dinner, both had grilled chicken, rice and steamed mixed vegetables.

When a cake was brought out for Meredith, everyone on board the boat joined Charmaine in singing "Happy Birthday", in broken English.

Charmaine streamed it live on Facebook to friends, colleagues, and family back home, including Rodney and his three children.

Bethany watched and sang along with them. When they were finished, even though her birthday had passed a week ago, everyone onboard the boat heard her shout, "Happy birthday, Mommy!"

It was the cutest thing...

"Aww, thanks, my love..."

"Can you show me outside now?"

"Sure…" Meredith put her coat on and walked out to the deck. Charmaine followed her.

Seeing Pudong skyline from up in their suite was one thing, but being so close to the skyscrapers out on the water was beyond magnificent.

As the boat slowly drifted past Shanghai's most iconic buildings—the Oriental Pearl TV Tower, the Shanghai International Convention Center, Jin Mao Tower, the International Finance Center, the Shanghai Center—Bethany watched and was awestruck.

"I wanna be there with you, Mommy!"

"I know, sweetie. Next time."

"Did you get me lots of nice things?"

"Yes, including beautiful matching dresses for us to wear to Christmas Eve mass."

Bethany's face lit up. "Yippie!"

"How are Gramps and Grammy?"

"Fine. Even though they make me go to bed too early, least they don't take my phone."

Meredith laughed. "Don't worry, I'll be home before you know it. Tell Gramps and Grammy I said hi and I love them."

"I will…"

"Sorry Bethany but Mommy's freezing. Time to go back inside. If I'm not too tired when we get back to the hotel, we can facetime again. If not, we'll do it again tomorrow."

"Okay. I miss you so much, Mommy."

"Miss you too, my sweet little girl."

Charmaine turned the phone around so Bethany could see her face. "Auntie Char misses you too!"

"Miss you too, Aunt Char."

"We'll see you soon enough. Until then, be a good girl for your grandparents."

"I will, Aunt Char…"

"Love you, Bethany!"

"Love you too…"

The call ended.

An hour later, they were back at the Waldorf on the Bund. They changed into pajamas, threw on the robes provided by the hotel and ate more complimentary chocolates in their room.

After a day full of activity, both women were exhausted. This was the perfect way to end a perfect day!

Before calling it a night, Charmaine Skyped with Rodney.

"Hi baby! How's the City Beautiful?"

"Even better than it looks online. The hotel's remarkable. I'm amazed at how clean this city is! It's spotless! You'd have to see it to believe it. Just wish you were here with me..."

Rodney frowned. "Me too. Can I see your room?"

"Meredith's in the shower, so now's a good time." Charmaine invited Rodney to view her cam.

Rodney whistled through his teeth. "Wow! Very nice, baby."

"Yeah. It's the perfect place for God's blessed and highly favored children. Wait till you see the view outside our room."

Rodney gasped. "Wow! So beautiful! How I wish to be there now."

"It's yours for the claiming, my dear Rodney."

"I know, but we need to be married first, before we can share a hotel room." Though they'd known each other for five years, Rodney was still separated when they first met. They officially became a couple just under three years ago, a few months after he was officially divorced.

Charmaine smiled sweetly. "I know, honey, just wishful thinking..."

"Believe me, I look forward to it just as much as you." Seeing the many bags spread out on the bed, he exclaimed, "Man, oh man, looks like someone did some serious shopping!"

"Yes, we did! And this is only day one!"

Rodney also went shopping earlier. But what he purchased didn't come in a big bag. The small box he left the store with would be given to Charmaine on New Year's Eve, when he proposed to her. The final payment for the ring he had on layaway the past six months was due today.

Rodney had every confidence that she would say yes to his proposal. He smiled at the thought. "Can I see what you got for me?"

"Ha! Not a chance! But I'll show you what I got for the kids."

Rodney feigned disappointment. "Okay."

Charmaine reached into a bag and plucked out the items one at a time. When she was finished, Rodney said, "They're gonna love it all!"

"Don't worry, you're gonna love what I got for you, too. But don't even think about bribing Wanda into asking me to show you, like you did when I was in Paris. I won't give in to your daughter this time."

Rodney burst out in laughter. "It suddenly feels like Christmas!"

107

"It'll be here before we know it." Charmaine smiled sweetly for her boyfriend again. Then, "Meredith's coming. I'll turn off the camera. Time for me to shower and hit the hay. I'm exhausted."

"Yeah. Time to get back to work myself." Rodney grew more serious. "Still planning on going to his church in the morning?"

"Yes. We'll be picked up at nine a.m. Not sure what to expect though."

"I don't have to remind you how the Martíns feel about it. Imogen, especially, isn't too thrilled that you're going there…"

"Everything will be fine. It's not like I'll be going to a mosque. It's a church."

Rodney still wasn't convinced. "Just be careful. And call me if anything bad happens…"

"You know I will, sweetness. I'm off now. Have a blessed and highly favored day, my dear. Talk to you tomorrow. Love you…"

"Love you too, Charmaine…"

15

AFTER ENJOYING ANOTHER SCRUMPTIOUS breakfast at the Grand Brasserie Restaurant, Charmaine and Meredith strolled outside the hotel to await their ride to church. It was five minutes before nine a.m.

The city of Shanghai greeted the American travelers with a beautiful, sunshiny 60-degree morning. It was a full ten degrees above Seattle's average temperature for November. But because it rained so much back home, it felt twenty degrees warmer now—at least that much!

There was nothing like seeing the *Paris of the Orient* bathed in bright colorful lights each night, especially this time of year with millions of wondrous Christmas lights added into the mix.

Yet, breathtakingly beautiful as it was, it couldn't compete with the sun's brilliant illumination.

It not only felt good on their faces, it gave Meredith a good reason to wear the expensive sunglasses she'd purchased the day before. They perfectly matched the brown Prada dress she had on.

Charmaine breathed warm air in through her nose. A smile formed on her face. "Thank you, Lord, for this perfect weather!"

A broad smile crossed Meredith's face as well. "Perfect indeed! But I must say the cold air last night felt just as good. There was just enough of a nip in the air to keep my Christmas spirits soaring!"

"Don't worry, Bestie, you'll be wearing your new coat again tonight. The message board inside said the low tonight will be in the low forties. Besides, why would you wanna cover up your beautiful new dress with a coat? You look stunning!"

"You, too, Bestie," Meredith said, complementing the light-orange, pea-soup green checkered dress Charmaine had on. She took a deep breath and exhaled. "Can't wait for round two later!"

"Me too! Especially after our massages…"

"I'd like to hit the gym first. Feels like I've gained five pounds already!"

"I heard that!"

Meredith grew more serious. "Thanks again for treating me to this most wonderful vacation, Bestie. So glad you talked me into coming here. It definitely was the right choice."

Charmaine grinned from ear to ear. "You know it's my pleasure!"

"I know. Just wish Bethany could be here with us. Love to bring her here someday…"

The glowing smile on Meredith's face crumpled when, at precisely 9 a.m., a late-model Toyota pulled up to the front of the Waldorf Astoria Hotel.

The facemask-wearing driver anxiously glanced at the photograph on his phone screen that Pastor Lau had texted to him, of the woman he was there to drive to church.

Then again, even without referencing the photo, the fact that she was presently the only ebony-skinned woman standing outside the hotel, not to mention at 5'9", she was taller than many men in China, made her easy to identify.

Standing alongside her was the other American woman Sam Yang was told to expect, only he didn't know what she looked like until just now. He rolled down the passenger front window and spoke loudly, so the two American women would hear his voice pressing through his facemask. "Charmaine?"

Charmaine raised her sunglasses and shot a quick glance at Meredith, then squinted to gain a better glimpse of the man in the car who knew her by name.

Even with a facemask on, she knew it wasn't Pastor Lau. For one thing, it wasn't his voice. And this man was far too young, a teenager perhaps. She shot him a sideways look. "Who are you?"

"Mark Lau's associate," the driver said, careful not to say 'Pastor' out in public.

Seeing a Bible in Charmaine's right hand, he gulped hard. Add to that that both women were dressed to the nines, and anyone curious enough to glance in their direction would easily deduce that they were going to church, or to some sort of Christian gathering.

Not good! Did Pastor Lau forget to warn them? Perspiration formed on his forehead; his eyes darted left and right looking for possible eavesdroppers. With his right hand, Sam motioned nervously for them to get in the car.

They exchanged indignant, "You've got to be kiddin' me?" glances. The embarrassment they felt for being met at this luxurious hotel in such a dirty vehicle was elevated to a whole new level, when the driver got out of the car and covered the back seat with a clean sheet for them to sit on.

Charmaine tried joking with Meredith, "Our outfits may be worth more than his car!"

Meredith didn't laugh. Something felt seriously wrong to her. She suddenly felt fearful, and fought strong urges to retreat inside the hotel and wait in the room until Charmaine returned later.

Even before the driver appeared, Charmaine knew her best friend didn't want to go to church with her. But she also knew Meredith wouldn't want her to be all alone in a strange country, especially with a driver there to receive them that neither of them knew.

The two Americans reluctantly got inside the car, unable to ignore the unpleasant condescending glances they received from some.

Thankfully, the car was cleaner on the inside.

Meredith just wanted to get this not-so-pleasant part of the trip over with, so Round Two of their shopping spree could begin.

Once they were settled in the back seat, Charmaine said, "This is my best friend, Meredith. And you are?"

The driver craned his neck back. "I'm Sam Yang. Pastor Lau sends his apology for not fetching you himself."

Charmaine placed her hands on her lap. "Where is he? Busy preparing his message?" This young man seemed friendly enough. He didn't appear dangerous in any way. But he was clearly jittery and paranoid.

Sam said, "We will meet him at church. He wanted to fetch you himself, but ever since he returned from the States, he believes he's being followed everywhere he goes. He thinks it's because of his American citizenship."

Followed? Meredith took a deep breath of air and exhaled. She felt panicked. "What do you mean?" She shot a desperate glance at Charmaine before her eyes volleyed fearfully back to the driver. "Followed by who?"

Sam Yang sighed. "Pastor Mark apologizes for the inconvenience, but it wasn't something he felt comfortable telling you on the phone, or in a text message. And you already know he doesn't use social media…"

Meredith's breathing became even more irregular. She gulped in more air. *Am I doing something illegal just by being in this man's car? If caught, could I be arrested? Why did Charmaine tell him my name?*

Charmaine saw the fear etched on her best friend's face, a face she spent nearly a half hour beautifying with the application of make-up. She reached for her hand. "It's okay, Bestie. We'll be fine. Pastor Lau's an honorable man."

Sam Yang overheard her and looked in the rearview mirror. "He's excited to see you both," he said, hoping to calm the nerves of his two passengers. "He's been talking about your visit all week."

Charmaine squeezed Meredith's hand. "We're excited to worship with you."

We shall see...the young man thought. Once their seatbelts were fastened, he drove off.

Meredith stared at the Waldorf Astoria out the back window until it faded from view. *Charmaine may be excited, but not me!* Once they were out of the Bund area, the unfamiliar landscape passing her by filled her mind with numerous desperate thoughts.

It took a while to finally break free of traffic. Once they did, what should have taken less than 20 minutes, from that point forward, took nearly an hour, as Sam Yang drove through a maze of sorts—constantly checking his mirrors—making sure no one was following them.

With two Americans inside his vehicle, he couldn't take any chances driving straight to the church. It was always risky enough bringing locals there. How much worse with foreigners who weren't even mindful of the vast persecution Chinese Christians faced on a daily basis?

Sam wasn't driving erratically, but his constant alertness didn't go unnoticed by his two passengers in the back seat.

Meredith, especially, became more alarmed as the seconds passed. She lowered her head and recited a few desperate "Hail Mary's" to calm her nerves. It didn't help.

Finally, Sam Yang pulled into a strip mall parking lot. He steadied his vehicle into one of the spaces and turned the engine off.

Eyes surveying the landscape all around him, the coast looked clear. "Here we are…"

Meredith raised an eyebrow. "Where's the church?"

Yang pointed to a dry cleaners/laundry mat. "Over there." He looked in the rearview mirror and saw the confused expressions on his passengers' faces. Unable to hold Meredith's stare, he looked away, wishing his facemask had covered his eyes as well.

Meredith shot a desperate glance at Charmaine. "What kind of church is this?"

Charmaine said, "Certainly not a blessed and highly favored one!" She was reminded of her "strip mall" church experience seven years ago, brief as it was, before God blessed them with their new building.

But at least it was a church, not a dry cleaners of all things! A moment of comedy pierced her uneasiness. *Ha! Exactly what we need after riding in this dirty car!*

Charmaine expected humble, but not this humble! If this was what Pastor Lau meant when he said his church was entirely different than hers, she wasn't sure if she wanted to see anymore.

Using her two hands, she motioned for her girlfriend to relax. "Everything'll be fine. I spent a considerable amount of time with Pastor Lau. I believe he's trustworthy. Once we see him, we'll both calm down."

Charmaine's words fell upon deaf ears. The dread Meredith felt before getting in this man's car was just taken to a whole new level.

Sam was the first one to exit the vehicle. The old blue jeans and sneakers he had on were dirt-stained, much like the outside of his vehicle.

Charmaine shook her head in disapproval. *Does he really plan on entering the House of the Lord dressed like that? Dry cleaners or not, is that his Sunday best?* Pastor Lau urged them to dress casually, but c'mon!

Meredith was too frightened to judge his appearance. Her father was a non-practicing Jew; her mother was Catholic.

One thing she respected about her parents was that they never pressured her to choose one religion over the other. They told her she would make the right decision at the right time in life.

She loved them for that. But if they knew the Protestant church she was about to enter was located at a dry cleaners, of all places, in the lesser part of Shanghai, Meredith felt certain they would fearfully reconsider.

How could God not be insulted by the very sight of this place? Will He judge me just for stepping foot inside? If I proceed, can I ever hope to receive His forgiveness? Will He punish my family back home for this great transgression?

Her parents had often warned that kidnap-for-ransom crimes were on the vast increase for Americans visiting foreign countries. In the back of her mind, she thought they were just being paranoid.

Were their alarming words coming to life before her eyes? *Are we heading into a situation we can't walk away from? After all, we are successful businesswomen!* Meredith prayed not...

Sam Yang plucked a few articles of clothing from the back seat. Pointing to Charmaine's Bible, he said, "I'll take that."

She did a double take, then reluctantly handed it over to him.

Yang looked both ways, then tucked it inside his jacket. "Follow me..."

There was a rigidness to him that both women found unsettling.

Meredith's eyes pleaded with Charmaine, "Do we have to?"

Yang studied her face carefully, wondering if she was a true believer or not. "Relax. You're among friends."

Against her strongest inner protests, Meredith got out of the car. As they ambled anxiously toward the laundry mat, everything inside told her to run from this place as quickly as she could.

But where could she possibly go when she had no idea where she even was? Fear slithered through her, like water filling a new garden hose for the first time. It had been a near perfect trip up until now.

Little did she know this was the beginning of the end of her luxurious Shanghai vacation...

Charmaine felt her best friend's hand trembling. Squeezing it a little harder, she said, "I'm trusting you, Lord!"

16

SAM YANG OPENED THE door for his two visitors, then did a quick visual sweep of the outside perimeter of the building, to make sure no one was spying on them.

With Christians under constant siege in China, it was impossible knowing for sure if government officials—or even common citizens—were doing 'round the clock' surveillance on them.

But it wasn't just that. The Peoples' Republic of China "social scored" all its citizens. Essentially, what this meant was, aside from monitoring credit scores, moral scores were also graded.

Everyone was ranked based on a social credit system that rated their trustworthiness, by using big data to build a high-trust society for its citizens and organizations to follow.

Just like private credit scores, social credit scores could change in real time, depending on an individual's actions and behavior on any given day, whether good or bad.

Everyone living in China was enrolled in this vast national database.

In short, it wasn't voluntary...

Essentially, social credit scores were assigned based on an individual's behavior, which ultimately equated into a variety of rewards or punishments based on the things they did, the places they went to, the things they purchased, and on and on.

Citizens were also scored on who they followed on social media and, conversely, on who followed them. Even medical records—to include monitoring whether females took their birth control pills—and the partners they chose were scored.

Personal data was collected from the Internet—to include all websites visited by netizens, all purchases made, chat rooms entered, and so on—then combined with data stored from surveillance cameras, which monitored facial recognition, body scanning and geo-tracking.

The social credit system, first announced in 2014, was aimed at reinforcing the idea that keeping trust was glorious in China and that breaking trust was disgraceful.

Females especially, welcomed having cameras on practically every street corner. Most claimed it made them feel a little safer.

While crimes like fraud and embezzlement naturally had major impacts on one's social credit score, and ultimately led to incarceration, other not-so-serious infractions were also factored in, to include reckless driving, smoking in non-smoking zones, spending too many hours playing video games, riding on trains without purchasing tickets, and posting things on social media the government didn't agree with.

Even wasting money on frivolous purchases was factored in. All helped determine social credit scores, which were adjusted in real time.

Some areas even had a social credit system for pet owners. Points were deducted for owners who walked their pets without leashes, or if they didn't clean up after them, or if their pets caused public disturbances.

Once the point allowance they were given was exhausted, their pets were temporarily confiscated, until the owners took responsible pet ownership classes and passed the various tests they were given.

Regardless of infraction, bad behavior was punished, to include being barred from purchasing plane tickets for domestic flights. They were also refused train tickets and rooms at China's best hotels. Other punishments included slower internet speeds at home and on their mobile phones.

More serious punishments included being publicly shamed and even blacklisted, thus banning them from good paying management jobs in state-owned firms and big banks. Companies were even encouraged to consult the blacklist before hiring people or giving them contracts.

Having a low social credit score also meant being banned from the best schools and universities. Worse, some Chinese universities even denied admission to students whose parents had bad social credit scores.

Good behavior, on the other hand, was rewarded either with money, VIP reservations at top-rated hotels, choice seating at China's many fancy restaurants, free rental cars, discounts on utility bills, fast internet speeds, better interest rates at banks, and on and on.

Those with good social credit scores who joined Chinese dating sites even had their profiles boosted, thus increasing their chances of finding the right soul mate.

While many loathed the system, even calling it Big Brother on steroids, others openly embraced it, claiming it was making them better citizens, and much better behaved. When stopped at crosswalks, for example, they made sure to bring their vehicles to a complete stop, or lose points.

Those with good social credit scores proudly displayed them on their mobile phones, as a bragging right of sorts.

The fact that citizens were also rewarded for informing authorities of any illegal activity in their neighborhoods—to include the unlawful gathering for religious services, heightened the concerns of Christians all the more.

And with nearly a billion and a half citizens living in China, they could never assume to be in the clear. But that's where God came in...

Charmaine and Meredith were presently unmindful of any of this.

"Be right with you," a petite middle-aged woman on the other side of the drycleaner counter said evenly, in broken English, without looking to see who just entered her store.

Ming was too focused on the endless stream of just-cleaned garments snaking past her, to divert her attention for even a second.

Ticket in hand, when the articles of clothing she was interested in appeared, she pushed a button which quickly stopped all motion.

She grabbed the three hangers holding the plastic-covered items, and handed them to a female customer, who quickly examined the just-pressed garments before handing over the money.

Yang opened the door so the woman could leave.

She nodded her thanks to him on the way out.

After helping two more customers, Ming handed five hangers of dry cleaning to Sam Yang, raised the countertop, and motioned for the two American women to enter.

Sam said to Charmaine and Meredith, "Follow her. I'll join you shortly."

Charmaine let her eyes wander in silence before they settled on Sam again.

He raised his free left hand as if to say, "relax," then left to deliver the just-cleaned garments.

Charmaine and Meredith begrudgingly followed the petite woman to the back of the store. She seemed even more paranoid than Sam was. And for good reason. As the owner of this establishment, if authorities ever discovered it was also a church, she would be in a world of trouble...

To help justify Sam's frequent comings and goings at this place, he worked part time delivering dry cleaning mostly to their many elderly customers. This way, if authorities ever grew suspicious and questioned him, his presence there would be justified.

But not all deliveries made by him were received by customers. A rather sizable stash of "uncollected" garments had stockpiled over the years, from customers who had either moved or died or simply forgot they'd dropped them there in the first place.

To keep the scheme going, Sam made a half-dozen fake deliveries each day with these articles of clothing. This was one of those deliveries that would be taken out the front door and later returned through the back door.

Members at this particular church location were also given clothing to take home with them—from this excess stash—which they brought back on their next scheduled visits.

Smuggling humans in and out of the dry cleaners was altogether different. If they were under surveillance by the Chinese government, seeing people entering and not leaving for several hours would cause red flags to go up, whether they carried just-pressed garments or not!

If ever caught in the act, not only would it endanger the church, authorities would soon discover that Sam was the son of a preacher, who was three years into a ten-year prison sentence, for his faith in Jesus.

That discovery alone would warrant further surveillance on him, and perhaps even the dry cleaners itself. Thankfully, it had never come to that.

When Charmaine and Meredith reached the back of the store, they found a small group of men and women of all ages congregating there. All had facemasks dangling from their necks.

The two visitors felt their pulse racing in their ears; their hearts pounded wildly in their chests. Since both were in excellent physical condition, even trained in martial arts, they weren't too concerned about being physically assaulted by anyone.

But knowing strength came in numbers, Meredith wished she had brought her mace with her. But she wasn't allowed to bring it on the plane.

Charmaine softly whispered, "I know You didn't bring me all this way for nothing, Lord! My trust is in You!"

Meredith heard her frantic plea and brushed off another shiver.

Ming promptly left them so she could get back to work. She would attend the last service of the day once her assistant manager, and fellow believer, arrived.

The curious stares the two women received from so many had more to do with what they were wearing than anything else. Clearly, they had no advance knowledge of what to expect at this place of worship.

In broken English, an older wrinkly-skinned gentleman in his 70s said, "You must be our American visitors."

"And you are?" Charmaine was trying to be cordial.

"I'm Zin Xhuang. This is my wife, Liu. Welcome to our church! Please make yourselves comfortable. You're among friends."

Even though the few remaining teeth he still had left were stained yellow, his smile was warm, sincere, endearing.

"My name's Charmaine." She extended her right hand. "This is my best friend, Meredith."

Liu took a moment to translate their words for everyone else. Not counting Sam Yang and Ming—the owner of the dry cleaners—the married couple for more than 50 years were the only ones in this small group who spoke English, broken as it was.

Then to her guests, Liu translated back. "They said welcome and nice meeting you both."

Meredith stared down at her feet, like she would rather be any place else on earth than at this undesirable place. She became increasingly petrified. "Where's your pastor friend?"

Charmaine frowned. "Yeah, where's Pastor Lau?"

"We will meet him soon. For now, please help yourself to tea and refreshments." Liu motioned toward the food table with a nod of her head. Her kind eyes made it look like she was always smiling, even when she wasn't. Her droopy skin was as wrinkled as her husband's.

Charmaine half smiled. "Thanks, but we had breakfast earlier back at the hotel."

Twenty minutes later, Sam Yang came barreling through the back door, quickly locking it. He placed the dry cleaning back on a rack, giving Xin the signal that the coast was clear.

In a swift motion, the old man moved a small chair, end table and throw rug in a corner of the room, revealing a small hatch in the floor.

When he opened it, Meredith inched forward and glanced down into the darkness. Her chest heaved up and down in fear. "What's down there?" she demanded to know.

"Church," Sam said, matter-of-factly.

Meredith panicked. "Down there?!"

Yang lowered his facemask, exposing his youthful acne-covered face. He smiled wearily, as the small group of believers slowly lowered themselves down on a wooden ladder, one by one, in total silence.

He handed smocks and facemasks to the two Americans. "Put these on. It's dusty down below. I wouldn't want you ruining your expensive-looking outfits. And please power down your cellphones. They are not permitted here."

Meredith's trembling increased. "I'd rather not."

Sam eyeballed her. *Is she going to be a problem?* "Fear not, nothing bad will happen to you. We're a peaceful group."

Meredith's mouth was so dry she had to swoosh her tongue around several times to make sure it still worked.

Charmaine placed a hand on her shoulder, hoping to comfort her best friend. But nothing could suppress the fear in her eyes, nor the mounting suspicion on her face.

"C'mon, Meredith, everyone seems friendly enough."

"I'm not sure, Charmaine…"

The first person to reach the bottom turned on a battery operated lamp on an old wooden table, allowing the two visitors to see the cement floor ten feet below.

Meredith swallowed back the ominous fear in her mouth. "Didn't you tell me some at your church think he's demon possessed?"

Charmaine silently rebuked her doubt-filled negativity. "Pastor Lau's not demon possessed. Besides, God will protect us. I'll go first."

Meredith hesitated. "I'd rather not…"

Charmaine pretended not to hear her. She put the smock and facemask on, then lowered herself down into the dark hole. She reached the bottom and looked up at her best friend. "It's okay, Meredith. It's safe down here."

Against her better judgment, Meredith put the smock and facemask on, removed her just-purchased $300 stiletto high heels and slowly climbed down the ladder. Her breathing became more erratic with each step she took.

Who would've thought that wearing hotel slippers would've been the better choice at this place! she thought sarcastically, silently saying a few more Hail Mary's to stop her trembling hands and legs.

Once again, it didn't help...

17

SAM YANG WAS THE last one to lower himself down the rickety old ladder. The moment his feet touched the floor, he glanced up and motioned for one of the employees, a fellow believer, to close the hatch.

He quickly covered it with the throw rug, small chair, and end table, then made sure there were no dust marks or scratches that might potentially lead outsiders to know there was a hatch beneath the rug, if it ever came to that. It wouldn't be opened again until the first service ended and the signal was given.

Meredith gulped hard again. It felt like a steel prison door had just been slammed shut, not a hatch, trapping her in this musty old dungeon. Her palms were sweaty; she felt like she was a breath away from having a full-blown panic attack.

A bright flashlight stabbed at the darkness, illuminating a 10-foot long corridor. It took a moment for everyone's eyes to adjust to the contrast from light to darkness, and for their nostrils to adjust to the damp mustiness pressing through their facemasks.

Meredith's eyes shifted this way and that, silently fearing someone might jump out of the darkness to attack her.

At the end of the corridor was a lone steel door. The man with the flashlight lightly rapped on it. Someone on the other side opened it immediately, allowing them entry.

The room was octagon-shaped, with four separate corridors and points of entry connecting other businesses, so fellow Christians and believers working at those places could all join underground at their scheduled times.

Battery-operated lights were mounted on cinder block walls providing illumination. A floor lamp rose above a small table holding the Bible from which Pastor Lau would read during his sermon.

On the floor next to the table was an industrial strength air-filtration unit. It removed most of the dust which normally hung thick in the air in the corridor.

Four space heaters were spread out near each door to provide warmth.

Scented candles were on small tables in the corners to help combat the ever-present mustiness. Those battling asthma and other lung and breathing conditions were given industrial-strength facemasks to wear.

Once everyone was inside the door was closed behind them.

Capable of holding 100 people per service, soon every seat would be taken. Much like Charmaine's church in Seattle, very rarely was there an empty seat for any service at this place.

Early arrivers sat on rickety, old-wooden benches chitchatting, or reading the Word of God in their native Mandarin, until the others arrived.

Charmaine's first thought was, *What kind of church is this?* But the warm glow of the reading lamp bathed the room in a welcoming light, creating an element of peace that was so palpable, it nearly pressed through the walls. She took a deep breath and relaxed.

Meredith felt no peace at all. This subterranean dump looked more like a fly-by-night operation to her than a church, only it was daytime. Nothing about this place comforted her in the least.

There were no crosses hanging on the walls, or any other religious artifacts. And where were the priests, nuns, and altar boys? Where were the comforting statues of Jesus, Mary, and Joseph? They were nowhere to be found. This place gave her the creeps.

Meredith wished she could close her eyes and disappear from this hell hole of sorts. *Why did I let Charmaine talk me into coming here?*

Pastor Lau lowered his facemask, revealing a welcoming smile on his face. Even underground, his eyes were kind and comforting. "Welcome to our humble church, ladies!"

Charmaine smiled in reply, hoping it would cover the uneasiness she felt for being here. "There you are! So nice to see you again, Pastor."

"Hard to believe it's been six weeks. Time sure flies. Now I can thank you in person for selling my house so quickly. You didn't disappoint."

Charmaine's eyes lit up. "And I can thank you in person as well. As you know, the extra two percent I earned paid for the trip."

A smile formed on Mark's face. "Happy to oblige, Charmaine."

"Truth be told, it was one of the easiest sales I've ever made." They embraced.

Mark shifted his attention onto Meredith. "Finally, we meet."

Meredith nodded her reply. Seeing her uneasiness, instead of hugging her, Mark extended his right hand. He felt her trembling.

"Enjoying our city so far?"

When Meredith remained silent, Charmaine said, "What can I say, Shanghai's amazing! You didn't even come close to giving it its full due. It's like visual food for the eyes to feast on."

Pastor Lau laughed. "Never heard it put that way, but I'm sure many would agree with you. It wasn't always like this. Once Shanghai, Macau and Hong Kong were transformed into rich metropolises, it was as if the peoples' hope had soared to the heights of the towering skyscrapers.

"A recent poll said eighty-three percent of Chinese residents think the future is bright and full of endless opportunities. Sadly, most have no clue that the Word of God teaches otherwise..."

Charmaine thought about the driver who took them to their hotel when they first arrived. If anyone was excited for China's future, it was him!

Pastor Lau tried once more to get Meredith to say something. "Are you still jetlagged?" When she remained silent, he said, "It always takes me a day or two to shake it off myself."

Charmaine interjected, "I'm sure we'll both be cured after our massages later this afternoon."

Pastor Lau chuckled politely, then grew more serious. "Let me begin by apologizing for not fetching you myself, and for not telling you up front that my church was located beneath a dry cleaners. I'm sure it's the last thing either of you expected."

Meredith snorted. "Well, yeah!"

Charmaine tried breaking the near-suffocating awkwardness. "Had we only known your church was underground, we would have taken your advice and dressed more casually for the occasion..."

Church, ha! Meredith thought, keeping it to herself. *What a disgrace!*

Pastor Lau looked down at his feet, before regaining eye contact with his two visitors. "I was afraid if I told you how we Christians suffered for our faith, it might have prevented you both from coming all this way..."

You got that right! Meredith felt anger rising to the surface, for being invited under false pretenses. If there was one good thing, the anger helped absorb some of the fear that had consumed her up to this point.

"Another reason we're dressed so casually is to avoid detection from outsiders. We must appear to them as friends and family, and not as a religious congregation in any way.

"We always wear facemasks out in public, because of the government's advanced facial and body recognition system. If there's one good thing China's constantly worsening air pollution problem did for us,

123

not to mention the recent pandemic, it's that most citizens now wear facemasks, which means we don't look too out of the ordinary.

"This place used to be a dry cleaners only. The laundry mat was added after the government increased its all-out war on churches. This helps keep a steady flow of customers coming and going at all times, who aren't members of our church, to hopefully keep authorities away."

Seeing a lump form in Meredith's throat, Pastor Lau said, "Sorry, again, for potentially placing you both in harm's way. Remember what I said at the Fujimoto's house about Christians here having the same Savior, but not the same freedom to serve Him like back in the States?"

Charmaine said, "Yes…"

He sighed. "What I didn't tell you was the government recently declared all-out war on Christians and on our places of worship. A simple online search would have opened your eyes to how bad things are here…"

Since Charmaine already knew which church they would be attending, she felt no need to search for other Christian churches in the city.

Besides, they were on vacation. What mattered most was finding the best places at which to shop and eat. Researching the fierce persecution Christians faced in China was never a passing thought...

Mark Lau silently thanked God for shielding it from them. Otherwise, they surely would have gone to France instead. "At any rate, when crosses were maliciously removed from churches, while most pastors quickly caved into the government pressure, hundreds tried standing up to the fierce aggression…"

Pastor Lau shot a quick glance at Sam Yang and sighed, "They never had a chance. The penalty was that thousands of pastors now languish in prisons across China, for their insubordination to the government and for their faith in Jesus. Four of them happen to be friends of mine and fellow pastors."

Charmaine briefly looked up at the ceiling before her eyes settled on Mark again. "Were they ever given a shot at freedom?"

After Liu translated her words to Mandarin for those who didn't speak English, they grew somber.

Pastor Lau nodded yes. "At first, all they had to do was renounce Jesus. If they only did that, they would serve month-long sentences before being set free without further penalty from the government."

Mark Lau shook his head sadly. "Tragically, *many* chose that option. That's when it became real to me, and I got to see first-hand Matthew seven, twenty-one through twenty-three coming to life before my very eyes."

Charmaine's brow furrowed, as her mind was taken back to his "I never knew you" sermon at the Monday night Bible study at her church.

"As for the rest, after refusing to renounce Christ three times, all were given stiff, ten-year sentences."

Sam Yang frowned. "One of them is my father…"

Pastor Lau lowered his head. "And one of the most honorable men I know, yet he sits in prison for his unwavering belief in Jesus."

Charmaine frowned. "Aww, sorry to hear that. When was the last time you saw your father?"

Sam's lower lip quivered. Sadness flooded his face. "Not since his trial three years ago. I visited him twice before he was sentenced. He forbade me from going there after that, for fear that they might put me under surveillance or even worse.

"I was only fifteen at the time. So it was difficult understanding what was happening. All I wanted was my father back. After his second refusal, his sentence was extended to six months in a prison labor camp."

Sam shook his head sadly. "I became angry with him. God too. I actually thought my father was being selfish! Imagine that? When he was given a ten-year sentence for his third refusal, it was as if my life had just ended. My father was my hero. I was completely devastated, especially since I couldn't visit him in prison…"

Sam wiped a tear from his left eye. "It took a while but, mostly thanks to Pastor Mark, I finally understood my father wasn't being selfish. He was being obedient to God by taking a stand for Him. Once I finally accepted this, my faith deepened and the love I already had for my father intensified." Sam lowered his head. "I miss him every day."

Pastor Lau grimaced. "Me too…"

Charmaine couldn't bear seeing the pained expression on the young man's face. If she looked at him a moment longer, she would burst out in tears. She wrapped an arm around Sam and held him, amid his soft sniffling.

Meredith's eyes grew as big as silver-dollar pancakes. Her heart ached for Sam, but, right now, she was too frightened at the thought of possibly going to jail just for being at this undesirable place. Had she known the consequences in advance, she would have never left her hotel room…

There was a rap on one of the doors. Meredith nearly jumped out of her skin. She kept waiting for authorities to storm in and arrest everyone. Her mouth felt dry like cotton again.

Charmaine reached for her hand. "It's okay, Bestie. No one seems alarmed. Take a deep breath and relax…"

A man opened the door and a dozen or so more people entered inside the room.

Mark greeted his newcomers, then said to his American visitors, "The others should be here soon. The reason we enter one small group at a time is that it's difficult having three-hundred people coming in and out for the three services we have here each day, especially in secret…

"I know how this must look to you both. It took some getting used to for us as well. But it's normal life for Christians living in China." Sighing, Pastor Lau said, "Are either of you familiar with R. C. Sproul?"

Charmaine shook her head. "No."

Meredith was still too petrified to speak. The expression on her face reflected her awful reality. She sat on a bench feeling increasingly claustrophobic. Her eyes kept volleying from her feet to the door that led her into this horrific place. The room started spinning.

Everyone was nice and sounded sincere enough, but the fact that they spoke a different language only amplified the anguish she felt. And even despite that they kept trying to assure her that she was among friends, she felt more like a prisoner than a welcomed guest!

"In my humble opinion," Pastor Lau remarked, "Doctor Sproul was one of the finest theologians our generation has ever known. I first heard about him at the conference I attended in Southern California with Kaito."

Charmaine nodded suspiciously.

"I felt so blessed to meet him shortly before his death. One thing he said that really resonated with me after I came to China was, 'Every time the gospel has been proclaimed boldly and accurately in church history, there has been persecution.'

"I know it sounds crazy but what most see here as devastating, we see as honoring God's command to preach the Gospel without compromise, even despite what we face."

Charmaine wanted to protest. How could that possibly be true when her church was so prosperous? They were fulfilling the very name God gave to Pastor Julian at the outset—*Blessed and Highly Favored.*

Aside from the mean-spirited few who constantly tried debunking the Martíns for preaching a prosperity gospel in order to gain the whole world at the peril of their souls, Charmaine couldn't think of a single time when her church had faced stiff persecution.

This was something she attributed to God's hand being on them.

Pastor Lau noticed Charmaine was a million miles away, deep in thought. He waited patiently for her to come back to earth.

Finally, she said, "I appreciate your bravery, Pastor, but what happens if this place ever gets raided by the police?"

Pastor Lau glanced at his flock and sighed, "We will willingly join our brothers and sisters in prison..." Charmaine was astounded. "Never forget, Charmaine, Jesus said in Matthew six that our treasures are found in Heaven, not on this fallen planet."

"Amen," she said, half-heartedly.

Meredith gasped. She wanted out of this god-forsaken place, so she could hide beneath the covers back at the Waldorf and decompress alone, until this awful feeling passed. Not even shopping appealed to her now.

It wasn't so much that she was at a dry cleaners, but that she was forced to climb down a flimsy ladder to a musty subterranean dungeon, in a just-purchased thousand dollar outfit, only to be told she might be in grave danger just for being there. *I'll never wear this outfit or shoes again! Thirteen hundred bucks down the drain!*

There was a rap on the last door leading into the sanctuary.

Meredith nearly jumped out of her skin again. Her nerves were completely shot.

A man opened it and the final group of people entered the room.

Pastor Lau smiled. "Now that we're all gathered, the service can begin."

Meredith shot up off the wooden bench she was sitting on. "Don't close that door. I demand to be taken back to my hotel immediately!" She feared if she didn't leave this hellish prison now, she might never get to.

Silence fell upon the subterranean gathering place. Those who didn't speak English—the majority—knew whatever she had said, it wasn't good. The tone of her voice dictated that much.

This happened on occasion with locals who were mindful of the government's attempt to squash Christianity like a giant pesky insect, but it was the first time with a foreigner, at least at this location.

When locals felt uncomfortable and wanted to leave, they never tried convincing them to stay. Instead, they let them go and prayed they wouldn't go straight to the authorities.

Pastor Lau glanced at Sam Yang. "I'll take her back, Pastor…"

Mark Lau said, "Xie xie." (Thank you).

Meredith glared at Charmaine. "Well, aren't you coming with me?"

Charmaine shot a desperate glance at Pastor Lau. He shrugged his shoulders, not knowing what to say to help the situation.

Seeing the fear in her best friend's eyes, she said, "I think I'll stay a while if it's okay with you. I wanna hear what he has to say."

Meredith shot her a desperate sideways look.

Charmaine placed her hands on Meredith's trembling shoulders. "Don't worry, Bestie, I promise to come straight back to the hotel after service, just in time for lunch."

Meredith shook her head in disgust. "So, let me get this straight—I came here just for you, yet you won't even leave with me? I can't believe how selfish you're being. Unbelievable!"

She was already teetering on the brink of the abyss. Now this? Enough was enough! "Should've gone to Paris without you!"

Sam Yang sent a text message to an employee aboveground, with the special code signifying that someone wanted to leave immediately, and the hatch needed to be opened.

His eyes settled on Meredith. "Ready?"

Meredith lowered her head, not wishing to look at Charmaine any longer. She was too upset.

Sam said, "Follow me…"

When Meredith climbed up the ladder, she tore off the smock and facemask, threw them to the floor in disgust, then removed her phone from her handbag, turned on her video camera, and started recording. She made sure to capture the shopping center before reaching Sam's car.

The camera remained on until she was dropped back at the Waldorf, thankfully without incident.

If Charmaine didn't make it back to the hotel later in the afternoon, she would contact the authorities and share the video with them.

She had no clue where the dry cleaners was located, but thanks to the video footage, the authorities would surely know.

Other than that, Charmaine was on her own!

18

PASTOR LAU GLANCED AT Charmaine. "Do you think your friend will contact the authorities?"

Charmaine bit her lower lip. Suddenly mindful of the dangers Chinese Christians faced, she shared his concern. "As long as Meredith makes it safely back to the hotel, me too, for that matter, I don't think so. Then again, I never saw her behave like that before..." *I hope not!*

Mark gulped, then cleared his throat. *Protect us, Lord!* "Let the worshippers arise in song and praise!" He glanced at Charmaine. "Just a reminder that many here don't speak English. They will sing in Mandarin."

Charmaine said, "By all means."

Pastor Lau nodded to the man standing by the old CD player at the back of the room. He pushed play and the karaoke version of the song *Give Thanks,* by Don Moen, started playing.

Charmaine's eyes wandered about the octagon-shaped room. Her first thought was, *Give thanks? For what? Being forced underground?*

Yet, the expressions on their faces, as they praised God with all their hearts, souls, and voices, were so remarkable, she was hard pressed to believe they were a persecuted church.

When they sang the chorus, "'And now let the weak say, 'I am strong' Let the poor say, 'I am rich, because of what the Lord has done for us,'" with their arms raised to Heaven, Charmaine was moved to tears.

It was the most beautiful sensation...

This wasn't the first time she'd sung songs to the Lord with fellow brothers and sisters, in different languages. One thing she loved about her church in Seattle was its mixed ethnicity.

But nothing compared to this experience. It felt more real now, more genuine, more heartfelt.

There was something about watching them leaning into God in this humble setting, from a position of complete nothingness, and doing it so joyously, so unassumingly, so unpretentiously!

Another thing she couldn't overlook was how no one purposely tried out-singing the others. Many sang softly with expressions on their faces that Charmaine could only describe as angelic-like.

It was clear they wanted all attention to remain on the One who'd rescued their souls from hell, and no one else. It was genuinely authentic.

Charmaine thought back to what Pastor Lau had said at the Monday night Bible study at her church, about some Christians not telling lies in church, just singing them! Not these people! No doubt they believed and lived every single word that came out of their mouths in song and praise!

They ended with, *Blessed Assurance*. When they sang the final stanza, "This is my story. This is my song. Praising my Savior all the day long," Charmaine wept like a baby…

Pastor Lau was touched by her deep show of emotion. "Singing hymns to God is a great privilege for any Christian, but doing it while suffering for Christ's sake, and doing it so joyfully, is a blessed thing to be sure."

Charmaine wiped her eyes with a tissue she found in her handbag. "It's one of the most beautiful experiences I've ever been a part of."

"Glory to God! Let us pray…" Pastor Lau lowered his head and prayed a lengthy prayer, which sounded nothing like Pastor Julian's lofty utterances to God.

When he was finished, he said, "I rejoice in having the distinct privilege of reading the Word of God to you today. Personally, there can be no greater honor bestowed on me. It's with that in mind that I'll ask you all to stand and open your Bibles to the book of Isaiah, chapter twenty-nine, verse thirteen…"

When everyone was ready, in Mandarin, Pastor Lau proclaimed, "The Lord says, 'These people come near to me with their mouth and honor me with their lips, but their hearts are far from me. Their worship of me is based on merely human rules they have been taught.'"

After repeating it in English for Charmaine, he said, "May the Lord bless the reading of His word…"

From there, he would speak in English, as Liu translated for her brothers and sisters in Mandarin. Some of the older folks would have preferred Shanghainese—the local dialect for many centuries—but it was slowly fading out of mainstream society.

A middle-aged woman signed for the two deaf people in attendance.

Letting his eyes settle on the group before him, Pastor Lau began, "Just like the passage states, *many* in the world profess faith in Christ. By merely listening to them, they dupe many into thinking they're solid Christians, and their faith is rooted solely in the Word of God, when nothing could be further from the truth.

"Let's be honest, we all know people like this. When asked, they unhesitatingly identify as Christians. Many are frequent churchgoers who sing all the songs and are among the first to shout 'Amen' or 'Hallelujah' when hearing the Word of God being preached. But, in reality, all they do is honor God with their lips with hearts that are so far away from Him, as evidenced by the lives they lead when they are not in church.

"Now, before you think I'm being judgmental, I'm merely heeding the warning Isaiah recorded. It was a warning that Christ Himself thought so important, He repeated it in Matthew fifteen, verses eight and nine.

"I assure you that while His words were spoken to the Pharisees and Sadducees, they were meant for all of us. This verse is what having 'profession' without 'possession' is all about, and could easily tie into what our Lord said in Matthew seven, twenty-one to twenty-three."

As Charmaine listened, Meredith's image surfaced in her mind. She professed faith in Christ. But was she really a Christian? She understood her best friend's reaction earlier, after unknowingly being taken to a location beneath a drycleaners. But these people were forced underground!

Members from her church in Seattle started popping in her mind, one after the next. Each time she blinked someone away, someone else's image surfaced—including some who behaved entirely differently outside the church than when they were in church.

Yet, they showed up each week in their Sunday best to praise the Lord, looking and acting like solid Christians. *Were they true believers? Or did they have 'profession' without 'possession'? Am I a true believer?*

Suddenly, Rodney came to mind. Charmaine pushed his image as far from her head as it would go, and refocused her attention on Pastor Lau.

"Prior to the government crackdown, I thought we were a closely-knit body of believers. On many levels we were, but when persecution visited our doorstep, many of our members, suddenly faced with the possibility of going to prison for their faith, became frightened and quickly scattered.

"It didn't take long before they stopped going to church altogether. Some who never missed a Sunday service suddenly wanted nothing to do with Christianity. They even refused to mention the name of Jesus in public places.

"Believe me when I say, up until that time, they had me convinced they were true believers. Naturally, I understood how they felt. When the government seized my church, and charged us with operating without government registration, I was so scared I couldn't breathe at times.

"The stress I felt knowing someone could break down my door at any moment to arrest me, or even worse, was unbearable at times.

"The things the un-persecuted church takes for granted. I can't fully express to you how blessed I felt to walk through the front doors of your church last October, carrying a Bible without fear of being arrested."

Charmaine froze. A shiver shot through her. She couldn't relate to what he'd just told her on any level.

"Most Christians get to drive to church in complete safety without always looking over their shoulders, hoping they aren't being followed by those who have the power to put them in prison for their faith.

"We don't have that luxury. Not only do we have to sneak into church, we're mindful that every minute we spend underground, someone could break down our doors and arrest us all for being caught in the act.

"While the government still allows religious gatherings, all groups must be affiliated with a government organization called the State Administration for Religious Affairs, and worship in institutions that are registered with the ruling Communist Party's religious affairs authorities.

"Churches that are registered need to have all sermons approved beforehand, making it more a Chinese church than a Christian one."

Pastor Lau sighed. "I confess, at that time, I had serious thoughts about going back to my safe and comfortable life in the States. When I decided to remain in China, my children—who still thought I was relatively sane at that time—suddenly thought I'd lost my mind.

"Day after day, I felt the full muscle of the Chinese government bearing down on me, weighing heavily on my shoulders. I frequently questioned why God had allowed such terrible things to happen to His faithful children."

Pastor Lau paused as Liu translated his words into Mandarin, then went on, "It's amazing how He sometimes answers prayers. It took a while, but as I kept serving Him through the storm, instead of looking for positive changes all around me, God used that time to shift my thinking to what was happening inwardly.

"If the Chinese government did any good, they separated the true believers from the false ones. Actually, God did it, but He used the unbelieving Communist Chinese government to do His bidding.

"As a side note, the fact that there is so little persecution in the States makes the false converts so much more difficult to identify."

Charmaine squirmed in her seat.

Pastor Lau noticed. "For those of us who didn't flee the persecution, God used it to strengthen our faith and strip us away from this fallen world, which, in turn, caused us to yearn to be with Him even more.

"When Christ becomes the prize, and Him alone, the persecution is so much easier to deal with, because we're constantly reminded that Heaven is our true Home, not this fallen world."

He paused again to let his words be translated.

Seeing the joyous expressions on every face caused Charmaine's heart to swell within her chest. *Why don't my pastors teach like this?*

Pastor Lau went on, "When our building was confiscated by the government, and later demolished, it was then that Isaiah twenty-nine, thirteen took on a whole new meaning for us..."

With his right pointer finger, Pastor Lau moved it back and forth around the small room. "These are the true followers of Jesus Christ. Some were initially among the deserters. Praise God, they overcame their fears of incarceration and eventually came back.

"My hope is that many more will follow. But in truth, if they don't, all it means was that they weren't true brothers and sisters in the faith.

"At any rate, now that most of the 'true' church has been forced to worship underground, the growth we've experienced has been nothing short of phenomenal. Not only in numbers, but also in substance.

"Even before the crackdown, the government placed harsh restrictions on the sermons we could preach from our pulpits. They also limit the donations we can collect and restrict proselytizing and charitable work in our communities. In some cases, they forbid religious education for minors.

"The government also began installing facial-recognition technology in all registered churches, so if any of their worshippers ever decide to go underground, they can eventually be tracked. Like I said earlier, that's why we always wear facemasks."

Charmaine was glad Meredith wasn't with her now. How much more freaked out would she be after hearing all this?

He went on, "The government crackdowns have only increased in recent months. I got word the other day that hundreds of Christian house churches were shut down in Beijing. The government seized all Bibles and even forced e-commerce retailers to stop selling them.

"Under new laws recently passed, there are potential fines equivalent of up to fifty thousand U.S. dollars imposed upon believers who are caught attending unregistered Christian meetings, including owners of apartment buildings renting units to believers. Part of the money from the sale of my house will be set aside to pay these fines, if it ever comes to that!

"Those attending state sanctioned aboveground churches may not fear government persecution like we do, but the price they pay is that they do not get to hear the true Word of God being preached each week."

Pastor Mark took a sip of water. "What the government allows them to say could hardly be considered by any stretch as the true Gospel. Even though so many American pastors preach a watered down message, at least Americans still have access to the true and full Gospel."

Charmaine said, "Sorry to hear about your situation, Pastor."

"I'm not. Not entirely, anyway." Pastor Lau grimaced. "It took losing my church to see just how lukewarm we really were up to that point. So, in that light, it was the best thing that could happen to us.

"This place isn't much to look at, but the Good fruit God's producing underground far outweighs anything I've ever experienced aboveground, because we're free to worship God without any outside interference."

"You really meet here every day?"

"Yes. We have three services per day. This is only one location. Millions worship underground in secret gathering places all throughout China. Compared to most other locations, this could be considered the 'Beverly Hills' of subterranean churches."

Charmaine looked around the room. "Wow, really?"

Pastor Lau grinned at her. "So you'll never hear us complaining?"

After Liu translated his words, heads nodded up and down.

He went on, "By having church seven days a week, I'm able to minister to many instead of only a few. And I get to preach Gospel-centered sermons and have Bible studies which haven't been tainted by the government. From a spiritual standpoint, we're infinitely stronger than we ever were in the past. Have you ever heard of Watchman Nee?"

Charmaine shook her head no.

"He was an evangelist and church planter in China. When chairman Mao came to power in nineteen forty-nine, Nee was considered a threat and labeled an imperialist. He was imprisoned on made-up charges and remained in prison right up until his death in nineteen seventy-two.

"Yet, even despite all that, God used him, and many others, to create a system of underground churches that has grown significantly since then. So many have come to know Christ through his ministry."

He paused so his words could be translated for the others, before saying, "The simple truth is that the Word of God cannot be bound. God truly does work all things for good for those who love Him and are called according to His purpose."

Charmaine was shocked hearing this. The expression on her face dictated that much. "Don't you ever fear getting caught?"

Pastor Lau nodded. "It can be frightening to think of the consequences we face, if caught, but in the final analysis, my danger isn't doing wrong in the eyes of the government, but in not taking a solid stand for my Maker.

"Despite what the unsaved world may do to me, if caught, I've been called to share the Word of God in season and out of season. The days of being lukewarm for me, us rather, are over.

"Besides, worshiping in hiding presents a certain mysteriousness most aboveground churches never get to experience. While risky, each time we meet, we feel like we're part of the early church who met in caves and catacombs. And there's something to be said about reading the Bible down here. It's like experiencing God's light breaking through the darkness."

Charmaine was on the verge of tears again.

"Don't feel bad for us, Charmaine. We're not victims, we're victors in Christ Jesus!" After it was translated, many shouted, "Amen!" with the most amazing smiles on their faces.

"Jesus suffered far worse than us. Yet, He never harbored a victim mentality, so why should we? At the very least, it would show weak faith in our Creator, as if He's not in complete control of all things at all times.

"Besides, if we turn sinners into victims, we push them away from the Gospel and from true accountability."

Charmaine shook her head in disbelief. *What strong faith these people have! So much stronger than mine!*

Pastor Lau shook his head. "It blows my mind at how far world leaders will go to try silencing Christianity, by dismissing the Bible as some fairytale that was written thousands of years ago.

"If so, why has it been banned in so many countries? And why do so many languish in prison for defending it? Would any of you willingly go to prison to defend Cinderella or Sleeping Beauty?"

He paused so his words could be translated for the others. Some chuckled politely. Pastor Lau smiled. "Foolish, I know. Even more foolish is that they hate Someone they proclaim doesn't even exist, when, in reality, the reason they hate Him so much is that He does!

"Well, they can keep putting Christians in prison for our faith, but they can never arrest the Word of God. Case in point: back in nineteen-fifty-three, the Bible was temporarily outlawed in China. At that time, more than seven-hundred thousand missionaries living here were kicked out."

"Charmaine was astounded to hear this. "Wow, so many!"

Pastor Lau smiled. "What looked hopeless at the time God used for His glory. Despite such persecution, because so many Gospel seeds were planted back then, the church has flourished. Did you know Christianity is growing faster here than anywhere else in the world?"

Charmaine shook her head. "Really? How can that be? I always thought China was an atheist country."

"It is. But even despite that, China will soon have more Christians than any country on the planet, as many as two hundred and fifty million! To put it in perspective, that's more than the total population of every country on the planet, except China, India, the United States and Indonesia."

Charmaine was astounded. "Talk about a plentiful harvest!"

"Indeed. It's one of the main reasons I'm still here, even at the expense of being persecuted and missing my children so much."

Pastor Lau paused to take another swig from his water bottle. "As you might imagine, the fact that we're so strong both in numbers and in substance frightens the Chinese government to no end. What they fail to comprehend is they didn't give us the salvation of God. Therefore, they cannot take it away from us. Not even Satan can do that.

"Whether man likes it or not, God's Word transforms lives wherever it goes. And it never comes back void. Simply put, nothing can stop the Creator of the universe from doing exactly as He pleases.

"The more the government tries squashing us, the more God raises up men and women like us to share the Gospel."

Mark's voice cracked, "I consider it the privilege of a lifetime to be one of them. It's an honor to willingly put my life on the line for my Maker. But it's not just me. My brothers and sisters here are just as willing…"

Charmaine closed her eyes and shook her head. *Now I understand what he meant back in Seattle about his church needing him!*

"Let's face it, Charmaine, it's easy to proclaim the Gospel when life is good, and all is well in the world. But I'm afraid that's when it becomes most watered down.

"One thing we've learned in our struggles is that God is never more present than when His children are suffering. It took a while, but we finally realized the circumstances we kept asking God to change, are the very circumstances God was using to change us."

After his words were translated into Mandarin, many said, "Amen". But it was softer than the way her church shouted their declarations to God.

But did that mean He didn't hear this humble group of underground gatherers as clearly as He heard the members of her church?

It suddenly seemed like a ludicrous thought...

He went on, "Once we understood this truth, we embraced all trials with an unwavering faith that God *will* work it all for good in His perfect timing. The spiritual growth has been so phenomenal underground that if we could worship aboveground again, I'm not sure we'd want to."

"Really?"

Pastor Lau nodded yes. "I've already given you a few examples, but it would be impossible for me to fully express to you how immeasurably blessed we are underground. Personally, as a Pastor, I can unequivocally say my preaching priorities have completely changed.

"Just knowing I can be arrested at any time forces me to carefully choose each topic and weigh each word I speak. There's no time for pulpit frivolity. My only concern is preaching the eternal Word of God..."

Charmaine shifted her position on the bench. "I'm simply amazed by your total dedication to serve God, no matter what..."

"When you take something away from people that means the world to them, they'll want it even more. For us, it's our faith in God. The fact that we willingly suffer for our faith should tell you how much it means to us."

Pastor Lau motioned with his hands to his fellow brothers and sisters. "I assure you we wouldn't trade what we have in Christ Jesus for anything this fallen world has to offer."

A smile formed on Charmaine's face. "I believe you, Pastor..."

Pastor Lau smiled back, then came to the point. "How about you?"

Charmaine's smile deteriorated. She grew hesitant.

Mark expected this sort of reaction from her. He pressed on, "A question I like to ask all newcomers to the church is, are the things you're living for worth Christ dying for?"

137

19

CHARMAINE WINCED, THEN GULPED hard. A shiver ran through her. *Could I ever walk away from the good life I have, like Mark had, if it ever came to that? Would I?*

Her face felt hot, and her palms were sweaty. "I think I'd better get back to the hotel. No telling what Meredith might do, or who she may call if I'm not back soon."

Pastor Lau nodded thoughtfully. "Yes, of course. And you don't want to be late for your massage…"

Charmaine smiled warmly. "But let me just say you've given me so much to think and pray about. I truly felt the Spirit of God here today."

"Happy to hear you say that. Will you visit us again before going back to the States?"

"I certainly hope so," Charmaine said, meaning it. "But as you might imagine, we have a full week of activities planned, so I'll have to get back to you on that. I'd still like to take you to Disney if I can."

"Let's see what happens. But if you decide to come back, call the dry cleaners asking for Sam. Tell Ming you're a tourist on vacation and you need to have laundry picked up at your hotel. Since all her customers are locals, that will be Sam's signal to come get you."

"Okay…"

Pastor Lau said, "Let us pray before you go."

"Absolutely."

He smiled, then lowered his head. "Thank you, Father, for the blessing of having Charmaine worship with us today. Now that Meredith is back at the hotel, calm her spirit, Lord, and give her peace. We know how difficult it is being exposed to this form of worship for the first time.

"We pray for the fortitude to withstand the increasing pressure from the Chinese government. We pray for more workers for the harvest, and that the seeds we keep planting underground will bring forth an abundance of Kingdom fruit aboveground.

"We pray, Lord, that You would empower us to reach the next generation of Christians, and for more of Your wisdom, to know how to handle the pressure we're constantly subjected to.

"Lastly, we want to thank You again, Father, for accepting Christ's ransom on the cross as the ultimate payment for our sins. Thank you, Jesus, for dying for us and for all who receive the salvation You freely offer through Your blood sacrifice. We're so grateful for the eternal assurance You have given us.

"Thank You, Holy Spirit, for convicting us deep inside when we sin against You, and for guiding and leading us down the narrow path which leads to our beloved Savior. And it's in His name that we praise and glorify You, Father, Amen!"

"Amen!"

Pastor Lau's soft and gentle words melted the deepest chambers of Charmaine's heart. It was a feeling she never encountered back home...

Sam Yang sent a coded text message to an aboveground employee, signaling that they were finished, and it was time to open the hatch.

"Thanks for joining us, Charmaine. I'm so grateful that you came."

"Me too, Pastor. It was eye-opening, to say the least."

Pastor Lau chuckled, hoping it was meant in a good way. "If you decide to come back and worship with us again, and I hope you will, can you do me a favor?"

"Sure..."

"Kindly leave your cellphone back at the hotel. After what happened earlier, we wouldn't want authorities tracking your location with it. Also leave your Bible there. We have plenty here."

"Yes, of course..." What would have sounded insanely absurd just two hours ago, now made perfect sense to her.

Pastor Lau smiled. "Hope you enjoy the remainder of the day with Meredith..."

"Should be interesting..." Charmaine hugged him. "Thanks again for the invite. I've never experienced anything quite like this."

"My hope is that you'll get to experience it again soon."

"Time will tell, right, Pastor?"

"Indeed, it will," said Mark.

At that, everyone leaving through the dry cleaners door followed Sam Yang out of the octagon-shaped room and down the corridor to the ladder.

Charmaine removed her smock, thankful that her new checkered dress was dust-free and otherwise untattered.

Riding back to the hotel, this time in the front seat of Sam Yang's car, mostly because of Meredith, Charmaine wasn't sure if she would return...

CHARMAINE ARRIVED BACK AT the Waldorf Astoria to find Meredith in rare form.

"Sorry if I'm a little tipsy. I'm on my third glass of merlot. When Sam dropped me off, I felt incredibly filthy. But instead of going up to the room to shower, I went straight to the bar…

"After silently toasting myself for escaping the bowels of the earth in a rundown section of a town I'm unfamiliar with, I drank it very quickly and asked the bartender to pour me another glass, which I enjoyed while listening to a jazz trio here in the lobby.

"Once the second glass kicked in, I felt more relaxed and my breathing finally stabilized. This is glass number three and I'm happy as can be!"

Charmaine reached for her hand. "Are you okay, Meredith?"

"Did you know the Grand Brasserie is known for having Shanghai's most celebrated Sunday brunch?"

Charmaine shook her head no. *Hmm, she's even worse than I thought!*

"Well, it is. Perhaps that would have been the better choice to make this morning…"

Like Charmaine, Meredith wasn't much of a drinker. Her words were slightly slurred. "I can't tell you how comforted I feel being back in the heart of Shanghai, surrounded by so many people and skyscrapers."

"I'm so sorry, Bestie. I had no idea what to expect earlier."

"I know. It's not your fault, Charmaine. We both were blindsided. But I'm still mad at you for not leaving with me."

"I understand how you feel. But in truth…"

Meredith held her right palm out. "I don't wanna know, Charmaine. Let's leave that dreadful experience buried underground where it belongs. You'll never get me to understand why anyone would cling so tightly to something that might put them in prison, or even mean death for them. How could that possibly be what God wants for them?"

Charmaine wanted to protest but now wasn't the time. It was time to get back on schedule. "Still up for shopping after our massages?"

Meredith lowered her head. "Hmm…"

"What if I contribute to your earring fetish?" Meredith had multiple holes in both ears. She never filled them when she was out showing properties, but it wasn't uncommon for every hole to be filled at all other times, including now.

After a long pause, Meredith took the final gulp of merlot. "Let's go."

After changing into more casual clothing, they rode the elevator down to the second floor to the spa, and received 60-minute massages, followed by 20-minute aroma-therapy massages, with essential stress relieving oils.

It was expensive, but the women who massaged them made every cent of the $225 they spent worthwhile.

Charmaine's body was relaxed, but her mind raced with many challenging thoughts from her underground experience earlier. But since Meredith had already insisted that she didn't want to know any details following her sudden departure, she kept them to herself.

But one thing was certain, Pastor Lau gave her much to think about and evaluate. *Reevaluate?*

After showering, instead of going to Huaihai Road—another popular shopping location featuring many high end fashion stores—as was planned, Meredith wanted to go to Nanjing Road again, namely back to Plaza 66.

Charmaine questioned her. "Did you forget to buy something?"

"No. I want to return the dress I wore earlier. Even an exchange will be fine. Believe me when I say, I'll never wear that brown dress again!"

There was no need to further elaborate. Charmaine knew exactly what she meant. "Okay, Bestie, as you wish."

An hour later, they were strolling Nanjing Road. Just as everything was starting to seem normal again, the mood was once again subdued when Meredith was the only one trying on new outfits, at least when it came to the high end fashions.

In the three hours they were out shopping, aside from the expensive green chandelier drop earrings Charmaine purchased for Meredith, at Prada, with oval and pear-shape gemstones cascading down them, the only things Charmaine purchased for herself were blue jeans, a few gray hoodies, a Shanghai tourist baseball cap, and white sneakers.

This concerned Meredith deeply. It's not like Charmaine suddenly became a cheapskate! It all came down to her underground experience…

Meredith prayed it was just a temporary phase she was going through, after being exposed to stark poverty. Either way, it didn't sit well with her.

But at least she was able to return the dress for a full store credit, which she used to purchase more outfits.

Back at the hotel, the inner battle raged on for Charmaine. The hotel room alone was partly responsible for fueling the burning conflict in her soul.

It took many years of hard work to finally get to enjoy a lifestyle that most could only dream of. Yet, it stood diametrically opposed to how her fellow believers in this country lived.

The message she heard preached earlier was entirely different from anything she'd ever heard before. It was all about denying self and resting in God's promises of future blessings.

Charmaine stared out the window at the bright Shanghai lights filling the radiant atmosphere. Sighing, she said, "Are the things I'm living for worth Christ dying for?"

Meredith said, "What?"

"Oh, nothing."

Whatever she said, Meredith knew it had something to do with their bizarre encounter earlier. She just wanted to forget the whole thing. "So, what time do you want to go shopping tomorrow?"

"If it's okay with you, can we go in the evening after dinner?"

"Sure. I'd love to see Shanghai lit up at night again. Perhaps we can go to a museum or take in a movie after lunch…"

Charmaine winced. "Actually, the reason I want to go shopping at night is that I plan on going back to Pastor Lau's church again tomorrow."

"What?!" Meredith couldn't believe what she was hearing. "You can't be serious, Charmaine!" They were the most frightening words she'd ever heard coming out of her best friend's mouth.

"I admit it didn't begin well, but it turned out being a life-altering day for me."

Meredith's heart raced again. The fear in her eyes was palpable. *I knew that's why she purchased the casual clothing!* "I thought this was supposed to be our vacation?"

Charmaine lowered her head. "It is, Bestie."

"That means spending time together!"

"I know. Nothing's changed, Meredith. I can't explain it, but I feel led to go there again. I need to check it out once more to satisfy this craving I have. After that, we can go shopping all night if you want, followed by Disney Land the next day, just as we had planned…"

"If you go there again tomorrow, Charmaine, there's no telling what I may do, if only out of concern for your safety and well-being..."

Charmaine knew precisely what she meant. "Do you still have the video you recorded on your phone?"

"Yes, why?"

"I know it's not your brand of Christianity, but I assure you Pastor Lau isn't a dangerous man. He's kind and caring and trusting. Can I please ask you to delete it?"

Meredith climbed into bed and pulled the bed sheet up to her neck. "Eventually, I will. For now, I'll keep it as an insurance policy…"

Charmaine felt a slight panic brewing beneath the surface, and silently prayed that her best friend in life wouldn't do something that could potentially create irreparable harm to so many.

Protect my new friends, Lord!

20

DAY TWO UNDERGROUND

CHARMAINE LOWERED HERSELF DOWN the ladder for the second straight day, feeling much less paranoid and more aptly dressed this time, to include a facemask and a Shanghai baseball cap.

Everyone was happy to see her again. As owner of the dry cleaners, Ming was especially happy that Charmaine had left her cellphone back at the hotel. It was replaced with a notepad and two pens in case one stopped working.

After opening the service with song and prayer, before delving into his message, Pastor Lau opened the session with a question for Charmaine. "It's so nice of you to come back. We're honored to have you again. Sorry to put you on the spot, but did you leave here yesterday with the same feeling you get after going to your church?"

"Not at all…"

"What would you say was different?"

When she hesitated, Pastor Lau said, "It's okay. You can be as frank as you want. As I'm sure you've noticed, our services are more like Bible studies and are geared more toward interaction among ourselves. So feel free to voice your opinions whenever you feel prompted to."

Charmaine liked the overall inclusivity. The problem was, due to the obvious language barrier, it was aimed mostly at herself and Pastor Lau only. And the time it took waiting for their words to be translated for the others further exacerbated the situation.

She took a deep breath. "Okay. I'd have to say the energy level. Don't get me wrong, the message you preached was powerful. Quite powerful! But I didn't leave yesterday with the sugar high I always get after hearing Pastor Julian preach. Sorry to say but compared to my pastors, your style's a little bland to me."

Mark laughed at the way she said it. After Liu translated her words for everyone else, they laughed even harder.

"I admit your pastors may preach the Gospel more articulately and with more flare and energy than I, but they can't preach a better Gospel, regardless of how eloquently they may speak, or how loud I might add."

Mark held the Bible in his hands. "Like the Apostle Paul said in Second Corinthians, chapter eleven, verse six, 'I may be unskilled as a speaker, but I'm not lacking in knowledge.'"

Charmaine opened her Bible to 2 Corinthians 11. After confirming his words in verse 6, her eyes were drawn to verse 5, namely two words, "super apostles". She read the verse softly to herself. *"But I don't consider myself inferior in any way to these 'super apostles' who teach such things."*

*Hmm…*She then read verse four. *"You happily put up with whatever anyone tells you, even if they preach a different Jesus than the one we preach, or a different kind of Spirit than the one you received, or a different kind of gospel than the one you believed."*

With her heart racing, she jotted 2 Corinthians 11 on her note pad to be read and studied back at the hotel later.

Pastor Lau placed the Bible on the table beside him, and waited for Charmaine to finish what she was doing.

When she looked up, he went on, "Aside from our different preaching styles, and energy levels, does it concern you that we preach from the same Book, yet with completely different motives?"

"Motives?"

Pastor Lau nodded. "The difference is people at your church always leave with sugar highs, to use your words, ready to take on the world. As for us, we leave feeling grateful, with contented, repentant hearts and spirits, always hopeful for what is to come in God's perfect timing.

"You know my words don't come from a jealousy standpoint, or from the mouth of someone who skated by in life. I achieved at an early age, but left it all behind to come here and preach the Gospel."

Charmaine nodded agreement.

"Truth be told, many here have more talent than me. If they lived in America, I'm certain they, too, would be successful…"

Charmaine flinched. "Hmm…"

"Sorry to say but the prosperity gospel that's preached at your church has nothing whatsoever to do with God's salvation, and everything to do with using the things carnal souls want to draw them in.

"Mindful of this, Satan takes full advantage, by using false teachers whose hearts have been trained to greedily entice unsteady souls to further their agendas."

"Agendas?"

"Yes. To gain the whole world at the peril of their souls. The message they preach has nothing to do with true Christianity. If anything, it's a false message desperate people want to hear. It preys upon the poor, the weak and the sick. And since most of the Body of Christ is impoverished, there will never be a shortage of souls to entice."

Charmaine smirked. "Are you saying my church isn't blessed?"

"From a worldly standpoint, you most certainly are. It would be impossible to argue against it. Spiritually…"

Charmaine raised an eyebrow. Clearly, she was skeptical. "Yes?"

"Let's start with the name of your church…"

The way he said it caused Charmaine to become even more defensive. "Really? You don't like our name?"

"Of course, in a spiritual sense, it's entirely appropriate for any Christian to say they are 'blessed and highly favored'. The fact that God chose us from the foundations of the world to be His children, how could we not think such things?

"The problem is most who proclaim that statement mean it in a worldly, materialistic way. And so I ask, Charmaine, what does it mean to you to be blessed and highly favored?"

"I believe it means having the favor of the Lord…"

"Go on…"

Charmaine rubbed her chin. "God has blessed me in so many ways. How could I not feel like Jesus' princess with the lifestyle I get to live?"

Pastor Lau grew more serious. "What if I told you those things might be keeping you from true fellowship with the Most High God?"

"Forgive me for saying this, Pastor," she sneered, "but aren't you being a little judgmental?"

"I understand why you might think that, but how can material wealth ever be viewed as a clear indicator of God's favor, when Christ was so poor that He didn't even have a place to lay his head?

"As you know, His earthly life began in a manger. When He arrived in Jerusalem at the end of His earthly ministry, it was on a donkey. Nothing in between the thirty-three years He walked among us—the hyphen period if you will—indicates that He tasted earthly riches on any level. Does that sound like prosperity living to you?"

Charmaine shook her head.

"Further, Jesus told His chosen Disciples that no servant was greater than his Master. By following Him, they had to deny self and carry their crosses daily. They lost livelihoods, income, places to live in, and so on. But by losing so much, they gained everything.

"Not counting Judas, whose betrayal was prophesied and therefore had to come to pass, the one thing the other Eleven didn't lose—couldn't lose by following Jesus—was their salvation. Unlike Judas, who followed Jesus but wasn't saved, the other Eleven were. And because they were saved, just like Christ didn't die in vain, neither did they!

"Sadly, this sort of message isn't being preached in many churches today. This is especially true in prosperity churches. To preach on denying 'self' and carrying our crosses is too gloomy, too negative for so many. Not only that, it doesn't line up with the messages they preach.

"False teachers don't want God but, in the name of religion, plan on getting everything their carnal hearts desire. They talk a good game and even have many good things to say. The real good ones speak truth more times than not.

"But you see, we're not called by God to preach half-truths or mostly truth; we're called to preach the true Gospel message, which is offensive to sinful, fleshly ears. Mostly due to self-centered desires, 'many'", he said, using his fingers as quotations, "who profess faith in Christ rebel against the Bible by twisting the scriptures to get what they want in this lifetime, without fear of what awaits them on the other side.

"Of course, you'll never hear false teachers say, 'Follow us at the peril of your souls.' Instead, they say things like, 'God wants you to be rich!' Or 'Partner with God.' Or 'You can't accomplish much without money.' Or 'As Kingdom kids, you can't wear tattered clothes.'

"I could go on and on. Where's the godliness with contentment Paul spoke of in First Timothy six, verse six? The prosperity Gospel has no concept of the sovereignty of God. I'll even go so far to say the god of the prosperity gospel is not the God of the Bible.

"Satan is the one behind it all. And believe me when I say, he isn't fighting religion. He's too crafty for that. And busy producing a counterfeit Christianity that's so much like the real one, so many are fooled by it. No wonder he's called the Master Deceiver."

Charmaine scratched her forehead. *Hmm, never thought of it like that.*

"The most frightening thing about these false teachers is they have a way of making others feel as if they are right with God when they really aren't, by confusing what true salvation is all about."

Pastor Lau shook his head sadly. "Anyone who isn't rooted in God's Word can easily be fooled and fall prey to their different gospels…"

"Can I ask, Pastor?"

"Yes, Charmaine?"

"What about those of us who really are blessed and highly favored from a materialistic standpoint?"

"Let me first say any blessing from God is a good thing. But are you suggesting that just because you live in a big house and drive a fancy car, you're more blessed spiritually or highly favored than the rest of us?

"Do you think your material possessions somehow prove to God your faith is stronger than ours, or that you're seen as more special in His eyes than we are?"

The way he said it made her feel foolish. "Sorry if I made it seem that way. It's just that…"

"Tell me, Charmaine, how does having a big house and luxury cars win souls for Jesus?"

Charmaine was noticeably fidgety. "When they see how much God has blessed me, most want the same things I have."

"That's precisely my point. Many at churches like yours preach more on the 'works' of Jesus, and how He can drastically improve your lives with many material things, than they do the actual 'words' of Jesus."

The way he said it caused Charmaine to gulp in air.

"Most who are spiritually blinded to the Truth will surely want the things you have. If you get them to think that openly proclaiming Jesus and professing faith in Him will help them obtain those things, they'll shout Jesus from the rooftops of the world.

"Not because they were filthy sinners before God saved them— although they'll surely confess that much—but mostly because they want what you have, which leads me back to yesterday's text…

"These people may look and sound like genuinely authentic Christians in every way but, in truth, they honor God with their lips, but their hearts remain far from Him. Teaching their flocks that those with the most toys have the greatest faith is vital to keeping the business known as the prosperity gospel rolling."

"Why do you say that?"

"Think about it, Charmaine. You're considered one of the true success stories at your church, right?"

She nodded yes.

"If you weren't successful, and you asked your pastors why this was the case, what would they tell you?"

"They would say I lack in faith…"

"Exactly. This may sting a little, as an American citizen, it stings me too, but one of the most destructive exports our country has ever produced are these false preachers. Many high profile pastors vouch for them and the rest of the world receives them warmly, without first considering the potential damage having them there would create.

"Don't get me wrong, like I said at the Fujimoto's house during dinner, there are many solid charismatic preachers in the world. But far too many aren't so solid."

"What about my pastors?"

Pastor Lau shook his head softly. "Sorry to say but perhaps churches like yours need to import more sound theology, and cease from exporting the name it and claim it prosperity gospel that's constantly preached…

"When I was in seminary school, I researched this movement and was shocked by some of the things I discovered."

"For instance?"

"When asked by one of his critics why he drove a Rolls Royce, without hesitation, an American pastor being interviewed said, 'If Jesus was here now, that's what He would drive!' Doesn't that sound a little off to you?"

Charmaine sulked sheepishly.

Pastor Lau shook his head. "Yet, many likeminded proponents tend to agree with him, thinking the more stuff they stockpile, the more blessed they are, when God's Word states the exact opposite.

"I don't have to tell you some so-called pastors in the States live in sprawling mansions, own vast amounts of property, and even have their own private airplanes."

Pastor Lau waited for his words to be translated into Mandarin for everyone else, then said, "If anything, we're told to store up treasures in heaven, not here on earth."

Charmaine thought about the four homes her pastors owned, including one in the Caribbean. They also had a garage full of fancy cars, motorcycles, four wheelers, and closets full of lavishly tailored wardrobes.

Pastor Lau went on, "Here's another woeful example of one of the more successful prosperity preachers in your country. He once bragged that one of his books sold exceedingly well in some Muslim countries. A handful of Muslims even joined his church after reading it."

Charmaine flinched and raised an eyebrow. "Isn't that a good thing?"

"Absolutely, if it serves to bring a genuinely repentant sinner to faith in Christ. But I'm afraid the reason it did so well is that it was a feel-good book full of watered-down religion and self-improvement, all in the name of Christianity."

Mark shook his head. "If I ever wrote a book on God's Word, I'm certain unrepentant people everywhere would hate it. Wanna know why?"

Charmaine nodded for him to continue.

"Because the gospel is inherently offensive to fleshly ears. Trying to make it more acceptable to the world would require altering the message itself. Who is anyone to do that? The simple truth is, if you want to be loved by everyone, tell them how much God loves them unconditionally, in every way, and that He would never harm them.

"On the other hand, to be scorned by many, tell them the truth that because of their sins they are deserving of hell and, unless they repent, the fierce fullness of God's eternal wrath remains on them.

"As followers of Christ, we must always be mindful that God's message isn't the world's message. Sadly, it isn't even the message many churches in the world teach. This explains why the overall view so many professing Christians have toward the Bible is greatly flawed.

"As a pastor, I do no one any favor by downplaying the truth of God's wrath, nor neglect to mention the severity of His judgment on all who die still in their sins. Refusing to talk about hell doesn't make that awfully wretched place disappear. It's a very real place, whether someone chooses to believe it or not! It simply cannot be blinked away."

Sadness filled Pastor Lau's face. "Why is it that so many pastors refuse to warn their congregations of these horrific truths? To answer this question, allow me to use a metaphor to describe the vast differences between churches like ours, versus many prosperity-minded churches.

"But first, open your Bibles to Second Timothy four, verses three through five. Pastor Lau waited a few seconds, then read aloud, 'For the time will come when people will not put up with sound doctrine. Instead, to suit their own desires, they will gather around them a great number of teachers to say what their itching ears want to hear.'

"Verse four, 'They will turn their ears away from the truth and turn aside to myths.' Verse five, 'But you, keep your head in all situations, endure hardship, do the work of an evangelist, discharge all the duties of your ministry.'

"The metaphor I'd like to use would be sailing on two ships, a cruise ship and a battleship. In my humble opinion, the first two verses represent cruise ship Christianity. The last verse represents a battleship Christianity.

"I've read the Bible many times. Nowhere is it recorded that Jesus commanded us to retreat into a life of luxury. Don't get me wrong, it's okay for Christians sailing on battleships to take occasional breaks. It's even necessary. But not for a lifetime.

"Whereas prosperity churches sail mostly on cruise ships, seeking worldly comfort and the desire to be catered to, we're honored to live radically for our King, by being soldiers on His front line on an enemy planet.

"But because we belong to Him, we also know the metaphoric battleship on which we sail will one day take us straight to Heaven."

Looking directly at Charmaine, Pastor Lau asked, "So the question begs, would you prefer to be taken to Heaven on a cruise ship or a battleship?"

Charmaine flinched but didn't answer the question. Her heart was palpitating too wildly in her chest to speak.

"In closing out this session, forgive me for saying this, but are you even aware that the things you pray for, and your pastor encourages, are the very things Satan offered to Jesus in the wilderness for forty days? The Bible's crystal clear that He rejected every last one of them!"

BAM! It was like being slammed in the head with a two by four. But it also stirred Charmaine deep in her spirit. *Is this man actually saying the things I always thought were God's blessings for me, may not have come from Him after all?* It was a sobering thought.

Pastor Lau knew his comment had landed hard.

It was as if her entire countenance had been changed, like her soul was hearing Truth spoken for the very first time...

Pastor Lau placed his Bible on the small table. "We will break for lunch now. Hope you will join us this time."

Charmaine smiled. "Even though you made me lose my appetite, I'd love to join you, Pastor, even if only for the fellowship."

Mark chuckled politely. "Sorry for that. If you'd like to stay for the next service, we can further discuss this topic. Much like your church, every seat will be taken again, so if you want to join us, I'll gladly have an extra chair brought down here for you. That is, if you wouldn't mind sitting close to me."

"As much as I should be getting back to Meredith so she doesn't worry about me, I'd love to continue the discussion with you, Pastor..."

Mark suddenly looked deeply concerned. "May I ask?"

Charmaine read his mind. "The video, right?"

He nodded yes.

"Truthfully, I asked her last night if it was still on her phone..."

After Liu, the beloved wife of Zin Xhuang, translated her words into Mandarin, many sat more erectly on the benches, as if bracing themselves for what she would say next.

Mark also stiffened up. "And what did she say?"

"Something along the lines that she'll keep it on her phone for now, as in insurance policy. You know, for my protection..."

"Do you think she would ever share it with the authorities."

"I don't think so. But I must say, she was even more frightened last night when I told her I wanted to come back again today. She thinks I'm crazy. Furious as she is, she wouldn't want to see me getting into trouble, especially so far away from home..."

Mark Lau lowered his head. "Let us pray. As the first service ends, we thank You, Father, for supernaturally protecting us and keeping us from harm. We pray that Meredith wasn't so freaked out yesterday that she'll do something foolish with the video she took on her phone. Bless her, Lord. If she hasn't been truly saved, rescue her, as only You can.

"Despite the constant persecution we face, we know You are fighting so many battles for us that we're not even aware of. We trust that no matter what happens, You will work it all for good, because we love You and belong to You.

"How blessed we are to be called Your children, oh God! You forever remain worthy of every ounce of honor, glory, praise, and worship we possess. May we never cease from adoring You and magnifying Your holy name, in Christ's name we pray...And all God's people said..."

"Amen!" At that, everyone dispersed...

As Charmaine climbed the ladder, her vision was blurred from so many tears stinging her eyes. Whereas Pastor Julian's prayers were all about receiving from the Lord, Pastor Lau's prayer was geared more toward giving praise and thanksgiving back to Him.

It was evident that nothing mattered more to him! His words touched something deep inside her in a way that Pastor Julian never could...

21

AFTER A QUICK HOME-cooked chop suey lunch aboveground in the back of the dry cleaners, which Charmaine barely touched, she lowered herself down the ladder with everyone else for the next service.

After opening the session in prayer, in Mandarin Pastor Lau said, "Romans eight, thirty-one declares, 'If God is for us…'"

The 100 others in the room confidently shouted, "Who can be against us!"

The declaration from this usually soft-spoken group was so loud it made Charmaine jump. She had no idea what they had said until Pastor Lau repeated his words for her in English…

Charmaine, too, responded with a resounding, "Who can be against us!" Her eyes wandered the octagon-shaped room. This group of worshipers seemed just as friendly as the first group. They showered her with curious nods and smiles.

When Charmaine's eyes settled on Pastor Lau, he said, "Tell me, Charmaine, what does this verse mean to you?"

"Just what it says, Pastor. If God is for us, our plans will ultimately succeed, regardless of who may be against us."

"I agree with you, except for one word…"

Again, one word? She was brought back to his sermon on Matthew 7:21-23, and the one word he focused on, *many.* "And that word is?"

"Before I tell you, please understand that adding or deleting a single word from Scripture can have serious consequences regarding properly understanding and applying its true meaning to our lives."

Charmaine looked confused. "And what might that word be?"

After her words were translated for everyone else, Mark said, "Our."

She shot him a sideways look; her eyes drifted up toward the ceiling, as she slowly repeated her words back to herself. "Am I wrong?"

Pastor Lau crossed his right leg over his left. "The way we understand it is if God is for us, *His* plans will ultimately succeed in our lives, not the other way around."

Charmaine rubbed her chin. "What's the difference between the two?"

"Guess you could say it all comes down to who's in control of your decision-making. Yes, I'm referring to the 'servant versus the self-centered Christian' mindset we discussed earlier. Thy will or my will? What can I do for You versus what can You do for me?"

"Now that you put it that way, I see your point."

"Psalm thirty-seven, four declares, 'Delight in the LORD...'"

Charmaine sat straight up on the chair that was brought in just for her. "'And he will give you the desires of your heart.' Charmaine smiled brightly. "It's one of my all-time favorites."

Pastor Lau said, "Mine too. But the key to understanding this passage is by understanding the first five words, 'Delight yourself in the Lord'.

"If only we'll do that, He will give us the desires of our hearts, because our desires will be in line with what He wants for us. In other words, the things we'll want will be the very things God wants for us."

Charmaine scratched her head. "Never thought of it that way..."

"Have you ever studied the life of the Apostle Paul?"

"Sort of, but not really. I love what he wrote in Philippians four-thirteen, 'I can do all things through Christ who strengthens me.'"

Mark nodded. "Another one of my favorites. But I wonder, did you also commit verses eleven and twelve to memory?"

Charmaine looked perplexed by the question. "No, why?"

"Do you even know what they say?"

"Not off hand, sorry..."

"Much like Psalm thirty-seven four, I'm afraid Philippians four-thirteen is one of the most misconstrued, misunderstood, taken out of context verses in all of Scripture."

Charmaine blinked a speck of airborne dust from her left eye. "Why do you say that?"

Pastor Lau opened his Bible, then flipped back and forth a few pages until he found the Book of Philippians. Charmaine did the same.

"Would you mind reading verses eleven and twelve for us?"

Charmaine cleared her throat. "Philippians four, verse eleven, 'Not that I am speaking of being in need, for I have learned in whatever situation I am to be content.' Verse twelve, 'I know how to be brought low, and I know how to abound. In any and every circumstance, I have learned the secret of facing plenty and hunger, abundance and need.'"

"Thank you, Charmaine. Which leads to verse thirteen. 'I can do all things through Christ who strengthens me.' As you can see, Paul's words had nothing to do with being blessed and highly favored from a worldly standpoint, and everything to do with his total dependency on his Maker in every situation, whether good or bad.

"Many back in our country think of that verse only when something good happens to them. Let's take a professional football player, for example. He scores a touchdown, then spikes the ball and flexes his muscles while strutting in the end zone, shouting that verse for all to hear, proud as a peacock. I've seen it many times. How about you?"

Charmaine nodded yes.

"I'm quite certain the Apostle's words weren't intended for self-centered ambitions. As I'm sure you know, Paul's life prior to following Christ was the envy of most in the world. He was a pillar of society. He had it all—wealth, social status, education, influence. He was even considered a Hebrew among Hebrews.

"Then came his Road to Damascus experience. After his conversion, not only did his name change from 'Saul' to 'Paul,' he went from being highly esteemed—or 'blessed and highly favored' as it's become known in many circles today—to being constantly persecuted.

"Life was anything but easy for him from that point forward. Even in prison—the very place he put believers before his conversion—he willingly called himself a bond servant of the Most High, as he faithfully preached the Gospel message to his jailers with great joy in his heart.

"Instead of feeling victimized, being in prison became an extension of his ministry. Even when he wasn't in prison, he suffered mightily for the Cause. Five different times the Jewish leaders gave him thirty-nine lashes. Three times he was beaten with rods. He was even stoned once.

"On top of that, he was shipwrecked three times, and once spent a whole night and day adrift at sea. He traveled on many long journeys, endured many sleepless nights, often went without food and water, and without enough clothing to keep him warm.

"And get this, he was often abandoned from those who claimed to be believers but really weren't. Does this sound like a life of pride and prosperity to you?"

Charmaine shook her head no.

"Talk about being transformed by the power of the Holy Spirit! Much like the millions now languishing in prison all over the world for their faith in God, Paul knew it was his Maker's will for him to be there.

"He was able to endure all these things because Christ strengthened him in every situation. His life presented a great example of the true Christian walk for all of us. I'm sure his story strengthens our brothers and sisters presently suffering the same fate he did.

"Remember I quoted the late R.C. Sproul, that every time the gospel has been proclaimed boldly and accurately in church history, there has been persecution?'"

Charmaine nodded yes.

"Prior to coming here, the only persecution I ever suffered in the States was verbal backlash from sharing the Gospel with family members and friends. Of course, Christians are persecuted for their faith in the States, but not to the extent that they languish in prison or are killed because of their belief in Jesus.

"It's more of a politically incorrect thing, where Christians are verbally mocked or criticized for sharing their faith out in public places, like I was, or when nativity scenes are removed from places where they had been set up for many years.

"Compared to what we experience here, I'd call that mild persecution at best. But that's how it begins—step by step, little by little. It wasn't until I relocated here and started spreading the Gospel, that I fully understood what Doctor Sproul meant.

"Don't get me wrong, I was mindful of the persecuted church in China before coming here. Terrible as it was back then, it's so much worse now.

"We're not the only religious group that's being persecuted. The government wants forced submission from all groups. Religious groups who are unwilling to be controlled by them are ultimately dismantled. But with Satan's help, the focus has recently shifted more on Christians."

"Why do you think that is?"

"Simple. It's not anti-Allah, anti-Buddha or anti-Dali Lama, it's anti-Christ!"

"That's interesting…"

Pastor Lau took a small sip of water. "Naturally, the more they persecuted us, the more I sought to learn about the persecuted church around the world. Even if it hasn't reached America yet, it stretches far beyond China's borders. Truth be told, we're not even in the 'Top Ten' of persecuted countries…

"I'm afraid if the persecution we face here ever comes to America, it will be extremely difficult for those who diligently strive to suck the marrow out of life by achieving all they can before this life is over, to accept being persecuted for their faith as coming from God.

"I'll even say Doctor Sproul's words probably wouldn't be too well received by this particular group of churchgoers. But to those of us who suffer for our faith, it makes perfect sense."

Charmaine scratched her nose. "I don't get it. How could anyone see that as God being for them? According to my pastors, God wants all His children to be happy, living in perfect health, with sustaining wealth..."

"Happy. Healthy. Wealthy. Let's start with being happy. How can I always be happy, Charmaine, when I'm hunted by the Chinese government for my belief in Jesus, knowing if I'm ever caught in the act, I'll end up in prison with my fellow brothers and sisters?

"How can I be happy when I hear about the torture they're constantly subjected to? How can I be happy knowing some in prison have had body organs harvested against their will and sold for profit? How can I be happy seeing Sam weeping and praying it never happens to his father?"

Charmaine looked shocked.

Pastor Lau's friendly eyes turned sad. "These heroes in the faith are in prison for one reason and one reason only, for their belief in Jesus, not a lack of faith. I assure you they have more faith than the rest of us.

"The simple truth is, the more evil I see in this crazy, fallen world, the less happy I become. But even despite all that, nothing can rob me of the joy I have in Christ Jesus. I believe joy is one of the supernatural buffers the Creator gives to all who belong to Him for sustained Christian living.

"In that regard, a joyless life isn't a Christian life. I'm afraid too many fail to realize joy and happiness are two very different things. Happiness is more of an emotional response which comes and goes, depending on how life treats us.

"If I'm always happy, that would make me an imbalanced Christian at best, a phony cheerleader, if you will. But because Christ was resurrected from the grave I, we, can always be joyful, even here underground.

"Regarding the next two things, 'abundant health and wealth' let me just say nothing could be further from the truth. If there's one thing persecuted Christians understand better than everyone else, it's the Apostle Paul's words, 'To live is Christ and to die is gain.'"

Pastor Lau glanced at Charmaine. "Have you ever really given much thought to that passage of Scripture?"

Everything inside her wanted to scream, "Yes," but if she did, it wouldn't be true. "Not really…"

"Personally, it's one of my favorites. 'To live is Christ and to die is gain.' What a powerful statement! If you exchange Christ with any other word, Paul's declaration could no longer end in gain, only loss.

"For example, if to live is happiness, perfect health, and wealth, to die would be loss, plain and simple!"

Charmaine felt nauseated. Everything she firmly-believed was crashing down all around her. She was starting to sense she had been misled spiritually all her life. It was difficult juggling the many emotions running rampant inside her body all at once.

Pastor Lau went on, "Paul's ministry spanned more than thirty years. He suffered most of those years. Yet, he counted every success prior to his 'Road to Damascus' transformation as loss, rubbish even, when compared to knowing Christ personally and intimately.

"Now you can better understand why the many languishing in prison are able to cope with their situation, dire and gloomy as it is. Just like the beloved apostle, they cling to the very same eternal promises he did.

"Even for those of us not in prison, as a persecuted church, we identify more with Paul's earthly ministry than most churches in the West could ever hope to. Look around. Do you think anyone here lacks faith in God?"

Charmaine let her eyes wander throughout the dimly lit room. "Not that I can see."

"Yet, with all due respect, when I was at your church, I heard your pastor say if anyone lacks in life, it's because they lack in faith."

Charmaine silently gasped. "Hmm..."

"Do you think Sam's father lacks faith in his Maker?"

Charmaine shook her head no.

"Even facing long prison sentences, I assure you the many now languishing in prison for their faith will never deny our Lord."

Sam Yang interjected, "But it's not only those in prison. I watched on TV the other day as authorities entered a Christian household in the eastern province of Shandong. After removing all things 'religious', they posted portraits of Mao Zedong and Xi Jinping declaring, 'These are the greatest gods. If you want to worship somebody, they are the ones!'"

A woman seated on a bench in the third row then shared something she saw on the news, as Liu Xhuang translated it to English for Charmaine. "I saw officials visit the home of an elderly Christian woman in Shangqiu

City. After discovering an image of a cross posted on her door, they ordered it removed.

"When she refused, they tore it down immediately, then unmercifully cancelled her minimum living allowance and her poverty alleviation, leaving the poor woman with nothing."

Pastor Lau said, "Could this be viewed as having weak faith? Definitely not! If anything, the world could learn a valuable lesson from these stalwart Christians who risk their lives each day to stand up for the Gospel. These are yet more examples of true heroes in the faith."

Charmaine scratched her scalp. "Wait, I'm confused. How could going to prison possibly be God's will for anyone?"

"To be truly contented in this world is having the willingness and openness to live whatever life God chooses for us. This doesn't always mean success, popularity, prosperity, or wellness. In fact, it seldom does. For some, it means going to prison..."

Charmaine shifted uncomfortably in her seat.

"Let me give you an example. The Bibles we have access to were smuggled into the country, by a dear brother of mine who was part of a Christian advocacy group back in the States. What makes them so special is that they have been properly-translated."

Pastor Lau shook his head sadly. "Tragically, millions of these Bibles were confiscated, and later destroyed, by Chinese authorities. Rumor has it they refused to even recycle them, fearing bad luck or karma or whatever. All were burned.

"It ended up costing many of these brave smugglers their freedom. Their sentences were much longer than the others, including my friend, Jonah. He may never get out of prison.

"Their lives may appear tragic to most unbelievers, yet the end result of their actions has been nothing short of transformational. Whenever word gets back to Jonah of the impact his efforts have had on so many, it gives him strength to carry on. His life very much reminds me of the Apostle Paul's, who, in my opinion, was the greatest Christian ever.

"The only Bibles the government still allows for all aboveground churches have been so grossly mistranslated, it's nearly impossible for anyone reading them to understand the soul-saving Gospel of Jesus Christ.

"Thanks to heroes in the faith like them, we have access to properly translated Bibles. By far, they are our most prized and cherished possessions. They never leave this subterranean gathering place.

"The biggest project we fund is an underground movement who cleverly prints each of the sixty-six books of the Bible, either in booklet or pamphlet form, depending on size.

"The first batch was published under the title, *Life Necessities—Volumes one through sixty-six*. But the Chinese government eventually connected the dots and realized it was the Holy Bible in disguise, so the name was changed. It keeps changing with each new publication."

Pastor Lau pointed to a closet door. "We keep them hidden in that storage closet under lock and key. If authorities ever discover them, we'll be in a world of trouble. We're already considered as criminals by the Chinese government, terrorists even, for illegal assembly without their permission. Even the police call us evil.

"If ever discovered, I feel certain we would be treated as harshly as if we were stashing narcotics. Which is why we guard them as if they were more precious than all the gold in Fort Knox, which they are. At least to us…"

Charmaine's mind was completely blown. "Wow, you truly value the Word of God."

A warm glow covered his face. "It's everything to us. Nothing matters more to us than getting them into the hands of others. Instead of purchasing big homes and luxury cars, these are our most prized investments."

After his words were translated for the others, Mark said, "Whatever extra money we have goes toward printing them."

Charmaine could only shake her head in awe. There was no need to ask if part of the money from the sale of his house would go toward this project. She had no doubt that it would.

Pastor Lau remarked, "It's a risky endeavor letting members take these books and pamphlets home with them, to be sure, and even a greater risk distributing them to outsiders, but seeing how life transforming it's been for all who read them, it's well worth the risk we take.

"Some have only one or two of these booklets in their possession. They cling to them for dear life. Yet, most Christians in the world have full access to the Holy Bible, but take it for granted by letting it collect dust on coffee tables or on bookshelves.

"I assure you those who are in prison for their faith bring more glory to God than anyone seeking worldly, material things. Their lives become powerful witnesses of God's glory and power in the ugly places of life. Everyone there gets to see His strength in their weakness."

Charmaine was confused. "How's that?"

"By not renouncing Jesus, no matter what pressure is brought to bear, that's when God gets the glory. In my humble opinion, they are the true 'highly blessed and favored' servants of God."

"Wow! That's deep…"

"Let me just say in closing this session that the awful importance of this life isn't about how much money you can make or how many properties you can own, Charmaine, but that it determines eternity.

"So, with that in mind, the question begs, are you a 'How can You serve me, Lord' type of Christian? Or a 'How can I serve You, Lord' follower? As for us, we believe we're called to serve, not be served."

Charmaine felt her stomach doing backflips…

Pastor Lau prayed for everyone and Charmaine left for the Waldorf Astoria. But the damage had already been done.

The call had already been made.

The decision was final…

22

"HI SADIE, IS PASTOR Julian busy?"

Sadie chuckled. "What kind of question is that? You know he's always busy, Rodney!"

"Yes, I know. But is he available? It's kind of an emergency. I'm on my lunch break, so my time's limited."

Pastor Julian's secretary glanced away from her computer screen. What she saw on Rodney's face was concerning. "Is everything okay?"

Rodney slumped his shoulders. "I hope so. It's about Charmaine…"

Sadie's brow furrowed. She looked surprised. "I saw her Facebook posts. Looks like she's having a blast in China, spending lots of money. Is she in any kind of trouble?"

Rodney bit his lower lip. "I'd rather discuss it with Pastor first, if you don't mind. Can you ask if he can spare a few minutes?"

Sadie glanced up at the clock on the wall to her left. "His meeting with the bankers just ended. He and Imogen have a lunch meeting at one, followed by a doctor's appointment which, hopefully, will reveal the baby's gender. I'm excited just thinking about it!"

Rodney was curious to know himself, but the worried expression on his face told Sadie he wasn't in the mood to discuss it now.

Sadie got up out of her plush chair. "I'm about to go to lunch myself. Let me check and see if he can squeeze you in before he leaves."

"Thanks, Sadie, I appreciate it."

"Think nothing of it…"

Sadie walked the long corridor to Pastor Julian's office; her mind raced with one question: Did Charmaine meet some rich man in China and cheat on him? She quickly dismissed the notion. She would never do that! Besides, Rodney looked more concerned for his girlfriend than dejected.

Stop thinking negative thoughts! The slightly overweight Caucasian woman peeked her head inside to find Pastor Julian sitting at his desk, pen in hand, scribbling something onto a legal pad.

He looked up from his notes over reading glasses. "Yes, Sadie?"

"Sorry to disturb you, Pastor. Rodney Williams is here to see you."

Julian looked at his watch. "You know I'm about to leave…"

"He insists it's important. It's about Charmaine."

Julian adjusted his reading glasses. "Is she okay?"

Sadie placed her hands on her wide hips. "He hopes so..."

Like everyone else at church, Julian knew *who* Charmaine planned on visiting in China. He dropped his pen onto the legal pad and leaned back in his leather chair. "Bring him in."

"Right away, Pastor."

A few moments later, Rodney appeared in Julian's massive office.

Whereas Sadie was properly dressed in a simple light brown floral dress with button down sweater, the same couldn't be said of Rodney. But since he was on his lunch break, Julian let it slide.

The lead pastor was more concerned about the downcast expression on Rodney's face than the sanitation engineer apparel he wore. Normally, he would rebuke him for bringing a negative spirit into his office. Already sensing what he would say, Julian braced himself. "Hey, Rodney, take a seat. What can I do for you?"

"Sorry to disturb you, Pastor. I know you're busy..."

Pastor Julian glanced at his watch, then came to the point. "It's okay. Is Charmaine in any kind of danger?"

Rodney sighed. "According to her best friend, I believe she may be. Meredith messaged me on Facebook last night, saying they went to Pastor Lau's church, which, of course, we already knew..."

Julian shook his head ever so faintly. The name alone had a sigh connected to it. "And?"

"Turns out it was at a dry cleaners, of all places..."

A dry cleaners? Julian tried putting a positive spin on it. "That's not so terrible, Rodney." He leaned back in his leather chair and stared at the wall opposite him, as if recalling a memory in midair. "You saw the photographs and videos taken at our former location. It wasn't much more than that."

"True, Pastor, but here's the kicker: his church is located *beneath* the dry cleaners?"

Pastor Julian's eyes widened. "Are you kidding me?"

Rodney shook his head. "Afraid not. When I called Meredith on messenger, she was crying hysterically. For starters, Pastor Lau never even bothered picking them up at the hotel. The driver who met them said the reason he was there, instead of Pastor Lau, was their belief that he was being monitored by the Chinese government.

"So Meredith's nerves were already on edge even before they arrived at the drycleaners. It went from bad to worse when they were ushered to the back of the store. One of the cultists—her words, not mine—moved a chair and throw rug, which led to a secret hole in the floor. Everyone lowered themselves down on a flimsy wooden ladder into a dark hole."

Pastor Julian leaned up further in his chair. He was mindful that part of the Body of Christ lived in stark poverty. He also knew millions of Christians were being persecuted, and were forced to worship in underground churches.

But he was called to represent the "positive" side of the Body, the prosperous side. As far as he was concerned, the "lesser side" was someone else's department. "What happened next?"

Rodney sighed. "The short time she was underground, she couldn't stop trembling. Just before the so-called service started, Meredith demanded to be taken back to the hotel. She begged Charmaine to leave with her, but she wanted to stay."

Even as the words came out of his mouth, Rodney still couldn't believe it. "Frightened as Meredith was underground, it only intensified on the way back to the hotel. She kept looking out the car windows hoping the police wouldn't pull them over and arrest her. Said she felt like a criminal just for going there."

"Poor woman…"

Rodney nodded agreement. "When she arrived back at the hotel, she was so traumatized she went straight to the bar and had three glasses of wine. Meredith's been to our church a few times. In truth, as a practicing Catholic, some of the things we do freak her out; like speaking in tongues, for example."

Rodney looked down at his hands. "But it's nothing compared to what she experienced over there. According to Charmaine, Pastor Lau's teachings are way different than yours."

"No big surprise there," he scoffed. Then his curiosity got the best of him. "In what way?"

"She didn't really say. But she claims she's been completely transformed by his preaching."

Pastor Julian gritted his teeth. "What?! You've got to be kidding me?"

Rodney dropped his head. "Wish I was, Pastor…" There was a brief pause. "I haven't told you the worst part yet."

"Tell me, Rodney!"

"Charmaine went back again today…"

Pastor Julian's eyes widened again. "You can't be serious?!"

"That's when Meredith messaged me. She thinks Pastor Lau's trying to brainwash Charmaine into possibly becoming an extortion victim.

"As you can imagine, Meredith no longer feels safe there. She's fearful of someone breaking down the door and arresting her. She wants out of China ASAP! I was up half the night tossing and turning in bed. I feel powerless being so far away."

Pastor Julian grabbed the pen off his desk and circled his lips with it, deep in thought. Rodney remained silent. Finally, the lead pastor said, "When was the last time you spoke to Charmaine?"

"Two days ago, before she went to sleep. She gave me no reason to be concerned for her well-being. When I asked her to compare churches, she said it couldn't compare on any level. I took it as a compliment. She never mentioned that his church was underground."

Pastor Julian stroked his chin very slowly. "Of course, it can't compare to our church, Rodney…"

"Yeah. Anyway, I went to sleep that night having no reason to worry. Meredith's message changed everything…"

"It's certainly a cause for concern…"

Rodney's mouth twisted in frustration. "Charmaine finally replied to my messages late last night when I was sleeping. She told me not to worry, that she was perfectly safe and in good hands. Said she didn't mean to seem distant, but she was enjoying her quiet time with God. She said the trip was just what she needed…

"Other than that, I've heard nothing else from her. She never answers my calls. Meredith said she was gone most of the day, and she didn't bring her cellphone with her. She wasn't allowed to."

Pastor Julian gulped hard. "Are you kidding me?"

Rodney shook his head. "That explains why she wasn't online all day."

"This isn't good." Suddenly, the $50K Charmaine had committed for the next church expansion, as seed money, loomed large in Julian's mind. "Did Pastor Lau ask Charmaine for money?"

"Meredith made no mention of it. Then again, she only spent a short amount of time with them, so how could she possibly know?"

Julian frowned. His mind raced with numerous troubling thoughts. *Should've never invited him up on stage! It's been a nightmare ever since!*

"Keep trying to call her, Rodney. If she doesn't answer soon, perhaps I'll fly to China myself to rescue her from that man."

A smile formed on Rodney's face, brief and weary as it was. "You'd do that for her?"

"Of course! She's one of our key players. Besides, that man's already created a sizable rift at our church. How much worse if he has Charmaine all to herself on his own turf? If he brainwashes her before she returns to the States, who knows what might happen..."

Julian looked at his diamond-crusted Rolex watch. "I gotta go, Rodney, but I'll try contacting her after we leave the doctor's office."

"Oh yeah, Sadie told me. Today's the day, right?"

Julian nodded. "We finally decided we both want to know."

"What are you hoping for?"

"In truth, it doesn't matter. But in the back of my mind, it would be nice if the first child was a boy."

Rodney forced a smile. "With so many praying for you, I'm sure Imogen will give birth to a perfectly healthy baby—whether it's a boy or girl..."

The comment earned Rodney a smile. "Amen to that! But for now, let's keep praying for Charmaine. In the meantime, if you hear anything, let me know, and vice versa."

"You got it, Pastor. Thanks again for everything you do."

"You're welcome, Rodney. Keep the faith..."

At that, both men left the church building and went their separate ways.

AFTER IT WAS CONFIRMED by her doctor that they would be having a healthy baby boy, Julian took Imogen to one of Seattle's landmark fine-dining destinations—Canlis—which just happened to be her favorite restaurant.

With the morning sickness part of the pregnancy finally behind her, this was the perfect place to celebrate.

Imogen savored every forkful of food that went into her mouth.

For $400, including tip, Julian hoped so.

When they got home, Julian tried calling Charmaine on Skype. After a few rings, he was informed she wasn't online. After two more failed attempts, he was convinced something wasn't right.

"I think it's time to take a trip to the Far East, my love." Rubbing his wife's belly, he said, "Are you up to joining me? It'll be a long flight, but just think of the maternity clothes you can buy over there, not to mention the new outfits we can get for Prince."

"When you thinking of leaving?"

"I'm thinking tomorrow. You know the damage that man has already caused. It's time to stop the bleeding. The sooner the better."

Imogen grimaced, then tensed up. "He's the last person I want to see, Julian…"

"I understand, my love. I don't want to see him, either! But it's time to confront him to his face, mano a mano."

"How long do you plan on staying there?"

Julian kissed his wife on the left cheek. "As long as it takes. I can always have Pastor Jeremiah preach on Sunday, if it ever comes to that. So, what do you say? Wanna join me?"

If there was one thing everyone knew about Imogen, it's that she was a shopaholic in every sense of the word. And with Shanghai being one of the most extravagant shopping meccas on the planet, it was the perfect carrot for Julian to use for getting his wife to join him on this emergency trip.

Imogen kissed Julian back, on the lips this time. "Let's do it then…"

23

TWO DAYS LATER

"THANK YOU FOR CALLING the Shanghai Waldorf Astoria Hotel on the Bund. My name is Chen, how may I be of maximum service to you today?"

Julian Martín said, "Hi, Chen, I'm calling for Meredith Geiger."

"Room number please?"

Julian looked at Imogen. She mouthed the words, "Fifteen-seventeen," which he then repeated back to the desk clerk.

Taking a moment to verify the guest's name, she said, "One moment, sir, while I connect you."

The phone rang four times before Meredith answered. "Hello?"

"Hi Meredith, it's Pastor Julian. We just arrived. We're in the limousine headed to the hotel."

"Oh, thank God, it's you! I almost didn't answer the phone. I kept staring at it hoping it wasn't the police."

"Didn't mean to startle you. I asked the limo driver to call the hotel for me."

"I would have preferred that you contacted me on social media, so I'd know it's you. My nerves are already shot. I can't sleep at night."

Julian easily detected the unbridled fear in her voice. This was all Pastor Lau's fault. "Relax, Meredith, you're safe now."

Meredith took a deep breath. "Those are the first comforting words I've heard since early Sunday morning."

Julian shook his head. "I understand why you're on edge. Rodney messaged me on the plane. He was frantic after reading your message. Is it true Charmaine went underground again?"

"Yeah. Hard to fathom, I know. Thankfully, she didn't go there yesterday. But she stayed in our suite all day reading the Bible in her own little world. Another wasted vacation day…

"I told her last night that we had to have a serious talk in the morning. I was already in bed with a migraine headache, and wasn't in the mood to have a discussion with her…"

Imogen had her right ear close to the receiver listening. "And what did she say?"

168

"She agreed. But that didn't stop her from going there again. I saw her quietly tiptoeing out of the room thirty minutes ago. She left a handwritten note on the table saying she would be back in time for dinner, and we could talk then."

Meredith sighed. "It was the last straw. That's when I messaged Rodney again. We were having such a wonderful time together. As quickly as Shanghai had grown on me, everything changed Sunday morning. I don't know what she sees in those people, I really don't."

"We understand. Contacting Rodney was the right thing to do. Imogen and I can't believe how Charmaine, of all people, would be vulnerable enough to listen to anything that man had to say, especially after what he did to my wife at our church a few weeks ago. I don't trust him."

Meredith frowned. "Neither do I. What concerns me most is how he managed to manipulate her so easily. Charmaine's a strong-willed individual, certainly not someone who's easily controlled."

Julian snorted into the phone. "Which is why she can't know we're here for now. If that man has advanced knowledge that we're here, perhaps he'll place her in hiding until after we leave. We must expect anything at this point…"

Meredith stared at herself in the mirror across the room. She looked terrible! "I agree, Pastor."

"We should be at the hotel within the hour. But Imogen needs a nap. Not easy flying halfway around the world being five months pregnant."

"I understand."

Julian rubbed his throbbing head with his free hand. "Could use a nap myself. But let's meet before Charmaine gets back to the hotel. Perhaps an early dinner?"

Meredith breathed another sigh of relief. "Sure. Just let me know when you're ready. I feel so much better now that the two of you are here."

"Us too," Imogen said.

"I'm tired of feeling cooped up in my room. Think I'll go to the gym and take out my frustration on the elliptical bike."

Imogen smiled into the receiver. "Good idea. Enjoy your workout. See you shortly…"

As the call ended, Meredith silently chided herself under her breath for not telling the Martíns she was leaving China later this evening.

Julian and Imogen stared out the back windows of the spacious limousine, at the bustling metropolis unfolding before them.

In broken English, the driver pointed out some of Shanghai's most iconic landmarks to the Americans, as they inched along in traffic.

Beautiful as it all looked, they were too exhausted to fully appreciate it. Even the first-class amenities they got to enjoy on the long flight couldn't prevent fatigue from storming their bodies.

Their mental clocks were still on Seattle time, where it was just after midnight. Once the jet lag wore off, both would be captivated by the sprawling city and the countless ritzy landmark department stores they saw outside the limousine window.

With pockets full of cash money to burn, as the saying went, the Martíns had every intention of seriously upgrading their wardrobes in the coming days. Whatever wouldn't fit in their luggage would be shipped back to the States. But first they had to rescue Charmaine from the clutches of that demon-possessed wolf in sheep's clothing!

Julian kissed Imogen on the forehead. "Exhausted as we are, can you imagine how we'd feel if we were stacked like sardines in the back of the plane for ten hours, with so little space between us?"

Imogen yawned into her fisted hand. "I don't even wanna think about it, Julian…"

"Can you imagine how off kilter they must feel now? At least we got to stretch out on comfy beds for much of the flight."

Imogen shook her head. "Lord, have mercy on them…"

A smile crossed Julian's face that quickly turned into a yawn. "Twenty-five K's a lot of money to shell out for two plane tickets. I would have rather invested it into our own plane."

Imogen kissed her husband's forehead. "Someday soon, my love!"

Julian smiled at the thought. "After the next church expansion campaign, the next fundraiser will be for that!"

"I can't wait!"

"Me neither…"

The Martíns were no strangers to flying on private jets. They were members of a vast corporate jet sharing network. While they didn't own the planes, essentially, after paying a one-time acquisition fee of nearly a half-million dollars, they were entitled to 50 hours of flight time each year, on a fleet of more than 700 jets worldwide.

In addition to the acquisition cost, they were responsible for an $8K monthly management fee and an occupied hourly fee, which covered fuel, maintenance, catering, and landing costs.

For all that, whenever they traveled in North America, a plane could be made available to them in as little as four hours, which could accommodate up to 14 passengers.

Their membership also gave them access to affiliate programs in Europe and China. In a perfect world, they would have taken that route. But this time of year, international travel needed more advanced notice.

Hence, their flying commercial this trip...

Julian retrieved a ledger from his briefcase that only he and his wife knew about, containing the names of the top 100 givers at his church. He also had a backup file on his personal laptop in his office.

Penciled in at #37, as a potential six-figure annual giver in time, was Charmaine DeShields. Once she reached her goal of becoming a million-dollar earner, as someone who'd always tithed faithfully, the church could count on receiving six-figures from her on an annual basis.

What no one at the *Blessed and Highly Favored Full Gospel Church* knew was that the Martíns skimmed as much as one-tenth of all funds raised right off the top. The money was placed in a personal account just for them. This represented their "hush" retirement fund. If anyone ever discovered it, they would have a lot of explaining to do.

Despite the extremely generous annual salaries they received—$1.5M combined—part of this "hush money" helped offset their exorbitant $8K monthly jet share membership fees.

Just seeing Charmaine's name on the list caused Pastor Julian angst. After cultivating and grooming her for worldly success for more than seven years, he wasn't about to lose her, or her money now, to some third-world poacher who probably didn't have two nickels to rub together, or whatever the currency was called in China.

Not without putting up a fight!

Mark Lau had already caused too much damage at his church. Dozens had since left, including two of their high-profile members, Bonnie Devlin and Cedric, the NFL football player, amounting to thousands of dollars in lost tithes and offerings each week.

That alone provided the Martíns with all the motivation they needed to spend $25K for the two plane tickets. If they needed further justification, the thought of possibly losing one of the most influential members at their church to that swindler was more than enough.

The collateral damage from losing someone of her stature could be huge. And how would Julian explain an unsuccessful trip to the others...

Now that Pastor Lau was banned from their church, Charmaine was the final link to him. Once they plucked her out from underneath his evil clutches, the bleeding could finally stop.

That is, if he hadn't already polluted her mind to the point of no return, with his obvious scare tactics.

The very thought caused Julian to burn with anger...

Upon arriving at the hotel, he placed the ledger back in his briefcase next to the Bible he kept there. The driver retrieved the Martíns' belongings from the trunk of the vehicle, and handed them to a waiting bellhop at the Waldorf Astoria on the Bund.

Julian tipped the chauffer handsomely before he and Imogen ambled inside the hotel. After receiving the keys to their supreme riverside suite, Julian introduced himself and his wife to the concierge attendant on duty.

In their minds, other than themselves, the bellhops and concierge were the MVP's—Most Valuable Persons—at any prestigious hotel.

The Martíns both knew the key to excellent service, not to mention preferred limousine access, all started with them.

Pressing three crisp hundred dollar bills into the young man's hand, Julian said, "This is for you. All I want in return is that you take very good care of us. We expect to be treated like royalty as long as we're here."

"Yes, sir," came the reply, in broken English. The shock on his face was satisfying.

"How many others work the concierge desk?"

"There are three others, sir..."

Pressing six more hundred dollar bills into his hands, Julian said, "See to it that each receives two-hundred dollars."

"Yes, sir!" The man couldn't contain his astonishment. Being on-duty meant an extra $100 in his pocket. *My lucky day!*

Finally, he pressed another $500 in his hands. "This is for the bellhops. Please spread it around evenly, or as you see fit."

"Yes, sir," came the reply again. His face was fully aglow.

The reason the Martíns always tipped in advance was that they wanted everyone—guest and hotel employee alike—to regard them as very important guests, whenever they were seen strolling the massive lobby, lounging at the pool, or dining in their restaurants.

In short, they wanted to stand out among the rest.

Just seeing hotel employees tripping over themselves to serve them, thrilled Julian and Imogen immensely.

In their minds, they weren't being prideful or arrogant. As blessed and highly favored children of the Most High God, this was how they were supposed to be treated everywhere they went...

Julian constantly encouraged those who sowed richly into their ministry that their glamorous lifestyle was an example of what they could all look forward to, in God's perfect timing, so long as they spoke everything they desired into existence, without ever doubting for a second that it would eventually happen to them as well.

In short, if they wanted to be true partners with God in their pursuit of the same financial riches they now enjoyed, they needed to harbor that same mindset. The problem for most members at their church was that they didn't have access to a constant cash flow, like their leaders did.

Critics of the *Blessed and Highly Favored Church* often argued that the money the couple threw around like Monopoly money was supposed to be used for meeting the needs of the church, and for furthering God's Kingdom, not for their personal use.

Not only were they being irresponsible by spending exorbitant amounts of money on themselves that wasn't theirs to begin with, most of the $1,400 they just gave out in tip money, would be gambled away after work, as the recipients drank beer, smoked cigars, and played Mahjong into the wee hours of the night.

Everyone at the church knew their hard-earned money, by way of tithes and offerings, was what had allowed the Martíns to live so extravagantly in every sense of the word.

No one ever objected to it. It was all part of the plan...

But God objected to it in a mighty way. As Julian and Imogen got to live in the lap of luxury, it was all being recorded in Heaven's memory...

Someday soon, both would have to give a full account for every dollar they collected, spent, and siphoned off the top. Nothing would be forgotten or overlooked on the other side. Nothing!

24

THIRD DAY UNDERGROUND

MEANWHILE, CHARMAINE LOWERED HERSELF down the ladder for the third time. The suspicion and uneasiness she felt the first two days was completely gone, replaced with a deeper yearning to know her Maker more. In short, her focus wasn't on *her* wants for a change, only on His...

Much like the day before, Pastor Lau opened the session by asking Charmaine a question. "It's a well-established fact that your pastors think we can lose our salvation. But what do you believe?"

Charmaine took a moment to mull over his question in her mind. "Honestly, I'm not sure. Sometimes I think yes. Other times no."

The look on his face conveyed to Charmaine that he appreciated her honesty. "The simple truth is there are many solid believers on both sides of this debate. As for me, I happen to believe once God's gift of salvation has been given, it can never be taken away..."

Pointing to the group, Pastor Lau continued, "This is something we all believe. If you'll allow me to, I'll explain why we believe this way, using the scriptures as my guide."

Charmaine nodded for him to continue...

"I'll begin with two passages of Scripture. John six, thirty-seven proclaims: 'All that the Father gives Me will come to Me, and the one who comes to Me I will by no means cast out.' And in verse forty-four, Jesus declared, 'No one can come to Me unless the Father who sent Me draws them, and I will raise them up at the last day.'

"These verses clearly prove that no one can come to the Father or be saved, except through Christ Jesus. It also proves that all that the Father draws to Jesus will come to Him. In short, God sent His Son on a rescue Mission for all who would believe in Him, as chosen by His Father.

"Not a single person, having been drawn by the Father, will be left behind to perish. Disciplined, yes. Condemned, no chance of it."

A smile crossed Pastor Lau's face. "This is why we remain hopeful despite that we are hunted by the Chinese government. If you study these passages very carefully, it's easy to see that the one thing missing from God's salvation process is humanity.

"Don't get me wrong, we're involved but only because our sins put Jesus on the cross. But we have absolutely nothing to do with the salvation process itself, except to say that those who truly repent, believe and receive God's free Gift become the recipients of His amazing grace."

Charmaine looked skeptical. "I don't know, Pastor. I agree that no one can earn their salvation. I've always believed that. Ephesians two, eight and nine makes it perfectly clear. But I find it hard to believe those who stray from the faith, after being saved, cannot lose what was given to them. How can you explain this?"

Without hesitation, Pastor Lau said, "It means they were never saved to begin with…" Charmaine shifted uncomfortably in her seat. "Are you familiar with John seventeen?"

"Not off hand, but if you share it with me, I'm sure it'll ring a bell."

"It's one of my favorite chapters in the Bible. I think it shines a glaring light on our belief in having eternal assurance. With that in mind, I'll ask you all to stand as I read the inspired Word of God to you."

When Mark was finished, he said, "May the Lord bless the reading of His word. Please be seated. As you can see by the sub-titles, it's broken into three parts. In verses one through five, Christ prayed that He may be glorified. In verses six through nineteen, He prayed for His disciples. In verses twenty through twenty-six…"

Charmaine interjected, "He prayed for all believers, right?"

"Correct."

Charmaine sat up more erectly. A smile was hidden beneath her facemask.

"While our focus today will be on verse twelve, let me take a moment to briefly walk us through the first five verses. They are vitally important."

Pastor Lau let his eyes wander the room. "Shortly before His arrest, Christ prayed in verse one asking His Father to glorify Him so He may glorify His Father in return.

"In verse two, He confirmed that His Father granted Him authority over all people that He might give eternal life to all that the Father has given Him. In verse three, He once again proclaimed that eternal life belongs to those that know the Father as the only true God, and Jesus Christ whom He had sent.

"He said in verse four that He accomplished the work His Father had given to Him. What makes this verse so profoundly deep was that He did it all with no home to call His own, no worldly possessions, no paycheck

175

for His services, no health insurance, nothing! Those things mattered not to Jesus. Yet look at what He accomplished!"

Pastor Lau went on, "He really drove it home in verse five. Our Redeemer said, 'And now, Father, glorify me in your own presence with the glory that *I had with you before the world existed.*'

"Wow! Just wow! Having seen and tasted the things above, why would He want anything from this fallen, sinful world?

"The only thing He wanted was to save all who came to Him with broken hearts and repentant spirits. All five verses are salvation-based, and have nothing to do with obtaining the things of this world."

Shaking his head, Pastor Lau said, "Whenever I read these verses, I can't help but think of the 'many' out there who diligently strive for the pleasures of this world, as if obtaining worldly possessions was the work God had given them to do."

He eyeballed Charmaine carefully. "Not to come across as judgmental, but before we delve into the second part of this most profound chapter, I need to ask how many from your church would be willing to go to prison for their faith in God?"

"Good question. Honestly, I don't know…"

Pastor Lau took a sip of water. "As you mull it over in your mind, let me make it more personal by asking what *you* would do if you were arrested for your faith, but were given an ultimatum—like many here were—to leave prison if only you would deny Christ? Would you do it?"

Charmaine squirmed in her seat. "No. At least, I hope not…"

"What if you could do it and still be forgiven?"

Charmaine winced. "Is this a trick question?"

"No. It ties in perfectly with my eternal-assurance belief."

"Hmm, sorry Pastor, but how could anyone deny Christ and still be forgiven? Wouldn't that be a clear-cut case of using the grace of God as a license to keep on sinning, which in turn could be clear grounds for losing their salvation?"

Pastor Lau shook his head. "Not if they're truly saved. Romans eight, verse one states, 'Therefore, there is now no condemnation for those who are in Christ Jesus.'"

"I don't know, Pastor. On the surface, it sounds a little too easy to me."

"Need I remind you that Peter disowned Jesus three times on the night He was betrayed?"

Charmaine was conflicted. "Hmm…"

"Which leads to verse twelve in our text, Christ said regarding His disciples, 'I have guarded them, and not one of them has been lost except the son of destruction, that the Scripture might be fulfilled.' Yes, He was referring to Judas Iscariot..."

Charmaine nodded, already knowing that.

"When Christ said, 'None were lost,' it was meant in a spiritual sense, an eternal one, meaning none would be lost to His eternal Kingdom. Yet Peter not only denied Christ, he repudiated Him, turned his back on Him.

"Do you think Jesus was mindful that Peter would do this after His arrest? Not only did He know it, He warned Peter in advance that he would deny Him three times before the cock crowed."

Pastor Lau flipped back in his Bible to Luke 22:60-62. "This was after his third denial. 'Peter replied, 'Man, I do not know what you are saying!'' Immediately, while he was still speaking, the rooster crowed. And the Lord turned and looked at Peter. Then Peter remembered the word of the Lord, how He had said to him, 'Before the rooster crows, you will deny Me three times.' So Peter went out and wept bitterly.'"

Pastor Lau paused to let his words hang thick in the air. "It's important to understand that Jesus told His Father that not one of His twelve Disciples would be lost except the son of destruction, *after* telling Peter he would deny Him three times, but *before* He actually did it.

"In the end, Judas and Peter both betrayed their Lord." When Charmaine flinched, Pastor Lau clarified, "Yes, even though Judas is in torment, Jesus is still Lord and Savior over all creation, whether one is saved or condemned. This includes Judas, even Satan!

"But because Peter had eternal assurance, he was in no danger of losing what was given to him from the One who knit him together in His mother's womb. The reason? It wasn't Peter's 'sinful' hold of Jesus that assured him of his salvation, it was Christ's 'sinless' hold of him.

"Sadly, even after we are saved, just like Peter, we will still sin and fall short of the glory of God too many times to count. The simple truth is, we're not sinners because we sin, we sin because we're sinners."

Pausing a moment to let his words sink in, Mark said, "But here's the thing. Those of us who believe we have eternal assurance understand this. By being chosen by God, and because of what Christ did for us on the cross, we are eternally forgiven just like Peter was, and can never be eternally lost, even despite our many shortcomings in life.

"On the other hand, those who believe they can lose their salvation often grapple with whether they're truly saved or not, even though they are. The common factor linking them is both sides are Heaven bound when life on earth comes to an end. But only one side experiences sustaining peace here on this side of the grave."

Charmaine was feverishly taking notes. At times, her hands couldn't keep up with the thoughts running through her head. She suddenly wished she was a stenographer.

"The Apostle Paul is another good example of this. In Romans seven, Paul confessed his desire to do what was good, but he couldn't carry it out. He said he didn't do the good he wanted to do, but the evil he didn't want to do, this he kept on doing.

"In his inner being, Paul delighted in God's law; but he also saw another law at work in him, which waged war against the law of his mind and made him a prisoner of the law of sin that was at work within him.

"He went on to call himself a wretched man, and even asked, 'Who will rescue me from this body that is subject to death?' He answered his own question by proclaiming, 'Thanks be to God, who delivers me through Jesus Christ our Lord!'"

Pastor Lau let his eyes wander the subterranean octagon-shaped room. "Is there anyone here who cannot relate to Paul's words? It's important to point out that Paul said this, not Saul, meaning those words were recorded *after* he was saved, not *before*!

"The reason? Just like with Peter, it wasn't Paul's 'sinful' hold of Jesus that assured him of his salvation, it was Christ's 'sinless' hold of him. Now, this doesn't give any of us a license to sin. Truth is, though we're called to be holy and sinless, we still sin at times.

"Like I said, we're not sinners because we sin, we sin because we're sinners. The disciple John recorded in his first epistle, 'If we claim to be without sin, we deceive ourselves and the truth is not in us.'

"The next verse declares, 'If we confess our sins, he is faithful and just and will forgive us our sins and purify us from all unrighteousness.'

"The verse after that states, 'If we claim we have not sinned, we make him out to be a liar and his word is not in us.'"

Charmaine looked up from the pages of notes she had taken. "Where is that in first John?"

Pastor Lau replied, "Chapter one, verses eight through ten…"

Charmaine jotted it down. "Thank you, Pastor."

"Of course! It's important to note that this was written to the believers." A smile formed on Mark Lau's face. "What a wonderful promise from our Lord to all His true followers. Amen?"

Once it was translated in Mandarin, everyone shouted, "Amen!"

"Nothing has changed since the days of Peter and Paul. So I must reiterate, anyone having the eternal privilege of being known by God as one of His children, will not be lost even though we still sin against Him.

"Now, let's bring it into this present age, by revisiting the question I asked earlier about going to prison for your faith. Let's say, for example, your church was raided and you were arrested along with many others."

Charmaine shifted her weight on the bench she sat on. "Okay…"

"After spending three days in jail, you were given the chance to renounce Christ and gain your freedom after serving a month long sentence, like Sam's father and many others here were offered.

"For argument's sake, let's say you rejected the offer and were taken back to your jail cell. A month later, you were given another chance to renounce Christ. Once again, you rejected it, and received a six-month sentence this time.

"Six months later, after battling overpowering bouts of loneliness from having minimal contact with friends and loved ones, you were given one last ultimatum—either renounce Christ and be released immediately, or the offer would be taken off the table and you would have to serve a ten-year sentence.

"What would you do if you knew you had God's eternal assurance, which means, like Peter, regardless of what decision you made, as a blood-bought Christian, you could still be forgiven?

"Peter wasn't even in prison, yet he denied his Lord, the very One he was blessed to walk with for three years! Yet, he was still forgiven."

A lone tear rode down Charmaine's cheek.

Mark noticed and pressed on. "Just like him, if you're a true child of the Most High God, even if you renounced Christ to gain your freedom, it wouldn't make you any less saved. Like Peter and Paul, it isn't your 'sinful' hold on Christ that assures your salvation, it's Christ's 'sinless' hold of you.

"Like I said the other day, this is why I believe those who don't renounce Christ in prison, even knowing they could still be forgiven, are the true 'highly blessed and favored' ones. By not denying Jesus, that's when He gets the glory."

Tears filled his eyes. "As a redeemed sinner who has failed Jesus too many times to count, this passage convicts me in the deepest chambers of my spirit...Oh, to be chosen of God! Such love! Such amazing grace!"

Looking toward the ceiling, he uttered a simple "thank you" to his Master and Savior. Prior to his conversion, Mark Lau was a task oriented individual who seldom showed emotion. But that was then...Just seeing him wiping tears from his eyes forced tears to their eyes as well.

"I assure you, Charmaine, if you're called by the Most High God to be His child, nothing can prevent it from happening, not the forces of darkness, and certainly not faulty preaching...

"Jesus said in John chapter ten, 'My sheep listen to my voice; I know them, and they follow me. I give them eternal life, and they shall never perish; no one will snatch them out of my hand. My Father, who has given them to me, is greater than all; no one can snatch them out of my Father's hand. I and the Father are one.'

"This further proves that God is in control, not sinful man. He does the choosing, not us. The point I'm trying to make is that Christ paid too high a price to ever lose a single sheep He purchased with His own blood, especially since all were received of His Father. God shall not lose one of His elect, not one, even in that person's last moments!

"The thief on the cross is a perfect example of this. He may be the best example that grace doesn't depend on what we do or don't do, but on what God has done for us. This man lived a wretched life and knew he was fully deserving of God's judgment. Yet, what did Christ say to him on the cross?"

Charmaine briefly lowered her facemask. "Today, you will be with me in Paradise..."

Pastor Lau shot his visitor a thumbs up gesture. "In the end, it was his belief that Christ really was who He proclaimed to be that forgave his sins, at the very last moment, which gained him entry into Heaven.

"We are no different than he was. Jesus said in John three-eighteen that we're condemned already. If all of us were born physically alive yet spiritually dead, how can we choose anything for ourselves spiritually speaking?

"The answer is we can't. The only way any sinner can cross over from spiritual death to life is if God takes the first step through regeneration, meaning He turns our stone hearts to flesh, and opens our eyes and ears spiritually. Until this happens, we are incapable of choosing Jesus.

"The notion that any one of us chose Christ of our own accord runs contrary to what the scriptures teach. This fact bruises many egos and is a big reason why so many choose not to believe in God's predestination, when clearly it is written.

"Yes, we do choose Jesus, but only after we have been graciously regenerated from above can we 'accept' the Gospel message and 'receive' Christ as Lord and Savior. In this man's case, it just happened on a bloody cross. And just like with us, God chose him first, not the other way around.

"As sinners, if we had anything to do with God's redemptive plan, salvation would be unattainable, because we humans would instantly taint it. It would then be 'works' based, not God's grace, and it would be lost on day one!"

Pastor Lau paused to let his words hang thick in the air, then said, "Think about it, if we could lose our salvation, how would that make us any different from all other pagan religions in the world, whose followers constantly hope they can do enough or be good enough to earn God's favor in the end? What kind of security is that?"

Pastor Lau sensed a slight confusion in Charmaine. "Let me ask, how much credit can you take for your physical birth?"

Charmaine giggled under her facemask. "None."

"Well, the same is true when it comes to being born-again: the recipient can't take an ounce of credit for it. The only difference is, unlike when infants enter the world, all who truly believe and are born-again remember when it happens.

"How could we not when we suddenly cross over from spiritual death to life. Nothing can compare to it. As the saying goes, 'Those whom God keeps are well kept.' Yet, there are many who believe they took the first step toward God, when nothing could be further from the truth. I mean, what can anyone do if they are dead?"

"Nothing."

"Where do dead people end up..."

"The grave."

The way Charmaine said it made Pastor Lau chuckle. "Exactly! Prior to God taking the first step, my life was a complete mess. I drank too much, gambled, lied, cheated, stole, lusted after women with my eyes, and was guilty of committing a whole slew of other sins."

Pastor Lau nodded sadly. "I didn't care for God back then, or His will for my life, at least not with my whole heart. It was mostly lip service.

"Had God not taken the first step, I'd still be that same lost person I was back then. The reason I'm willing to be persecuted here in China is because I believe the many promises recorded in this blessed Book will come to pass, in God's perfect timing, for all who love Him.

"In fact, I risk my whole eternity on what it teaches. The reason? Because Jesus rose from the dead. This means, I win in the end. We all do! And what could be better than that?"

When his words were translated into Mandarin, many started weeping tears of joy. Charmaine was deeply touched by their selfless worship of the One who had saved them all from hell.

Pastor Lau said, "As much as I want to keep going on this topic, I'm sure the crowds are already gathering aboveground for the next service. But if you decide to stay, we can pick up where we left off after lunch."

"Of course, I want to stay! My soul feels like it's on fire!"

Pastor Lau said, "Praise God for that! Let's eat then, shall we?"

25

AFTER A QUICK HOME-cooked lunch aboveground in the back of the dry cleaners, with dozens of new church members, Charmaine lowered herself down the ladder for the next session. This time, she had questions to ask...

While eating her wonton soup and pork lo mein aboveground, her mind searched for scriptures that could possibly defend those who think they could lose their salvation.

Finding them, she decided to wait until everyone was listening. "Hope you don't mind, Pastor, if I ask some questions regarding salvation and whether or not it could ever be lost..."

Mark Lau smiled. "By all means! Fire away..."

"What about working out our salvation with fear and trembling?"

"Lucy told me you ran track and field back in high school." Charmaine nodded yes. "Me too, back in Portland. Since we're both former athletes, let me use a sports analogy to best describe this to you."

Mark Lau flexed his right arm. "See this muscle?" He glanced down at his arm. "What's left of it, anyway..."

Charmaine cracked up.

When his words were translated, everyone else laughed as well.

Mark smiled. "God placed this muscle in my body at birth. It's always been there. I had nothing to do with it. The more I exercise it, or work it out, as the Apostle Paul stated, the stronger it gets.

"Our faith can be likened to this muscle, or lack thereof. The more we exercise it, the stronger it gets. The less we exercise it, the weaker it gets. And just like the muscles in our bodies were placed there by God Almighty Himself, the same is true that the faith we have to believe in Him was also given to us by Him. It's something for which we can take no credit.

"Now, from a spiritual standpoint, once God's free-gift of salvation has been given, like our physical muscles, it's already there. The more we work it out with fear and trembling, the stronger and more effective our earthly ministries will be. It's as simple as that..."

"Hmm..." Charmaine liked his explanation, but she wasn't sure if she believed it or not. Referring to her notes, she pressed on, "What about where the Word says those who have been enlightened, and tasted the heavenly gift, and shared in the Holy Spirit, and tasted the goodness of the Word of God and the powers of the coming age, only to fall away?"

"Fair question. One I've asked myself too many times to count. When I think of folks praying a simple prayer asking Jesus into their hearts to save them from hell, I understand why they do it. I did it several times myself, before I was finally saved for real.

"When confronted with the possibility of going to hell, who wouldn't agree to saying a 'salvation prayer' if it would guarantee they'd never be sent to that wretched place?

"Most, after praying with someone to receive Christ as Lord and Savior, get emotional by thinking they've just been made right with God. But if there is no genuine repentance, in time, they will end up going back to their sinful lifestyles because their conversion wasn't genuine.

"In short, they honor God with their lips with hearts that remain far from Him. Are you familiar with the parable Jesus told His disciples, in Matthew chapter eighteen, when He compared the kingdom of heaven to a certain king and one of his servants who owed the king a massive debt, but didn't have the means to pay him back?"

Charmaine said, "Yes, I am."

"The king decreed that the man and his wife and children, and everything they owned, be sold so payment could be made. The servant fell down and worshiped the king, saying, 'Lord, have patience with me, and I will pay everything back.'

"The king was moved with compassion and forgave his massive debt. After being forgiven so much by the king, what did the servant do next?"

Sam Yang said, "He had a confrontation with a fellow servant…"

Pastor Lau nodded. "Someone who owed him a tiny fraction of what he owed the king. He took the man by the throat, saying, 'Pay what you owe me!' So his fellow-servant fell down and begged him, saying, 'have patience with me, and I will pay you back.'

"But the man cast him into prison till he could pay what was owed. When his fellow-servants saw what he did, they told the king what he had done. When he stood before the king again, it was a much different result.

"The next time he stood before the king, the result was entirely different. The king said, 'You wicked servant! I forgave all your debt, yet you couldn't show mercy on your fellow-servant for the small amount he owed you!' So the king became furious and delivered him to his tormentors, until he should pay all that was due.'"

184

Charmaine raised her hand in the air. "Wait! I'm confused. What does this have to do with saying a sinner's prayer?"

"This man took the king's forgiveness for granted. Being forgiven by God is at the heart of the Gospel. Instead of a life transformed by the power of the Holy Spirit, the instant the servant was away from the king, he went back to his old ways just like a dog returns to its vomit, or a pig runs back to the mud after just being cleaned.

"The same is true for all the unconverted in the world. After hearing the Gospel preached at church or on the internet or TV, many feel a certain conviction in their souls to be forgiven.

"They're told if they repeat a simple prayer, it will make them square with God. Initially, many shout Jesus from the rooftops. You know, honoring Him with their lips.

"But since they have no true understanding of the Word of God, and there is no genuine repentance on their part, their prayer is nothing more than an act of desperation to keep them from going to hell, without the desire to turn away from their sinful lifestyles.

"In other words, they want what Jesus can give them, without wanting Jesus Himself and the many struggles He spoke of regarding all who would follow Him.

"Still blinded to the Truth, they ask for and think they've received God's salvation and forgiveness. This makes them feel as relieved as the desperate servant who was forgiven his massive debt to the king.

"But since his plea was desperate—not repentant—the moment he was out of the king's presence his true colors resurfaced. When the king sent the servant back to his tormentors, it's a microcosm of the false convert being sent to hell."

Mark shook his head sadly. "Which takes us back to your question. These people have been enlightened, they've tasted the heavenly gift, shared in the Holy Spirit, tasted the goodness of the word of God and the powers of the coming age, only to fall away.

"This doesn't mean they were saved, Charmaine. All it means is that they were exposed to God's goodness, yet they remained unconverted.

"Scripture is clear that it would be better for them to have never been exposed to His goodness than to taste it only to depart from it. It would be better for them had they never been exposed to it at all.

"Nothing's changed since the days these scriptures were recorded. Judas Iscariot wasn't the only one who walked away from Christ two thousand years ago. John six, verse sixty-six states that many of Jesus' followers, after personally witnessing the many great miracles He performed, not to mention the perfect life He lived, ultimately turned away and no longer followed Him.

"There's that word 'many' again. Think about it, if so many left Jesus after experiencing miracle after miracle while in His presence, why should we question that 'many' since that time, including in this present age, have done the same?

"I find it interesting that that passage was recorded in John six-sixty six, or six-six-six. The disciple also recorded in first John two, verse twenty-three, 'This is the antichrist, he who denies the Father and the Son. No one who denies the Son has the Father; whoever acknowledges the Son has the Father also.'

"Four verses above that, he recorded, 'They went out from us, but they were not of us; for if they had been of us, they would have continued with us. But they went out, that it might become plain that they all are not of us.' Once again, this doesn't mean they lost their salvation."

Charmaine shifted in her chair. "I know, they never had it to begin with, right?"

"Precisely. Again, they had profession without possession, which was why they ultimately fell away…"

It took a while for the translator to bring everyone up to speed. Hence, the delayed head nods.

"Now, let's briefly discuss those who stood by Jesus. I'm sure you know except for John, who was banished to the island of Patmos for his faith and his testimony, the rest died gruesome deaths for their faith. Do you think Jesus was mindful of how they would die?"

Charmaine opined, "Of course, He knew!"

Pastor Lau nodded agreement. "Once His disciples understood they had eternal assurance, their lives in the flesh suddenly became less significant, as their focus was switched onto the world to come.

"Each considered it a great honor to die for their King. But they died knowing they would be absent from the body and present with the Lord, just as the Apostle Paul said in Second Corinthians five-eight.

"These men were greatly flawed just like us, yet they knew they were saved. Otherwise, why die in the manner in which they did, if there was even the slightest chance they would be shut out of Heaven?

"Doesn't make much sense now, does it? While others who willingly die for their religions leave this world in a cloud of violence, those who are martyred for Christ leave quietly rejoicing, anticipating the eternal comfort they have in their King, our King.

"These men have been dead for two thousand years. All are with our Savior now. Do you think they would exchange God's unconditional love for their former lives on this fallen planet, where they were hated and persecuted to the point of death for their faith in Christ?"

Charmaine shook her head no. *Hmm...*

"While it's true that God loves all people, for those who aren't truly born-again, His love has an expiration date. In other words, for those who are perishing, God's love is conditional.

"Whether you love God or hate Him—faithful servant or staunch atheist—He still provides for everyone He created, even if most deny it or take it for granted. But this can *never* be mistaken for God's unconditional love.

"If you want to see first-hand the difference between the two, try dying in your sins. If you do that, instead of being welcomed Home as one of God's children, you will feel the full weight of His fierce eternal judgment constantly bearing down on you in a place called hell."

Pastor Lau silently gasped. "Certainly not unconditional love by any stretch of the imagination. Wouldn't you agree?"

Charmaine brushed off a shiver then softly said, "Yes."

"But the Good News is, if you truly are saved, meaning you belong to Christ Jesus, God's love for you is both unconditional and eternal! Imagine being completely smothered in His unceasing love, while living in perfect peace and harmony for all eternity, when life on this fallen planet comes to an end..."

Pastor Lau smiled. "Could something so spectacular ever be measured in worldly terms? I think not. That's precisely what's in store for all whose names are found written in the Lamb's Book of Life! Hallelujah!

"I confess it used to bother me how God sometimes blessed those who hated Him more than His own children. But knowing what He has in store for all who love Him, they can have this world. All we want is Jesus!

"Following Him gives us something so much better to look forward to. We're convinced beyond a shadow of a doubt the persecution we now face won't follow us into eternity. Soon, we'll truly be free.

"As brothers and sisters in Christ Jesus, just knowing we'll spend eternity together makes the love we share infinitely more genuine than what this world offers. In other words, the love we share for each other isn't tied to anything worldly.

"Knowing we have eternal assurance makes carrying our crosses daily a whole lot easier. Once you fully understand what it means to carry your cross, to the point of death, I might add, serving Him becomes joyful, even when suffering becomes part of the journey."

"Wow! You make it sound so easy…"

"In no way is it easy, Charmaine, but it's definitely worth it!"

Charmaine shook her head in confusion. Everything he said sounded logical enough. But in the back of her mind, she was still unsure about the eternal assurance he kept speaking of.

Mark Lau sensed what she was thinking. It was time to ask her one last question…

26

"KEEPING IN LINE WITH carrying our crosses daily, people see all sorts of things when they look to the old-rugged cross. I wonder, Charmaine, what do you see?"

"I see Jesus dying for the sins of the world. And you, Pastor?"

Pastor Lau nodded agreement. "I agree, at least for those who truly believe in Him. But can I tell you what I don't see?"

"Okay."

"The desire for anything of this world. Nor do I see anything good in me. How could I, when my sin was so offensive that the only way I could ever be saved, was for God to crush His own Son on the cross for *my* transgressions?"

Pastor Lau shook his head. "Imagine that, the Creator of the universe doing all that for sinful old me. You see, Charmaine, what happened at Calvary was the truest manifestation of God's love for all His redeemed children. As one of them, I can't help but reflect on how His grace was at work in my life long before I was even aware of it."

Pastor Lau got choked up. "Though He foresaw my great sin and depravity, He still loved me. And to prove it, He sent Jesus to die brutally on the cross, so when God looks at me, He doesn't see my sin, He sees His Son dying in my place, as if He committed my sins, not me.

"What great love! Once we view the cross from the perspective that we all deserve hell, and had it not been for God's love for our souls, that's exactly where we would end up, our perspective is forever changed. The world becomes less and less and Christ becomes more and more."

"Wow!" The way he said it brought tears to Charmaine's eyes. *I've been looking to the cross for all the wrong reasons...*

This was yet another way he was in direct opposition with her pastors at her church in Seattle. Pastor Julian, especially, was known for saying Jesus died on the cross for the many material things they wanted in life. It was one of his core beliefs he projected onto others, including her.

Charmaine took a moment to formulate her thoughts. "Pastor, your teachings are so profound. I admit much of what you teach is opposite to what my pastors teach. I wonder, what would it take to get all pastors on the same page?"

Pastor Lau rubbed his chin and momentarily looked up to the dark ceiling. "Okay, remember what I said at the Bible study at your church about the only generation in total agreement with everything the Word of God teaches, are those who have already passed on into eternity?"

Charmaine nodded yes. *How could I forget?*

"Imagine if, before graduating from seminary school, aspiring pastors were required to spend five minutes in hell viewing the cross from a condemned vantagepoint, knowing those sent there were without hope. One minute even!"

Seeing Charmaine's eyes double in size, he pressed on, "One thing I can promise is there would never be a need to visit that wretched place a second time. Once would be frighteningly enough.

"Please don't think I'm being disrespectful, but I wonder what would happen if your pastors were sent to hell for just a few seconds, and saw 'many' who thought they were saved—perhaps even some who sat under their teachings before death came to collect them?

"Upon coming back from that place of torment, do you think they'd still preach the same prosperity-driven message?"

Charmaine lowered her head and shook it softly.

"I'll answer it for you. Not a chance! If God gave them the same clarity of thinking all doomed sinners sent to that place had, with the full understanding that they were beyond hope, I'm quite certain they would come back completely changed, and would preach the truth and nothing but the truth from the pulpit from that day forward. Even if it caused some to leave the church, they still wouldn't compromise."

BAM! Charmaine gasped. Her heart raced at such a horrific thought! It felt like she was just kicked in the gut with a steel-tipped boot. But in a good way for a change. God had just used his words to pluck her out of the "God's Favorite Princess" mindset she harbored all this time.

She became teary eyed. "Now I know why I'm here. Because of what you just said. I've never heard anything so profoundly truthful in all my life."

Pastor Lau smiled at her, then continued, "Getting back to my belief in eternal assurance, perhaps the best argument I can make can be found in the four words found in Matthew seven, 'I never knew you.'

"Yes, those four frightening words again," Pastor Lau said evenly. "I'm sure you still recall when I said at the Monday night Bible study at your church, of how Jesus didn't say 'some' or 'few', He said many…"

Charmaine nodded.

"While many point to this passage to confirm their belief that we can lose our salvation, I think it proves otherwise. In fact, I think it makes a very strong case in favor of God's eternal assurance."

There was this puzzled expression on Charmaine's face. She tilted her head in mild protest. "Okay, I'll bite. How?"

"Think about it, the fact that Christ didn't say, 'I once knew you' or 'I knew you before you strayed away from me', but 'I never knew you' confirms they *never* belonged to Him at any time, even if they fooled many into thinking they did.

"I can't say it enough. Those who honor God with their lips, when their hearts are far away from God, have profession without possession. There is no middle ground or in between. Either you're saved or you're not. In other words, nothing is ever lost.

"Of course, Jesus is ever mindful of everyone who has ever walked the face of the Earth. After all, He created us. This includes the very woman who gave birth to Him two thousand years ago.

"I don't know about you, but the prospect of being born of someone You first created is too profound for my feeble mind to absorb, let alone fully understand. Yet, mind-numbing as it sounds, that's precisely what happened in the life of the virgin Mary.

"Have you ever really thought about that? Being born of a woman that You first created? Not only had Mary never been touched before the Spirit of God overshadowed her, the very One she gave birth to first created her!"

"Wow!" Charmaine exclaimed again, "Can't say I have. I mean, I knew it, but just like everything else you teach, you have a way of taking it so deep, it makes me want to go deeper into the Word myself."

Unlike Pastor Julian. Where was the Gospel message in his sermons? Where was the call to repentance?

Mark smiled at his visitor again. "The thing you must understand is, as part of the triune Godhead, He created everyone. But by no means does Christ recognize everyone as His Father's children. That distinction is reserved only for those who are truly born again.

"For everyone else, His words 'I never knew you' were meant in a relational way. Only those who have truly been converted and belong to Jesus relationally, will get to spend eternity with Him.

"In the end, we will be content to hear Christ's words found in Matthew twenty-five, thirty-four: 'Then the King will say to those on His right hand, 'Come, you blessed of My Father, inherit the kingdom prepared for you from the foundation of the world...'"

Pastor Lau waited for his words to be translated. Smiles formed on their weary faces. "Amen!"

Seeing them all beaming made Charmaine feel slightly jealous. *Do they have something I don't have after all?*

"See how blessed we really are? We're comforted knowing there is nothing entered anywhere in the records of eternity that stands against any soul that truly believes in the Lord Jesus Christ! This includes us!"

Pastor Lau grimaced and shook his head. "The same is true that every promise God made in the Bible to those who reject Him regarding their demise, will come to pass exactly as they were written...

"For proof of this, all we have to do is continue on in the passage. Our Lord went on to say in verse forty-one: 'Then He will also say to those on the left hand, 'Depart from Me, you cursed, into the everlasting fire prepared for the devil and his angels...'

"In verse forty-six, Christ went on to say, 'And these will go away into everlasting punishment, but the righteous into eternal life.'"

Charmaine lowered her head for the longest time, completely blown away by what she'd just heard. Her body quaked in terror.

Pastor Lau sensed what was happening, and kept going. "If you don't meet Jesus in salvation, Charmaine, you *will* meet Him in judgment. Don't let some spiritual hypocrite keep you out of Heaven."

With her spiritual eyes fully open, Charmaine shivered at the thought. She squirmed in her seat. "How can I know for sure if I'm saved or not?"

Pastor Lau didn't hesitate, "Perhaps the reason some can't remember crossing over from spiritual death to life, is because it never happened, which means they may be false converts without even knowing it.

"If you are truly born again and you came face to face with your 'old self', you would be repulsed by who you once were. But if this has never happened, have you really crossed over from spiritual death to life?"

BAM! It all made sense now. *I can't believe the God I've been praying to all my life isn't even the God of the Bible!*

She thought back to what Pastor Lau said at the Monday night Bible study, about some people doing everything at church but getting saved. She sighed, knowing that person was her!

Charmaine was shattered by this realization. She felt completely gutted. The repentant woman felt deeply convicted in her soul and broke into loud sobbing. She fell completely prostrate before her Maker.

Being underground made her feel even lower than she already was. If she could lower herself even more, she would do it.

With her body pressed against the dusty floor and her face buried in the palms of her hands, from this position of complete humility and brokenness, in between sniffles, she cried out to Jesus.

"Sorry, Lord, for making my relationship with You all about me. I no longer feel blessed and highly favored. I feel prideful and dirty in Your presence. And utterly boastful. I'm so ashamed of myself...

"The things of this world I craved and placed before You all these years seem so meaningless and insignificant, compared to what You did for me on the cross. I took your ultimate sacrifice for granted by twisting it to make it all about me."

In a soft whisper, Liu Xhuang translated Charmaine's words for everyone else. Tears streamed down her cheeks one after the next. Her constant sniffling made translating even more difficult.

Charmaine went on, "If I'm not truly saved, there's nothing more I want now than to receive your salvation through Christ Jesus, just like my brothers and sisters here with me have already done.

"Forgive me, Father, and have mercy on me, a sinner. Cleanse my soul with the blood of Jesus. Save me for real, Lord, as only You can. Show me how to be a better servant for Your glory, and no longer for mine."

Pastor Lau observed and listened with the others, as they all brushed joyful tears from their eyes. Under the circumstances, how could they not rejoice?

After a while, their new sister in Christ picked herself up off the floor. "Thanks for opening my eyes, Pastor. I finally feel saved for real, like I just came running out of the grave!" She was still sniffling.

"You're welcome, Charmaine, but I can't take any credit. It was all God. He softened your heart and opened your spiritual eyes and ears, not me. He gave you regeneration, not me. He granted you faith and repentance, not me. Therefore, He gets all the glory, not me.

193

"I'm called to share the Gospel in season and out of season and leave the results to Him. But let me just say having the privilege of witnessing what just happened between you and God is something none of us will soon forget."

Heads nodded all throughout the room after his words were translated.

Charmaine spoke softly, "Believe me when I say, of all the things I came to China for, the very last thing on my mind was to get saved. Why would I need something I thought I already had?"

Sam Yang said, "There's nothing like knowing you are a true child of God!"

"Amen to that, Sam. Now I know why I kept coming back here. I praise God for this church. I'll never be the same."

Charmaine wiped new tears from her eyes. "As much as I would love to come back tomorrow, I should probably spend the day with Meredith. I feel bad for always leaving her alone. I'm sure she's furious with me now. I need to do my best to make it up to her."

Pastor Lau replied, "I agree."

Charmaine stared at Pastor Lau with a level of admiration and respect that everyone gathered in the subterranean church easily recognized. "I understand now more than ever how badly you are needed at this place. So, if we don't go to Disney Land, can I at least take you to dinner before I go back to the States?"

Mark Lau looked down at his feet. "As much as I'd love that, I think it's best if we don't. For one thing, I don't want you to potentially be linked to me by the Chinese government, And there's also Meredith to think about, namely the video she took.

"With that in mind, I think it would be wise to focus the remainder of your time on her. Tell you what, the day you leave, we can meet for breakfast at your hotel. How's that?"

"Sounds good! One more thing before I go…"

"Yes?"

Charmaine was ashamed and looked down at her feet. "I need to apologize for something I did when you were at my church."

"What is it?"

"Before Imogen prophesied over you, I told her you lacked passion and energy for the Word of God. I wanted her to reinvigorate you and get you to strive for the good life again. That was part of her so-called prophecy to you. Please forgive me for that."

"Think nothing of it. Truth is, I'm not surprised to hear you say that."

Charmaine wanted to say, "Really?" but instead broke into the warmest of smiles. "Please don't ever change your style. I love you just the way you are."

"Likewise, my sister."

Charmaine asked Liu, "Could you please tell everyone that I've never felt closer to God than when worshipping underground with you all."

After the kind, Chinese woman was finished translating, many heads nodded their sincere appreciation at her.

Charmaine went on, "It took twenty years to build my real estate business into a successful enterprise, but only a little more than a week in a foreign country with all of you, to be reminded that what I had built would one day fade away.

"From a worldly viewpoint, most might think my church in the States had it right, and you had it all wrong. I no longer think that way. While we always address ourselves as brothers and sisters in Christ at my church, in truth, we're more like business associates than anything else."

After her words were translated, Charmaine said, "As much as I look forward to getting back to the States, to begin life anew in Christ Jesus, part of me wishes to remain with you a little longer..."

Waiting for her words to be translated, Charmaine could only smile.

They nodded their heads and flashed bright smiles back at her. Some were missing several teeth. It was the most amazing thing.

Because they worshipped the same Jesus, and had the same Spirit dwelling inside, the expressions on the tear-stained faces of those Charmaine knew by face only, projected a love for her that was profoundly intense, even despite the language barrier between them.

The feeling was mutual. The love she had in her heart for them, as true brothers and sisters in Christ, was an eternal love which could never be measured in worldly terms. In the long run, Jesus was the only mode of communication they needed. They would understand each other perfectly clear on the other side someday...

"Lord willing, we'll get to do this again—sooner rather than later..."

After Charmaine's words were translated, they gathered around her and laid hands on her to pray for her.

At that, Charmaine followed Sam Yang out to his car, so he could take her back to her hotel, not knowing this would be the last time they would ever worship together on this side of eternity...

AFTER A FOUR-HOUR nap in their suite, Imogen called Meredith. "How was your workout?"

"Just what I needed, thank you."

"We can be ready for dinner in a half-hour."

"Sounds good, Imogen. We can meet at Grand Brasserie if you want. It's located on the ground floor. The food's really good."

"Sounds perfect. See you shortly..."

When the Martíns arrived, Meredith was already there waiting for them. Relief flooded her soul. But she couldn't disguise the fear in her eyes. Nor did she want to. "I can't thank you enough for coming all this way. Charmaine's lucky to have you both."

Julian said, "We're honored to be here, Meredith. And we want to thank you again for alerting us to the situation. You did the right thing by contacting Rodney. She's blessed to have a friend like you."

Meredith took a deep breath and exhaled. "For the life in me, I can't understand why she feels so drawn to those people. I admit they're nice, but they gave me the willies.

"Because of them, Charmaine wears a facemask everywhere she goes. I understand wearing it outside, but the only time she removes it is up in the room. I should have never let her talk me into coming here."

Imogen reached for Meredith's left hand. "That's why we're here, to fix things! After that, the four of us can go sightseeing and do some shopping. I'd like to check out the place you and Charmaine went to. I saw the selfies and videos on Facebook."

Meredith replied, "Nanjing Road is a very nice place for shopping." This was said without the slightest detection of enthusiasm in her voice.

Julian leaned back in his seat and stretched his arms above his head. "I don't care where we go, so long as I can find a good tailor to design a few suits for me."

"I'm going home..." Meredith blurted out.

Imogen winced and blinked hard. "What? When?"

"My flight leaves at eleven-thirty tonight. I just want to be with my daughter and forget all about this horrible experience."

Meredith's lower lip started quivering. "Hope you don't feel like you wasted your time because of me..."

The Martíns exchanged curious glances. Rodney told Julian she wanted out of China ASAP, so he wasn't as surprised as his wife was.

He took a small sip of water. "Not at all. We understand completely. Go home and be with your daughter. We'll fix this!"

Meredith lowered her head. "Thank you…"

After lunch, Imogen felt tired again. She kissed her husband on the lips. "I'm going up to rest a while. Let me know when she arrives…"

"I will…"

Meredith said, "Time for me to start packing…Thanks for the meal."

"Our pleasure. And thanks again for alerting us. You very well may have saved Charmaine from grave spiritual danger."

Having been fully exposed to the potential grave danger herself, there was no need for Julian to further elaborate. "You're welcome, Pastor."

At that, the two women rode the elevator together up to their floors.

Julian took a seat in the lobby and waited for Charmaine to arrive. He pulled out his laptop to review the first few chapters of a book he was writing titled, *It's Yours for the Asking, Church! So what are you waiting for?!*

Try as he might, he couldn't focus on his notes. The words staring back at him became one big blur. All he could think about was Charmaine, and the damage the man she was spending so much time with had already done to his church.

The very thought caused anger to burn deep within him again. *It stops today!*

27

AT 6 P.M. SAM YANG dropped Charmaine back at the Waldorf Astoria Hotel, after being stuck in traffic for nearly three hours.

The instant she entered the lobby, the Martíns spotted her. Thanks to Meredith, they knew to expect the facemask. They also knew she'd spent the day underground at Pastor Lau's so-called church, doing who knew what.

In that light, they weren't expecting to see her wearing anything Prada or Versace. But blue jeans, a gray hoodie, baseball cap and plain white sneakers? Really? In the lobby of this classy establishment?

The only time the Martíns ever saw Charmaine dressed this way, was when she volunteered to help paint the new daycare center on campus before it opened.

Even so, Julian wanted to remind her by saying, "You know image is everything for the children of God, especially for members of our church, even halfway around the world!"

It was yet another sign that Charmaine wasn't in her right mind. He grimaced. He was already frustrated for having to wait two hours in the lobby before she finally showed up.

Then again, he couldn't fault her for this—she didn't know they were there. But he did blame her, and Pastor Lau, for the potential psychological damage both had caused to Meredith this week. He could see it in her eyes. *Poor woman!*

Julian glanced briefly at his diamond-crusted Rolex watch, then spoke into his mobile device, "She's here. Time for your pastor to rescue one of his lost sheep."

A shout of "Amens" streamed through his cellphone, as 20 of Charmaine's closest friends from church listened to their pastor on a Zoom video conference call.

With Seattle being 15 hours behind Shanghai, it was 3 a.m. in Washington. Most listened in bed and left their video cameras off.

At any rate, their dedication to praying for one of their own so early in the morning was commendable…

When Rodney Williams messaged the Martíns, informing that Charmaine went underground for the third time, Julian sensed the situation was so dire he urged Rodney to set up this meeting so they could all pray that God would rescue her, which He did, but from the false gospel she was exposed to all her life, not the other way around.

Rodney felt honored to coordinate their request. How could he not, when his two spiritual mentors were willing to travel all that way just to rescue his misinformed girlfriend? "Wish I could be there now. Had it not been for my job, I'd be with you..."

"Don't worry, Rodney. Imogen and I have it all under control. By the way, Meredith's leaving tonight. She's had enough."

"Can't say I'm surprised..."

"Gotta go. I'll update you later."

The smile on Rodney's face projected both relief and great admiration for his charismatic leader. "God bless you, Pastor!"

The call ended. With so many praying, no doubt they would be successful in rescuing Charmaine from the man who was no longer welcome at their church.

Who else would travel halfway around the world for one of their own? Talk about leaving the 99 to go after the one that was lost? It only made them love the Martíns even more.

Julian kissed Imogen, who'd already awakened from her short nap and joined her husband and Meredith in the lobby. "Wait here."

He rose from the chair he was seated on, festively dressed in gray slacks, a white dress shirt that was unbuttoned at the top, hidden beneath a red Polo sweater. He approached Charmaine thinking, *What a sermon this'll make when I get back!*

Charmaine blinked hard upon seeing her pastor, not sure at first glance if it was him or not. Realizing it *was* Julian, she couldn't have looked more surprised. Head tilted; chills shot up and down her spine.

She lowered her facemask. "Pastor Julian, what are you doing here?"

"Surprised to see me?" There was this unmistakable glow on her face that was impossible to overlook.

"Shocked would be a better word." Charmaine was happy to see her pastor, but there was this nervous energy swirling about him that she was unfamiliar with.

Usually, when he wasn't preaching, he was cool, calm and collected. Unlike now. He seemed uptight, edgy.

In seven years, this was the first time she ever felt uneasy being in his presence. She spotted Imogen seated on a plush lobby chair, a few feet away from the 20-foot Christmas tree and gingerbread house table.

This didn't surprise her. But what caused her heart to sink in her chest was seeing Meredith sitting on the chair next to her, her luggage on the ground beside her. Her head was down.

Worse, Imogen held her hand consoling her as if they were the best of friends when, not counting the few after service meet-and-greets at church, this was only their first time meeting.

Charmaine approached the two women. She wanted to cordially greet Imogen, but seeing the strange, *What-in-the-world-happened-to-you* expression on her face, she focused her attention on Meredith.

Squatting before her best friend, Charmaine rested on her haunches. "I had every intention of being back in time for dinner and shopping. We were stuck in traffic for nearly three hours. I would have called, but you know I didn't bring my phone with me."

She placed her right hand on Meredith's leg. "Something amazing happened to me earlier, Bestie…"

Imogen grimaced. *Something amazing happened?*

Amazing or not, Meredith wasn't the slightest bit interested in hearing about anything that happened underground with *those* people. She just wanted out of China. Seeing Charmaine's facemask further heightened the situation, and reinforced her will to want to leave this country.

Charmaine glanced at the luggage beside her. "Going somewhere?"

"Home. Flight leaves at eleven-thirty."

Charmaine exhaled loudly. "Please don't go!"

Meredith glared angrily at Charmaine. "I've had enough of this trip. When I saw you sneaking out of the room early this morning, after I made it perfectly clear that we had to have a serious talk, it was the last straw! I don't want to spend another day in this country!"

"You know where I went, Meredith."

"Yeah, to be brainwashed by those cultists!"

Charmaine surveyed the massive lobby. Now mindful of the many dangers Christians faced in this country, her friend's indiscretion could prove dangerous. She hoped no one was listening. "Don't say that, Meredith. It's not true."

"Sure seems that way to me. Clearly, you're *not* the same person I came here with. It's like you've had a mental breakdown or something."

Charmaine knew her friend was still traumatized by her dry cleaners experience, which Meredith still refused to call a church. But enough to cut her vacation short?

There was no need to ask if she was the reason the Martíns were in China. What other reason could there be?

Charmaine glanced at Pastor Julian. "When did you arrive?"

Julian checked his watch; not that he needed to, it was purely out of habit. "Earlier today, when you were underground with that so-called pastor."

She ignored the sarcasm. "But why?"

Julian glanced briefly at Meredith. "Out of concern for you; your spiritual well-being, to be precise."

Charmaine flinched. His tone of voice determined that her spiritual well-being probably had little to do with it. "I'm perfectly fine, Pastor. Couldn't be better, in fact, spiritually speaking."

"Why's that?"

"Later." Her eyes volleyed back to Meredith. "Please don't go, Bestie! I know it's all my fault. But we flew all this way to spend quality time together. You said yourself you like Shanghai even more than Paris..."

"Yes, before you ruined it all!"

"We still have a few days left. We can go shopping all day tomorrow if you want. I already told Pastor Lau not to expect me."

Meredith looked over at Imogen. She was glad her pastors got to see how one of their own was dressed. It further confirmed her premonition that she'd had some sort of mental breakdown. The old Charmaine would never be seen wearing that sort of clothing at a place like this!

"Shopping? Ha! Where, at more surplus stores? Or will you change your mind again and stay in the room all day reading the Bible?"

Imogen observed and listened and could only shake her head...

Charmaine deflected her snide remark and pressed on, "Is there anything I can do to get you to change your mind?"

Meredith tilted her eyes up. "Sorry. My mind's made up. Grateful as I am for the trip, I don't want to spend another day here. I just want to go home and be with Bethany..."

"Meredith, please? What about my birthday dinner?"

Meredith became even more emphatic. "Birthday dinner? Seriously? How could you possibly think about that now? Do you know how scared to death I was all this time thinking someone might knock on the door to arrest me, or handcuff me down in the lobby and take me to jail, if I was foolish enough to go to the gym or the restaurant? Do you even care?"

"Of course, I care, Bestie!"

Meredith snickered. Her eyes narrowed. "Thanks to you, I had to order room service for all my meals. Here I am in one of the most beautiful cities on earth and I'm too afraid the leave the room, let alone dare leave the hotel to go sightseeing!

"When you went underground the second time, I was tempted to go to the Grand Theater or to the casino. I even got dressed and was ready to go, anything to calm my nerves.

"I was even tempted to travel eight-hundred miles on the bullet train to Beijing, just to get away from this place. But I was too paralyzed with fear to leave the hotel."

Meredith shook her head in disgust. "Even if I had the guts, Beijing wouldn't have been far enough away! It's still China! I finally went to the gym earlier, but only after your pastors arrived.

"Up until then, I felt all alone and paralyzed with fear! Even with your pastors here, I won't feel totally safe until I'm on the plane headed back to the States."

Glancing quickly at Imogen again, Meredith's eyes volleyed back to Charmaine. "This was supposed to be *my* vacation! I'm not a criminal! I refuse to suffer the consequences from *your* involvement with *that* cult!"

Charmaine flinched, then surveyed the massive lobby again. "I understand how you feel, Meredith, but it's not a cult." *Perhaps it's best you leave, after all?*

"Call it what you want, Charmaine. The last thing I need is to be labeled an accomplice. I have a daughter to raise…"

"Can I at least accompany you to the airport?"

"No need. I'm sure you and your pastors have much to discuss," Meredith opined, nervously. "I only contacted them out of concern for you. Actually, I messaged Rodney on Facebook. He did the rest…" She broke eye contact and stared at her hands folded on her lap.

Charmaine steadied her gaze back to Pastor Julian. What she saw in his eyes was unsettling. She shook her head in disbelief, silently wondering what their true motive was for coming all this way?

She took a deep breath, hoping her growing agitation wouldn't cause her to say something she might later regret.

Her eyes settled back onto Meredith. Her voice grew more desperate. "I know how this must look to you, Bestie, and I appreciate the concern, but I'm fine, really."

If you say so! Imogen kept her condescending thought to herself. All she could do was bite her tongue and hope for a good outcome. The last thing she needed was to upset the baby in her womb even more.

Meredith glared at Charmaine. "Besties don't do these things to each other!" She stuck her nose in the air and looked away. It very much sounded like she'd had enough of the friendship as well.

Meredith nodded at Julian, who then motioned with his right hand for the concierge to approach. "Could you please get a limo ready to take my friend to the airport?"

"Yes sir!" came the enthusiastic reply.

Your friend? You don't even know her! Charmaine couldn't quite describe how she felt. Whatever it was, it was strong and unrelenting.

Julian pressed a twenty-dollar bill into his hands. "See that she's treated with the best of care."

"Certainly, sir!" the young man said again, standing at full attention, as if saluting a commanding officer. It was a bit much.

When Meredith rose from her seat, Charmaine panicked, "Please, Bestie, this is the last thing I ever wanted." She tried embracing her friend, but Meredith's arms remained limp at her side.

It was evident that she wasn't in the forgiving mood. It was awkward to say the least. "By the way, I already gave you a birthday gift…"

Charmaine was confused. "What do you mean?"

"I deleted the video from my phone…"

Charmaine sighed relief.

The Martíns looked at each other. Neither one knew what Meredith was talking about. But seeing Charmaine sighing relief, it was evident to them both that it was a big deal.

In truth, the main reason Meredith deleted the video was that she didn't want it to cause her potential trouble at the airport.

At that, without saying another word, she followed a hotel employee, who pulled her luggage to a waiting limousine outside.

Charmaine watched her friend lower herself down in the vehicle, wondering how much permanent damage, if any, had been done to their friendship. The still-terrified look on her face determined that a great chasm now existed between them.

Could this be considered spiritual persecution? Charmaine prayed not. But how could she think otherwise, when Meredith never bothered glancing at her one last time, as the driver left for Hongqiao International Airport? She looked the other way.

Charmaine felt like bawling her eyes out. She was surprised she was able to refrain. It wouldn't last…

Julian noticed. But instead of trying to comfort her, he said, "Now, what were you saying about being totally transformed spiritually, or something along those lines?"

Charmaine's eyes darted left and right, surveying the massive lobby. "Not now, Pastor. This isn't the place to have this discussion. Never know who's listening."

Julian glanced at his wife. Imogen shrugged her shoulders.

"Besides, I wasn't expecting you. You gave me no time to prepare my list of questions."

Julian shot another confused glance at his wife.

Imogen mouthed the words, "List of questions?"

Julian was the one to shrug his shoulders this time…

Charmaine knew her comment had the desired effect. "But don't worry, I have every intention of revisiting this conversation with you."

"Why don't we meet for breakfast in the morning?" asked Julian.

"Sure, the food at the Grand Brasserie is really good…"

Imogen said, "We know. We met Meredith there for an early dinner."

Charmaine snickered under her breath. "I see. Let's meet there, then."

"What time?"

"Eight a.m.?"

"See you then…"

"Good night, Pastors."

"Good night," Imogen said.

Charmaine went up to her room. Seeing Meredith's side of the walk-in closet cleaned out brought tears to her eyes. She understood why her best friend was so freaked out. But the last thing she wanted was for her to cut her vacation short, all because of this.

She sat on the bed and had a good cry. Wiping tears from her eyes with a tissue, if Meredith thought she was crazy now, what would she think when she tried explaining that the church she'd deeply loved and wanted her to join back in Seattle had it all wrong, and that it took spending three days beneath a dry cleaners in China—with a persecuted church—to finally understand what the Bible really taught?

Charmaine flushed that thought from her mind and made a cup of jasmine tea.

She stared out at the Pudong skyline across the river. The view remained stunningly spectacular. Yet, as much as she appreciated it, it no longer had a hold on her like it had the first few nights.

The river that was a constant flurry of activity each morning with cargo and fishing ships going up and down the crowded waterway, one after the next, were replaced each evening with dinner cruise and neon party ships.

Another tear escaped her eye, when she spotted the boat that she took Meredith on for her birthday dinner celebration, the night before they went to church and their lives were radically uprooted...

She easily recognized the dinner cruise ship by its funky neon lights.

Dinner cruise ships...

Charmaine thought back to what Pastor Lau said the other day. Clearly, his church was sailing on a battleship, while hers was on a cruise ship.

Prior to taking this trip, much like the boats sailing up and down the Huangpu River, a Christianity cruise ship was the only thing she knew.

Pastor Lau's question rushed to the forefront of her mind. *Would I prefer to be taken to Heaven on a cruise ship or a battleship?*

Suddenly, his challenge back in the States to research prosperity churches flooded her mind. "If not, you should," he had said.

Charmaine logged onto *YouTube* and typed in *False Prosperity Churches*. What she discovered frighten her to the core!

Pastor Lau was right!

28

THE FOLLOWING MORNING

AFTER FILLING THEIR PLATES full of food, Julian blessed the meal, then said, "Now, what were you saying yesterday about being transformed spiritually?"

Charmaine took her time eating a strawberry before answering. "My eyes and ears have finally been opened to the true Gospel of Jesus Christ."

"True gospel?"

"Yes. One that isn't centered on my own selfish desires..."

Julian glanced quickly at Imogen, then at the notebook Charmaine had brought with her, before steadying his eyes back on her.

With frustration in his voice, he said, "And this from the man who blasphemed our church and rebuked my wife, and one of your pastors, I might add, in front of a full congregation?"

Charmaine scanned the restaurant making sure no one was listening. Normally she could get fiery with the best of them. But knowing common citizens were rewarded in this country for turning in those who broke the law, she remained calm.

Satisfied that the coast was clear—at least she hoped it was—she glanced at Imogen. "That was never his intention, Pastor. He was only defending the Word of God..."

Pastor Julian shook his head in disbelief. "So, I was right! This really is a rescue mission..."

"Rescue mission?"

"Yes. From you possibly becoming an extortion victim," came the reply. The luminous glow Julian was known for was gone. His eyes projected anger for Pastor Lau, and a deeper concern for his lost sheep.

He can't be serious? Charmaine snorted frustration. "Extortion? I thought we were talking about the Gospel?"

"We are, but my gut tells me Pastor Lau's a dangerous man."

Imogen stared at Charmaine until she could no longer hold her gaze— her eyes drifted down to the floor. "Mine too..."

Charmaine gulped hard. "How can you say that, when neither of you know him?"

Imogen shook her head in disbelief. "I won't even dignify that with a reply, not after what he did to me!"

Julian leaned back in his chair. His eyes narrowed. "Are you saying you side with what he did?" Both felt disrespected by her.

"Of course, I'm not happy that you were humiliated, Pastor, especially with so many eyes on you," she said to Imogen. "But I understand why he did it. You forced his hand, so to speak."

Imogen gasped, then raised her hands in the air. "You can't be serious?!"

Charmaine took a sip of coffee. "You're entitled to your opinion, but I assure you Pastor Lau's one of God's true servants. Not only is he kind and tenderhearted, he's well-versed in the scriptures. I assure you he's not the judgmental, mean-spirited man I thought he was at the outset."

A smile crossed her face. "Thanks to him, I have a clearer, more balanced understanding of what the Word of God teaches. He made me realize so much of what I thought I already knew, I didn't know at all."

Her words stung Julian at first. Anger settled in again. *What am I, chopped liver?* "Can you be more specific?"

Where do I begin? "Okay, one thing I learned is what makes me blessed and highly favored is that God didn't choose me from the foundation of the world to be His princess, but His servant."

The Martíns exchanged more astonished glances. Her greatly toned-down wardrobe was further proof that she believed what she was saying. They had to act quickly and un-brainwash her before it was too late.

Imogen leaned forward in her seat. "Of course, we're all God's servants, and we all make up the Body of Christ. But God chose to prosper our church. This entitles us to His richest blessings."

Charmaine took another small sip of coffee. "I know that's what you preach, Imogen, but I no longer believe it, at least not the way you do."

"How am I supposed to take that? Your words are hurtful, Charmaine, judgmental even."

"I'm not trying to sound disrespectful. All I'm saying is I don't need some lofty title connected to my name to assure me of the salvation I have in Christ Jesus."

Charmaine searched Imogen's eyes ever so gently. "I no longer wish to be referred to as 'God's princess', especially His favorite one!"

Imogen was rendered speechless. She sipped her tea unable to mask her disappointment over her outlandish comments.

Charmaine noticed. "What's wrong with calling myself a servant of the Most High God? When I stand before Jesus at the end of the age, He won't say to me, 'Well done thy good and faithful princess, Realtor, evangelist, prophetess, only servant. In that light, identifying as His servant is good enough for me. How arrogant I was!

"Pastor Lau quoted Charles Spurgeon the other day. He said, 'If God has called me to be His servant, why stoop to being a king or president?' Blew my mind! A week ago I would have rolled my eyes..."

When neither replied, Charmaine referenced her notes and went on. "Another big change that took place is in my prayer life..."

Imogen scratched her head in befuddlement. Charmaine was the last person she ever thought would be deceived by an outsider the likes of him. "Oh, yeah, in what way?"

"It started the other day with something Pastor Lau said."

Julian stiffened in his seat and shrugged his shoulders. "Okay, I give. What did he say?"

Charmaine smiled. "He said the sweetest part of his day was spending intimate time communicating with the One who loved him more than anyone else could, and learning everything he could about Him..."

Julian nodded agreement, as if he used that same approach himself.

Charmaine quickly removed that thought from his mind. "I remember saying, 'Amen,' before realizing how different his approach was to mine; yours too, for that matter."

She frowned. "The difference is he approaches God's throne seeking *His* will for his life, while we approach it from a position of royalty and with selfish expectations. Instead of asking, 'How can I serve you, Lord?' like the early church did, we ask how He can serve us?"

Julian clenched his fists, but remained silent. Everything she was openly condemning was vital for his prosperity system to succeed. Once again, he felt greatly disrespected by her, insulted even.

Charmaine ignored his posturing and went on, "If the chief goal for Christians is intimacy with God, the fact that Pastor Lau doesn't have material anchors constantly weighing him down, gives him a significant advantage over us.

"I assure you, Pastors, this doesn't show a lack of faith on his part, as you might think; if anything, he has more faith in God, genuine faith, than the three of us combined."

The Martíns exchanged more awkward glances. They never thought the day would come when *she*, of all people, would openly rebuke them like this, especially out in a public place!

Even though no one else heard her, she was starting to sound like their critics back in the States, namely Kaito Fujimoto.

Charmaine remained undeterred by them. "I'm convinced God used Pastor Lau to remove the scales from my eyes, by showing me just how far away I was from Him on so many levels, even if it didn't appear that way in the eyes of others."

Imogen said, "Everyone knows how much you love Jesus."

"Yeah, I always thought so too. I was very good at honoring Him with my lips." Sadness covered her face. "But my heart was far away from Him all that time, without even knowing it."

Julian swallowed the food in his mouth. "What are you getting at?"

Charmaine shot a quick glance at Imogen. The uncertain expression on her face forced her eyes back to Pastor Julian. "If, and that's a big 'if' I was saved before taking this trip, it was just barely."

Imogen grew defensive, as if she had the ability to peer into Charmaine's soul. "How can you say that? Of course, you're saved!"

"No doubt everyone back home would agree with you on that. I surely thought I was. But, in truth, had I not come here, there's a very real chance I may have been one of the 'many' Jesus preached on in Matthew seven."

When neither replied, she went on, "Instead of hearing preaching that convicted me of my sin, like I've heard all this week, all I got from the two of you were prosperity-based messages, week in and week out. You made me think I was saved when I'm not sure I really was."

Charmaine took a bite of her mushroom and cheese omelet and a sip of orange juice. "Lucy Fujimoto recently told me something she never fully understood until she left our church. Pastor Lau merely confirmed it for me here.

"What she said was, if we don't preach about sin and God's judgment on it, how can we possibly present Christ as a Savior from sin and the wrath of God? Do you agree with this, Pastors?"

Julian stared down at the table shaking his head in utter amazement.

When neither answered, she went on, "I now agree with what Pastor Lau said at our church, that the greatest miracle in a believer's life has nothing to do with the things both of you teach. It's when we cross over from spiritual death to life, as if coming out of the grave.

209

"When that happens, it's impossible to forget. The reason I know this is that I felt Jesus calling me out of the grave here in China. Believe me when I say, Pastors, I never felt that sensation back home. If anything, I felt more blessed, at least in a worldly sense, than saved.

"Which is why I must repeat, if I *was* saved under your preaching before coming here, it was by the skin of my teeth."

Charmaine took a deep breath and exhaled. "Not a comforting thought, wouldn't you agree, Pastors?"

Julian shook his head in utter defiance. He couldn't believe what his ears were hearing.

Charmaine sighed. *I should be mad, not you!* "I think what frightens me most is knowing had my faith not come under such loving scrutiny, I would have never thought the need to question the salvation I thought I had, not to mention the things the two of you teach."

Imogen raised an eyebrow. "Loving scrutiny?"

Charmaine nodded. "Pastor Lau gave me the uncompromising truth, but in love. In other words, he told me the things my human side didn't want to hear, which in turn opened my spiritual eyes to the true Gospel message."

She glanced down at her notes again. "Now I can state with absolute certainty that I have the eternal assurance the Bible speaks about, something else you never taught.

"This means, even when I'm on my deathbed, I'll never have to ask, 'Did I do or give enough' to please God enough to save me from hell?"

A smile curled onto her lips. "God's salvation is all about what He did for me, not the other way around! I assure you both there's nothing greater than knowing I'm saved for real. No more second guessing for me."

"What are you talking about, Charmaine?! I always preach on God's grace and that we must be saved!"

"Yes, Julian, you do, but your messages are designed to save us from hell, not from our sins, into the good life, not a life of sacrifice." Charmaine frowned. "When was the last time either of you preached on denying 'self' and carrying our crosses like Jesus commanded us to do?

"I'm talking about selfless sacrifice that doesn't benefit us financially? Not to sound disrespectful, but could the reason you never preach on that topic have anything to do with the fact that it stands in stark opposition to the perfect health-and-wealth messages you always preach?"

There was no reply from either of them. Both looked nauseated.

Charmaine went on, "I want you both to know the days of filling God's ears only with temporal things are over for me. All I want from this point forward is to know God more and what He wants from me, not what I want from Him."

Julian grunted under his breath and shook his head in disgust.

"Don't get me wrong, I didn't need Pastor Lau telling me God knows me perfectly well. I've always believed that. Psalm one thirty nine alone makes it crystal clear."

Charmaine took a deep breath. "But what really sunk in on this trip was how little I know about Him, and how little interest I had in knowing Him from a servant standpoint. Aside from the fact that God created me and sent His Son to die for my sins, I'm ashamed to admit I don't know much else about Him, nothing truthful, anyway."

Eyeballing the Martíns very carefully, she said, "You taught me to approach God's throne as if He was a genie in a bottle, lying in wait to grant the wildest desires of my heart!" *What a joke!*

"You no longer believe that?"

"How can I, Imogen, when it's not what the scriptures teach? How could I ever hope to know Him better, when all I did was strive for things that benefited my fleshly life, at the expense of my spiritual life?"

Normally, when the three of them were together, the Martíns did most of the talking as Charmaine listened with great interest, even taking notes.

It's as if the roles were suddenly reversed. Only they weren't listening to her with any great interest.

The last thing Charmaine ever wanted was to disrespect her pastors. But even if they didn't know it, her words were being spoken in love. "It pains me to say this, but many of the things that used to excite me about being a Christian, things I always thought were signs of having strong faith, now fill me with shame and regret.

"Especially when I think back to the many times you told us never to pray 'Thy will be done.' You claimed it limited God's power in our lives. Really? If praying God's will be done was good enough for Jesus, it's certainly good enough for me!

"Now I'm just grateful for the privilege of spending time with my Lord and seeking His will for my life. Nothing matters more to me than that."

Charmaine bit her lower lip and referenced her notes again. "Another thing Pastor Lau told me that really rocked my foundation was the things you teach us to name and claim, then speak into existence, are the very things Satan offered to Jesus in the wilderness for forty days. Could this mean the message you teach doesn't originate in the Word of God?"

Julian's mouth was agape. For many years, their critics back home had accused them of these very same things. He was having difficulty processing that Charmaine had been turned into one of them. He silently wondered what would come out of her mouth next.

"The two of you know Psalm thirty-seven four is one of my favorite scriptures. Well, thanks to Pastor Lau, I have a better understanding of what it really means. He taught me the first five words, 'Delight yourself in the Lord,' is the key to understanding the passage.

"If we'll only do that, God will give us the desires of our heart, because our desires will be in line with what He wants for us. In other words, instead of focusing on self-centered passions and desires, the things we want will be the very things God wants for us. I had it all backwards...

"Jeremiah seventeen, nine, another verse I never heard you preach on, says the human heart is wickedly evil, which means our desires apart from God are worldly, temporal, and definitely not from above?"

Charmaine smiled warmly. "It took worshipping underground with true brothers and sisters in Christ, to finally realize the vast majority of the things my heart desired weren't the things God wanted for me. My many possessions had become major roadblocks to true fellowship with Him. Then again, it wasn't that I had so many things, they had me!"

Julian lowered his head and shook it from side to side. *Man, oh man!* "What are you saying? Do you plan on leaving the privileged life you have and taking a vow of poverty, like Pastor Lau?"

"Only God knows what the future holds. For now, Pastor, I have no plans of walking away from my business. But I do plan on changing my approach to things."

Imogen scratched her nose. "In what way?"

"In all ways. After this life-altering experience, I'm no longer interested in creating my own personal heaven here on earth. I feel it's a contradiction of words. For instance, you know the mansion I've been claiming for three straight years four doors down from the Wilshires?"

The glow on Imogen's face was gone. It was obvious to Charmaine she couldn't disagree with her any more vehemently.

"Well, if it ever goes on the market, I'm no longer interested as a potential buyer. What business do I, as a single woman with no children, have wanting a six-bedroom house in the first place?" *The Bibles that could be purchased with that kind of money...*

Imogen shook her head quietly, sadly...*Who is this person?*

Charmaine said, "It's time for me to grow up and mature as a Christian..."

Julian glanced at his wife. The expression on his face screamed, *We flew halfway around the world for this?* "Mature?"

Charmaine nodded yes. "By letting the Word of God say what it says without asking it to do or say what I want it to say. It means fully submitting to God's authority, regardless of the consequences.

"Anything else is living a Christian lie, at least on some levels. No more building on sand for me!"

Imogen glanced at her husband again, and raised her hands in defeat. "Okay, Charmaine, humor me, how were you building on sand?"

Charmaine lowered her head, as if she wanted to cry. "After all these years as a supposed Christ follower, I have so few treasures waiting for me in Heaven. Fifty years from now, the many things I've stored up for myself here on earth won't mean a thing.

"Yet, the many rewards I've lost, that I would have rightly stored up in Paradise had I only kept my big mouth shut, are forever gone. It's like the waves of my foolish pride swept them all away. Sorry to say, but the same is true for the two of you as well..."

Julian stiffened up again. His soft brown eyes darkened. "Oh yeah. How's that?"

"Sorry to say, but you may think you're building on rock when, in reality, you're building on sand, just like I was..."

Imogen's jaw nearly hit the table. She didn't know how much more of this nonsense she, or the baby, could take.

Julian's nostrils flared as he brushed off the accusation. "Are you saying we failed you as Pastors?"

Charmaine slumped her shoulders. "On many levels, I'd have to say yes."

The waitress approached with a coffee pot. "More coffee?"

Charmaine covered her cup with her hand. "No, thank you."

Julian put his right hand up in polite refusal.

The warm smile on the young Chinese woman's face faded. She wasn't used to seeing the energetic couple, who tipped so generously, looking so distraught and long-faced. The good vibes they'd given off since their arrival now felt anything but "good".

Whatever they'd just heard, they couldn't hide the obvious pain it had caused them. She cleared the table in silence and quickly left them, hoping against all hope that the confidence this couple had unknowingly instilled in her wouldn't suddenly dry up, forcing the deep depression she'd battled all her life to resurface.

The very thought frightened her, leaving her feeling totally dejected. *Where's the dynamic couple I kept bragging to my family and friends about?*

Imogen wiped her mouth with a cloth napkin. "I've heard all I care to hear. I need to protect our son from all this negativity."

Charmaine gasped. "Son?"

Julian said, "Yeah. We found out the day before coming here."

"Wow, congratulations to you both! That's wonderful news..."

"Thank you, Charmaine..."

Imogen didn't reply. She was too upset. Her sparkling green eyes weren't so sparkly. She kissed her husband's hand. "I'll be up in the room, darling."

The expectant mother glared at Charmaine. Her brow furrowed and her face quaked ever so softly. Without saying another word, she excused herself from the table and walked to the bank of elevators.

Julian finished his coffee. "Think I should join her..."

"I understand, Pastor. Think I'll head up to my room as well..."

As Charmaine rode the elevator back up to her suite, she couldn't help but wonder if Julian and Imogen were truly saved, or were they nothing more than false teachers, wolves in sheep's clothing?

She didn't like what her gut was telling her...

29

THE PHONE IN CHARMAINE'S suite rang. "Hello?"

It was Julian. "Can I interest you in an afternoon tea and dessert down in the Salon de Ville? It's a quaint European-style tearoom on the second floor. I checked it out yesterday. Imogen and I had planned on going, but she's not up to it now."

Charmaine didn't want to be disturbed now. When she returned from breakfast, she plopped down in the chaise lounge chair and read her Bible.

For the past two hours, she was stuck on John 15:18-25, where Jesus warned His disciples that no servant was greater than his Master. He also warned them that the world would hate and persecute them because they hated and persecuted Him first.

As it turned out, Pastor Lau was right—she really did need to be still more often. By so doing, she was learning more of who God really was, not who she wanted Him to be. Yes, it all came down to being still...

The proof was that this was the first time she ever spent two hours meditating on only eight Bible verses in her life.

As much as Charmaine wanted to dedicate the remainder of the day to studying the Word, since she was the reason the Martíns were in Shanghai in the first place, if for only that reason, she owed it to Julian to make time for him now. "Sounds good. I'm a little hungry. Besides, I could use a break from my reading."

Reading? Curious as he was to inquire, after their breakfast debacle, Julian left it alone. "Great. See you there in ten minutes."

"Okay." Charmaine made sure to bring her notes with her, just in case.

The instant they stepped foot inside Salon de Ville, the woman who'd worked the day before fawned all over Julian, as if he were a Grammy winning pop star. Julian had introduced himself to her the day before, while making the rounds as he waited for Charmaine to arrive.

He told the woman he would be bringing his wife the following day, and even tipped her $50 in advance. She was thrilled to see him again. And he was so tall and handsome!

"I told you I'd be back! Only not with my wife. She's not feeling well. She's resting up in our penthouse suite. But I'd like to introduce you to my dear friend, Charmaine. She's a top member of my church…"

"The middle aged Chinese woman said, "Nice to meet you, Charmaine. I'm Jinjing."

"Nice meeting you, too." The smile on Charmaine's face was clearly forced.

Jinjing may not have picked up on it, but Julian did. He brushed it off and pressed another fifty dollar bill in her hand, then requested the table closest to a 6-foot decorated Christmas tree.

Jinjing was all smiles as she walked them to their table.

Charmaine witnessed the cash exchange and practically rolled her eyes.

Once they were settled sipping herbs and ginger tea, in real china cups, they took a moment to listen as a man played soft Christmas music on a harp. It was soothing.

Julian took a sip of tea. "Normally, Imogen would never miss afternoon tea and desserts. Especially now that she's pregnant. Our plan was to take ballroom dance lessons then come here before going shopping later."

"Ballroom lessons? Here in the hotel?"

"No. At the local park. People from all over the world participate. Hopefully, we'll get to do it before we head back to the States."

Charmaine smiled wearily, sensing what her pastor would say next.

Finally, Julian said, "I want you to know my wife's been crying off and on the past three hours up in our room. She feels betrayed by you, and disrespected for siding with Pastor Lau.

"I know her hormones are out of whack, due to the pregnancy, but she also feels judged by you. Do you know she hasn't prophesied over anyone since your friend openly rebuked her?"

Charmaine pursed her lips. "I'm sorry, Pastor. Like I said earlier, it wasn't my intent to come across that way. All I was doing was standing on what the Word teaches."

Julian felt insulted again, but he was still willing to cross swords with her a little while longer. "Didn't Mark teach you about judging others, especially your own pastors?"

Charmaine saw that he was hurt, but this was too important. "Actually he did, while we were having lunch up in the dry cleaners the other day, after service. He taught me what the Bible had to say about judging others, and when it's scripturally appropriate."

"Oh, really now?" *Having lunch up in the dry cleaners? And you haven't been brainwashed?*

Charmaine shifted her weight in her chair. "Let me begin by saying you rightly taught that we're not to judge the unsaved. If we do, we'll be judged for the very same things we judge them for, right?"

Pastor Julian suppressed a yawn. "Every Christian knows that!"

"You also rightly taught that whenever we see fellow believers habitually sinning, while we're not to judge them, per se, we're to call them out, but in private, at least at first...

"If they repent, great. If they rebel, we are to go to the church. If they still rebel after that, they are to be put outside the church."

Pastor Julian nodded agreement again.

Charmaine paused when a waiter carefully placed a three-tiered stand full of delicious finger foods on their cloth-covered table.

The top tier was full of delectable cakes, mousses, pastries, and Christmas tree cookies for the holiday season.

The middle tier had homemade scones and three small bowls full of assorted jellies. The lower tier held savory finger sandwiches.

When the server left them, Julian blessed the food. Charmaine plucked a ham and cheese sandwich off the bottom tier and took a bite. "If I keep eating like this, it'll take a year to lose everything I've gained in China."

Julian laughed and reached for a scone. "If Imogen was here, there wouldn't be a crumb left on all three trays when we left!"

Charmaine laughed, but it was more reserved than the robust laughter she was known for. While this was the first moment of normalcy they'd shared since their surprise sneak-attack on her, both were clearly still on edge. So, where were we?"

Julian took a moment to swallow the food in his mouth. "You were talking about judging others..."

"Right. One thing you never taught me was what the Bible has to say about judging pastors, by way of checking their words and actions to what the Word of God teaches. Because of this lack of knowledge, I always thought it was wrong to confront any pastor, especially my own."

She briefly looked away from Julian before her eyes settled on him again. "Pastor Lau taught me the exact opposite is true."

Julian became defensive. "Really now?"

Charmaine took a sip of her drink. "Honestly, Pastor, when he first told me this, it made me think of times when I literally bit my tongue, after hearing or seeing things in church that didn't seem right to me…"

Julian's face reddened. "Oh yeah, like what?"

"Okay, here's one, why do you allow some of our members to dance on dollar bills on the steps leading up to what's supposed to be the altar of God? By doing that, aren't they defiling something that's supposed to be holy? This has always bothered me."

Charmaine lowered her head in shame. "Wanna know why I never confronted you with this in the past?" Julian rubbed his forehead without answering. "Things were going so well for me and I didn't want to rock the boat. Imagine that? So many lost treasures…"

Charmaine was on the verge of tears. "As much as I blame you for allowing it to happen in the first place, I blame myself just as much for keeping my mouth shut all this time. Of course, I always knew before coming here that not all pastors were saved. I've even heard you say it."

She pursed her lips. "But I'm starting to think the percentage of false teachers in the world are higher than I imagined. Even many who are saved preach messages that are more self-serving than they are in tune with what the Word of God teaches."

Julian scoffed at her words, knowing they were meant for him.

"From now on, I'll be sure to test the spirits and compare everything I hear to what the Word says. If it lines up, I'll receive it gladly. If not, I'll wholeheartedly reject it."

Julian licked the inside of his mouth with his tongue. Clearly, he was offended. "Sounds to me like someone who thinks he's above reproach!"

"Pastor Lau?" Charmaine shook her head. "Not at all. If anything, he urged me to check everything he said in the Bible. If his words differed from the scriptures, not only should I reject them, he said he wasn't worthy of his calling as a Pastor, and he deserved whatever judgement he got from man, and God, for his gross misrepresentation."

Julian rolled his eyes. "Come on, Charmaine, you're a member of one of the most prestigious churches on the planet! God's blessings surround us from every angle. If anyone has God's ear, and favor, it's us! As your pastor, I'm quite proud of this!"

I bet you are! "How blessed are we really, Pastor?"

Julian looked at her incredulously. "Don't be fooled, Charmaine! You're a successful woman. You have money. You're always quick to point out to others the big reason for your success stems from your membership at my church. Have you ever considered this man's trying to cherry-pick you away from us?"

Charmaine took a bite of a Christmas tree cookie. *How do I know you're not doing the same?*

"I'm sure *his* church can't compare to *ours*…"

"You're right about that, Pastor," she said, almost dismissively. "There is no comparison…"

Julian wanted to ask, "If his church is so great, why is it underground?" Realizing they were forced underground, he backpedaled, "How many members do they have?"

"Not sure. I haven't met everyone. But they have three services per day, seven days a week, with a hundred people per service."

"Seven days a week?" *And this isn't a cult?*

Charmaine nodded. "His church is part of a huge underground network with millions of believers. I assure you they're every bit as enthusiastic about serving the Lord as we are in our *golden cathedral*."

Pastor Julian couldn't ignore the way she said, 'golden cathedral'. He didn't need to be a brain surgeon to know she was being sarcastic.

"Honestly, I felt closer to my Maker underground in China than I ever did at our church. Compared to the many soul-stirring messages I've heard preached this week, it seems all you preach on is sunshine and rainbows."

Julian blinked a few times. "Not sure I follow you…"

"Guess what I'm saying is you can have this world and its many material trappings. I no longer want it. All I want from now on is to serve Jesus properly…"

Julian pointed a finger at Charmaine. "Can't you see you're being brainwashed? This man's robbing your mind of the fertile phrases that were planted there many years ago!"

Must've been dirty then, if it needed washing! Charmaine wanted to be offended by his authoritarian, unkind gesture, but she let it go; she needed to remain on point. "I assure you I haven't been brainwashed! My mind and soul are very much intact."

Julian felt anger rise to the surface and bit his tongue, not wanting to say something he might later regret.

Charmaine looked her pastor square in the eye. "Who would have thought the mental break I needed from my busy life would be found in an underground church in Shanghai, beneath a dry cleaners, of all places!

"I admit I was uncomfortable the first time I climbed down into that dark hole. Not gonna lie, I was scared."

Well, yeah?! Julian thought, swallowing the food in his mouth. "Meredith told us all about it."

"I can only imagine her recollection of it."

"It was pretty desperate. That's why we came here. For you." Julian massaged his chin with two fingers. It could wait no longer. "Did they try extorting money from you?"

Extort? "Never once did anyone ask me for money. They took up an offering which I gladly contributed to. Every cent goes toward meeting their meager needs. The rest is used to purchase Bibles and properly translated booklets that are printed in Mandarin." *Not on redecorating!*

"How much did you give him?"

"Him?"

"Pastor Lau, I mean..."

"I thought I was giving to God? And isn't it supposed to be between me and God?"

"Yes, of course. Sorry for asking."

"Pastor Lau has no interest in the things of this world." *Unlike you!* "All he wants is to remain obedient to God, without being bogged down with worldly distractions.

"He said the spiritual battles true children of God face in this life are difficult enough to cope with. Longing for the things of this world is nothing more than a self-centered chasing after the wind."

Pastor Julian stretched his arms above his head. "Sounds like someone who's never been exposed to the finer things in life."

"First off, that's not true. He had a good life as an engineer back in the States. He wasn't a millionaire like you, but he was comfortable enough. He chose to walk away from his former life less than a year after receiving a big promotion, to serve the Lord over here. I admire him for it.

"Another thing I admire is that even though he just made a substantial sum of money from the sale of his house, his meager lifestyle hasn't changed one bit. I'll be surprised if he keeps a single dime for himself."

Charmaine shook her head. "Just so you know, Pastor Lau's not against anyone having wealth and possessions. He totally agrees that when God gives these things and the ability to enjoy them, not enjoying them or being ungrateful for them would nullify the blessing."

Julian yawned. *Finally, something we agree on!*

Charmaine took a moment to reference her notes. "But he also believes what James four states, in verse three, 'When you ask, you do not receive, because you ask with wrong motives, that you may spend what you get on your pleasures.'"

Julian readjusted his weight in his chair. "Come on, Charmaine, how many times have you heard me say it takes great faith to obtain the good things in life…"

Charmaine couldn't believe her ears. *Did he just say that? Talk about twisting the scriptures!* "That's easy for you to say, Pastor. By being at the top, you and Imogen will keep flourishing in your system no matter what."

Julian winced. *My system?*

Charmaine briefly looked down at her notes. "But what about everyone else at church who are still 'living in lack', as you like to say?"

"Man, oh Man! I can't believe this! You're starting to sound like our critics back home!" Julian glanced at his watch. "He really got to you, didn't he?"

Charmaine nodded yes. "God used him to open my spiritual eyes and ears to what the true Christian life is all about. Thanks to him, I firmly believe it has nothing to do with the glamorous gospel message you preach. It's so obvious to me now…"

She gazed deep into Julian's eyes. "I wonder, Pastor, how many from our church would ever resort to living underground or willingly go to prison for their faith, if it ever came to that?"

Julian was clearly baffled by her question. "You know God hasn't called us to that…"

"Why? Because we have greater faith than our persecuted brothers and sisters around the world?"

"There are many contributing factors, but I'm sure that's part of it."

His comment bothered her. "I respectfully disagree with you, Pastor. No one at our church has more faith than these people have. Their hunger for the Word, despite the dire consequences they face on a daily basis, inspires me in a way I've never felt at our church. It's made the things of this world I've always held so dear suddenly seem meaningless."

"That's an easy sell coming from a man who has nothing…"

"Once again, I disagree. Pastor Lau only seeks the things from above, the important things, the eternal things. In that light, he has so much more than you and I combined. Did you know there will soon be more Christians in this country than all other countries on the planet, including the U.S.?"

Julian glanced at his watch again. "I think I read that somewhere," he said, rather dismissively.

Doesn't any of this interest you? Charmaine sighed. It was time to really get his attention. "I wonder if your preaching style would change if you were required to spend thirty seconds in hell…"

Julian flinched at the thought. It was the very last thing he thought she would ask. He took a moment to think it through, before dismissing it as utter nonsense. He clenched his teeth. "I want to meet this so-called pastor again," he demanded.

Charmaine was concerned at how her blunt question put no fear in his eyes; the only thing she saw there was arrogance. "I'm sure that can be arranged. But don't be mad at Pastor Lau. He's not the reason for the big changes you see in me. If you want to get mad at anyone, get mad at God. After all, He's the cause of it all…"

Julian ignored her latest rant. "How about tomorrow?"

"Perhaps the two of you can meet once he finishes with his three services?"

With his pride jolted, Julian wanted to say, "Shouldn't he be setting up a meeting with me!" Mindful that his church might potentially lose $50K in seed money, not to mention thousands of dollars more annually to some underground church in China, he thought better of it. "That would be fine. We can meet up in my suite."

"As you say."

"Perhaps you and Imogen can go shopping to clear your heads. That is what you came here for, Christmas shopping, right?"

"Initially, yes, Pastor. But God had other plans for me…"

Julian snorted frustration. "This conversation's over!" He dropped a hundred dollar bill on the table, and excused himself. "Tell your friend I insist on meeting him tomorrow. Good afternoon."

"I'll be sure to tell him, Pastor…"

30

AT 7:15 P.M. THE next evening, Pastor Julian stood outside the hotel in a light drizzle, waiting for Mark Lau to arrive.

Charmaine, too, for that matter. She left a message for the Martíns late in the afternoon saying she would be back later, but didn't say where she was going. She went for a long walk to clear her head and think things through, before meeting Pastor Lau at a local coffee shop after his third church service, to let him know she would be leaving in the morning.

As much as she wanted to remain in Shanghai, the way her two pastors kept smothering her—to the point of suffocation—she no longer felt comfortable being around them. They acted more like overbearing parents than pastors.

Julian nervously checked his watch every few seconds, bothered that Mark was late, even if only 15 minutes...and counting. *Take your time, but don't waste mine!*

Julian squinted upon seeing a late-model vehicle pulling up to the front entryway. He inched his head forward, trying to make out the passenger in the car. It looked like Charmaine, but with a facemask on, he wasn't sure.

When the man driving the vehicle owned by Sam Yang inched closer, Julian realized it was her. He grimaced and shook his head. It figured. Of course, they were together!

Julian scoffed at the vehicle the man drove. If ever there was a cringeworthy moment! *And to think someone driving that piece of junk taught Bible study at my church!*

Charmaine spotted her pastor and waved at him. She wasn't surprised seeing him standing beneath an umbrella being held by a hotel employee, as if he was royalty.

Pastor Julian motioned for her to roll down the window. "Have him do valet parking. I'll pay for it," he said.

Charmaine relayed the message to Pastor Lau. He quickly nodded his appreciation.

"Treat them both like royalty," Julian insisted to the two bellhops waiting there with him. Both had already been given US $20 bills.

"With pleasure, sir." They wasted no time opening umbrellas to shield Pastor Lau and Charmaine from the rain.

Pastor Lau tried waving him off, saying it was unnecessary, but the young man persisted.

Charmaine felt equally uncomfortable. She wished the rain-drenched winds could blow the uneasiness between the two men away. It worsened with each step they took. *Aren't we supposed to be on the same side?*

"Hello Pastor. Nice to see you again." Julian extended his right hand cordially, trying to ignore the tension he felt being in this man's company again. It was identical to how he felt a few months ago.

Mark Lau felt it too. Then again, after everything Charmaine told him earlier about her conversation with her two pastors, he expected it. "Good to see you again, as well…"

"How was your day, Charmaine?"

"Quite productive, Pastor. And yours?"

Julian flinched, hoping they didn't notice. "Likewise."

Once they were inside the lobby, three more hotel employees followed closely behind Pastor Julian, making sure his every need was being met and that nothing was overlooked.

The satisfaction on the American pastor's face, from being the center of attention, was evident to all onlookers. At 6'4", Julian towered over most people in China. And the way he walked with long, determined strides, made him look even taller than his height.

Clearly, he was enjoying it, even despite whose presence he was in...

Pastor Lau, on the other and, wasn't impressed or intimidated by any of it. Nor was he envious of Julian's flamboyant style or his worldly stature. Far from it. On the contrary, he was embarrassed by the sudden rush of attention, and felt entirely out of place.

His greatest concern was that someone might recognize his face among all the hoopla. Already on the Chinese government's radar, all it would take was a simple facial recognition search to possibly reveal his identity as a pastor of an underground church. *Not good!*

He prayed that wouldn't happen...

With her Christian perspective radically changed, Charmaine was equally put off by her pastor's over-the-top attitude. The full-court press theatrics that once appealed to her now looked so wrong. It wasn't the true Christian way. It saddened her knowing that when she checked in the other day, she'd displayed similar antics! The very thought made her cringe.

But what irritated her most was the way Julian looked down on Pastor Mark, physically and metaphorically. If he was trying to hide that he placed himself above his Chinese counterpart a secret, he failed miserably.

Imogen cringed when she spotted them walking her way. Just seeing Mark's face again nauseated her. She nearly dry-heaved.

Even six weeks later, she still couldn't suppress the anger that burned within her. She dreaded this even more than the excruciating pain she was certain to feel four months from now, when she gave birth to her son.

She glared at him with detective eyes, as if he was the enemy, which, in her mind, he was! "Hello, Pastor." Her tone was both cold and clinical. She couldn't even force a smile at this point.

Pastor Lau extended his right hand, and greeted her cordially. "Nice to see you again, Imogen. You're really starting to show. How many months now?"

"Five." Imogen covered her belly with her hands, as if trying to shield her child from him, blocking all access.

She shifted her gaze to Charmaine, someone else she was unhappy with. The difference between the two of them was that she cared for Charmaine. Thanks to this monster, she wasn't in her right mind.

Once they got her back to the States, they could work hard on bringing her back to her old self. Until then, they had to do their best to swallow their pride and treat her with kid gloves.

Imogen reached for Charmaine's hand. "Let's go shopping. A limo will take us…"

Charmaine reluctantly nodded yes. Then to Pastor Lau, "Will I see you tomorrow?"

Pastor Lau looked at her. He knew what she meant. She hadn't yet told her pastors she would be leaving in the morning. The plan was to meet for breakfast before Charmaine left for the airport. "If the Lord wills, yes."

Charmaine replied with a warm smile.

Julian glanced at his wife. He knew she was hurt. How could she not be, seeing one of their better students treating the enemy with a greater respect than she had for them?

Charmaine said to Imogen, "I won't be long. All I need is a quick shower. Let's meet back here in an hour."

"Sounds good." Imogen watched Charmaine walk to the bank of elevators. Then to Julian, "If you need me, I'll be right here waiting for Charmaine."

Julian kissed his wife on the lips. "We'll be fine, my love. Enjoy your dinner and shopping with Charmaine."

Eyeballing Pastor Lau, she said, "We will…" Without saying another word, Imogen left them.

Julian said, "Why don't we adjourn to my suite?"

"As you wish," Pastor Lau replied, evenly.

Once the two men were inside the elevator car, Julian didn't have to tell the conductor which button to push. He knew to take them to the top floor, to his supreme riverside suite.

The two pastors rode in total silence. The more it ascended upward, the more Mark's stomach churned. The elevator ride had nothing to do with it.

Julian glared down at his Chinese colleague, sensing more and more that he was trying to poach Charmaine away from them.

Once they reached the suite, Julian said, "Hungry, Pastor?"

Mark smiled cautiously. "I was told to bring my appetite with me."

Julian chuckled at the comment. "Do you like lobster thermidor? My wife and I had it the first day we were here. It was scrumptious."

"Sounds good."

"What would you like to drink with it?"

"Hot tea would be nice."

"And for dessert?"

"No dessert for me. The meal will be enough."

"Okay, as you wish."

Julian called room service and placed the order. Twenty-five minutes later, there was a knock on the door.

Julian rose from the sofa. "That was fast. They told me it would take at least an hour on the phone."

"I see," Pastor Lau said, and left it at that.

Julian opened the door. "Thanks for the quick delivery!" His voice was robust.

"You're welcome, sir," the sweaty-browed waiter said in reply, fully expecting a generous tip for his prompt service.

Julian didn't disappoint. He pressed a 50 dollar bill in his hand, and glanced at his counterpart to make sure he witnessed the cash exchange, hoping it might lead to his first step to living a more robust lifestyle again.

He thought to himself, *The many blessings this man's missing out on, and is fully entitled to, as one of God's earthly shepherds! With a little personal training, I could teach him how to live so much better, instead of squandering away so much!*

"Xie xie," the waiter said, leaving as quickly as he'd arrived.

Mark Lau remained unimpressed by any of it. This was yet another reminder that they didn't share the same spirit. Both men honored God with their lips. But he feared Julian's heart was far away from His Maker.

"Smells delicious. Would you bless the food, Pastor Lau?"

After Mark blessed the food, they ate in silence, until Julian finally came to the point, "I'm curious, Pastor, what was your motivation for inviting Charmaine to China?"

"I thought it might be good for her to see how Christians worship the One True God from a different perspective."

"By 'different perspective', do you mean underground?"

"That's part of it, sure."

Julian wasn't buying it. "Could the fact that she's so successful have anything to do with it? Is that why you asked her to sell your house?"

"What do you mean by that?"

"You know, hoping it might lead to her giving you so much more over time than she earned in commission?"

He can't be serious! "That had nothing to do with it, actually."

There was another prolonged silence, as the men ate their meals. Finally, Julian said, "Can I ask you something off the record?"

"Why off the record?"

"You know, with no one else listening..."

"I know what you mean. But even if others were here, my answer still wouldn't change regardless of question."

Julian practically rolled his eyes. "Why do you choose to live this way? At the end of the day, what's in it for you?"

Mark's face lit up. "Heaven!" Seeing Julian wasn't satisfied with his answer, he said. "Were you aware that I walked away from a successful engineering career back in Seattle, to preach the Word of God over here?"

"Yes, I heard. So why the vow of poverty?"

A glow appeared on his face that could have easily illuminated the subterranean church at which he pastored. "Jesus could have labeled me a lost cause and banished me to eternal suffering in hell. He would have been perfectly just if He did."

Lau became teary eyed and paused a moment to catch his breath. "But He didn't. Instead, He died for me, a sinner!

"What you see as tragic here in China, I see as God's blessing. While I didn't think that way when the government removed us from our church, seeing how God has worked so miraculously through the persecution of His saints, makes me grateful now that He allowed it to happen.

"So when I tell you all I want is Jesus, my words are one-hundred percent true. You can have this world and its many material trappings, Julian. it's no longer for me. All I want is Jesus. He is my treasure! He's my gift, my life!"

Pastor Lau wiped his mouth with a cloth napkin. "Now, may I ask why you felt the need to fly halfway around the world to check up on Charmaine? It's not like she came here to join a cult."

Kaito Fujimoto's face came to Julian's mind. "Can't be too sure these days, right?"

"Agreed. But you can rest assured knowing the things you hold so close to your heart no longer interest me in the least. And they never find their way into my preaching, not in a good way, anyway. I preach Christ crucified, nothing more."

"Of course, I preach that, too. That goes without saying," Julian said, almost dismissively. "But God also called me to preach the blessed lifestyle to my people. You saw the splendor of my church."

"Yes, I did…" came the reply, softly.

"Wait till you see it next time you're in Seattle! It'll be even bigger! God's about to really bless us again…"

"I know all about it. Charmaine told me…"

Julian stuck his chest out like a peacock's. "What can I say? I come from the United States of Amiracle!"

If his hope was to elicit laughter from Mark, it fell upon deaf ears. He brushed it off. "How can I make it clear to you, Pastor, the only treasures I seek are on the other side, the Good side, the eternal side?"

"Okay, humor me. What caused the sudden change of heart?"

"That's simple. It all came down to having a proper understanding of what the Bible teaches. In the past, your many possessions might have filled me with envy and resentment, but no longer. For where your heart is, your treasure is also…"

Julian snorted frustration. "I know that, Pastor but, come on, you and I both know it takes money to run a church, especially one as big as mine. Not to brag, but we need nearly a half million each month just to meet our overhead."

Lau took a sip of hot tea. "You'd be surprised at how little I live on. God has shown me over the years that it's not what I can live with that makes me most successful, but what I can live without."

Julian put a chunk of lobster in his mouth. He chewed on it a few times then swallowed it. "I admire you for putting such a positive spin on your meager situation, but let's be honest, you and I both know Charmaine could greatly benefit your situation here..."

Mark nodded agreement. "I'm sure she could, but that was never my focus for inviting her. If I really wanted money, the five-hundred thousand dollars from the sale of my house would have already been transferred here. Having the privilege of teaching her the Word of God is all I seek."

Julian sneered. "You make it sound so self-righteous..."

"Not at all. I'm curious, Julian, when was the last time you suffered for Jesus, I mean really suffered?"

"My life isn't as easy as you might think, Pastor. I have my share of enemies badmouthing me online and in the press. Some even protest outside my church on occasion."

Mark took a sip of his tea. "Why are they protesting?"

Julian frowned. "You know, the sermons I preach, my lavish lifestyle, and so on. Everyone at my church knows they're doing the devil's work. Still, it isn't always easy dealing with their hate speech.

"So, in that sense, I'm paying a steep price just like you. Which is why I feel so justified living the blessed lifestyle. I need to remove all suffering from my life so I can be more like the risen Christ."

Pastor Lau nearly choked on the tea in his mouth. "I've never heard anything so ridiculous in my life! It's remarkable how you and I read from the same Book, yet our interpretations of Scripture couldn't be more polarizing."

"You can say that again." This was said with the same, condescending tone Julian had used before.

Mark looked briefly down at his plate. "I don't see the point in preaching on things that won't mean anything fifty years from now..."

"What do you mean by that?"

Mark looked him squarely in the eye. "Whereas you define success in worldly riches, my success comes from winning souls to Jesus."

Julian's face reddened. "Are you saying I preach a false gospel?"

"Based on what I experienced at your church, and from the words you speak now, how could I not?"

"Stay away from Charmaine!" Julian snapped. "Thanks to you, she's all messed up in the head. I see it in her eyes!"

"Messed up?"

"Look, I'm asking you nicely not to make it any worse for her!"

"You're giving me too much credit, Julian. I had nothing to do with the changes you see in her. It's beyond my control. Yours too, for that matter. This kind of transformation can only be attributed to the work of the Holy Spirit.

"Besides, Charmaine's old enough to decide for herself what's best for her, and where God wants her to go from here. All I want is to see her keep growing in Christ Jesus. Nothing more. Her money has nothing to do with it." Mark searched Julian's eyes very carefully. "Can you say the same?"

Julian shook his head in disgust. He became puffed up with pride. "Oh, I see, you think you're better than me, is that it?"

Mark shook his head. "I'm just a sinner saved by God's grace. Nothing more."

Julian scoffed, "I know, a redeemed wretch, right?"

"Precisely!"

Julian became even more red-faced. "You're a real piece of work!"

"For that, I can only praise God for His Divine sanctification."

"Something smells fishy, and it's not the lobster thermidor."

"I agree with you there, Julian."

"I can't seem to wrap my mind around how you could possibly blame God for all that's happened in your country! Frankly, as a Christian, I find it offensive."

"Blame Him? Offensive?"

"Let me rephrase. It's hard for me to believe the God we both serve, who Himself is 'love', would let so much persecution befall His supposed children over here…"

Ignoring the "supposed" part, Lau replied, "Do you believe God is sovereign?"

"Of course, I do."

"Okay, so as a sovereign Being, if He wanted to prevent it from happening, nothing could come against Him, right?"

Julian shook his head, sensing where his dinner guest was going with all this…

"God could have prevented it, Julian, but He allowed it to continue for a reason. I confess at the outset, my constant prayer was that He would remove this dark cloud from us, so we could keep serving Him.

"It took a while, but once I saw things more clearly, I knew it was done to strengthen not weaken us. How could we be angry with God when our faith has grown by leaps and bounds underground? Just as importantly, the things of this world have become smaller and smaller to us."

Julian wiped his mouth with a cloth napkin. "No disrespect, Mark, but how can you be absolutely sure it isn't His judgment on you, for having such weak faith?"

"Weak faith? Are you kidding me?" Mark took a few deep breaths to calm himself down.

"Sorry, just trying to get you to see things from my perspective."

"You want perspective, Julian? Okay, here it is: Try telling the many here languishing in prison they have weak faith! Some have lost vital organs which were sold after being harvested." *Wonder how long you'd last in prison before caving in and renouncing Jesus, just to be free again?*

"It took being persecuted, Julian, fiercely persecuted, to finally learn to take God at His full Word in every situation, whether good or bad. How about you? Can you say the same?"

Julian looked at his watch. "Of course. Doesn't my lifestyle prove that much?"

Pastor Lau sighed. Clearly, they weren't on the same page. "Let me ask, would you still trust God if He took everything away from you?"

"Of course! But as you know, Mark, we all represent the Body of Christ. We all have different talents and gifts. God called me to be a city on a hill, a bright and shiny beacon for everyone within the greater Seattle vicinity to see..." *Not a basement dweller like you!*

Mark shook his head in frustration. "Christ's words weren't meant from a structural standpoint, Julian. We are called to be the cities on a hill, not the buildings at which we gather."

Julian became more firm. "Listen, you may be called to suffer, but squandering away many blessings isn't God's plan for me."

Mark rubbed his chin. "What if I told you if anyone was squandering away God's greatest blessings, it was you..."

Julian snorted, then rolled his eyes. *Now I've heard everything! Clearly, this man's delusional.* "If you say so..."

"Hear me out, Julian. How do you plan on explaining to God, on Judgment Day, how you squandered away so much money that was meant to further God's kingdom here on earth?"

When Julian didn't comment, Mark went on, "The simple truth is when life is perfect, as your life seems to so many people, there's no need to seek the Lord's comfort. Why should you when you have enough worldly comfort for a thousand people?

"The greatest comfort in my life is the eternal assurance I have through Christ Jesus. God's truest blessings are found on the other side of the grave for those who are truly saved."

"I'm not one of your followers, Mark, I'm a pastor too..."

"I have no followers. The only One we follow is Christ. I'm one of His under-shepherds only. Sorry to have to say this, Julian, but your critics don't attack you because you follow Jesus, they attack you for turning your church into a perpetual money machine for you and your wife...

"The persecution we face is infinitely more intense and has nothing to do with worldly riches. We're persecuted for preaching the Truth, nothing more! There's no comparing the two."

Julian became angry. "Do you have any idea how many salvations take place at my church every Sunday, on average?"

"No I don't. Neither do you, for that matter. Only God knows the heart. And do you mean salvations or conversions?"

"Hmmm....What's the difference between the two?"

Pastor Lau sighed. "In a word: eternal."

Julian pushed back from the table. "I think you should go now..."

"As you wish..."

31

MEANWHILE, THINGS WEREN'T GOING much better for Charmaine and Imogen. The driver took them to Nanjing Road.

After Imogen had inquired, he had recommended a popular restaurant named Taikang Dumpling.

As it turned out, it was a good choice. The food was as delicious as the driver had promised. But it was there that everything took a turn for the worse. Again. The food had nothing to do with it.

Halfway through the meal, a meal that was spent mostly in silence, Imogen reached for Charmaine's hand. "Not to come across as insensitive, but we're really worried about you. Sure you're okay?"

Charmaine smiled. "I appreciate the concern, Imogen, I really do, but in truth, I've never been better. I never expected this trip to be so life-transforming. I'll never be the same..."

"How do you expect me to take that?"

"I'm still processing it all. But one of the most seismic differences between our church and Pastor Lau's could be found in Julian's recent Facebook post."

Imogen looked confused. "Which one?"

"You know, where he reminded us, much like he does at the monthly prayer sessions, that Jesus died for the new homes and vehicles we seek. How many times has he followed that statement up with Jesus' last words, 'It is finished', as if that's why Christ died for sinners?"

Charmaine glanced out the restaurant window. "I saw it while riding the elevator up to my room, after my second underground service. You know I always share your posts, oftentimes without even reading them. That's how blind my loyalty has been to you both all these years."

Charmaine saw the smug look on Imogen's face but ignored it. "After spending time with persecuted Christians who have nothing, I realized just how shallow and self-serving his post really was...and deceptive!

"I mean, could obtaining material possessions really be the reason why Christ died on the cross two-thousand years ago? Now, before you tell me my friends in China lack faith, let me just say it's by choice they have nothing. A lack of faith or talent has nothing at all to do with it."

Charmaine closed her eyes and shook her head. "Even more disturbing than your husband's post was the steady stream of replies I read back in my hotel room. It sickened me. Especially after reading Mrs. Davenport's lengthy reply to his post about wanting a million dollars, a new house, a vacation home in the Cascade Mountains, two new cars, and on and on.

"She even numbered her desires in chronological order." Charmaine looked at Imogen, who was clearly frustrated. "Wanna know what number six was?"

Imogen stared back as if she wasn't sure she wanted to know. Finally, she shrugged her shoulders. "What was it?"

"That God would restore her marriage and deliver her husband from alcoholism. I know you saw it; you 'heart' liked it and commented, 'You go girl! You gotta dream big to achieve big!'"

Imogen grew defensive. Charmaine was even more belligerent now than she was back at the hotel the day before. She never dared disrespect her like this back in the States. It made her loathe Mark Lau even more. "You know how badly he treats her when he's drunk."

Charmaine took a deep breath and, as calmly as she could, went on, "That's not the point, Imogen. They're married! Since they're one in God's eyes, shouldn't the salvation of his soul and his deliverance from alcoholism have been her first prayer request, instead of number six?"

Imogen looked away in embarrassment.

"Even without focusing on number six, the Davenport's are on a fixed income. Like many at our church, they live well beyond their means and can barely pay their bills. Yet, she faithfully sows into the church, hoping she'll be the next one to be financially blessed.

"Nellie recently confided in me after a Wednesday night Bible study that the Davenports were in over their heads in debt trying to finance their lavish lifestyle, until God finally blessed them with great riches. She said they were never in debt before joining the church.

"When I met with Mrs. Davenport, she assured me she wasn't being negative and it wasn't a lack of faith on her part. Even with her husband's daily struggle with alcoholism, she assured me she had total faith that everything she kept praying for would one day be hers."

Charmaine shook her head in disgust. "I listened to her, but the lack of results in her life caused me not to believe her. Wanna know how I tried fixing the situation?"

Imogen stared at Charmaine incredulously, but remained silent.

"I told her to rebuke the creditors calling her at all hours of the day, until she could finally pay them. This was yet another act of blind loyalty on my part, to you and your husband."

Charmaine momentarily looked up at the ceiling before her eyes centered on Imogen again. "I can't tell you how much I regret it now. If I could have a do-over, the conversation would be so much different."

"In what way?"

"Well, for starters, Imogen, I wouldn't have your backs this time. Do you remember my comment to your post?"

When Imogen gasped and looked away, Charmaine pressed on, "To know God better, and to be contented with what I already have, without being envious of the things I don't have, plain and simple. I owe this radical change of thinking to Pastor Lau's teachings...

"The thing is, had I gone to Paris instead of China, I no doubt would have shared Julian's post all over social media, declaring even bigger and better things for myself, hoping newcomers to the church would follow my lead and do the same."

Charmaine looked down at her dinner plate. "How blinded I was! This 'Fake-it-until-you-make-it' approach we use isn't biblical. You know better than me that the vast majority at our church aren't wealthy by any stretch of the imagination. It's like all we're doing is selling them lottery tickets. Where's the Godliness without contentment?"

Imogen scratched her head in disgust. How much more pride could she possibly swallow?

"It saddens me realizing how I'd placed my worldly possessions above the Lord, in that I used them as tools, visuals even, to recruit others to join the church, by promising that they, too, could obtain the very same blessings I had, by becoming members themselves.

"Not only is this false advertising on our end, where's the Gospel message in that approach, Imogen? Where's the denying 'self' and carrying our crosses daily? What about the suffering for our faith?"

Imogen folded her arms across her chest.

"I've lost so many eternal rewards over the years, from constantly letting my left hand know what my right hand was doing, just to be praised by others for my kindness and generosity.

"When I think back to the last prayer meeting at our church, when I rudely disrupted the service, even as many still had their heads bowed in

235

prayer, so I could brag about something that should have been kept a secret between myself and God all along, I want to vomit."

Charmaine lowered her head in shame. "Then to call Kaito as everyone listened, as I made my intentions known to him, it was the height of pride and arrogance on my part. I'm sure you still remember…

"But what pains me even more than that is wondering how many people I prayed with over the years, to receive Christ as Lord and Savior, who are just as lost now as they were when I prayed for them.

"It's not a good feeling knowing I'm guilty of creating false converts who honor God with their lips, but their hearts are far away from Him.

"Oh, how I wish I could take back every falsehood I'd ever spread about the Word of God, and replace it with the true Gospel message. It's like a knife in my heart. Those days are over!

"Not only is the 'blessed and highly favored' mindset I've harbored all these years idolatrous and self-centered, it's a slap in the face to the multitudes of Christians in prison, not to mention the multitudes of others who are dirt poor—who have nothing—yet are storing up vast treasures for themselves in Heaven.

"Such blessings can never be measured in worldly terms." Charmaine eyeballed Imogen. "Now that I understand the true Gospel message, if ever there were hero servants, it's them."

Imogen scoffed. She looked offended.

"This is going to sting a bit, but the church I've loved so much, that was such a huge part of my life for seven years, has done more damage to my walk with God than good. It sickens me knowing the bright and shiny edifice that used to feed my soul, and make me feel so proud, now seems so dark and gloomy. It no longer appeals to me."

Imogen looked like she was about to burst out in tears.

"I want you to know I don't blame the two of you for my past actions. I was a willing participant in the prosperity scheme you teach. Therefore, I'm just as guilty myself. Achieving success had become a form of worship all to itself, a recruiting tool, which I now see as mass idolatry at the highest levels."

Sighing, she said, "Another thing I learned in China was that the two of you had become idols to me. In a way, I even idolized myself…"

Imogen blinked hard. Before she could reply, Charmaine said, "It's true. The view I had of myself, the church, and the two of you was off the charts." She shook her head remorsefully. "You know, it's funny, all those addiction classes we have at church for our struggling members that I thought I never needed, I realize I need more than most.

"Only my addiction wasn't drugs or alcohol or gambling or pornography. It was my constant strive for success. How could I ever truly be contented when I always wanted a little more? I praise God for using Pastor Lau to deliver me from my serious success addiction…"

Imogen's eyes grew wide with shock. "What? Did you just say success addiction?"

"Yes."

Imogen snorted. "I've never heard anything more ridiculous in all my life! You've said many outlandish things since we arrived, but this has to be the most outlandish so far. I wish to go back to the hotel."

"What about shopping?"

"I'm no longer in the mood. Besides, Julian took me shopping last night after he parted company with you. We went to Huaihai Road and had the most wonderful time! We spent a fortune…"

If Imogen was trying to make her feel guilty or jealous, it wasn't working. If anything, Charmaine felt this deeply increasing pain in her heart for her two pastors.

Imogen paid the bill and they left the restaurant.

The limousine driver looked in his rearview mirror. "Where to, ladies?"

Imogen looked at Charmaine, who shrugged her shoulders. "Take us back to the hotel at once."

"As you wish…" The driver was mildly surprised at how quickly her mood had changed. He wasn't expecting to take them back to the hotel until the wee hours of the night.

The last time he experienced something similar, was when he drove a European couple to the casino. They were the happiest couple on earth on the way in, but the most miserable couple on the way out, much like the two women in the back seat now.

He wondered what had caused the sudden mood change. He wasn't about to ask. His job was to drive them from A to B. Nothing more.

Charmaine was about to make things even worse. "I want you to know I'm cutting my trip short."

Imogen's eyes widened. "Really?" When are you leaving?"

"Tomorrow morning."

"Why?"

"I'd like to be home for my birthday, so I can spend it with Rodney. I also want to apologize again to Meredith." What Charmaine didn't say was she wanted to get away from them.

Imogen looked more hurt than shocked. "What's your flight number?"

"I can't remember. I think it leaves at noon, connecting through Hong Kong. I'll leave the hotel at nine."

Charmaine hated dumping so much on Imogen, especially since she was 5 months pregnant, but these things needed to be said.

Hopefully, God would use her loving rebuke to finally open Imogen's eyes spiritually, so she would finally see how off track she was…

When they arrived back at the Waldorf Astoria, the mood was somber. Imogen tipped the driver and went inside the lobby without saying another word to Charmaine. She was too upset to talk!

"Well, good night then. Hope you and Julian have a blessed and restful evening."

Yeah, sure you do!

As Charmaine went back to her suite to pack her things, Imogen sat on the couch next to her husband. Julian didn't need to ask how it went with Charmaine. The downtrodden expression on her face, not to mention that she came back empty handed, meant there was no need to ask.

After a while, his curiosity got the best of him. "Well?"

Imogen frowned. "It's worse than we thought, honey! I can't take her criticisms anymore."

Julian rubbed his wife's throbbing back. "I know."

"It's gotten to where I don't want to be around her anymore, at least not until whatever's taken root in her soul eventually passes."

Imogen craned her neck back to see her husband. "Are you ready for her latest bombshell?" Before Julian could answer, she said, "She's decided to cut her trip short, and will be leaving in the morning."

"What?"

"You heard me…"

Julian panicked. "Could you imagine the potential damage she could do by sharing her experience with everyone at church, especially if we're not there to defend ourselves? We need to find out what flight she's taking and transfer our tickets."

"You do it, honey, I'm too stressed and tired…"

Julian kissed his wife on the lips. "Rest now, my love, I'll take care of everything. By the way, my meeting didn't go much better than yours…"

238

Imogen sighed and left it alone.

After the evening she just had, she didn't want to know a single detail of her husband's meeting with that man! She hated Mark Lau for what he did to Charmaine and, to a lesser extent, to Meredith Geiger.

Every premonition Imogen had about the so-called pastor pointed in one direction—he was a wolf in sheep's clothing...

32

CHARMAINE WOKE EXTRA EARLY to meet Pastor Lau at 6 a.m. at the hotel for breakfast. It sounded mean, but her hope was that they could finish breakfast and Mark could leave the hotel before the Martíns saw him. If they bumped into each other, nothing good would come of it.

She was standing by the gingerbread table, sniffing in the tantalizing aroma from the house made of pure chocolate, when he arrived. Her face lit up when he entered the hotel lobby. "Good morning, Pastor!"

"Good morning to you, as well." They embraced.

Once they were seated, Charmaine wasted no time inquiring. "So, how'd it go last night with Julian? I'm dying to know." She was careful not to say, "Pastor."

"Let me put it this way, when it comes to being ordered to leave places by pastors at your church, I'm still batting a thousand! Or should I say, three strikes I'm out!"

Charmaine wasn't surprised, but you'd never know it by the shocked expression on her face. "Are you saying he asked you to leave?"

"Yes. He basically thinks I invited you here to take advantage of you. He even said the reason I let you sell my house was so it would ultimately benefit my situation down the road. Something along those lines."

Charmaine knew what he meant by "situation". He meant his church.

Mark looked at the ala carte menu. "How was your shopping excursion with Imogen?"

"It never happened. We made it as far as Nanjing Road. Everything quickly soured at the restaurant we ate at. By the time we finished our meals, Imogen was so disgusted, she wanted to go back to the hotel."

"Truth be told, I had trouble sleeping last night. I felt bad for unloading on her so much, especially with her being pregnant and all. But I wanted her to know how I felt before returning to our busy lives back home. She needs to know the changes in me are real and permanent."

Mark let his kind eyes settle on Charmaine. "Did you tell her in love?"

"I think so. I hope so."

"Let me just say that while I strongly disagree with the government's opposition to the Christian faith, my hope is that I'll never turn the mission field into the enemy, despite that they put hate in my heart at times. The same is true with your pastors and much of what they teach."

Charmaine looked confused. "Okay, so what approach should I take with the people at my church? If I even remain there, that is…"

"First, let me say that I believe one of the hardest people to convert are those who think they're saved but really aren't. But I also believe there isn't a heart anywhere on the planet that God cannot conquer.

"There's no life He cannot change. No past He cannot forgive. And Christ would never reject anyone who came to Him sincerely and repentantly broken. After all, he saved us, right?"

Charmaine nodded, then became teary-eyed.

"Our hearts must never stop aching for anyone going through the motions of Christianity without ever seeing the Light of the true Gospel. If we're going to win them to Christ, we must do it in love…"

"Once again, pastor, you're spot on. I'm really going to miss your preaching."

"You will be greatly missed as well."

Charmaine wiped her eyes with a tissue, then pulled a wad of cash from her handbag. Keeping a hundred dollars for herself, she placed the rest—$2,700 to be exact—in Pastor Lau's hands. "Please accept this as a blessing for being such a blessing in my life!"

Mark's face lit up. "Thanks so much for your kind generosity. I'm most grateful. How would you like the funds to be used?"

"However God puts it on your heart. All I ask is that we keep it between us."

Pastor Lau broke into the warmest of smiles. "Absolutely! I'm sure Kaito never told you he gives ten percent of what he earns to help fund this ministry, above his tithes to his church. Am I right?"

Charmaine shrugged her shoulders. "I had no idea…"

"Well, since I'm the one telling you, he's in no danger of losing a reward in Heaven. Even so, knowing him, I know he'd rather keep it a private matter, between God, himself and me…"

Charmaine took a sip of milk tea. "Now that I'm heading back to my lavish lifestyle, how can I keep from being tempted by the worldly things that had such a huge grip on me for so many years?"

"Good question, and an easy one to answer. By always focusing on the life to come. If the earth is God's footstool, how indescribably majestic will Heaven be for all who end up there?

"Not even the most beautiful house on the planet on the most beautiful beach can compare to what awaits us on the other side, Charmaine.

"Mostly because the church has all but abandoned teaching about a final destination from our pulpits, we are perhaps the first generation of Christians who have lost sight of our long term goal, which is to finally go Home and be with our Creator.

"How tragic that so many Christians are so comfortable and have become so deeply entrenched in this fallen world, that they rarely give eternity or Heaven a passing thought. Everyone wants to go to Heaven, but they live as if they never want to die. Last time I checked, the only way anyone can go to Heaven is by dying in the flesh."

Charmaine chuckled softly. "Very good point, you make."

"Now, when it comes to describing God's eternal domain, like all Christians, my knowledge is limited. The Bible provides us with many clues, but certainly not enough to form a complete composite.

"But here's something I do know—the gifts God placed in us for His glory and for the furthering of His Kingdom here on earth, are the very things we will bring into eternity with us. Imagine looking and feeling our very best in a place where we will never grow tired of worshipping God the Father, Jesus the Son, and the Holy Spirit...

"Not only that, we'll have the ability to think in Heaven, feel and emote, but without ever shedding tears, getting sick or battling boredom. The instant you step into eternity, you will still be you; but not the sinless you. No, you'll be the redeemed version of yourself, personality and all!"

Mark Lau shook his head in amazement. "I don't know about you, but this excites me very much."

A smile curled onto Charmaine's lips. "Just the thought that Jesus is preparing mansions for us in Heaven is cause for excitement..."

"Well, some translations say 'mansions' while other translations say 'rooms'. Personally, I never think about the size of the place Jesus is preparing just for me. All I know is it will be perfectly suited for me in every way, which means I'll be perfectly satisfied with every last detail.

"First Corinthians two, verse nine declares, '...No eye has seen, no ear has heard, no mind has conceived what God has prepared for those who love Him.'" Mark's face was aglow. "In that light, regardless of how big or small the place Jesus is preparing for me may be, I know I will be perfectly satisfied with it.

"Remember, I went from living in a four-bedroom house in the States to a studio apartment here. I can't fully express how much I have come to love my tiny living space.

"What makes it so special is that I get to spend intimate time with my Savior, without dealing with life's many interruptions. I think this is a good analogy of what awaits us on the other side. It's not the size of the place that will matter, but that Jesus prepared it for us."

"Wow!" Tears rushed to Charmaine's eyes.

Pastor Lau shook his head. "How could anyone choose the things of this world over that? Yes indeed, Heaven will truly be our greatest adventure! Our best days are still ahead of us!

"So, let me ask, when was the last time you introduced someone to Jesus, with no strings attached, hoping that God would rescue them not only from hell, but also from their sins, without bringing perfect health and wealth into the equation?"

Charmaine looked sad. "Not sure if I've ever done that, Pastor."

"The more you focus on the grand prize—Heaven with Jesus—the easier it will be for you to properly witness and win souls for Him. That's my challenge to you once you arrive back in the States."

Charmaine beamed. "Challenge accepted!"

"Very good. With these truths settled in your mind, how would you like to leave this planet? In other words, what's the last thing you would ever want to do, before stepping foot inside Heaven?"

Charmaine scratched her chin. "Hmm, that's a good question. Perhaps donate a large amount of money to a good cause."

Mark nodded thoughtfully. "As for me, what could be better than leading someone to faith in Christ just moments before stepping foot into eternity, and meeting Jesus face to face?"

Wow! Charmaine dabbed at her eyes with a cloth napkin. "Thanks for letting God use you so mightily on my behalf, Pastor. Lord willing, I'll get to come back and worship with you again in the future."

Pastor Lau said, "If it's God's will for you to come back, there isn't a force in all the universe that can prevent it from happening."

"Amen to that!" Charmaine took another sip of her milk tea. "By the way, when I get home, I plan on sending more money so you can print more Bibles and booklets in Mandarin. How can I do it?"

Mark's face lit up again. "Kaito has all my banking information in the States. If God puts it on your heart to donate, he can surely help you."

"Ever since you told me about your friend who's now in prison for smuggling Bibles into China, it's been on my heart to help you."

"I assure you it's a worthy cause. Your reward in Heaven will be great!"

Tears flooded Charmaine's eyes again. "After forfeiting so many eternal rewards over the years, your words comfort me to no end, Pastor."

"Glory to God," came the reply.

Toward the end of the meal, Julian joined them. "Good morning!"

Charmaine was startled by his voice. "Good morning, Pastor. We've already finished eating, but you're welcome to join us…"

"It's okay," Julian said, flatly. "I'll eat later with Imogen. Just wanted you to know we've decided to head back today as well. We even managed to get booked on the same flight as you."

Charmaine gasped. Her pulse raced in her ears.

Noticing the "*how-did-you-know-what-flight-I'm-taking*" look on her face, Julian said, "It wasn't too difficult. You told Imogen your flight was around noon, connecting through Hong Kong."

Charmaine shot a desperate look at Mark. He lowered his head.

Julian knew he'd just touched a nerve. But as her pastor, it was time to pull in the reins. She was already too far out there for twenty people.

He shot a quick, angry glance at Pastor Lau, before his eyes settled back onto Charmaine. "Anyway, just wanted to give you a head's up. No need to worry about transportation. We can share a limo ride to the airport. Let's meet at the concierge desk at nine. Okay?"

Charmaine sighed, then nodded sadly, angrily…

When Julian left them, she said, "See what I mean? They won't leave me alone. I'm surprised but not surprised that they are also leaving."

Mark said, "I should go now. My flock awaits me."

Charmaine started weeping. "Whether I remain at my church or not, I want you to know from this moment on I'll always consider you my real pastor. If I didn't live halfway around the world, I'd join your church in a heartbeat!"

"So kind of you to say, Charmaine. To God be the glory!"

"I know that, Pastor. But you were the one He chose to straighten me out spiritually. Despite the recent fallout with Meredith and my pastors, which I can only assume is spiritual persecution, I wish to thank you from the deepest chambers of my heart for inviting me to your city.

"The impact's been nothing short of profound! Thanks to you, I believe in the eternal assurance I have in Christ Jesus. Like you told me underground," she said, in a soft whisper, "it makes all the difference!"

Tears flooded Mark's eyes. His joy knew no bounds.

They embraced.

Mark wiped his eyes with a napkin. "If we don't see each other again on this side, we'll surely see each other again on the other side."

"Amen to that, Pastor! Either way, I'll look forward to it very much."

"Me too."

After one more endearing embrace, Charmaine said, "Time for me to finish packing."

"And time for me to go to work. God bless and keep you always."

"You, as well, Pastor."

Mark Lau left the Waldorf Astoria Hotel not knowing how prophetic his words would turn out to be...

33

THE LIMOUSINE RIDE TO THE airport was tension-filled, to say the least. Charmaine was annoyed that her pastors managed to get booked on the very same flight she would be on.

She felt manipulated, spied on, as if they were the Chinese government and she was one of their defiant citizens.

The guilt she felt for hurting their feelings the past three days was replaced with agitation. *Should I tell them? Oh, why not!*

"When I get home, I plan on wiring some of the money I've earmarked for the church-expansion project to Pastor Lau, so he can purchase Bibles that have been properly translated for his fellow countrymen and women."

Julian blinked hard, then shrugged his shoulders in silence.

Imogen answered for her husband. "How much is some?" Her tone made it crystal clear that she was still furious. She eyeballed Charmaine. The Adidas warm up suit she had on was a good choice for the long flight, but the "Shanghai" baseball cap was a bit much.

"I'm still praying about it, but I know it's what God wants me to do."

When Pastor Julian grimaced, Charmaine said, "Did you hear me, Pastor? The money will be used to print Bibles in this country…"

Julian snapped, "I knew he was swindling you! I even told you that!"

Charmaine grew more incredulous. *Really?* "Hmm, if you must know, in the week I was here, he never once asked me for anything."

Charmaine saw the stinging pain in her pastor's eyes. She felt bad, but not enough to apologize for wanting to give money to print properly translated Bibles and other booklets in China?

Surely that would be better stewardship on her part than renovating and expanding a church she now believed preached a false gospel message to the multitudes who hoped to be blessed and highly favored like their pastors. *Don't turn the mission field into the enemy!*

Charmaine braced herself when Julian's face went flush in disbelief. He gulped hard but remained silent. "Don't worry, anything I give won't interfere with my regular tithing. So long as I'm a member of your church, I'll keep tithing faithfully. Aside from that, I'm free to send offerings to wherever God leads me."

So long as she's a member? Julian thought about the others who'd left the church after being exposed to Mark Lau's false teachings, including some of his most faithful tithers. "Are you thinking about leaving?"

"I didn't say that. I'm just saying…"

Imogen looked out the window, totally put off by the one who used to be one of their best students. "Are you saying our new church expansion is unworthy of your giving?"

"First of all, it's the third renovation since I've been there. Not that I'm keeping score, but if I'm not mistaken, not counting those in the front rows with the greatest means, I've probably contributed more to those projects than most other members have over the years."

Imogen glared at her. "The church is grateful to you for that, Charmaine, not to mention God Almighty Himself."

Really? "Not to sound disrespectful, Pastor, but shouldn't helping persecuted Christians here in China be more important than renovating a building that already outshines all others in our city?"

Julian asked, "Can you at least wait until we get back to the States before doing something you may end up regretting?"

Charmaine sighed. *Regretting?* "Can I ask you something, Pastors?"

"Shoot."

"Are either of you willing to die for your faith in Jesus?" Charmaine had already asked Julian this question the other day back at the hotel. But she wanted to see their joint reactions.

Imogen snorted loudly. "What kind of question is that? Of course, we would! Jesus is our Lord and Savior!"

"Would either of you willingly go to prison for Him?"

Pastor Julian winced. He was caught completely off guard by her follow up question. "Yes, of course!"

Charmaine wasn't convinced. "I've had lots of time to think about those two questions. It saddens me to say before coming here, I don't think I would have willingly gone to prison for my belief in Jesus."

Imogen practically rolled her eyes. "What are you getting at?"

"Please hear me out, Pastors. Because my faith was rooted more in the world than in the Word, if our church was ever raided, like Pastor Lau's was, and we were thrown in jail for our faith, I don't think I'd have the strength to stay in prison like many here willingly do.

"Honestly, it would be difficult going from a privileged lifestyle to prison. Sadly, I think I speak for most members at our church."

247

Imogen looked at her husband, before her eyes resettled on Charmaine. "I don't follow you."

"Many of Pastor Lau's good friends and fellow pastors are serving long prison sentences for their faith in Jesus. Initially, all they had to do was renounce Christ and they could leave their jail cells."

Charmaine studied their faces very carefully. "But they didn't. It made me wonder what we would do if it ever happened to us. I'd like to think I'd be strong at first…"

"Meaning?"

"Personally, Imogen, if I knew I always had the option to leave, just knowing I could still be forgiven the way Peter was after denying Christ three times, it would provide me with a false strength.

"But what if the day came when that option was taken off the table? What if after a few weeks, my jailers told me it was now or never, meaning either I renounce Jesus or spend many years in jail?

"How can we call ourselves blessed and highly favored if we're unwilling to suffer for our Savior, to include going to prison, if it ever came to that? Pastor Lau taught me that this life wasn't meant to be our best ever. That will come on the other side in Heaven."

Julian grabbed his knees and squeezed them. "What are you getting at, Charmaine?"

"If my Maker wants me to suffer for His glory, I'm now willing to deny 'self' and carry my cross daily. How about you?"

He rolled his eyes. "Of course! I'm your pastor!"

Once again, Charmaine wasn't convinced. "I'd like your permission to speak to the church when I get back, about taking up a collection for properly translated Bibles to send to China…"

Pastor Julian frowned inwardly, then glanced at his wife. All Imogen could do was shrug her shoulders. His eyes volleyed back to Charmaine, "I don't see a problem with that, once we finish with our campaign…"

You don't see a problem with that? Charmaine was completely blown away by his reply. "Campaign or not, I'm sure you can see the great need over here, right?"

Julian sighed. "Yes, of course, we do…"

"Good. I know you can't speak for the others, but as our lead pastors, you can set a good example by giving a sizable offering to the cause. If anyone can afford to donate, it's you. I've never refused to give to your campaigns. So, how much can I put you down for?"

Julian glanced at his wife as if Charmaine had just asked him to donate a kidney.

Imogen rolled her eyes in disgust again.

Julian said to Charmaine, "Let's discuss it further when we get back home. Like I said, we have our own fundraising campaign to think about."

"Okay, sure. As you wish." Charmaine had no further questions. What was the point? It was increasingly evident that they were no longer on the same page, at least not spiritually. Her concern for her two pastors had just risen to greater heights. Her spirit silently grieved for them...

They rode in silence the remainder of the way to the airport.

Charmaine sent a text message to Rodney: *Sorry for the limited contact the past few days. Please don't think I was ignoring you. I needed this alone time with the Lord. It's been life-transforming. I have so much to tell you that needs to be said in person. Here's the updated flight info. Hope to see you soon, sweetness. Love you...*

After practically ignoring him all week, Charmaine just hoped her boyfriend would be at Sea-Tac Airport to receive her when she landed...

34

HONG KONG INTERNATIONAL AIRPORT

THE NINETY-MINUTE FLIGHT southwest, from Shanghai to Hong Kong, went rather smoothly. After much finagling on his part, Julian managed to upgrade Charmaine from business to first class, even securing the seat next to Imogen's for her to occupy.

Julian sat to her left, separated by an aisle. In her former life—before going to China—to be precise, she would have been extremely grateful for the upgrade, honored even, especially being seated so closely to her two spiritual mentors. But not now.

Charmaine felt trapped and couldn't wait to finally get away from them, so she could think things through without them breathing down her neck. The last thing she wanted was to be ganged-up on again. She wasn't in the mood to defend herself from yet another spiritual debate with the Martíns. It could wait until they were back in the States.

But the main reason Charmaine didn't want to be seated with them was that she had so much to think and pray about. That plus she had every intention of poring over the many pages of notes she took in the few short, blessed days she was fortunate to worship underground with brothers and sisters she loved so dearly, and considered more of her church family than even her church family back in Seattle.

With this new hungering and thirsting to know her Maker even more intimately, she would have preferred reading her Bible on the relatively short flight. But the last thing she needed was to be labeled a Christian by the Chinese government, and potentially spied on, if she was blessed to return to Shanghai in the future. Lord willing…

Once her connecting flight—which wasn't on a Chinese carrier—was over international waters, she had every intention of reading straight out of the Bible, without fear of being spied on by the Chinese government.

Thankfully, the many pages of notes she took kept her plenty occupied on the plane. Even better, Imogen slept for most of the flight. A shiny gold-colored sequin sleep mask covered the upper part of her face and forehead.

Travelling halfway around the world five months pregnant had finally caught up to her. Or perhaps she was suffering from a shopping hangover.

Or maybe it was stress from being totally disrespected the past few days. It was probably a combination of all three...

Julian, on the other hand, was fidgety and kept shifting his weight in his seat, as if waiting for the perfect time to give one last spiel, to hopefully snap her out of whatever had taken root in her soul underground, so the Charmaine everyone knew and loved would resurface before they returned to the States.

Charmaine could almost see the words flowing up his throat and pressing on his lips, begging to be released. She caught him frequently peeking at her notes, curious as ever to know what she was reading.

She made no effort to shield them from him. She even tilted the pages to give him a better vantage point. If each page was full of Truth, why hide it?

Her hope was that the words on the sheets of paper might serve to convict him deep in his spirit, and create in him a true spirit of repentance, for preaching what she now knew was a false gospel for so many years.

Upon clearing customs at Hong Kong International Airport, she quickly realized her wish wouldn't be coming true anytime soon.

Much like he did in Shanghai, Julian tried pouring on the charm with a female ticket agent, doing all he could to have Charmaine upgraded to first class again.

"I'm sorry, sir. There are no available seats. As it is, the flight is overbooked." This was said very sweetly, empathetically even.

Julian pleaded with her, "Please, do me this favor. I'm a very powerful individual. I'm the lead pastor at one of the biggest and most successful churches in America."

The woman seemed unimpressed with his boastful words, but nevertheless flashed another courteous smile, exposing deep-set dimples on her cheeks. "I wish I could accommodate your request, sir, but again, the flight is overbooked."

Julian ignored her words and snorted frustration, which did nothing to help the situation.

Pausing to let his tone settle, he placed a hand on Charmaine's shoulder. "See this woman? She's one of the top members at my church. I'd really hate to see her confined to coach class for the long flight back to the States. I'm sure there's something you can do for me. I'm willing to pay whatever the amount."

The ticket agent nodded politely at Charmaine.

Charmaine looked down at the floor. She no longer desired, let alone drew comfort from, Julian's flowery words. "Actually, my seat's in business class…"

The ticket agent said, "We're offering free flight vouchers for anyone willing to take a later flight back to Seattle. If the three of you would be willing to give up your seats, I'm sure I can accommodate your request on a later flight to the States."

Before Charmaine could answer, Julian became visibly irate. "No, we're not willing! Can't you see my wife's five months pregnant?" he snapped. *Not a chance!* He glared at her. "Did you hear what I said? I'm willing to pay any price!"

Charmaine was mortified at how determined he was to have his way with her, and wished she could somehow shrink away from the conversation. She didn't want to wait for a later flight, either, but only because she didn't want to spend even more time with the Martíns than was absolutely necessary.

The courteous smile on the woman's face vanished, replaced with a more stern expression. "I heard you loud and clear, sir. As you can see, there are many others in line waiting to be checked in. Aside from taking a later flight, there's nothing more I can do for you. Sorry." *You may not be busy, but I am!*

Julian wanted to keep pleading with her, but her tone of voice conveyed to him that the conversation was over. His eyes suddenly became uncomfortably intense. He pounded the counter, startling the poor woman by his unprovoked aggression. "I'd like to speak to your supervisor."

"Sure, sir. If you would kindly wait over there, someone will be with you shortly." *Americans!*

Charmaine grimaced. This was a sad moment for her. As one of God's preachers, wasn't he supposed to be above this sort of erratic behavior, especially when out in public? Where was the calm, even keeled man she always knew when he was away from the pulpit?

Suddenly, Julian's motto, "A first-class effort will never produce a second-class result," loomed large in her mind. Only now she was witnessing a first-class passenger acting like a second class jerk! The way he kept misbehaving, even second class was being too generous.

She said, "I'm perfectly fine with my seat in business class. Even economy-class would be fine at this point."

At this point? Imogen gazed at Charmaine incredulously. Instead of stepping up to the plate and defending her husband, it was almost as if she was siding with the ticket agent. *It's Mark Lau all over again!* She would have another woman-to-woman talk with her back in the States. Hopefully by then, she would come back to her senses.

For now, it was time to try reasoning with her one last time. "You've never seen anything like the first-class accommodations on their transatlantic flights. Trust me, Charmaine, the suites are more luxurious than most other airlines! You'll never forget the experience. It's not as good as traveling by private jet, but it runs a close second."

"Like I said, Imogen, I'm perfectly satisfied with the business-class suite I have." This was said rather firmly.

Charmaine glanced at the flight attendant trying to silently apologize—using facial expressions—for their inappropriate behavior, all the while hoping to convey to her that she wanted to be seated as far away from them as possible.

Imogen shook her head in disappointment. The conversation they'd had in the limousine the night before about her husband's Facebook post, loomed large in her mind.

Clearly, Charmaine wasn't the woman she used to be. Not even close! The fact that she was surrendering her right to be blessed and highly favored stood diametrically opposed to what the Martíns taught their congregation. As one of their best students over the years, this lack of loyalty came as a slap across the face.

Julian snorted frustration once more, then let it go at that. *If you no longer think you're worthy of God's best, your loss!*

Charmaine knew what they both were thinking. She was just thankful to put an end to the argument.

She took a seat next to the Martíns and silently prayed the time would pass quickly, so she could board the plane and finally distance herself from them.

A handful of passengers stared at them disapprovingly, silently hoping there wouldn't be a repeat performance on the long flight to Seattle.

After what they'd just witnessed, Charmaine couldn't blame them. Instead of exuding the love of the Lord, her pastors looked like the most miserable couple on the planet.

Charmaine remembered something Pastor Lau had told her, "A joyless life isn't a Christian life, even when enduring persecution!"

The Martíns were anything but joyful now…

Charmaine never thought the day would come when Julian, of all people, would become so unglued. And for what? Because the poor woman couldn't upgrade her to first class? So what? No big deal! There were far greater tragedies in the world.

She frowned, knowing it was mostly penned-up frustration over the possibility of losing her as a member. Still, his actions were embarrassing and humiliating. Disrespectful as it sounded, now that she saw through their charade for what it really was—merely an act they put on in the name of Jesus—they were starting to annoy her.

Charmaine didn't want their off-the-wall antics robbing her of the peace she felt welling up inside, which she knew was the Holy Spirit at work in her, and nothing to do with the things they preached on.

And to think one of my long-term goals was to be just like them. Time to cross that off my bucket list, she mused. But something else was bothering her. The way Julian offered to pay any amount of money to upgrade her seat displayed bad stewardship on his part.

Was bribery one of the nine fruits of the Spirit outlined in Galatians 5:22-23? Last time she checked it wasn't. Where was the love, joy, peace, forbearance, kindness, goodness, faithfulness, gentleness, or self-control the Apostle Paul wrote about, even saying against such things there was no law?

Julian's behavior reflected none of those things! The only fruits he displayed came from a wild, out-of-control spirit. Instead of acting in a godly manner, he'd acted more like a spoiled brat than anything else! He was totally out of control.

And what about honoring her personal wishes to be left alone on the flight? Didn't that matter? Apparently not to the Martíns!

Charmaine frowned. Had it happened on the way to China, she would have been right there with her pastor, doing all she could to persuade the ticket counter agent to bump her up to first class, her "blessed and highly favored" attitude leading the way.

Her pastor's actions presented her with the perfect object lesson on how self-centered she used to be. It was a sickening thought.

She didn't need Pastor Lau telling her Julian's uncouth behavior was unacceptable for God's true children—whether out in public or in private.

Everything was different now…

Christ's death and resurrection is what made her right with God, not good works! No other sacrifice would do. By trusting in Him, that lone incident forgave all her sins—past, present, and future—sparing her soul from eternal condemnation.

It had nothing to do with what the Martíns preached from the pulpit each Sunday. Nor did it make her a princess on any level, but a redeemed servant. Pastor Lau was absolutely right—how was it possible to be a servant and a princess at the same time?

Her new mentor was also spot on in suggesting that harboring a "princess" mindset was one of the key factors to her reckless, prideful living all those years. He was also right to say that being rescued from hell was a cause for inward reflection, not outward spending!

Best simplified, whereas Cinderella was transformed from a servant into a princess, Charmaine was transformed from a princess into a servant.

And she was perfectly okay with it...

She felt blessed to call herself a servant of the Most High God! The only One she would have a high view of, from this point forward, was the One who rescued her soul from eternal damnation.

As much as she wanted to remain a member of the *Blessed and Highly Favored Full Gospel Church*, if only to share the true Gospel with her many friends there, how would they receive it, when one message was focused on this world, while the other was focused on the world to come?

One was earthly rich; the other was eternally rich! Since both messages came from the very same Book, it was cause for concern.

In no way did Pastor Lau speak as eloquently or with as much flare as Pastor Julian. But he clearly understood God's Word infinitely better...

Surely, he was storing up great treasures for himself on the other side. She couldn't say the same for the Martíns. All she knew was if they weren't truly saved, the only thing they would be storing up for themselves would be God's judgment.

Finally, the call she had been anticipating. "Ladies and gentlemen, at this time we would like to begin boarding our first-class and business-class passengers, and anyone else requiring special assistance."

Charmaine was so relieved, she felt like shouting "Hallelujah" at the top of her lungs. Now she could finally read the Word and seek God's guidance, without her pastors twisting the scriptures to fit their self-centered, worldly-minded, mass-accumulation agenda.

Imogen said, "That's us..."

Charmaine half-smiled. "Hope you enjoy the flight. See you back in Seattle."

Imogen sighed. "By the way, there's something I forgot to tell you back in Shanghai…"

Charmaine braced herself. "Yeah?"

"Though it's not due until January, of the one-point-three million that was promised the day you made your commitment, seven hundred and eighty thousand has already been received, as end-of-the-year write offs. Pretty awesome, huh?"

Charmaine silently gasped. In the end, it all came down to the money.

Imogen briefly looked down at the floor before reconnecting with her. "All I'm saying is if you're looking for another tax deduction, you may want to do the same…"

Really? Of all the things Imogen could have said, including apologizing for the way she and her husband had acted in China, this is what comes out of her mouth? *I really am nothing more than a commodity to them! Wow, just wow!*

Charmaine swallowed back anger. She was so agitated she could no longer look her pastors in the eyes. "Thanks for the update. Like Julian said, let's further discuss it back in Seattle, along with everything else…"

"Will Rodney be picking you up at the airport?" The way Imogen asked, it was as if she already knew the answer. "If not, we'll gladly have our driver take you home."

"Thanks, but I haven't seen Rodney in a week. I miss him and want him to take me home, as we had planned."

The way she felt now, if Rodney wasn't there to fetch her when her plane landed, she would rather walk home from the airport then spend 30 minutes with her pastors in a car, after the long flight.

Imogen shook her head. She wasn't at all surprised with her reply. After this insane trip, she fully expected it. "Have it your way then."

At that, the Martíns boarded the plane...

35

THREE HOURS LATER

FOR THE FIRST TIME since checking out of the hotel in Shanghai, Charmaine was finally free of the Martíns. As they reclined comfortably in separate pod-like suites in first class, her seat was still in the full, upright position, Bible open, with plenty of sheets of paper and a pen for taking notes.

Since business-class passengers were offered similar amenities as those in first class, she would recline later if she felt she needed a break.

With exception to her personal pod-like suite, the only real proof that she was seated in business class was that she was wearing the slippers that were provided for her, compliments of the airline. They even matched the Adidas warm-up suit she had on.

There would be plenty of time later to bask in the amenities afforded to her in business class if she so chose.

But for now, her soul was starved to learn more of the Word of God, from a servant's perspective, than anything else.

Charmaine chuckled to herself. After the shenanigans with the ticket counter agent back in Hong Kong, even being in the underbelly of the plane, among all the luggage, would have been preferable to being "trapped" in first class with the Martíns.

At least there she could meditate on what she was reading, without constantly being interrupted, or having her pastors breathing down her neck. As far as she knew, suitcases weren't capable of doing such things.

At any rate, being sandwiched between two classes of people on this flight presented her with a metaphoric optic of sorts.

After spending ten beautiful life-altering days with a group of persecuted individuals the world would surely regard as low class, or even from a lesser breed, and being shown true Christian love the moment she was introduced to them, Charmaine begged to differ.

If those up in first class represented the Martíns' brand of Christianity, and those behind her represented Pastor Lau's, she would unhesitatingly choose economy class in a heartbeat.

Then again, she no longer wished to be part of the lower, middle, or upper classes. The only class Charmaine DeShields wanted to be part of, from this point forward, was "servant" class.

Prior to taking this trip, she always gravitated toward those who were part of the Mutual Admiration Society (MAS)—those who'd beaten the odds to achieve the upper-class social status, much like she had done.

Charmaine never looked down on anyone in the lower tax brackets. She wasn't raised that way. If anything, whenever she fed the homeless back in Seattle, she often prayed that God would increase their faith so they, too, could experience the same blessed-and-highly-favored lifestyle for themselves someday.

She even brought them to church on occasion, and made sure to feed them in the church cafeteria, before dropping them back at wherever they happened to be staying that week.

Like Pastor Julian had always taught her, it was theirs for the taking; all anyone had to do was ask for the things they desired, in Jesus' mighty name, and never for a second doubt that it would eventually come to pass for them too, in God's perfect timing. *Blah, blah, blah!*

After wrestling in her mind, back and forth, as to whether or not to remain at the *Blessed and Highly Favored Full Gospel Church*, Charmaine felt this sudden disconnect from her two former pastors, and knew her days at their church were over.

How could she remain there when she no longer believed what the Martíns taught? She already knew if she tried sharing the true Gospel message at her Wednesday night Bible study, the time would surely come when they pulled the rug out from underneath her, and put someone else in charge who followed their off-track teachings.

No doubt her decision to leave would have a profound negative impact on her real estate business. Instead of feeling overcome with grief, a surge of peace flooded Charmaine's soul.

It was as if a huge suffocating weight was lifted off her shoulders—a heavy yoke she never even knew was there before taking this trip. This allowed her to breathe and think more freely.

Had someone told her beforehand there was even a remote possibility that all this would happen, she would have angrily rebuked the person who dared make such a foolish suggestion.

The sadness from knowing how much she would miss the church family she'd loved with all her heart, paled in comparison to the pain in her soul from knowing how greatly deceived her church family had been all this time, and would continue to be, if the Martíns weren't radically transformed by the power of the Holy Spirit, like she had recently been.

Roughly a quarter of the way into the twelve-hour flight to Seattle, Charmaine felt flustered and pulled the pamphlet out of her purse, documenting the $8.6M needed for the upcoming church expansion.

She shook her head in disgust, wondering how many churches could be funded in China with the $150K alone that would be spent on new furniture? Last time she checked, the furniture they had from the last renovation was still in excellent condition.

It was infinitely better than what most churches had at their disposal, especially churches like Pastor Lau's. Instead of campaigning to purchase new benches at his church, they hammered more nails in the rickety old benches they already had and placed worn cushions on top, to provide a little more comfort for their congregants.

It seemed to work just fine. Comfort wasn't what mattered most to them—it all came down to doing all they could with what little they had to reach more souls for Christ.

Unlike her pastors....

Former pastors, she corrected herself. *The Bibles that could be purchased with my fifty thousand dollars!* And with the potential of having as many as 250 million Christians in China in the not-too-distant future, she wanted to be part of that substantial growth!

While her decision to leave the *Blessed and Highly Favored Full Gospel Church* was firm, the only drawback was that she would be revoking a promise she'd made in front of so many people.

But how could she honor her commitment to give $50,000, knowing it would be hastily spent refurbishing a building that was already quite regal? How could she, in good conscience, sow into a ministry run by people who preached a false gospel to tens of thousands each week, by promising them earthly riches at the cost of spiritual decay for many?

After experiencing what true church fellowship was all about, Charmaine finally understood the true Gospel message had nothing to do with worldly success, or with raising money for new furniture every few years for the offices of the many pastors and their sizable staffs.

By being part of the inner sanctum, so to speak, she knew beyond a shadow of a doubt that the chief aim of the *Blessed and Highly Favored*

Full Gospel Church was financial independence for their members, not spiritual obedience.

In short, it was nothing more than a "prosperity-minded" gathering place, even though the percentages of those who became successful there, were no higher than in the secular world.

Now that she'd been given this not-so-lofty glimpse into their hearts and souls, Charmaine wouldn't be overly surprised to discover that the Martíns had been skimming money off the top for so many years, for their own personal use.

This was something she would discover on the other side...

36

HALFWAY ACROSS THE PACIFIC Ocean, Charmaine was reading 2 Corinthians 11:13-15 in her Bible, *For such men are false apostles, deceitful workmen, disguising themselves as apostles of Christ. And no wonder, for even Satan disguises himself as an angel of light. So it is no surprise if his servants, also, disguise themselves as servants of righteousness. Their end will correspond to their deeds.*

The instant she finished reading it, a shadow hovered above her, covering the page. Without even glancing up, she knew it was Julian again; a shiver shot up her spine.

This was his second time checking on her since the plane left Hong Kong. He apologized last time for his ill behavior back in China—if you could call it an apology. It sounded more like words coming from a man who believed he was 100 percent right, but didn't want to lose her as a member. Imogen also checked up on her, after one of her bathroom breaks. She, too, offered a half-hearted apology.

Julian flashed his made-for-TV smile. "Enjoying the flight so far?"

Charmaine looked up at him. "Yes, I am." *I thought I made it clear to you that I wish to be left alone!*

Julian's brow furrowed. "Why'd you say it like that?"

"Got a lot on my mind."

"Care to share? After all, I am your pastor." Their eyes locked. "Right?" It went beyond losing money at this point. It was personal—a battle for her heart, mind, and soul! *No way I'm losing her to that man!*

The business-class section on the plane had four suites per row. Aisles separated the two middle suites from the two window suites.

The man seated next to Charmaine, whose middle suite was situated a few inches in front of hers, and slightly tilted away from her window suite, was focused on the spreadsheets on his laptop screen.

Li Qiang was *not* happy seeing Julian towering over him again, his right hand resting on his personal pod, as he spoke to the woman across from him. He bristled in annoyance. His very presence came as a distraction, especially since he spoke so loudly, without the slightest consideration for anyone else on the plane.

Qiang had an urgent business meeting in Seattle in less than 10 hours and was trying to prepare his reports. He wanted to ask the man, "Are you a flight attendant? If not, please leave us alone!"

Charmaine nodded at him apologetically. He nodded his appreciation and refocused on his laptop screen. Then to Julian, "This isn't the right time or place. Besides, as you can see, I'm reading the Bible."

Julian winced. "There's always time for that, Charmaine."

Charmaine shot him a look as if she wanted to retaliate, but she remained silent. *Just one more proof!*

The desperation in his eyes was unsettling. If anything, it further confirmed her growing suspicion that her former pastor was indeed a false apostle, disguising himself as an apostle of Christ, the very thing Pastor Ogletree had accused Pastor Lau of being, after asking him to leave the Monday night Bible study seven weeks ago.

Julian got the message—hopefully for the last time—and rejoined his wife in first class. *Perhaps a nap is what I need...*

Feeling a deep conviction inside, Charmaine turned on her mobile device, logged into her bank and, at 37,000 feet above the earth's surface, transferred $10,000—the maximum amount online—to Pastor Lau's bank account in Seattle, from the $50,000 she had earmarked for her church.

She then sent a text message to Kaito Fujimoto on *WhatsApp*, authorizing her account manager to transfer the remaining $40,000, plus all interest earned to Pastor Lau's account, to be used as he saw fit.

Really? came Kaito's quick reply. *Are you referring to the money for the church expansion?*

Charmaine was surprised at how quickly he replied, since it was 3 a.m. in Seattle. *Yes! I know it's late, but can I call you?*

Kaito replied: *By all means...*

Before his cellphone rang, Kaito climbed out of bed and tiptoed out of the bedroom, so he wouldn't wake Lucy. "How are you, Charmaine?"

With a smile on her face Kaito couldn't see, she said, "Blessed and Highly Favored..." She paused, then said, "...to finally be one of God's redeemed wretches! And how's my dear brother in Christ?"

Chills shot up and down Kaito's spine. He was overjoyed. "Wow! What can I say? I'm blown away!"

Charmaine burst out in laughter. "Worshiping underground with Pastor Lau was the most amazing experience of my life! Thanks to him, I'll never be the same!"

"Praise God!"

"I'm flying back to the States now. Can't wait to tell you all about it, once the jetlag wears off. But for now, just know I've had a change of mind. Heart, rather.

"From an evangelistic standpoint, my money will do more to further God's Kingdom—by purchasing Bibles in China that have been properly translated in their own language—than if I gave it to my church."

More chills spread throughout his body. "Wow, Charmaine! I'm speechless!"

"When Mark told me there will soon be more Christians in China than any other place on earth, I saw a great opportunity to put my money to good use for a change. I have no doubt it'll be wisely spent in his care."

Kaito Fujimoto replied, "Agreed. The harvest is plentiful over there, but the workers so few. Here, too, for that matter! I keep praying that God's favor will spill over into Japan as well..."

"I will gladly join you in that prayer." Charmaine glanced at the man seated next to her. He was still focused on the charts on his laptop screen, but it seemed as if he was straining hard to hear her conversation.

Kaito turned on the bathroom light. His thin hair was messy. "Let me ask, since you're on your way back to the States, why don't you transfer the funds yourself when you get home?"

"You know how certain members of my church are, Kaito."

"Yes, I do..."

"Once they catch wind of it, they'll do all they can to get me to change my mind."

"Good point you make..."

"I already told the Martíns of my intent to send part of the money to Pastor Lau. Should have seen the looks on their faces."

The way she said it made Kaito laugh. Then it struck him. "Was this done on video chat?"

"No. Ready for this? The Martíns are on the plane with me."

The confused expression Kaito saw staring back at him in the mirror, didn't capture how he really felt. "What? They went with you? I haven't spoken to Mark since you arrived there, so I'm sort of in the dark."

"Not exactly. The first day we worshipped underground, Meredith was so freaked out that she cut her trip short. When Rodney told the Martíns I was being brainwashed, they flew to China to rescue me."

"Who told Rodney? Meredith?"

"Yes. Anyway, they asked me to wait until I was back in the States. But my mind's already made up. Which is why I want the transaction completed before I get back to Seattle."

Hallelujah! "I'll do as you wish, Charmaine. Just download the form I've attached, initial it in three places, and it will be done."

"Will do. I must say, in the three days Julian and Imogen were in China, their behavior was atrocious. Never saw them acting so poorly. Imogen even tried guilt-shaming me back in Hong Kong, saying much of the money that was pledged for the renovation project is already in-house. Makes me wonder what their chief motivation was for going there?"

Kaito turned off the bathroom light and went to the kitchen for a glass of water. "Valid point you make, Charmaine…"

"Funny thing is, they travelled all the way to China to rescue me from Pastor Lau's clutches. But as it turns out, God sent *me* all the way there to be rescued from *them*!"

Charmaine sighed. "They refuse to accept that God used Pastor Lau to deliver me from their false teachings."

"God sure works in mysterious ways."

"He sure does! You know how I always flaunted the Martíns as being two of the most anointed preachers on the planet…"

"You could say that!"

"Well, no longer. They now seem quite flawed to me. And pesky. Makes me wonder how well I knew them prior to taking this trip?"

"As a former member of your church, I understand completely."

"Then again, it's not that the Martíns had changed, I have! Even China had nothing to do with the radical changes in me—it was the work of the Holy Spirit."

A joyful smile formed on Kaito's face. "Exactly!"

"I can't stop thinking had I travelled all that way without attending Mark's church, for one thing, Meredith would be on the plane with me instead of the Martíns. And chances are good I'd still be spiritually lost."

"Aren't you forgetting something?"

Charmaine looked confused. "What?"

"That God chose you and not the other way around. You could be a Muslim living in a country that forbids the Bible from being preached. But if God's calling you to salvation, nothing or no one can prevent it from happening. Apparently, China was where He chose to reveal Himself to you."

"Wow, God chose sinful old me! How can I possibly wrap my head around such a profound statement? It's too magnificent!"

The man occupying the suite next to hers overheard her again, and silently snickered.

"One thing I discovered in China was the church I thought was so fully alive was more dead than most other churches on the planet. I no longer wish to be part of a sick church in a dying world."

Charmaine couldn't see the tears streaming down Kaito's cheeks, but she wouldn't be surprised to see them. This was a call he and Lucy had no doubt prayed for, for many years.

When her investment banker remained silent, Charmaine said, "I want to thank you for providing such excellent service all these years. Sorry if I don't say it enough. Perhaps because I always thought I was doing you more of a favor by remaining with you when everyone else left.

"In truth, the Martíns introduced me to other investment bankers, after you left the church, who also delivered impressive returns. I can't tell you how many times they pressured me to switch my accounts over to them."

"I'm not surprised. Others have told me similar stories..."

Charmaine took a swig from her vitamin water. "In truth, I threw a little money their way, mostly to get my pastors off my back, but I kept most of it with you. Never fully understood why until just now."

This caused even more joy to flood Kaito's heart. He knew exactly what she meant. "Thanks for sticking with me when no one else did..."

"You're welcome, brother. And thanks again for recommending me to sell Mark's house. It was one of the easiest sales I've ever made. Not only did it pay for this trip, and then some, thanks to his teaching, I know I'm Heaven-bound when my life is over. I'll never question it again!"

"Hallelujah!"

"By the way, Pastor Lau told me your church preaches the very same Gospel message he preaches."

Kaito took another gulp of water. "That would be correct! Only we don't have three services per day, seven days a week, like he does."

Charmaine laughed, then grew serious again. "The reason I ask is that I plan on becoming a member of your church, when I get back to Seattle."

Chills raced down Kaito's spine, tingling him everywhere. "That's the best news I've heard in a very long time. Have you considered the negative impact leaving that church will have on your business?"

"Yes, I have. Probably have to cancel my city bus campaign. Then again, perhaps God never wanted my image on all those city buses in the first place. If there's a good side to it, the six-bedroom house I've been praying for the past three years no longer appeals to me."

A smile formed on Kaito's face that quickly faded. "Aside from potentially losing clients at church, you should also expect to be scorned and ridiculed like I was…"

Charmaine took another sip of her drink. "Already thought about that, Kaito. Compared to what our friends in China deal with, it's nothing."

"Can't argue with you there." Kaito chuckled. "What can I say? I'm amazed at how far you've come in only a week. The many at my church who prayed for you all this week will rejoice at the news!"

"Glory to God!" Then, "Hey, I just received the form. It's late there. I'll let you get back to sleep."

"Sleep? How can I sleep now? I feel like running around the block ten times!" The way he said it caused Charmaine to burst out in laughter again. "I have the most amazing feeling inside. Answered prayer always does that to me, especially after three long years."

"Thanks, Kaito," was all she could say.

The call ended. Charmaine initialed in three places, then sent it to him with one last reply, before powering down her phone: *Just so you know, I plan on telling no one about this transaction! Naturally, the Martíns will know. Other than that, no more forfeiting treasures in Heaven for me!*

She looked out at the darkness outside the porthole and smiled, knowing she was doing the right thing. It felt good to be giving without wanting or expecting anything in return…

Now that she had a new, well-balanced understanding of what the Bible taught, even if there were no rewards to be gained on the other side, the love she had in her heart for her Savior was so strong, the very honor and privilege of serving Him was all the reward she wanted…

Meanwhile, Kaito was so excited he wanted to wake Lucy and share the wonderful news with her, but she was sound asleep. It could wait until daybreak. He climbed in bed, held his wife, and silently praised God for using his best friend, Mark, to transform Charmaine's life.

"Thank you, Lord!" Kaito whispered skyward in the darkness.

37

AFTER FINISHING HER MEAL, Charmaine reclined her seat back. With her body in the perfect reclining position, and a blanket draped over her for warmth, she resumed reading her Bible.

Just as she was turning the page, the plane suddenly dropped, after hitting a pocket of dry air, causing a few "oohs" and "aahs" to reverberate throughout the cabin from startled passengers.

Charmaine was "oohing" and "aahing" along with them. When the turbulence continued, she placed her Bible on her tray table and looked out the porthole to her right. Some of the papers she had for taking notes scattered onto the floor. It was the least of her concerns.

It was pitch black outside. The only thing she could see was the blinking light at the end of the plane's wing slightly behind her. The way it oscillated up and down caused even more fear to pulsate through her. She gulped hard and clenched tightly onto the armrests.

Like all other white-knuckled passengers on board, Charmaine was totally unaware that the wings on a plane this size could flap 30 feet or so up and down—like that of a bird's—with great ease, without ever breaking free from the fuselage.

Whenever pressure was applied—namely turbulence—airplane wings were engineered to work like shocks on a vehicle driving on a bumpy road; they could oscillate with great flexibility until ultimately springing the aircraft back to its resting or cruising place.

Before newly-manufactured planes were added to the fleet of any airline carrier, they first underwent static, stress, and fatigue testing. Under severe duress, the wings on a plane could reach greater than 150 percent of their designed stress levels, before ultimately cracking like branches.

In short, they were engineered to sustain most of the elements into which they were being flown, without breaking, to include fierce, sustained turbulence.

The captain turned on the fasten seatbelt sign, then said over the intercom, "Flight attendants, prepare the cabin…"

As her co-attendants got busy clearing dinner trays, the lead flight attendant calmly said over the intercom, "Ladies and gentlemen, as you can see, the captain has turned on the fasten seatbelt sign. At this time, please make sure your seats, beds and tray tables are in their full and upright position. Sorry for the inconvenience. Hopefully, it won't be too much longer."

The man seated next to Charmaine, whose eyes had been glued onto his laptop screen the entire flight, looked more annoyed by the distraction than anything else. He powered down his computer and stowed it in the compartment to the left of his seat, antsy for the pilots to do their jobs so he could get back to work.

After a few minutes of battling through several pockets of unstable air, the pilots finally managed to level off the aircraft.

The lead pilot spoke into the intercom. "From the flight deck, this is your captain speaking again. Sorry for the bumpy ride earlier. Usually we can anticipate rough pockets of unstable air on the horizon, but on occasion, they do sneak up on us.

"As you can see, I've once again turned off the fasten seatbelt sign, so you're free to move about the cabin. However, as a precaution, I'll ask that you keep your seatbelts fastened whenever seated, in case we encounter more unforeseen turbulence. Thanks, and enjoy the remainder of the flight…"

Not even thirty minutes after everyone had resumed watching movies, going online, reading, reclining, whatever, there was more turbulence.

Only it was worse this time…

Like a sustained earthquake—air quake rather—the turbulence intensified, shredding the nerves of every passenger on board, including the pilots and flight crew. With an average span of 20 years of service each between them, the first round was nothing out of the ordinary.

This was altogether different…

Before some could even fasten their seatbelts, they were thrust from their seats. Terror-laden screams filled the cabin, replacing the "oohs" and "aahs" heard last time the plane violently shook. Passengers who were still seated looked around the cabin with unbridled fear in their eyes.

A few overhead compartment doors popped open spewing out their contents, hitting some passengers in the head, including a flight attendant who suffered a bloody nose and a concussion after being struck by a heavy carryon bag.

Oxygen masks fell from above each seat. Few reached for them. Most were too fearful to let go of whatever they were clinging to for dear life, to hopefully avoid being thrown about the fuselage along with the handful of others like hopeless, powerless ragdolls.

In the cockpit, the malfunction light flashed on the dashboard, warning that the problem was with the rudder at the tail of the aircraft, which controlled the plane's movements from left to right, directing the airflow to keep it flying straight.

Because of its immense size, the Boeing 777 jumbo jet had both an upper and lower rudder, which were meant to move in unison. For whatever reason, the lower rudder had deflected 13 degrees to the left and was stuck there, causing the pilots to lose directional control of the plane.

Whereas the rudder kept the aircraft flying horizontally, airplanes turned because of the banking created by ailerons—small-hinged sections on the outboard portion of a plane's wings which were situated next to the landing flaps.

Ailerons worked in opposition. As one wing tipped up, the other tipped down. This dual motion caused the aircraft to bank, which allowed the flight path to curve in the direction of the pilot's choosing.

Hydraulics controlled much of the plane, including the rudder. Trying to fly the plane without complete control of the full hydraulics was next to impossible. Having a vast ocean beneath them, with no place to attempt an emergency landing, only exasperated the situation in the flight deck.

The senior captain was doing all he could to keep the plane level and straight, using foot pedals to control the upper rudder, and control columns to move the ailerons on the wings of the plane.

Each time he momentarily managed to level off the aircraft, he had to repeat the same process a few seconds later. It was amazing how he was able to keep the plane semi horizontal at all.

After 30 minutes, he felt like he'd just finished participating in a decathlon. The constant motion had turned his legs into jelly.

The mounting stress from the dire predicament only increased the fatigue rummaging through his body. He was forced to relinquish control to his co-pilot. After a while, despite her most valiant efforts she, too, was physically spent and signaled for the flight engineer to take over.

At times, the plane banked sharply from left to right, before bobbing up and down like a float riding waves on the water.

Whenever they were forced to increase engine speed, the nose of the plane pointed straight up toward Heaven, before quickly nosediving down when the pilots cut back on the speed.

This went on for several minutes. All three pilots were mindful that they wouldn't be able to control the aircraft too much longer, which meant they needed to find a place to land in the soonest possible time.

Anchorage, Alaska was the closest possible landing location. But could they keep the aircraft airborne for the next 45 minutes?

They hoped it wouldn't be a bridge too far...

The female first officer tried fingering through the Cockpit Operating Manual (COM) which provided a list of procedures when problems occurred. She seriously doubted if there was a procedure for this problem.

Even if there was, her hands shook so much that she wouldn't be able to read it. Her stomach was doing backflips, her mouth was dry as cotton, her pulse raced, sensing the end might be near...

JULIAN MARTÍN MANAGED TO fasten his seatbelt. Imogen wasn't so fortunate. Even though the captain had informed passengers to keep their seatbelts fastened whenever seated, being pregnant made it quite uncomfortable. On top of that, she had an upset stomach.

Just as she had finally dozed off, she was thrust out of her bed in the front row. With no seat in front of her to stop her, her body slammed into the lavatory wall, throwing out her right hip. She screamed in agony.

Julian frantically stretched his left hand as far as it would go, trying to grasp hold of Imogen's right hand. But it was more reactionary than anything else—there was too great a distance between them.

Even if he could reach her, she was too fearful to attempt meeting him halfway. Body pinned against the wall her hands covered her belly, trying to protect the little prince inside her womb.

She couldn't speak—she was too frightened to even scream. Her lips were so dry, they were stuck together. Her throat had constricted. Tears streamed out from beneath the gold silky sleep mask covering her eyes, as she pleaded with the God she never knew—at least not in a soul-saving way—commanding Him to rescue everyone on board the flight.

Julian fully understood why his wife kept the mask on—everything on the other side of it was nothing short of terrifying! But he was desperate to look in her eyes, hoping to draw strength and be comforted by her.

Imogen's silence, coupled by the fact that the flight attendants were in no position to cater to his every whim, made him feel all alone in the world, with no one there to comfort him. This caused even more fear to swell throughout his trembling body.

Julian leaned to the right and stretched his neck as far as it would go, just enough to see out of the pod encapsulating him. He saw Charmaine 10 rows behind him gripping the armrests with her hands. Her eyes were closed in prayer.

He closed his eyes and did the same, "Father God," he shouted loudly, "I command You, in the name of Jesus, to stop this plane from going down, this very instant! My life's work isn't yet finished. There's still so much I want to accomplish for Your glory. Please save me, so I can give Prince the good life You promised to all Your children!" It was as if he was the potter and the Creator of the universe was the clay...

Because of the god-awful grinding noise in the cabin, Imogen couldn't hear most of her husband's desperate plea, only a few words and syllables here and there, as he decreed this and declared that. But even without hearing it all, she pretty much knew what he had said.

She lowered her sleep mask to get a quick glance at him. The confidence her husband had always displayed when praying was gone. He even stuttered at times, when making his self-centered declarations.

He no longer resembled the man who addressed thousands of people every weekend from the pulpit. If anything, he looked like a scared, hopeless, little boy who wanted his Mommy.

Up until now, the only assurance Julian had in life was self-assurance. From an eternal perspective, it meant nothing, nothing but condemnation, that is. Seeing the desperate, hopeless expression on his face, it's like he knew his prayer to God had been as ineffective as pouring gasoline on a fire, hoping to extinguish it.

But what frightened Imogen more than anything else was that he looked nothing like a man convinced his soul was safe in the hands of the living God, regardless of what happened in the coming moments.

From her vantagepoint, Imogen spotted Charmaine. Their eyes connected. Charmaine could tell she was writhing in pain. She was able to read her lips, "My hip! My hip!"

Charmaine watched Julian crawling on his hands and knees to try helping his wife to her feet. The way she shooed him away, the pain must have been so excruciating that she preferred remaining on the floor with her back and hip pressed up against the lavatory wall as leverage.

Charmaine wanted to join her former pastors in the first-class section and pray with them both. But the plane was shaking so violently, if she

271

tried getting out of her seat, she feared she might be strewn about the fuselage only to end up badly-injured herself.

The agitation in Charmaine's voice earlier was replaced with a deep sadness for Julian and Imogen that started at the center of her chest and quickly spread out everywhere. Tears fell freely from her eyes one after the next, clouding her vision.

What she felt for the Martíns was the worst kind of pain. It was a spiritual pain from someone who was fully mindful of the eternal consequences they both faced.

More than anything, she wanted to share the Gospel with them one last time. But after the way they seemingly rejected everything she had told them the past couple of days, all she could do was pray for them.

Even 10 rows back, Imogen knew Charmaine pitied her. She could see it in her eyes. Imogen thought back to what she had said the other day, about never having to second guess the eternal assurance she had in Christ Jesus, no matter what situation she faced in life.

Imogen couldn't deny that Charmaine looked like someone who had every confidence of being eternally welcomed by Jesus on the other side, if this really was the end for them.

She couldn't say the same for herself or her husband...

Imogen blinked her away, and looked down at the 5-carat diamond her husband had recently placed on her finger, as it lay on her belly covering her unborn son, protecting him.

If the pilots didn't find a way to right the ship, so to speak, the ring she wore so proudly would end up at the bottom of the ocean, along with their fancy luggage, expensive wardrobes, and the three boxes full of costly gifts they had purchased in Shanghai, mostly for Prince.

Good thing me and Charmaine didn't go shopping after all, she scoffed. *Might have ended up being more worthless purchases!*

Imogen covered her eyes again with the sleep mask as a possible distraction. It didn't help. With or without it on, her mind kept playing cruel tricks on her, by forcing her to recall the many things she'd placed above the Lord.

There were too many to count...

As the seconds passed, Imogen was slowly coming to grips with the realization that she might never get to experience the many joys of motherhood, even after so many had prayed for her to get pregnant.

If the plane went down, the child she felt intimately connected to in her womb the past five months, would be a son she would never get to raise. She had no doubt Prince's soul would go to be with Jesus.

But what about her own soul? Would it go to Heaven? Or would it be sent to…could it be? A shiver shot through her…

The fact that she even had to question her salvation at this desperate "moment-of-truth" time in her life—when all the chips were down—wasn't a cause for optimism.

With a sorrowful expression on her face, the prospect of meeting her Maker now frightened her more than the prospect of the plane crashing into the ocean below.

Julian was thinking similar thoughts. If God didn't answer his desperate prayer, his command rather, he would lose everything he and his wife had worked so hard for—the four homes they owned, one in the Caribbean, the garage full of cars, motorcycles and four wheelers, the lavish tailored wardrobes, and on and on.

This caused him unspeakable anguish, especially since the jet plane he coveted in his heart, which he hoped to have within three years, might never come to fruition. Not counting fatherhood, what would have been his crowning achievement as a Pastor, was starting to seem more and more plausible that it might never happen.

Now fearing for his very life, Julian wanted to contact his church, and urge them all to pray for them to be rescued, but his cellphone became one of the flying objects scattered about the cabin.

He was too frightened to look for it…

Deep down inside the Martíns knew they never had the favor of the Most High God, even if it appeared to many that they did. This wasn't some new eye-popping revelation that was suddenly thrust upon them, now that their lives were seemingly in peril.

Even despite their vast spiritual blindness, both were mindful of what they were doing all along, namely twisting what the Bible taught and using it for their own personal gain.

In private, they knew they'd strayed off track long ago. They promised each other they would come clean at some point, and get right with God, by fleeing the life they knew wasn't pleasing to their Maker.

But the numerous temptations this all-consuming "selfie-driven" world offered them, including the insatiable desire for great riches, was so powerful that it kept them from seeking God with all their minds, hearts, and souls.

Their combined obsession for the good life forced them to refrain from sharing certain parts of the Bible that stood opposed to the glamorous lifestyles they led, and taught others to diligently strive for.

The end result of their unceasing perversion was that it kept them bound in darkness, even though they had occupied the brightest edifice in all of Seattle!

In the back of their minds, both were in their 30s and figured they still had plenty of time to make things right, even though their Bibles told them tomorrow was promised to no one.

With the possibility of being mere moments away from their hearts no longer beating inside their chests, they no longer thought that way.

This filled them both with an all-consuming dread. If everyone back in Seattle—their flock—could only see them now...

38

THERE WAS MORE TURBULENCE, followed by a god-awful popping sound, then a screeching noise that sounded like grinding metal.

The passengers onboard felt each movement, each new thrust. The constant banking from side to side caused many to vomit. That sensation, unpleasant as it was, seemed mild when compared to the sensation of feeling that they were all teetering on the brink of total disaster.

Charmaine observed, as the man seated next to her powered down his computer again. But instead of stowing it this time, Li Qiang closed it and kept it on his tray table which he never bothered closing.

He laid his head on top of it, looking completely terrified, sensing his life's work might soon come to an abrupt end. It was eerie…

Charmaine's human side was as terrified as this man looked, not to mention everyone else on board the plane. Her mind thought back to when she went on a mission trip to South America.

The day before they returned to the States, she went bungee jumping with Rodney and a few others from church. Moments before she took the plunge, she became paralyzed with fear.

It took much coaxing from Rodney, and her instructor, before she finally found the courage to leap off the bridge.

As she inched closer and closer to the river down below, with nothing but a huge elastic cord strapped around her waist, her fear escalated.

But once the cord had stretched itself to the maximum, the pull of gravity slowly brought the harness securing her back up to safety. Adrenaline kicked in and her fear gave way to unbridled excitement.

There was no bungee cord or harness strapped to the plane to pull them back from the surface below and save them now. But she had something infinitely better to hold on to—Someone rather!

Though Jesus wasn't with her physically, she had every confidence knowing if the plane on which she was traveling never recovered—which seemed more and more a distinct possibility—with her soul intact and eternally secure, she felt this incredible peace knowing whatever happened in the next few moments, she had nothing to lose and everything to gain.

Charmaine couldn't help but wonder if anyone else on board this flight would be with her this day in Paradise. There had to be others who trusted in Jesus for their salvation. As much as she wanted to include her former pastors into the tally, she couldn't do it.

She reached for her cell phone. It was time to call Rodney and tell him she loved him, just in case. Meredith too.

As her phone rang, Charmaine glanced down at the man seated next to her again. His head was still resting on his laptop on the tray table looking in her direction. Head at a sideways tilt, the Bible on her tray table was perfectly level with his eyes.

Now fearing for his life, Li Qiang silently wondered if the message contained within its pages—the very message his only brother was in prison for preaching—really had the power to save souls.

He lowered his facemask. "Can you share the Gospel with me?"

Charmaine blinked hard, as if it would increase her hearing. "What?"

Meanwhile, Rodney was awakened from a deep sleep and answered his phone. He was a little discombobulated and thought Charmaine had already landed, and was calling for a ride from the airport.

The deep, steady, churning, racing, grinding, high-pitch frequency noise streaming through his phone, rustled his senses, and quickly changed his thinking. He was filled with unbridled fear.

Rodney bolted up in bed. "Charmaine! What's wrong, baby?" He heard a man yell in broken English, "Can you share the Gospel with me?"

"Wait, Rodney…" Then to the man next to her, "Are you referring to the salvation God promised to all who would believe in Christ Jesus?"

The man nodded yes.

Wow! Thank you, Lord! "It would be my honor to share it with you. But it'll have to be the quick version, just in case."

The Chinese man nodded yes again. The fear in his eyes was evident.

Charmaine's body trembled in fear; her voice quaked knowing the end kept creeping up on them, but this was too important.

Rodney yelled into the phone, "What's that loud noise? What's going on, Charmaine? Are you okay, baby?"

She kept her cellphone an inch away from her mouth so Rodney could hear her words. "The long and short of why Christ came to earth was to save sinners. If you want the same salvation I—and hopefully others on this plane—have, you must fully understand that your sins are what put enmity between you and God."

"I do."

Rodney was completely dumbfounded. *What in the world?*

"Good, because if you don't satisfy God's anger toward your sins by trusting in Christ for forgiveness, if this plane crashes, your soul *will* end up in hell…"

Li Qiang nodded yes. Beads of sweat were visible on his forehead.

If this plane crashes? Rodney was wiping sleep from his eyes, and nearly poked his left eye out.

"In other words," Charmaine shouted above the deafening noise, "either Christ will satisfy God's anger, or your sins will in hell! It's vitally important that you understand this!"

Li Qiang said, "I do."

Rodney became more panicked. "Who are you talking to, baby, me or someone else?"

"To both of you!" she shouted into her receiver. Then to the man seated next to her, "Truth be told, I just got saved for real the other day. I came to China a false convert without even knowing it."

False convert? What? Rodney got out of bed and started pacing the bedroom floor.

The plane rattled and shook even more violently. It was a wonder it hadn't splintered and broken into a million pieces by now.

Li shot a desperate look at Charmaine, as if trying to remind her of the dire situation.

Charmaine took a deep, exasperated breath. "Do you believe only Jesus has the power to save your soul from utter destruction, and that all other roads lead to hell?"

The man became teary eyed. "Yes…"

"Praise God!" Had the man whose name she did not know—there wasn't enough time for proper introductions—been sitting back in his pod suite, she wouldn't be able to see his face, and they wouldn't be having this conversation now.

She placed her left hand on his shoulder. His body shook erratically to the rhythm of the plane. "If you really believe what I just told you, confess to God that you're a sinner and repent of your sins while there's still time. Only then can you receive Christ's full pardon. Do it now!"

Li Qiang nodded his gratitude, then sobbed uncontrollably. Full of utter remorse, he felt condemned in his trespasses against the just and holy

God his brother faithfully served and had spent the last seven years in prison for, while he got to live the good life.

For the first time ever, he was deeply grieved in his spirit and felt the full conviction of the Holy Spirit deep in his soul.

In his native Mandarin, he repented of every sin he ever committed in life, especially the sin of criticizing his brother's faith for so many years, and for mocking and rejecting the Gospel each time his brother tried sharing it with him.

Now fully convinced that it had saved his brother's soul way back when, he wanted that very same salvation for himself!

As Li Qiang prayed to his Maker, Charmaine shouted into the phone receiver, "Hello? Sweetness, are you there? Hello?"

She looked at her phone screen. The connection was dropped. She tried calling Rodney back, but couldn't obtain a signal.

With trembling hands, she tried calling Meredith, but to no avail.

Meanwhile, Rodney scratched his head in befuddlement. Knowing there was nothing he could do to help Charmaine, he wept uncontrollably and prayed to God, asking Him to save his girlfriend's life.

Li Qiang, on the other hand, felt like the thief on the cross his brother frequently spoke of. After a life full of sinful living and rejecting all things "Jesus", he was forgiven by God at the last possible moment, and would enter Paradise to be with his Lord, the instant the aircraft he was on made impact with the watery surface below.

Just knowing he would see His Savior very soon, and his brother now languishing in prison at the time of God's choosing, filled him with a gratitude he never felt in his 57 years living on Planet Earth.

While he was saved by the skin of his teeth, as the saying went, he would rather be a janitor in Heaven than a millionaire in hell!

Even though their roles would be reversed in Paradise, with him being the pauper this time, he longed to see his brother again someday, his brother twice over. *What a great and glorious time that will be!*

"Thank you, Jesus, for having mercy on this sinner's soul!"

Now that he had the eternal assurance the Bible spoke of, Li Qiang felt more secure on this increasingly doomed flight than he ever did when reaching the highest pinnacles in life.

He glanced up at Charmaine with tears streaming down his cheeks, and smiled at her, with a peaceful expression on his face that wasn't there a few moments ago.

Charmaine didn't have to ask why. She silently rejoiced.

She dreaded to think what type of conversation she might have had with this man, had they met on the flight to China instead of on the way back, before she was spiritually enlightened by Pastor Lau.

Perhaps she would have commanded God to rescue them both from peril, like the Martíns were no doubt doing, which would have ended up sending the two of them straight to hell...

Then again, like Kaito said on the phone earlier, if God's hand was on him for salvation, no force in the universe could prevent it from happening, not even a doomed flight.

For proof of this, all she had to do was look at his face. Truly, this man had just crossed over from spiritual death to life! *Hallelujah!*

Charmaine recalled what Pastor Lau had said about leading others to faith in Christ—at the very last minute—before life came to an end. Joy flooded her soul, even despite the incredible situation she now faced.

Another thing he told her over lunch one day, was that some would lead many to Jesus, while some would lead only one. But that one soul was so precious to God that its Heavenly value was priceless, as was the reward given to everyone God used to win him or her to Jesus.

Charmaine had no way of knowing just how stubborn this man's heart was, or that God had sent many of His servants to preach the Gospel to him. Nor did she know he had rebuked them all, and that his own brother was languishing in prison for his faith in Christ.

All she knew was that she got to share the Gospel with someone, without wanting anything in return or without adding anything "worldly" to it, as Pastor Lau had challenged her to do from this point forward.

For now, only God knew what had transpired between the two of them, or that she'd just stored up another reward in Heaven that could never be stolen or forfeited, due to her big mouth or foolish pride.

Soon, very soon, she would discover she wasn't the only one who would store up treasures over this one salvation; everyone—his brother especially—who prayed for him every day in prison, without fail, would also receive Heavenly rewards, which ultimately would be laid at the feet of their King and Savior, on that great and glorious day...

Even frightened to the point of hyperventilating, Charmaine half-smiled at the thought, brief as it was. "Thank you, Jesus, for letting me transfer the funds before I..." She stopped. "Use it for Your glory, and for the furthering of Your kingdom here on Earth, Amen!"

Joyous as Charmaine felt among the chaos, she was deeply saddened that she couldn't talk to her boyfriend one last time. There was so much she wanted to tell him, if indeed this was the end for her. Meredith too!

She wiped a tear from her eye. *Save them both, Lord, as only you can!*

39

THERE WAS MORE TURBULENCE. The plane carrying more than 300 souls swerved from side to side, like a model airplane with bottle rockets strapped to its sides, not knowing where it was headed.

The lead pilot cut back on the engine speed again but, like all other attempts, it proved just as fruitless.

All three pilots were ever mindful that if the rudder broke off the tail wing at any time, control of the aircraft would be lost.

Before the lead captain could update the flight crew and passengers in the cabin, that's precisely what happened. As it turned out, their worst fears had come true. Anchorage, Alaska had just become a bridge too far…

Loud sobs and prolonged screams filled the fuselage from terror-laden passengers, when the plane suddenly spiraled sharply downward in a tailspin.

The pilots did all they could to pull the aircraft out of it, but to no avail. They exchanged fearful glances knowing the flight they were piloting had just become a doomed one.

With expressions of total resignation on their faces, as their bodies shook from fear and from the constant erratic movements, the three pilots nodded their professional appreciation to each other, knowing this would be their last flight.

All wondered what would become of them in the next life? Was it possible they might come back again as pilots?

They would soon see how warped their thinking really was…

The chief pilot yelled into the microphone to the Anchorage tower, "Mayday! Mayday! We're going down! We're going down!"

Then to the cabin, he fearfully bemoaned, "Brace for impact!"

The sound of engines grinding and screeching metal being twisted like straw grew more pronounced, as the plane began its rapid descent, at maximum velocity, into the frigid Bering Sea below.

Everyone on board held their collective breath, or shrieked in terror, hoping the pilots could find a way to reverse course and head east again, instead of straight down.

But as the seconds slowly passed, hope kept fading, as the vehicle they were traveling on inched closer and closer toward the surface below.

Most were too frightened to open their eyes. They prayed to their gods for a last-minute miracle.

In their native tongues, some pleaded with Buddha to save them.

Others cried out to Allah.

Others prayed that the science behind the engineering would find a last-minute way to divert the aircraft, thus preventing it from crashing.

"Save me, Jesus!" was the desperate plea of some, who would soon learn they never really knew Him at all.

"Someone save us, anyone!" was the outcry of others.

Those who believed in reincarnation tried calming their nerves and hearts, by wondering who or what they would come back as in the next life. It wasn't helping...

Some became so fear-stricken that they fell unconscious. Others suffered massive heart attacks and died. Even if the plane miraculously freed itself from the tailspin and managed to survive, they were already gone.

Regardless of what god they prayed to, it was so loud inside the cabin no one heard their desperate cries for help, thus amplifying the situation.

But the Creator of the universe heard every word uttered to the false gods they worshipped, and every single thought, as if they had actually been spoken to Him. It was all recorded in Heaven's limitless memory.

Their desperate prayers to their false gods would all go unanswered. There would be no last-minute miracle, no saving the aircraft.

They were mere moments away from being convinced that He was the only true God. Worse, the love He had shown them every minute of every day, in the span of time in which He allowed them to be alive, was about to be removed from them in the twinkling of an eye.

With the large body of water steadily inching up on them, just waiting to receive them, everyone on board knew there would be no rescuing the aircraft from its apparent death spiral.

Even more frightening, the soul-splitting horror they all felt now would increase infinitely, the instant they stepped into eternity...

AS THE PLANE KEPT inching its way toward what would soon become a watery grave below, the downward spiral threw Julian's equilibrium off. He started vomiting.

Dreadful as that sensation was, it couldn't compare to the horror he felt knowing the God he preached from the pulpit each Sunday was but a warped version of the One true God of the Bible, someone Julian never knew personally, relationally, intimately.

By delighting more in God's gifts than God Himself, Julian had set up another god above the Most High, a false genie-in-a-bottle type of god, headed up by Satan himself. He should have been more focused on winning souls to Christ, not exploiting them for his benefit.

The sheer desperation he felt from more than a decade of profaning the pulpit and using it for personal gain was so overpowering, it nearly choked off his air and oxygen supply.

He glanced at his wife again. The gravity from the plane spiraling downward kept her body pinned against the lavatory wall, only now at the midway point. One hand still covered her belly, the other massaged her right hip, as she wept hysterically.

It very much felt like they were speeding down a steep roller-coaster hill; only roller coasters eventually climbed again, before ultimately leveling off. Good thing she couldn't see her husband's face. If she could, her anguish would only intensify.

Now beyond convinced the plane wouldn't break out of its death spiral, even that couldn't get Julian to think forward and genuinely repent at the very last moment, by asking for God's grace and forgiveness.

Like everyone else on this now-doomed flight, the world they knew was spiraling away; the Martíns were a few short breaths away from no longer being part of the beautiful life they'd created together.

The countless material possessions that had consumed them all their lives couldn't save them now.

Worse, their desperate pleas to be "saved" had nothing to do with the afterlife or with anything spiritual. Nor were their words uttered with even a trace of genuine repentance for their many years of sinful living.

As the man seated next to Charmaine genuinely repented of his sins before a just and holy God, the Martíns kept asking God—commanding Him rather—over and over, not to save their souls but the plane they were traveling on, so they could get back to the lives they cherished so much.

Their spiritual blindness was so great that instead of looking forward and contemplating life on the other side, which was a few ticks away from becoming their new, grim, eternal reality, they still couldn't let go of the world that had elevated them both to such lofty heights.

That's where their hearts and treasures were, not on the things of God.

The final proof of this was, even faced with this dire predicament, the one thought that kept running through their minds now was, *Why didn't we wait and take the next flight home?*

CHARMAINE FORCED HER HEAD up one last time to the first-class area. Imogen gazed back at her in total despair, crying hysterically as the grinding and screaming intensified.

What Charmaine saw on her former pastor's face went beyond the excruciating pain she felt from her injury. The greedy confidence she was known for was replaced with sheer terror. It was etched onto her face like a new tattoo. It was eerie.

For someone who'd always taught the finer things in life had to first be spoken into existence—without ever doubting—before it could ever come to fruition, she sure looked doubtful now.

Had Charmaine not taken this trip, perhaps she would be wavering back and forth in her mind right now, wondering if her soul was truly safe or in peril. She had zero doubt now...

Imogen, on the other hand, looked like someone who'd just realized all modes of communication with God were about to be permanently cut off.

Julian couldn't save her.

Her church family couldn't save her.

Not even her desperate commands skyward could save her now.

Charmaine thought back to when Pastor Lau rebuked her at her church a month and a half ago, as many watched and listened. *Looks like the false prophetess is about to be silenced for good, just like he had prayed*, she thought sadly, frighteningly.

Charmaine couldn't see Julian, but he no doubt felt as hopeless as his wife looked. The last verse of 2 Corinthians 11:13-15 she was reading earlier when his shadow covered the page came to mind. "*Their end will correspond to their deeds...*"

That's precisely how Imogen looked, as if she'd anticipated the most dreadful of outcomes. Her heart ached for her former pastors, and for everyone else on board the plane whose names weren't written in the Lamb's Book of Life.

Like the Martíns had done, Charmaine also questioned why she hadn't waited for the later flight. But instead of harping on it, she was just grateful that Meredith wasn't with her now. If so, chances were good she, too, would soon be eternally doomed like many on this plane.

After pushing "REDIAL" numerous times on her phone, her joy knew no bounds when she was miraculously reconnected with Rodney.

Fearing the signal could be lost at any time, she shouted into the receiver, "Rodney, listen to me! The plane I'm on is going down. I'm sure you know the Martíns are on the flight with me. I don't think we're gonna make it."

Rodney had been frantically pacing his bedroom floor ever since the last call was dropped. He pulled the phone from his ear and stared at it, as if the phone were to blame for speaking such outlandish words. "What?!"

Charmaine started weeping. "Please listen to me, sweetness, it's vitally important. The Martíns *are* false teachers. Everything Pastor Lau said about them was right. We had it all wrong. The Fujimotos were wise to leave the church when they did. You must do the same!"

Rodney's knees grew weak. His head started spinning. "False teachers? What do you mean, baby?"

In between sniffles, she said, "I hope to see you again on the other side. But for that to happen, you must repent, truly repent! Ask Kaito to share the Gospel with you, so you don't end up in hell someday with the Martíns! Take Meredith with you! Your kids too!"

Rodney looked at his phone again, unable to comprehend what he was hearing. *What in the world?*

Charmaine heard loud static in her ear. The call was about to be dropped again. "I love you, sweetness, and I already miss you!"

The line went dead.

Rodney collapsed to the floor and wept uncontrollably, knowing this would be the last conversation he would ever have with his girlfriend.

He never felt such pain, such anguish in his heart like he did now. The more he thought about the love of his life's horrific predicament, the more shattered he was, gutted even. "I never got to ask you to marry me."

Sensing her boyfriend's hopeless condition, Charmaine wiped tears from her eyes and silently prayed again that she would see Rodney on the other side, at the time of God's choosing.

Now moments away from being eternally comforted, she resigned herself to letting go of the things of this world, in anticipation of the world to come. Knowing the plane would surely crash, but not knowing exactly when it would make impact, made her heart jackhammer inside her chest.

Yet, she felt this peace that surpassed all understanding. It was a supernatural peace that only those who truly belonged to God ever got to experience.

Even though it was pitch dark outside, she pulled the porthole cover down with her right hand, not wishing to see the blinking light on the wing behind her any longer.

She thought about the Place she would soon be transported to. An eternal dwelling place at which she would be the best version of herself, the sinless version. She would still think, feel, and emote, only in perfect peace and health with the Lord Jesus Christ, just like Pastor Lau had said.

With one trembling hand gripping the seat in front of her and the other clenched onto the back of her new brother in Christ, Charmaine started singing the song, "*Amazing Grace*".

Amid the constant screaming and whimpering inside the cabin, Li recognized the hymn and sang along with her in his own language.

Much like with her brothers and sisters underground, she didn't understand his Mandarin. But because they were singing the same Gospel hymn, she knew exactly what he was saying...

With trembling hands and a heart full of joy, she recited the Bible verse Pastor Lau had shared with her at lunch the other day, found in Psalm 116:15: "*Precious in the sight of the LORD is the death of his faithful servants.*"

Hallelujah! Charmaine glanced down at her brother in Christ one last time, and smiled faintly. Her face quaked in terror, but the overriding peace he saw in her eyes told another story.

He said, "I thank God for putting you next to me on this plane."

"Me too, brother. Me too..."

Yes, that was his name—Brother, her brother in Christ! Whatever name he was given at birth mattered not to her, because it couldn't compare to being known as a friend and brother in Christ Jesus.

Convinced they were Heaven bound, both just wanted to get it over with, so they could begin life anew in eternity with their Lord and Savior, the One whose blood had protected their souls from the second death, as promised to all believers in Revelation, chapters 20 and 21.

Even among the horror, they were greatly comforted by this eternal truth...

Charmaine smiled at him wearily. "Let's close our eyes now. Next time we open them, we'll be together in Paradise! How awesome is that?"

"Amazing!" he cried, joyfully. "Thank you so much…"

The very last words Charmaine DeShields ever uttered in this lifetime were, "See you on the other side, brother!"

The plane slammed into the Bering Sea at more than 500 miles per hour, quickly turning the massive Boeing 777 jumbo jet into a crumbled speck of rubble in the vast body of water, a grain of sand, really.

Not a soul on board survived…

Flames shot out everywhere. The four massive engines kept roaring until they were ultimately silenced. Once the burning mass was completely gobbled up by the ocean, the flames from the 35,000 gallons of jet fuel still in the tanks would be extinguished.

But for everyone on board, whose names weren't found written in the Lamb's Book of Life, the flames of hell would never be extinguished…

40

AS PROMISED IN THE Word of God, Charmaine DeShields, Li Qiang, and everyone else onboard the doomed flight, whose names were written in the Lamb's Book of Life, were absent from their bodies and instantly present with the Lord.

Stepping into eternity was as seamless as the Apostle Paul had promised it would be—it happened in the twinkling of an eye. Their last horrific breaths on Planet Earth quickly became their first glorious breaths in Paradise, where Jesus had gone to prepare places just for them!

At the exact point of impact, their souls disconnected from their earthly bodies and were instantly transported to Heaven, to be eternally comforted by their Savior.

From this point forward, they would experience the endless joys everyone "blessed and highly favored" enough to inhabit that Place got to enjoy. They were finally Home, and not even their wildest thoughts of their new eternal dwelling place came close to hitting the mark.

It was infinitely more glorious than what they could have ever imagined it to be...

There wasn't a desire anywhere on the planet they just left that could ever entice them to want to leave this newly inherited Place, nor a force anywhere in the universe that could ever pluck them out of it.

Wanting to return to the sin-stained world they'd just left was as absurd as humans looking at ant holes from up in space, through giant telescopes, and being envious of what the ants had...

But the most important thing was that they were with Jesus, and were now the objects of God's limitless agape love. This intense love would be focused directly on them and would only increase as the ages passed...

And what could be better than that?

1 Corinthians 3:15, "*For no one can lay any foundation other than the one already laid, which is Jesus Christ. If any man builds on this foundation using gold, silver, costly stones, wood, hay or straw, his work will be shown for what it is, because the Day will bring it to light. It will be revealed with fire, and the fire will test the quality of each man's work.*

If what he has built survives, he will receive his reward. If it is burned up, he will suffer loss; he himself will be saved, but only as one escaping through the flames."

EVERYONE ELSE ON BOARD the flight—the vast majority—whose names weren't found written in the Lamb's Book of Life, were instantly transferred to Hades, where they would remain until the Great White Judgment Day of God Almighty. This transition was just as seamless, only theirs was a horrific transition.

Tragically, Julian and Imogen Martín were among this condemned majority, without their unborn child, whose soul had ascended to Heaven at the precise point of impact.

Soon, along with billions of other souls—including "many" who were avid churchgoers—both would stand before Jesus, the Savior they often preached about but never really knew, and be forced to give a full account of all the things they did in life.

The days of smooth talking and finagling and bargaining were over for the two false teachers. There would be no outmaneuvering their Maker.

Nothing would be hidden from a just and holy God, not a single thing! The many worldly things the Martíns had placed before the Lord while back on the planet from which they'd just been transported, would never be removed from their minds.

Those things would torment them forevermore, without reprieve.

Only there would be no consoling each other as they waited, fully anticipating God's fierce judgment. There would be no more "together" for Julian and Imogen. Both were placed in total isolation completely terrified and fearfully alone.

But what they felt now was nothing compared to what lay ahead. Instead of Jesus being their Redeemer, He would be their eternal Judge.

With quaking souls, they would stand naked before the Lord, and be forced to give an account of everything they had done in the flesh. Not a single sin would be overlooked or forgotten.

After that, with no hope of redemption, along with all other doomed sinners, they would bow before Jesus and their tongues would confess Him as King of kings and Lord of lords.

Then, without a shred of mercy, they would be thrown into the eternal lake of fire, where they would become the objects of God's fierce, eternal wrath which would only intensify as the ages passed, without reprieve…

And what could be worse than that?

In the end, Christ's last three words on the cross, "It is finished," that Julian and Imogen Martín had used solely for personal gain, would haunt them forevermore.

But not nearly as much as the four words they never preached on in their ten years as false teachers—*I never knew you*!

Just knowing they would hear those four horrifically soul-shredding words on Judgment Day, from the Lord Jesus Christ Himself—with no chance of escape or forgiveness—was so terrifying, the couple wished they could be blinked out of existence before that great and terrible day came to pass. But they didn't have that option.

Like everyone else sent there, they knew they were eternally doomed...

Cause of physical death on their earthly death certificates: *plane crash.*
Cause of second "spiritual" death recorded in Heaven: *sin.*

Revelation 20:11-13: "*Then I saw a great white throne and him who was seated on it. From his presence earth and sky fled away, and no place was found for them. 12 And I saw the dead, great and small, standing before the throne, and books were opened. Then another book was opened, which is the book of life. And the dead were judged by what was written in the books, according to what they had done. 13 And the sea gave up the dead who were in it, Death and Hades gave up the dead who were in them, and they were judged, each one of them, according to what they had done.*"

Epilogue

ONE MONTH LATER

WITH NO BODIES RECOVERED from the plane crash, a lavish memorial service was held for Julian and Imogen Martín, and Charmaine DeShields, at the *Blessed and Highly Favored Full Gospel Church.*

Images of the three, whose lives were prematurely cut short, were splashed about everywhere. It took three separate services for the tens of thousands of mourners to pay their final respects to their fallen faithful leaders, who'd lost their lives while rescuing one of their lost sheep.

Many glowed at the thought of the Martíns receiving numerous blessings in Glory for laying down their lives for Charmaine the way they both had. They could almost see Jesus hugging them extra tight for that lone selfless act.

They were totally oblivious that the Martíns weren't looking down from Heaven and smiling, after hearing so many endearing things being said about them from friends and fellow congregants, as some had alluded to during the emotional service.

In fact, the couple they'd loved and respected so much were nowhere near God's eternal dwelling Place. Instead of praising the King of Glory with all of Heaven's saints, Julian and Imogen were totally crushed in spirit, as they fearfully awaited God's fierce judgment.

All they could do now was rehearse in their minds over and over again the many good things they did in Jesus' name back on Planet Earth, trying to find a spiritual loophole of sorts to help them on Judgment Day, as they pleaded with their Maker for mercy.

Yet, like all other doomed sinners sent there, after laying out their best "individual" defenses, by reminding Jesus of the many things they did in His name back on earth, their souls would shrivel up in terror when the King of Majesty rendered judgment against them, by declaring that He never knew them as His own.

If the many gathered to honor them were aware of this, their souls would shrivel up too.

Next in line to become lead pastor, Jeremiah Ogletree should have been the one presiding over the memorial service. But after making a shocking discovery on Julian Martín's laptop while moving into his office, he quickly declined.

The secret file documenting the millions of dollars that had been funneled into a personal account the Martíns had opened years ago, troubled Jeremiah deeply. He couldn't fathom how his good friends and mentors had defrauded the church he'd loved with all his heart and soul.

After sharing the criminal news with everyone else, the deeply distressed man felt he had no choice but to step down as lead pastor. The Ogletrees were there to pay their final respects. Other than that, their days at the *Blessed and Highly Favored Full Gospel Church* were over.

ROCKED BY THE SUDDEN loss of three people who meant everything to him—in the blink of an eye—with his soul completely shredded, whereas the troubling secret file discovery forced Jeremiah Ogletree to leave the church and reconsider his true spiritual condition, for Rodney Williams it was the two harrowing phone calls with his girlfriend, on what turned out to be her final moments on Planet Earth.

First, he listened in horror as she prayed with someone on the plane seated next to her, to receive Christ as Lord and Savior. The way she witnessed to him was unlike anything he'd ever heard come out of Charmaine's mouth before. Clearly, she was a different person.

Then, on her second frantic call, she accused the Martíns of being false prophets, then urged him to meet with the Fujimotos, so he wouldn't end up in hell with Julian and Imogen someday.

Following his late girlfriend's advice, Rodney went to their house a few days later, and listened thoughtfully as Kaito took his time sharing the Gospel with him. That was when God revealed Himself to Rodney for the very first time, by using the very same Gospel message he'd been exposed to all his life, but never truly understood.

With his spiritual blinders removed, he repented of his sinful living and joined the Fujimotos at Grace Bible Church the following Sunday.

After his second visit, Rodney became a member. He spent much of his free time with the Ogletrees and Meredith Geiger, sharing the Gospel with them. While Meredith didn't feel comfortable joining him at church, she welcomed him warmly to her home on a few occasions.

Rodney started praying without ceasing that God would do for the three of them, what He had done for him—which was save their souls from utter destruction.

He didn't stop praying until God finally answered his prayers...

Whereas Meredith ultimated became a member of Grace Bible Church, the Ogletrees chose not to join. The reason they declined had nothing to do with the church or with Pastor Donnelson's teachings, and everything to do with Jeremiah's wish to be a lead pastor someplace else.

But regardless of where they ended up, one thing was certain—the Gospel Jeremiah would preach would be the Gospel of the Bible, not some man-centered version of what he once preached.

CHARMAINE DESHIELDS ENDED UP having two memorial services in her honor. After informing Pastor Donnelson of her intent to join their church, Kaito Fujimoto was given permission to hold a simple memorial service for his good friend at Grace Bible Church.

Though most in attendance didn't know Charmaine personally, after hearing about her miraculous transformation, and of her intent to join their church, the sanctuary was full of people there to honor the passing of their honorary member.

Kaito cleared his throat and, after thanking everyone for coming said, "Ever since I left the Blessed and Highly Favored Full Gospel Church, nearly three years ago, Lucy and I prayed without ceasing that God would use us to open Charmaine's eyes to the true Gospel message, one that was seldom if ever preached at her church, I'm afraid."

Kaito noticed Jeremiah Ogletree and Rodney Williams both flinching in one of the front row pews. Though they were now on the same page spiritually, clearly, they were embarrassed for their former church.

Meredith Geiger sat next to the Fujimotos in the same pew, with her daughter, Bethany.

Fujimoto continued, "I'm grateful to the many of you gathered here who never met Charmaine, but nevertheless prayed for her. In the end, God answered our prayers. Only He sent her halfway around the world and used our beloved brother, Mark Lau, to finally win her to Christ."

Polite laughter filled the church.

"Instead of harping on Charmaine's many life achievements, I'd like to ask our dear friend and former associate pastor to share what happened to Charmaine in China before her death. Pastor?"

Pastor Lau approached the lectern and gripped it with both hands. "It's good to be back and see so many familiar faces again. I still pray for you each day, and consider you my extended church family..."

Mark was showered with smiles from many seated before him.

He grew more reflective. "I first met Charmaine on my last visit to the States, a few days before I buried my late father-in-law. I asked her to sell a house I owned in Kenmore.

"We made a deal that if she sold it before the first of December, she would forgo her upcoming trip to Paris and travel to Shanghai instead. I used the fact that Shanghai was one of the world's premier shopping meccas, to rouse her curiosity.

"But in truth, what I wanted most was for her to spend a few days underground with my church, hoping it would transform her life spiritually. I can only praise God for doing just that!

"As it turned out, Charmaine sold my house three weeks before the deadline. She was a very good real estate agent. My delight knew no bounds when, using part of the commission, she fulfilled her promise by travelling to Shanghai with her best friend, Meredith…"

Mark nodded at Meredith. She nodded back, then lowered her head.

Pastor Lau went on, "While both women went there for the sole purpose of shopping, God had other plans for Charmaine. In the few short days she worshipped with us, she left an indelible impression upon all our hearts. Personally, I'm going to miss her vibrant smile.

"Without a doubt, the highlight for us was after three days of hearing the true Gospel message being preached underground, she fell completely prostrate before the Lord and cried out to Him for forgiveness. It was a beautiful experience I'll never forget.

"It was as if God had used the first two days to get her to unlearn the many false-hoods she was taught for so many years, before finally opening her eyes spiritually to who He really was.

"I just wish many of you would have had the chance to meet the 'new' Charmaine on this side of the grave. But lament not, brothers and sisters, we'll have an eternity to get to know her, and each other, infinitely better than we ever could in human form, once we reach the other side."

The endearing smile on Mark Lau's face could only be worn by someone who was thoroughly convinced the person he was there to remember was indeed in Heaven.

"Like Kaito alluded to, instead of harping on our beloved sister's many past accomplishments, we need only focus on the spiritual success she enjoyed in what turned out to be her final days on earth, to hopefully demonstrate what awaits all who truly belong to God on the other side.

"I told Charmaine at lunch one day, in between services, that I wanted Psalm one sixteen, verse fifteen etched onto my tombstone when I died. It says, 'Precious in the sight of the Lord is the death of his faithful servants.'

"She was so impacted by that Scripture that she told me she wanted it etched on her tombstone as well..." Pastor Lau got choked up and started weeping. "Just never thought it would happen to her first."

He took a moment to collect himself, then said, "Not that I needed proof that her conversion was genuine, but if I did, her actions on the plane before it went down erased all doubt. Only I'd like Kaito to share this part with you. After all, his hands were in the details."

Mark Lau stepped aside, and Kaito cleared his throat. "Shortly before the plane made impact, Charmaine messaged me saying she had a change of heart, and that she wanted the entire fifty thousand dollars she had earmarked for her church renovation project to be transferred to Pastor Lau instead, so he could print more Bibles in China.

"Mark and I had nothing to do with her decision. It was all hers. She also said she had no intention of telling anyone about it; she wanted it to remain between herself and God. The only reason she told me was that she wanted me to complete the transaction before she arrived back in the States, so no one could talk her out of it...

"She also gave Mark most of the cash she had leftover before leaving China, nearly three thousand dollars. He never asked for it. She did it all on her own. Now, in no way am I implying that our dear sister was saved by performing good works. Not at all! No one is ever saved that way. But as God's children, we're saved unto them."

Many "Amens" were uttered throughout the sanctuary.

"And if that wasn't enough, when Rodney told me how Charmaine had led someone to faith in Christ on the plane, even as it was going down, how could this not be attributed to the Spirit at work within her?

"Charmaine told me on the last conversation we ever had, that her greatest regret was the numerous treasures she had forfeited in Heaven, from always letting her right hand know what her left hand was doing. Believe me when I say, it pained her deeply..."

A smile formed on Kaito's face. "Jesus Himself said, 'By their fruits you will know them.' I can attest that Charmaine didn't leave China the same woman she was when she first arrived there. Not even close.

"Her selfless actions on the plane are further examples of a life transformed by the power of the Holy Spirit. Even better, the eternal rewards she'll receive go beyond winning that one soul to Christ.

"Every salvation that takes place as a result of her giving to Pastor Lau, for properly translated Bibles, will mean even more rewards for her in Heaven. So, you see, even in death, our dear sister will keep storing up treasures which can never be forfeited due to her own personal pride!

"Talk about an enduring legacy?! Wow! Just wow! I think it's safe to assume she stored up more rewards in her final moments on this planet, than she did her entire life leading up to that point...

"Bottom line, from a spiritual standpoint, the last few days of Charmaine's life were more productive than the first thirty-one years had been. Her life should be an example to all of us that it's never too late for Christians to turn things around and readjust our spiritual compasses so we, too, can have an even greater impact on God's Kingdom here on earth, while we're still alive."

Kaito sighed. "I don't know about you, but Charmaine's life and death has forced me to reflect on the many rewards I've lost on the other side because of personal pride and ego. I know I've been guilty of this too many times to count. How about you?"

Many heads nodded agreement.

"While we humans have no idea who or how many people God ultimately uses to rescue lost sinners—like we once were—we can rest assured knowing every good work we perform toward this ultimate task is recorded in Heaven's memory. Even if we're not directly involved, our indirect actions always result in rewards in Glory.

"How awesome is that?!" Shooting a quick glance at Pastor Ogletree and Rodney Williams, Kaito said, "As you all know by now, Charmaine told me before the plane went down of her intent to end her membership at the Blessed and Highly Favored Full Gospel Church, upon returning to the States, so she could join our church.

"To those of you who didn't know her, it's impossible for me to fully express just how miraculous this really is! Charmaine was no fan of our church. Truth is, before going to China, she never understood what possessed me and Lucy to leave the liveliest church in all of Seattle, to join a completely dead one like ours! Her words, not mine!"

Laughter filled the sanctuary.

"In all seriousness, she felt sorry for me and Lucy for the longest time. Yet, in the end, ours was the church she wanted to join. Go figure. One more proof of her genuine conversion.

"And so, my dear brothers and sisters, as the memorial service draws to a close, let us use Charmaine's recent spiritual transformation as an example of not only what awaits us on the other side, but what kind of legacy we want to leave behind when God calls us Home! Amen?"

"Amen!"

PASTOR LAU BRACED HIMSELF when Meredith approached him. Bethany was by her side. Like Rodney and Jeremiah, Meredith attended both memorial services with her daughter. She couldn't ignore the stark contrast between the two. One was a celebration of Charmaine's many life achievements. The other was a celebration of her ascent to Heaven.

Meredith reached for her daughter's hand, then said to Mark, "When I first heard Charmaine died in the plane crash, I was devastated. My first thought was had I remained in China with her, I'd be dead too.

"Once that grim thought passed, I couldn't help but feel that God had spared my life, but judged hers for worshipping underground with a bunch of cultists. I was furious with you, and blamed you for her death!"

Mark glanced briefly at Bethany. Once eye contact was made, the youngster looked down at her feet. "I understand how you feel, Meredith."

Tears formed in Meredith's eyes. "But why did Pastor Julian and his wife also have to die? What crime did they commit to deserve such a horrific fate? All they did was try to rescue one of their own. Certainly, nothing worthy of a death sentence!

"Had I not inserted them into my nightmare, they'd still be alive and I'd be dead. That's what I'm having the greatest difficulty coming to grips with. Sometimes I feel paralyzed with guilt."

Mark placed his hands on her shoulders. "Their deaths are not your fault, Meredith. It goes without saying that had you been on that flight, you wouldn't be here now. But do you really think it happened by mere chance or circumstance?"

Meredith dabbed at her eyes with a tissue. "Not sure I follow you…"

"Let me assure you that God didn't overlook the fact that you *weren't* on board the plane when it crashed. Though we humans cannot fully understand God's plans, that doesn't change the fact that He is sovereign, and in complete control of all things at all times.

"What I'm trying to say is the reason you're still alive is that God has ordained it. The same is true for why the Martíns are no longer here."

"Hmm…"

"It's true, Meredith. Now that God has chosen to keep you alive, what will you do with the remainder of your life? If you haven't yet done so, I'd take this new lease on life you were given to get right with God, then do all you can to have a positive impact for His Kingdom in the days you have left on this planet, however few or many they may be…"

Meredith glanced down at Bethany briefly and smiled. Then to Mark, "Rodney has been such a blessing to me since Charmaine's death. Mostly thanks to his persuasive teachings, I'm a believer now!"

Mark gasped. His eyes widened. "Really?"

Meredith nodded. "I still have so much to learn and many questions which need answering, but I can say with confidence that Jesus is my Lord and Savior!"

Seeing that Mark was on the verge of tears, she said, "I asked the Fujimotos not to tell you. I wanted to tell you myself. I must say, as a new member of their church, Pastor Donnelson is some preacher!"

"Indeed he is! You're in very good hands with him." Mark was struck with a thought. "How cool that your conversion, Rodney's too, equates to even more eternal rewards for Charmaine, even in her absence!"

Meredith smiled. "Well, if I understood Kaito's message correctly, wouldn't it mean you'll also receive rewards for your involvement? I mean, had God not used you to rescue Charmaine, none of this would have happened, right?"

Pastor Lau beamed from ear to ear. "That would be correct. But more than anything, I look forward to placing them at the feet of Jesus. After all, had it not been for Him, I would still be on the fast track to hell."

The way he said it brought tears to Meredith's eyes and put a smile on her face. "Thank you, Jesus!" was all she could say.

"Amen to that!" came the reply of the joyful pastor. Amid the constant persecution Mark Lau faced at his subterranean church in China, if someone asked him to properly describe how he felt now, he would say it was even better than winning the Super Bowl! *Hallelujah*!

Beloved, do not believe every spirit, but test the spirits,
whether they are of God; because many false prophets
have gone out into the world (1 John 4:1).

If you were

on that plane,

where would your soul

be transferred to?

Tomorrow is promised

to no one...

A Sincere Debt of Gratitude...

First, to my dear friend and brother in Christ for nearly 25 years, Dean Jason Arcamo: For the past 3 years, Jason has worked at the U.S. Embassy in the Philippines. Due to the Corona virus, he returned to the States last March, with his wife and three kids, for what they thought might only be a month or two.

They ended up staying for six months...

What made this "unplanned" trip so remarkable was, even though the Arcamos aren't Florida residents, the bulk of their time was spent in the Sunshine State. Even better, the house they rented was within walking distance from my residence. Only God could have choreographed something like this in a time of global pandemic.

In the days leading up to their arrival, I was at the point where my brain was fatigued from trying to juggle two books at the same time. The handful of days Jason and I spent together editing, beta reading and proofreading this book—into the wee hours of the morning—were instrumental to helping me finish on time.

Thank you, brother, for all your help and for providing that wonderful time of refreshing. The change of pace and fresh perspective you offered was just what I needed. I consider our friendship as one of the greatest blessings in my life. Truly, you are a friend and brother in every sense of the word.

I would be remiss if I didn't thank his wife (and better half), Joy, for the delicious Filipino meals she prepared, and for putting up with us as we toiled with the looming deadline. It was great spending quality time with you and the kids again. I appreciate you so much, my dear sister.

Next, I would like to extend a special thanks to my editor, Susan Axel Bedsaul, whom I happened to meet at the church at which Jason had pastored before relocating to Manila. I'm sure my crazy deadlines make her scratch her head at times, yet she is always gracious with her time when I need her most.

You are a true blessing to me, Sister Susan! Who would have thought when we were first introduced, way back when, that it would lead to all this? I look forward to tackling many more projects with you in the future.

Lord willing...

I would also like to thank the many beta readers who helped with the pre-editing process, and everyone else who has ever helped with any of my books over the years, in any capacity. I am grateful to each of you, and pray God's richest blessings for you all...

Lastly, I am grateful to all my readers, especially those whose eyes and ears were opened to the true Gospel message for the very first time, or whose spiritual walks have been strengthened from reading my books. That's why they were written in the first place, to share God's Word and bring Him glory!

Personally, after what Christ did for me on the cross, sharing the Gospel message in my books is not only the greatest of honors, but also the least I can do to glorify my King for rescuing me, a sinner, from the very place I would have deservingly been sent to when my life on earth came to an end—hell!

Can there be a greater blessing in life than having God's eternal assurance? I think not! This "redeemed wretch" is eternally grateful to You, Lord! Truly, You are an awesome Savior, and I will serve You all the days of my life, in good times and in bad, for You and You alone are worthy to be praised, honored, and glorified...

About the author

Patrick Higgins is an Amazon bestseller and award-winning author of the end times prophetic series, *Chaos In The Blink Of An Eye*. The "CHAOS" in our present world is well documented in this timely series, which won the Radiqx Press Spirit-Filled Fiction Award of Excellence, soon after the first installment was published. To date, more than 2000 positive ratings/reviews have been posted on Amazon and Goodreads, on the first 6 installments...and counting!

Once completed, there will be 12 installments...

He also wrote *I Never Knew You*, *The Pelican Trees*, *Coffee In Manila*, and *The Unannounced Christmas Visitor*, which won both the International Publishers Awards (IPA) and the 2018 Readers' Favorite Gold Medal Awards in Christian fiction.

While the stories he writes all have different themes and take place in different settings, the one thread that links them all together is his heart for Jesus and his yearning for the lost.

With that in mind, it is his wish that the message his stories convey will greatly impact each reader, by challenging you not only to contemplate life on this side of the grave, but on the other side as well. After all, each of us will spend eternity at one of two places, based solely upon a single decision which must be made this side of the grave. That decision will be made crystal clear to each reader of these books.

Higgins is currently writing many other books, both fiction and non-fiction, including a sequel to *Coffee in Manila*, which will shine a bright, sobering spotlight on the diabolical human trafficking industry.

To contact author: patrick12272003@gmail.com
Like on Facebook: https://www.facebook.com/patrick12272003
https://www.facebook.com/TheUnannouncedChristmasVisitor
Follow on Twitter: https://twitter.com/patrick12272003
Follow on Instagram: @patrick12272003

Looking for an editor?
Contact Susan Axel Bedsaul, the Complete Editor
Excellent Results. Reasonable Rates – fuddydudsto2@outlook.com

What readers are saying on Amazon and Goodreads...

Thank you so much, Brother, for writing this book. It shows why the prosperity gospel is so wrong. It also shows that God loves us so much that He will do what it takes so we can know we are saved, like he did with Charmaine. I won't say anymore and give the story away but please everyone, make sure you are saved. You never know when it could be your last chance. Get this book...

Dawn Galloway – Amazon review

One of the most powerful books I have read! This book is so powerful, and should make everyone who calls themselves a Christian really stop and think. Do we want to know CHRIST for what He can do for us, or for what CHRIST would want us to do for the Father? JESUS' life was all about pleasing the Father. That is what our lives should be about, too. Thank you, Patrick Higgins, for this powerful book! I will be reading many more of your books.

Sandra K. Baney – Amazon review

One of the best Christian fiction books I have read to date. I could not stop reading! It bared the soul and touched the spirit. The characters were real and relatable, even sadly, the false prophets.

Luvstoread – Amazon review

Spellbinding! From the many gospel truths shared to the surprise conclusion, I couldn't put the book down. 5 Stars absolutely awesome!

Lynn Cooper – Amazon review

I love reading Patrick Higgins books but this one stood out above the rest. It answers questions that a lot of us have. The book from start to finish did not leave out the true gospel message. It shouted out loud and clear the love and sovereignty of God the Father and Jesus Christ. I recommend this book to everyone. May it be just as much of a blessing to you as it was to me.

Jan B. – Amazon review

Awesome book! I don't usually make comments but I couldn't put this book down until I finished it. The most important thing in life is a relationship with God our Father through His son Jesus and knowing for certain that you understand the

Gospel and to know you are truly saved. This book is a must read for everyone, Christian and non-Christian, it will make you examine your life and if you are truly born again.

Kindle customer – Amazon review

Eye opener! There's so much truth brought to light with his words. Scriptures are listed to anyone wanting to verify his authenticity. Hard to put down.

_____DebA Okla – Amazon review

Truly a rewarding read. Biblically sound, thought provoking and a road map to eternal life. Without a doubt, one of the absolute best books I have ever read.

Kindle Customer Lin – Amazon review

Excellent book. Thought provoking story. The contrast between prosperity, lukewarm Christians and the faithful, persecuted Christians in China makes it worth the read.

Book – Amazon review

Patrick Higgins has an anointing! "I Never Knew You" is so profound. It has truly challenged me to evaluate all aspects of my walk in this Christian life. I was truly blessed and plan to share this book with family and friends.

Kindle customer – Amazon review

Wow! Just wow! Thank you, Patrick! Wow! Very touching! This impacted my soul and was very uplifting!! Our God is an awesome God! Amen!

Raina – Amazon review

I love this book! It tells the true meaning of God and how you too can spend eternity with him. It's a must read!

Amazon Customer – Amazon review

This book was so real, really made you evaluate your relationship with God. I would even recommend to person that are unsaved. Excellent!

Marie – Amazon review

I wish this was preached all the time in our churches. The prosperity gospel isn't always so blatant. Sometimes it's more subtle, but it's still there. Listen well because your eternal life depends on the true gospel. The gospel was laid out beautifully in this book.

Joan Warren – Amazon review

This book fully explains the beautiful message of salvation through Jesus Christ. Thank you, Mr. Higgins for writing this story. It clearly leads it's readers away from the "name it and claim it" teaching of so many false teachers and leads it's readers directly to God Almighty. It was impossible not to care about these characters even as the book neared it's conclusion. This is an important book for our troubled times.

KSH – Amazon review

Everyone should read this book! I Never Knew You. I can't begin to fathom the sorrow of hearing those words spoken to me by Jesus! Nor even hearing them spoken to others. Family, friends, strangers. To hear them spoken to anyone that I had the chance to tell about Him and the way to salvation...and didn't even try? That is unthinkable.

And yet, like the pastors of the megachurch in this book, there are real-life pastors who are leading their people astray. I have watched them on Christian stations giving messages that sound more like success seminars than sermons. The central character is a faithful member of that church, but God has plans to save her despite that fact, so that she never has to hear Him say, "I never knew you."

Brenda Hughes – Amazon review

The truth! Amazing! I couldn't put it down! I certainly will follow this author. God bless him for the truth he isn't afraid to write.

Sharon – Amazon review

This book is such a blessing...it points out all of the hypocrisies of the prosperity preachers against the true word of God. One prosperity preacher kept popping into my mind while reading it. I finished this book in one day as I could not put it down.

Anna – Amazon review

305

Powerful writing that makes you very inter reflective. Once I started, I was compelled to finish to the end without stopping. It's so well written that you feel what the characters do, even found myself crying for them. Definitely makes you think.

Pam C. – Amazon review

A must read! I pray that "many" eyes are opened upon reading this amazing novel. Thank you, Mr. Higgins, for a wonderful spiritual experience. I will recommend to all!

Eric W. – Amazon review

It renewed my spiritual hunger. I really enjoyed this book a lot. I got a better understanding of Matthew 7:23 and other biblical verses. I don't know. I really enjoyed being a parishioner of Pastor Lau's church. I can easily see room for a sequel.

Joose59 – Amazon review

A wonderful read! This book has the capacity to soften hearts and lead unbelievers to Jesus and eternal life. For the Christian, it will increase your faith as you are given much on which to contemplate and meditate. If your questioning your salvation, wondering about the 'gospel' or the Christian life, then you should read this book. You'll be glad you did.

Amazon review

Heart stopping truth! Riveting story of the two ways of life. Truth, peace, and choices! Eternal decisions, peace or pain, death or life!

Crhoads – Amazon review

As a Christian I often look for Kindle books that are both evangelistic and true to God's Holy Word. Patrick Higgins has been faithful to both and I thoroughly enjoyed this book. The persecuted church has so often been ignored in the US because of our materialistic culture. This book has reminded me again what our earthly mission should be and that is to reach others for Christ by sharing His wonderful gospel of grace. To God be all glory and honor.

Bigdawg – Amazon review

Amazing! I love this author and have read several of his books but this one has by far touched my heart and soul the most. As I walk in my journey to know Jesus more, I have struggled in my prayers to turn my heart more fully to Him. I finally found the perfect word I was searching for 3\4 through the book when Charmaine realized she needed to be a SERVANT to the Lord and not make it about her, but Him. Now my journey continues...

M. Rene Puetz – Amazon review

This is one that will flare some up! If we are questioning our faith, maybe we should. I enjoyed this very much. So insightful and true. It is truly frightening what is happening right under our noses...

Virginia Rawls – Amazon review

I knew this book would be exceptional by its title alone. I was part of the Word of Faith movement till God convicted me, and I left that church. I would like to thank Patrick Higgins for his excellent description on how to accept Jesus as your Savior. I hope many come to the Lord from reading this book. I hope that Mr. Higgins continues to publish word that will still be reverent 10, 20, or 30 years from now, if the Lord tarries.

Avid reader – Amazon review

I have read several of Patrick Higgins' books, and I love the way he writes for the LORD. This book was no exception. I enjoyed this book so very much, started it too late on a Saturday, but finished it the next day because I had to know what happened to the lead character. This books really teaches a lesson on false teachers, and the way they can lead you to destruction instead of the narrow path to our LORD and Savior Jesus, Yeshua.

The two pastors in this false church were really leading their flock astray in a big way, and I hate to say this but I was delighted with the end of this story. "I Never Knew You" was put forth in full when they met their maker. Bravo Patrick, another wonderful story to help the church follow the path our LORD has set forth for us to follow, pick up your cross daily and follow me. Come quickly LORD, we are waiting patiently for you.

Marilousie Gilley – Goodreads review

Make sure you are getting the true Gospel...Don't take someone else's spin on the scriptures as the truth, read it for yourself and check that they are in the Word and not in the world...Your soul is at stake... don't follow after false teachers...Follow Jesus and Him only...You will find that all that glitters is not gold... The main character in this story found out the truth, before it was too late...others were stubborn to their own peril...It is a wake up call....and It begs the question, What are you feeding your soul, and to what or who are you bowing down to? Time is getting short folks, do you have the right Jesus?

Book Zilla – Amazon review

A must read! I could not put this book down! I even ordered the paperback book so that I can add these truths to my daily Bible study. Thank you, Patrick Higgins, for sharing your love and faith in Christ with your readers! I am so blessed to have stumbled upon, or should I say "God put this book before me"; I have no doubt God wanted me to read this book at this specific moment. I look forward to reading more books by this author.

Anne Crumley – Amazon review

Phenomenal! Praise God for Mr. Higgins. The words and love shared in this book as a tribute to our Lord and Savior Jesus Christ, are truly immeasurable. This book made me check myself as a Christ follower many times over. Hallelujah!!

BTurn – Amazon review

Amazing! Just amazing! Spellbinding, as one person said is so true. One of the best Christian fiction books I've read in a while. I would recommend this book to all those who think that they are saved but aren't truly saved. God's blessing to you, brother Patrick for opening eyes to the truth of God's Holy Word.

Mary Dobbs – Amazon review

If you only read one book this year, make it this one! I'm a big fan of the author and must say that to me, this is his best work yet. From the very beginning, the story was a page-turner for me. There were parts of the story where I cried along with her and praised God that the author had written it. The story is impactful, filled with messages of faith and salvation, and will stay on your mind after you finish the last page.

J. E. Grace – Amazon review

Printed in Great Britain
by Amazon